The River

Refl...

Mark Godfrey

Published by Leaf by Leaf
an imprint of Cinnamon Press
Meirion House
Tanygrisiau
Blaenau Ffestiniog
Gwynedd, LL41 3SU
www.cinnamonpress.com

British Library Cataloguing in Publication Data. A CIP record for this book can be obtained from the British Library.

Designed and typeset in Garamond by Cinnamon Press.

Cover design by Adam Craig © Adam Craig.

Cinnamon Press is represented in the UK by Inpress Ltd and in Wales by the Books Council of Wales.

Acknowledgements

I owe thanks to a great many people whose influence, guidance, love and support has knowingly or otherwise enabled me to live and write. Here are a few to whom I owe the most heartfelt thanks.

My family: My wife, Ann; my father Christopher and mother Sheila; my children Jonathan and Charlotte; my sisters Sarah and Anna. And every other member of the Godfrey/ Lawrence/Thomas/Carling clan, especially those in nappies and those not yet born.

My friends: Clare and Mick, John and Cath, Roger and Sarah, Penny and Jon, Clare and Sean, Martin, Richard and Adam, Peter.

Special mentions: Ben and Sheila for providing the river; Sarah Willis for asking what I was prepared to give up in order to do this; Roger Finnigan for reading the manuscript and believing I should persist with it; Angela Macmillan and Sarah Coley at *The Reader* magazine for publishing my first short story; Tim Lyons for being my first writing partner; the members of my writing group: Daragh, Gill, Joely, Melissa, Ravi, Rosemary and Toni; Andrew Michael Hurley for his tutorship and encouragement.

Authors: This novel owes a monumental debt to the work of Richard J Evans and Steven Pinker, as well as Timothy Snyder, Nicholas Stargardt and David Cesarani. I hope I have done justice to the factual in this work of fiction.

Publishers: Jan, Adam and Rowan at Cinnamon Press for taking on this project at the most difficult of times. Your trust in this book means the world.

Finally: Great Ormond Street and Harefield hospitals, who have literally enabled me to live.

The River Reflects

For Ann

The river is ceaseless, the ocean inexorable—sifting the grime —dissolving the salt—moving matter as if merely a thing— until the thing becomes other matter—and other matter becomes another thing—and that thing becomes us—and we become like the river reflected, both light and dark.

Chapter One

We sit in silence. The gathering darkness of the evening has crept into the room and softened the harsh lines of the argument. I watch Alexander's face crease into a tired smile.

'What will you do?'

This time the impatient snap to his voice is absent. He's asked me three times, and with the argument spinning and circling and almost dying of boredom, I have lost the will to attempt an answer. I look at him and say nothing. I exaggerate the weariness in my expression. It's the only response I can give, hoping that he too is fed up of a discussion that should have timed-out an hour ago and continued only because neither of us quite had the heart to walk out on it.

'You have to make a decision.'

Not again, I say to myself. I stretch my arms, hoping for some release.

He breathes out: a long exhale, deliberate, conveying the weight of his resignation. And did I catch the slight accompanying twitch of the lip that might signal contempt? It's said that once that so much as flickers across the face of your spouse you might as well call the lawyers.

But maybe I'm looking for it, examining every move he makes for evidence? We're past the anger and entrenchment; we're tired now, and stuck, and both of us know nothing will change this side of the morning. He loves me, I'm sure—he's said it twice—although I haven't said it back.

So I say it: three little words that mean everything in the right context.

He smiles. 'So will you do it?'

'No,' I say, wishing I hadn't bothered, wondering how an expression of love concedes an argument.

I reach for a cigarette, the sixth or seventh of the evening. I won't enjoy it. It's a mechanical act. Two or three during the course of an evening are to be savoured. After that the effect is lost and guilt supersedes pleasure as I rotesuck my way to an early grave.

He gets up and walks to the window. It's his habit when things are tense between us. He has to pass me in my chair. I watch as he gets closer, maybe in expectation of something, a touch on the arm or a genuine, warm smile. But he doesn't offer so much as a glance as he passes. Perhaps he can't bring himself to. I stare at the far wall, the one with my series of paintings about rejuvenation, a group of three semi-abstract oils that mingle dystopia with optimism. A defining statement, or so I'd hoped. They're on our wall because no one would buy them.

Which is where the argument began. My gallery hadn't paid me for the paintings that had sold. Alex said I had to 'do something,' meaning sanctions, threats, lawyers. I said, it's not deliberate, they've always been bad at admin. He told me to go somewhere else where they can 'organise shit.' I said they're having a tough time and I should support them through it, not tip them over the edge. He said my career is going 'down the tubes' while they 'play at being shopkeepers.'

So it went. The truth is, they picked me up years ago when no one else would. They believe in me, love my work, and I like them. They're more interested in art than commerce and I owe them my patience.

'You owe them nothing.'

'I want to owe them, I'm loyal.' Then I added the spiteful aside, the one that felt good when it was delivered, no matter how bad I feel now: 'why do you think I'm still with you?'

'Because you love me?' It was a genuine question and something in me retracted the moment I realised he did care what the answer might be.

I'd stung him, but having gained the upper hand I wasn't about to surrender it by giving the easy answer.

Which was when he started telling me he loved me.

Now, while he stares aimlessly—or pointedly?—out of the window, I draw hard on the cigarette, hearing the faint crackle that primes me for the hit that's to follow. But there's no hit, no satisfaction. I hold the smoke down in the hope of extracting some pleasure from it. I exhale the disappointment, the final inch of breath made audible.

'What?' he says, turning back from the window.

'Nothing.'

'You sighed.'

'I'm smoking.'

He opens his mouth as if to follow up, but closes it again, perhaps, belatedly, making the connection.

'Can I have one?' He doesn't smoke. Or, at least, he smokes once a year, every June 30th, the anniversary of him giving up five years ago. It used to be something we did together. I wave in the direction of the packet.

He takes one and looks for the lighter. It's on the coffee table, inches from the cigarettes and I suppress the instinct to get up and hand it to him.

'Where is…' he says, still looking. I don't answer as only a fool could fail to find it. 'Ah,' he says, picking it up, 'hidden behind your Chagall catalogue.'

I wonder about the tone of voice. Forced jollity? Or is it peevishness, as if I'd hidden it deliberately in anticipation of him choosing this moment to break a five-year abstinence?

'And I thought I'd hidden it so well.'

'I was joking,' he says.

'So was I.'

We manage a faint laugh. The argument about who is likelier to take the other too literally was one we'd had last week and it ended in a civilised draw.

He goes back to the window and I gaze, distractedly now, at my paintings. I want to remark on him taking a cigarette, but daren't. It was tonight's argument that had provoked him to want one, that much is obvious, and any reference, however oblique, would risk opening that up again. It's comforting to believe he chose this moment to evoke our past, when we were happier, when smoking was a shared pleasure.

And if I'm mistaken in that, I don't want to know.

'There's an odd looking man hanging about on the street,' he says.

'Odd?'

'I don't mean odd as in weird. In fact he looks implausibly normal, which is what's odd.'

It's a curious change of subject and a welcome distraction. I join him at the window.

'There.' He points to a figure partly sheltered from the light of a streetlamp by the shade of a tree, about three doors down. 'He's been there for a while.'

I wonder what's remarkable about a man standing on our street. He's well dressed and looks like he's minding his own business, maybe waiting for a taxi or a rendezvous. I see that his shoes, the part of him that isn't shaded, shine with an abnormally brilliant lustre, but that quirk apart, his appearance seems innocuous enough.

'Tell me what's odd about him.'

Alexander looks towards the man. A hint of a smirk crosses his lips and I realise he's ready to enjoy himself, as if we've begun a new game.

'To start with, he's been there for several minutes.' He raises a hand to stop me butting in. I wasn't about to, but the habit of the night's argument has formed. 'No big deal in itself I admit, but think about it: if he's waiting for someone, why do it half way down the street? A corner is more logical.' He holds a hand up again.

'I wasn't…' I say, and smile in spite of myself.

'And look at the way he's dressed: he's smart. It's eleven-o-clock. No one sets off for a posh do at this time. He's just standing there. He's going nowhere.'

I tell him I'm not convinced.

'Look at his raincoat. It's a fine, warm night.'

'There's a man over the road wears a parka all year round, some people do.'

'He's a cold-blooded, skinflint who only owns the one jacket.' He jerks his thumb towards the man in the street. 'This guy is properly tailored. He'll have coats and jackets for every occasion and weather.'

'Time for bed, Sherlock,' I say. He likes to be called Sherlock; it's one of our endearments. It feels like we've contrived a truce and, although the discussion will resuscitate tomorrow, this is the opportunity to close it for the night.

He gently squeezes past me, the sharp defensive movements of earlier no longer required. I reach up to draw the curtains and look again down the street. It may be a coincidence but, at the moment I glance in the man's direction, his head jerks away, as though guiltily, like I'd caught him staring at me.

I dream of the man in the street and wake with a curious, unaccountably palpable urge to know if he's still there. Five-thirty. It's light, birds are singing, and the rumble of traffic hasn't begun, save a distant, solitary vehicle that is probably a refuse van. Alex is still asleep, so I go downstairs to throw open the curtains of the living room.

Why am I doing this? Having been so dismissive of anything unusual about this man's presence, what possesses me now to believe he'd still be there? Was it the moment when he seemed to turn his face away? Is it the question of whether he had been looking at me? Was that when the benign appearance of a well-dressed man on our street became an entity in my mind's eye? And if he had been looking at me, why?

I banish the thought for its ridiculousness. There wouldn't have been any intent. He was perhaps embarrassed to be caught staring, but he has to be looking at something while he stands there in the night.

'He stands there in the night.' I roll the words around my head until I'm almost chewing them, aware I have the beginnings of an obsession. I tell myself to shut up and go back to bed for another hour before the alarm goes off. But I think back to the dream and, as more of it filters back into consciousness, realise I know the answer, the reason he's stuck in my head: it's the needle-sharp glints of light burned into my mind; it's the shoes.

I've been seeing the shoes in my dreams and now I see them in daylight, in my imagination. So shiny, like burnished metal, as alive in my head as if I'd closed my eyes after looking at the sun.

As I grab a curtain to pull it back, I have a premonition of what will be revealed: the man, standing in the garden, staring straight back at me. Only this time he won't avert his gaze. Instead, he will look at me, face fixed and hollow, eyes glassy and emotionless. I pant with the shock of it, the fear, then I upbraid myself for my irrationality. My knuckles have whitened from the tightness of my grip on the curtain and I force myself to relax.

Sliding a finger between the two curtains, I slowly part them and press my eyebrow against the cloth, anticipating the moment when the chink of light widens enough for me to see the view outside. At first there is nothing, but the field of vision is still too narrow to be sure. This is so stupid, and I feel so weak that I decide, in a rush, to pull the curtain back with a flourish and expose myself to whatever, whoever, may be lurking there. First one curtain, then the other. I watch them slide back on their runners and fasten my gaze on the horror outside.

There's nothing, except the flutter of a startled wood pigeon. Our modest street-side garden with its familiar small trees and shrubs is peculiarly empty, as though the absence of the imaginary figure owes more to it having vanished than never having been there. And now the strangest disappointment. Something about my fear not materialising has left me thwarted. I look up and down the street, willing the man into existence, hoping he will emerge from behind a tree, or hedge, or van, or a neighbour's garden, or from somewhere, anywhere.

With my attention fixed on the view from the window, I don't sense the movement behind me.

'Sylvia.' The voice is initially chilling, but I recognise it at the same moment I turn and see Alexander. 'What's the matter?'

'You surprised me,' I say.

'I only live here.'

I laugh and reach over to hug him. I say I wasn't expecting him. He asks why I'm up so early and, after hesitating, weighing whether the desire to share a burden is worth the risk of embarrassment, I decide to tell him the truth: that it's because of the man on the street and I think I've been spooked by him.

This has the potential to open up a new argument because he won't understand and I won't be able to find any better words of explanation. But all he says is, 'I told you there was something odd about him.'

'I had a dream about him.'

'Oh?' he says, but I know his heart isn't in it. He's something of a fundamentalist in his belief that the more fascinating someone believes their dream, the more tedious it will be in the retelling.

'I don't remember the detail,' I say.

'But you woke up worrying he might still be there?' He smiles and puts an arm around my shoulder, but I stiffen, feeling faintly stupid.

'It's okay,' he says, 'he's bugging me too.'

I look at him, surprised by this admission. He isn't bugged by much. Normally he's so sure of himself or, at least, good at maintaining the appearance of being sure. He makes money by exuding certainty, which is useful since I don't earn much.

I make us coffee and I take mine up to my studio. The leftovers from last night's argument are still hanging around and I decide to get away before anything reactivates. As I make my way from the room Alex doesn't challenge me and I guess he realises nothing has changed and it would be wiser for him to leave me alone.

The studio is on the second floor. More accurately, it is the entirety of the second floor, running the length and breadth of the house, with a house-width window at one end overlooking the river. At the other end are skylight windows that would give a view of the street if they weren't too high to look out from. I own this space in almost every sense, since the house was built for an artist and is governed by a covenant that forbids its sale to anyone other than an artist. My husband's money may have bought it but the entitlement to live here is mine.

This is where I feel safe. It's a place where I'm in control. It's my dominion, my territory, a place where everything is an extension of me, where every item and artefact, every tool and gadget, every piece of furniture and lighting, is chosen and arranged by me alone. It's where I'm the one with the knowledge of the whats, the whys and the hows, the one who understands it all, who fits the elements together. It's my consciousness, character, my very nature on display. I feel privileged here, and lucky.

I look out over the river. It is my companion, an irresistible, mesmerising presence, with its ever shifting, yet unchanging, repertoire of low and high tides, eddies, pools, fast streams and slack water—but always the same slow flow, sedate and grey-brown, sometimes blue, drawn inexorably to the sea.

On the river path there's the unending procession of walkers and joggers who come past in singles and twos, or sometimes packs from a school, or in a tangle of leads from a dog walk service. However early I wake or however late I stay up, there's someone out there, making their contribution to the continuous flow of my life. How kind of them.

I walk back between the painting zone and drawing zone, between the larger of my two easels—currently set up for a manga style group portrait in acrylic of the G7 leaders—and my drawing table and chair, the place where I find my greatest composure, where the concentration of work most perfectly stills the restless spirit and frees the mind.

The drawing table is an extravagance since I could have bought a perfectly good one for a fraction of the price, but it's comfortable and tactile, seductive even, with its drawers and holders, as well as its artfully designed combination of wood, steel and glass, and its smooth, silent mechanisms for adjusting height and tilt. To its side is my computer. I press the space bar to wake it up.

The overnight email traffic is predictable: summer sale; holiday offers; last chance to vote; a petition to sign. Easy to deal with at least. But there's one, sent at 01.08, which makes me hesitate. Its subject line reads: 'Can we meet?' It hangs there challenging me to open it. I struggle to work out why I'm tempted. Nearly all spam is efficiently diverted into my specially trained junk mailbox and it is rare for anything like this to get through. So, why? Who? I click to open the message, half expecting to unleash some horrible consequence, some malware, spyware, virus or other unintelligible cyber gunk sure to wreck my computer and ruin my day. But it opens like any normal email.

12 June 2014 01.08

Dear Ms West

I have been following your career for a while. You produce very promising work and your solo show in Camden earlier this year dispelled any notion of you as a purveyor of pretty images, revealing you to be an artist of serious intent. I was very impressed.

Consequently, you have been shortlisted for a private project of mine, one that I have been nurturing off and on for some time. I would prefer not to say any more via this medium and propose instead a meeting between yourself and a representative of mine at your earliest convenience.

I will say that the commission is a substantial one and will require the artist who is selected to devote their entire energy to the project for a period of not less than one year.

If you would wish to take this a stage further and meet my representative, please reply with a date, time and location, and he will be there.

I read it again. During the first reading my concentration on the later paragraphs was overshadowed by the phrases in the first: 'promising work,' 'purveyor of pretty images'. Who is this man? It has to be a man. I've been producing art, professionally, for fifteen years and I'm beyond 'promising'. Anyone who thinks I ever produced 'pretty images' has missed the point. Have I only now become a 'serious' artist, is that what he's saying?

As I read it a third time the words 'very impressed' gain weight and the prospect of a year long commission registers. I play around with what that might mean financially and how it would affect the schedule of other projects.

But who is this person? I still think it's a man, but I suppose you never know. Why write an email in the style of a letter but put no name at the end? I google the 'name' that appears in my inbox, but I guess it's an account set up to disguise the sender's identity and it's no surprise when nothing comes back.

But is there anything to be lost by meeting this 'representative'? I click 'reply' and hover my hands above the keyboard. Then I sit back. This needs more thought, not least about where to meet. And is it really a good idea? Does this person know or understand my work? Is this some elaborate fishing exercise? Is someone getting a kick out of seeing how many desperate artists will respond to the prospect, however vague and sinister, of a full year's commissioned work?

I wonder who else may be on this shortlist. Anyone I know? I sit up and start a message to people in my network, to see if anyone else has been approached. But I delete it. Something stops me. I feel both chosen and toyed with, but I want to believe it's the former, that some nameless person out there is so taken with my work he wants to engage me for a whole year.

I walk back to the window. Watching the river solves most dilemmas, I find. And not just dilemmas: creative impasses; hurt feelings; self-doubt and loss of perspective —metaphorically speaking—are drawn to the river's unrelenting flow and carried to sea.

On the opposite bank I see a man, standing still, looking downriver towards Hammersmith Bridge. Only, from his angle, on the river's inside curve, with the trees in full leaf, he can't see the bridge. Is he lost? He looks out of place, that's for sure. Then: fuck.

I pick up a pair of binoculars from the windowsill. I'm never sure whether I'm an invader of people's privacy or a student of the mores of riverside life, but I keep them there for whenever something catches my interest, and often, as now, it is to confirm what I already think.

When I told myself he was too smartly dressed to be walking along that stretch of the river, I felt a chill. The binoculars tell me I was right. The raincoat and shoes give him away, the shoes still surprisingly immaculate after their walk along the dirt track that constitutes the footpath on that side of the river.

Has he slept? Did he go and come back? I watch him and expect him to look towards me. Or maybe that's exactly what he has been doing? That's why he's looking pointlessly in the direction of the bridge: he saw me come to the window and switched his gaze, just as he did last night.

He turns, a graceful pirouette as though having made a snap decision, his eyes blankly scanning the bank in front of him, and as he completes his turn and readjusts his focus of attention, he raises his head and starts walking slowly upriver.

Am I going crazy, or has he deliberately avoided lifting his head in my direction, even though it would be the natural thing to do given the direction of his turn? He carries on walking, still slowly, face fixed squarely forward. I watch him for a minute or so during which he doesn't stop or deviate or take any interest in anything on the river or its opposite bank; in other words, anything that will cause his head to tilt in my direction. He's retreating and, finally, he's gone.

Placing the binoculars back on the sill, turning from the window, rushing across the floor to the computer, I have the one burning, implausible but inescapable thought. I reopen the email, click reply, and in less than thirty seconds have specified a date, a time and a location.

He says nothing. He sits there with his stage farce open-mouthed look. He's saying 'are you fucking nuts?' without the words. Next thing we're in my studio and he's leaning over my shoulder as we open the email.

'Alex,' I say, and stop. I want him to back off. I want him to calm down. I didn't want to tell him; except I had to tell someone and it would be wrong to hide it. But now he's trying to take over.

'What?' he says.

'Space,' I say. It's my word meaning that he's crowding me, hassling me, flustering me, making me talk gibberish. After years together it's a word I've made him understand.

'Sorry,' he says, and leans back.

He reads it in a flash.

'He's a stalker,' he says, and puts his arms up like there's nothing else to say on the subject.

'Will you read it again?' I say, 'and this time with an open mind.'

As though to punish me, he reads it aloud very slowly. For the first two paragraphs he injects a sneer into his voice, but this fades during the last two. He reaches the end and I sense a subtle shift in him.

'I don't buy it.'

I look at him, waiting for the expansion.

'He's more or less admitted to having stalked you.'

'You mean that someone who's been following my career is automatically a stalker?'

'He's outside the fucking house.'

I feel my temper rise. I want to point out that he's conflated the man outside with the content of the email. I want to tell him that he thinks he's so clever yet he's dispensed with reason. But I don't because, much as I would love the opportunity to counter-patronise him for an argument lacking in rationality, I'm viscerally aware of the inconvenient truth: I've reached the same conclusion.

'What?' he says.

'It's an unorthodox approach, I admit,' I see him jumping to get back in, 'and it's true he could be a stalker, but...'

'There's no "but", Sylvia. Email him back and tell him you're not interested and then ignore him. If he doesn't back off we call the police.'

21

'But, Alexander,' I continue, relishing the retaliatory use of his full name, 'he might be genuinely interested in my art. Some people are. Did you know that? Some people even buy it occasionally. Are you aware of that? If I want to meet him and find out exactly what he's proposing—in a wide open public place where the whole world can bear witness to whatever evil plan he has in mind—I will.'

He softens at last. I knew he would. When he knows I'm angry with him he conciliates. He may assume control too quickly, and his instant judgements are infuriating, but he isn't a bully.

'I'm coming with you,' he says.

'No,' I say, 'trust me.'

'It's him I don't trust.'

'Neither do I. But I'm prepared to try.' I look at him and reach for his hand.

He yields reluctantly, but when his palm relaxes I feel its warmth and I know I've won him over, for now.

Chapter Two

I arrive early, stop outside for a smoke, then go inside and take a walk round the British Galleries. When the impulse to meet this 'representative' first struck it was partly because I'd already pencilled in the Victoria and Albert Museum as a meeting place. This is the backwards way round thinking that I long since ceased sharing with my highly sequential husband. When I told him the venue, minus the thought process leading to it, he surprised me by nodding his approval, but still felt the need to say 'good choice' in the manner he reserves for when he grants an endorsement while implying that it is his idea. But still, we've come a distance since the out-of-your-tiny-mind attitude he kicked off with.

I plough through the rooms, desultorily and without interest, just about noting the familiar pieces along the way. It's not that Alex has ruined it; in fact we parted well, as though the argument of the last couple of days hadn't happened. But I'm preoccupied with the meeting and unable to shake off a nagging fear.

I have convinced myself that the tearooms of this vast museum are as safe a meeting place as any, the likelihood of an attack being close to zero. But that's not it. My actual fear, the one I struggle to disclose even to myself, is that this mystery person is telling the truth, and I really have been shortlisted in a competition for a year's commission. Some instinct tells me he isn't bogus; my real fear isn't him, but me: I may not measure up and I'll blow the opportunity.

Walking through the tearooms, a cup of coffee on a tray, more a prop than because I need the caffeine, I am looking for a smartly dressed man in shiny shoes. Failing to see anyone fitting the description, I settle into the Poynter room, my favourite, its blue Dutch tiles and dark wood panelling closing around me like a comfort wrap.

The museum throngs and resounds in the background, a multitude of people and languages, milling together, some no doubt discovering the treasures for the first time, some rediscovering their favourites, all pursuing their interests, drawn by a fascination for civilisation, history and the human capacity for learning and accomplishment. It's a world in artefacts. But something also saddens me when I come here, something that took me a while to understand but eventually came to me when staring at an eighteenth century silk gown in a fashion gallery and thinking of the person who would have worn it. I wondered what she would have been thinking as she put it on for the first time, imagining the giddy expectation as she prepared for her first appearance at court. And how did her life ahead look to her? And how quickly was it over? Set against the span of history, her life, though privileged, was small and fleeting. All around is the permanence of the dead.

Maybe it's not the man with the shiny shoes I'm waiting for. Maybe his appearance was a harmless coincidence. But it doesn't matter, whoever it is will be in the museum by now, making their way towards me, and the mystery will soon be over. I imagine him, or maybe her, about to turn the corner and loom into view this very second. I count to three. No one appears.

I look away, look back again, and there he is. It's unmistakeable; it's the same raincoat, the same shoes. As he sees me—harder for him, scanning a whole room, than for me, covering the entrances—he smiles with such unexpected familiarity, a mix of knowingness and beneficence, that my mind goes into reverse and I doubt, after all, if it can be the same man.

He quickens his step as he walks, almost glides, towards me. He moves with such grace, and when he reaches me he extends an arm. I take his hand and he makes no attempt to squeeze mine, just holds his in the air allowing me the sensation of caressing, rather than shaking, until he withdraws it, smiles again, and meets my eye.

'Victor,' he says.

'Sylvia,' I say.

'I know,' he says, raising an eyebrow, almost conspiratorially. He's relishing the moment, and my doubts fully resolve: I was expecting someone sinister and I'm presented with someone of impeccable charm. Close up, it has to be said, he is older than I had imagined. I might previously have believed him to be in his mid-thirties, not that I'd really thought about it, but Victor is, as far as I can tell, a youthful looking fifty year old.

He removes his coat and declines my polite but nervous suggestion that he gets himself a drink. He sits and looks around the room.

'Good choice,' he says. I shudder at the echo of Alex's phrase. 'Don't look alarmed, I have good feelings about our meeting.' He smiles. There's something reassuring about how he says this. Presumptuous, maybe, but what the hell? Here I am, I have surrendered to the intrigue, I may as well play my part for all it's worth.

I tell him that his methods are scary, that my husband went ballistic and I shouldn't be here.

'But you are here, aren't you,' he says, with a faint but pointed narrowing of the eyes. He doesn't say it to catch me out; he says it as if to imply that I quite enjoy the adventure. I smile back at him, and my nerves settle.

'You have a number of questions, of course. This is what I propose.' He leans forward, thrusting his arms out, cufflinks now exposed from beneath the sleeves of his suit jacket, his shirt pure white and smooth. 'I will give you some background, some explanation, some idea of how the process will proceed, and if I miss anything, you ask. How's that?'

I nod acceptance. It seems so logical, so well prepared of him, so considerate.

'First, please accept my apologies for staking out your house.' I should look annoyed but my response is shrugged indifference. 'No, it was bad,' he says, 'very bad form indeed. But it's a risk we take to find the right person.'

I half expect him to continue his justification, but a change in his manner tells me that line is ended.

'We,' he says, 'are our sponsor and myself. Our sponsor is a person who wishes to remain unknown. Suffice to say we are talking about someone of standing, of means, and someone who knows about art. Some considerable effort has been expended to reach this point, and a great many artists have disqualified themselves by being too modish, too trivial, too abstract, too figurative, too stuck in one medium, too political, not political enough, too whimsical, too frightening, too vacuous, too egotistical, too self-regarding, too crude, too subtle, too drunk and so on.' He waves a hand to suggest these are top-of-the-head examples from an extended catalogue of disqualifications.

'Surprised you have anyone left,' I say.

'I think we surprised ourselves,' he says, in all seriousness, 'for a while we thought there was no one in whom we could trust.' He looks at me, a trace of uncertainty on his face, a flicker of something almost vulnerable.

'It's true,' he says, reading my expression, 'you are all we have.'

I want to laugh. He's being so serious and the situation is so ridiculous. I'm flattered—I think—and horrified. I look at his face and into his eyes and catch a glimpse behind the charm. I don't know what it is, but it seems to arise from some recess of his brain, and manifests in the faintest tremor on his upper lip.

'I'm sorry, I didn't mean to sound so melodramatic.'

I tell him it's okay, and ask, 'But why me?'

He leans back and looks at me, almost into me. It seems he's on the verge of something. A revelation? Something he isn't meant to tell me but now wants to? There's an expectation, but it's cut off when he says he'll get that drink after all. A glass of wine, he says, and asks me if I'd like one.

'Join me.' The charm is back on.

By the time he returns with a bottle and two glasses, I have been sitting self-consciously, darting looks around the room at the other snackers, drinkers and diners, wondering what the answer to the question will be. I think back to feeling flattered, but flattered by who? By some deluded madman and his accomplice? I'm past thinking he's a danger, but I'm not past suspecting him of being plain crazy.

He places the glasses in the centre of the table and seems to be creating some ceremony out of the pouring of the wine. Eventually it is clear he's taking care to measure out exactly equal amounts. Satisfied, he pushes one of the glasses towards me.

'To business,' he says, raising a glass. I pick mine up and raise it to chink his, wondering whether the toasting of a transaction, still nearer the beginning than the end, is quite the right thing to do.

'You have the right psychological profile.' It's a statement that could be a compliment but, right now, out of the blue, sounds weird. I gulp more of the wine than I intend.

'I had better explain,' he says. 'We have studied your art, your website, your life history, including your family background, education, husband, the fact you don't drive a car, the petitions you have signed, the causes you espouse, your press interviews—there's a surprising amount of information for someone who is not, shall we say, in the superstar league—and you fit precisely.' He sips his wine, and from the gleam in his eye, as he rolls the liquid around his mouth before swallowing, I assume he's expecting my approval.

'I'm happy not to be in the "superstar league",' I say, 'fame is not my spur.'

'We know. That's the beauty of psychological profiling.' His smile widens. I would get angry with most men at this moment, including my husband. The smugness would infuriate me and I would normally say something— intending a witty put-down, but usually settling for an insult —designed to shut them up. But I want the job. I have no idea why. I don't really need the money since Alex earns enough for both of us, and I have no idea what the job is. Something about this strange man, his shiny shoes, his secrecy, his impulsive desire to share a bottle of wine and his mysterious so called sponsor, has snared me.

'Could you look any more pleased with yourself?' I say, laughing.

'British sense of humour, I love it.'

He looks at me closely, as though examining me, perhaps measuring me against this profile of theirs.

'What are you doing?' I ask.

He sips his wine. I sip mine.

'You are strong, stronger than you think. I am sure of it.'

My smile feels weak and I expect him to revise his view immediately. He's hit a nerve. I feel exposed for the first time since we settled down together. But it isn't him who's exposed me, at least not intentionally: it's me. I fear I'm not the one they're looking for at all.

'Strong,' he says, with a little, fast nod, 'even though you doubt it.'

I want to change the subject. 'So, where are you from?'

'From? How do you mean?' He looks puzzled by the question. At last, I think, I have him at a disadvantage.

'You mentioned the British sense of humour, as if you were a foreigner. Although, you do sound English.' I notice his poise returning, which is a disappointment since his discomfort was, briefly, gratifying.

'I have, shall we say, origins, but they are so long ago and I have never known a country other than this one.' He stares at me—probably working out that I don't think he's quite answered the question. 'I am a British citizen,' he says, at last, his eyes glazing over as he picks up his glass for another sip. 'The thing is,' and I know we've returned to the subject of "why me?", 'is that you are unusually sensitive to the feelings of others.'

'Empathy is important to me.' He looks blank. 'In my work as well as in life, I mean.'

He throws up his arms and I half expect him to shout something, but he settles and leans towards me with his eyes now sharply focused. 'I despise that word,' he says. 'Please don't use it again.'

I instinctively apologise and promise to remember, before checking myself and thinking it shouldn't be me who's doing the apologising. I drink more of the wine and wonder when it will start kicking in, and how that might change the conversation. Will he get angry? Will I say something stupid?

'Empathy is a nothing word,' he says, 'it is a noble feeling but it has been trivialised by sofa journalists, soft-soap do-gooders and lifestyle gurus who pretend it's meaningful whilst turning it into a cliché, a word in a vacuum.

'What I am talking about is this: if I take, say, a pet rat from my pocket and pin its tail to the table and start burning it with a cigarette lighter, burning its fur to begin with, then burning into the flesh, making it squeal in agony, until slowly, ever so slowly, I bring it to the point of death, will you feel for the rat? I dare say you would. But you have sat and watched. What is your empathy worth if you sit and do nothing?'

I jump to my feet. I tell him I want nothing more of this charade, that I don't want anything to do with someone who can even think such a sadistic thought. I pick up my bag and turn to leave.

He grabs my arm. A surprisingly firm grip, yet not aggressive, and I yield; a struggle will make a spectacle of us.

'Sylvia,' he says, 'you are the one.'

'The chosen one?' I say, putting as much emphasis as I can on the word 'chosen' to convey, I hope, the right note of sarcasm.

'Please sit down,' he says. He's pleading, and I soften. 'There is much more to discuss, much more to say, and I promise no more gimmicks.'

'Was that some kind of a test?' I'm still angry but I put my bag down.

'No,' he says, 'not a test. We already know.'

I collapse back into the chair and thrust my head into my hands. I smile at Victor to ease off attention from a nearby table.

'Thank you.'

'Not you,' I say at a whisper, 'I don't want the whole restaurant thinking we're having some kind of bloody domestic.'

'Great creative alliances need passion.' His hand reaches to touch my arm, the contrast with his earlier grab is mesmerising, the soft pads of his fingers gently, but decisively, touching my forearm. Once more his presumption precedes my submission and I smile again, this one signalling that our conversation is back on.

'Where was I?'

'Victor, I think we're still pretty much at the beginning.' I don't want to sound tart so I smile once more as I say it.

'I've told you about the sponsor, I've told you about our exhaustive search for the right person, and I've told you about me.' He looks at me hard-faced, then laughs.

I maintain my smile as best I can. I'm relieved he's aware of his obfuscation, but don't quite share the joke.

'Okay,' he says, turning off the laugh and thrusting his cuffs forward, 'I will give you the bones of what is proposed.' His face is stern. 'No interruptions.'

'Promise,' I say. Having to play the obedient child now we're at the crux of the matter isn't too much of a sacrifice.

'You have been told it will run for a year. That is a minimum. We don't expect it to run to two years but it will probably continue well into a second year. You have to give it your undivided attention. By that I mean you will do no other work whatsoever during the period in which you are engaged by us. I mean, literally nothing. No idle sketches, no treatments, no proposals. Nothing. Not even at the end of a day, during what you might consider free time. We will own you completely for the duration. Is that understood?'

I tell him that I understand perfectly, but the condition seems extreme. Surely if I fulfil the terms of the project my free time is to do as I please? He looks at me and draws breath slowly, as though carefully weighing up the limits of his authority.

'We will allow you four weeks holiday in the year,' he says, 'other than that the terms are rigid, set in stone, just as I have described.' He comes closer. 'Sylvia, this will be exhausting, mentally, emotionally and physically. You have to be strong.' He smiles and reaches for my forearm again. 'You will be strong, I know it.'

There are several questions begging to be asked, but since he's giving me the outline and I've promised not to interrupt, I make a mental note and let him continue.

'The details of what we require will become apparent in stages. I will brief you at the beginning and end of each stage. The subject of the whole project will be revealed to you at the start of stage one. I will not tell you today.

'If you agree to these conditions, a sum of five thousand pounds will be transferred into your bank account before close of business today. You will be allowed one opportunity to quit: when the full subject brief is first known to you. That seems to us only fair. What is more, if you pull out at that point, you can keep the five thousand; that is our gesture of good faith. But after that, once you have said yes, we will not permit you to say no.

'Payment for the year will be no less than a six figure sum. If it runs beyond the year, further payment will be in proportion.

'Finally, no one must know. We make an exception for your husband, but no one else. You have to impress upon him that he is to maintain total silence. It would be best if he were kept out of your studio for the duration, but we are reasonable people and we know that he has certain rights within the matrimonial home.' He smiles at this last remark, enjoying the mix of irony and innuendo. Testing out his British sense of humour, perhaps.

'That's a lot to think about,' he says, 'and I realise you must now have questions. But have I made myself clear?'

As crystal, I think. Or mud, depending how you look at it. 'I seem to have an incentive to work slowly.'

'But you won't.' I know that he means it's not in my nature.

'My husband,' I say, 'is not the most containable person. If he wants to tell someone, he will.'

Victor holds out his arms. 'You will impress upon him the importance and he will understand.'

I wonder if they have a profile on Alex. If he gives his word he will honour it, I know that. But seeking his acquiescence for a project that is still so faintly sketched will be bound to incite one of his cross-examinations, the outcome of which is entirely unpredictable and out of my control.

Still, I ask the question that has been butting itself against the front of my mind since Victor mentioned it.

'Why will it be so exhausting? I've always worked long hours, I've done big projects before, or juggled several smaller projects, and I'm used to working to hard, fixed deadlines. What is so demanding about this, particularly since it has no definite end point?'

Victor drains the last of his wine and refills our glasses. I watch the sudden deliberation in his movements, along with an avoidance of eye contact, which, I know already from our short acquaintance, is uncharacteristic, and I wait for his reply.

'A year is a long time,' he says, 'and our sponsor is demanding.'

He lifts his glass and drinks. It appears to be the only answer I will get. I pick up my glass and take a large sip. I want to get out now, go home and sift things through my mind in my own time.

'In a hurry?' he says.

He's noticed the change in me. Maybe it's the alcohol, and the feeling I'm no longer in control of myself, even less this bizarre process, or maybe it just feels like the end of a conversation that deep down I should never have got into, but the delicate balance of intrigue and fear has tilted and slid from my grasp and all I can hear is Alex asking me if I'm out of my tiny fucking mind.

'Sylvia,' he says, and leans forward, his face serious and concerned, 'we need you, you have a part to play and you will play it well. Trust me.'

Once more he touches my arm and this time I tug it away, as though he's administering a burn. 'I'm sorry,' he says, and looks hurt.

'No, I'm sorry,' I say, 'I need to be alone.'

I can see he's disappointed. Moments later we're on our feet. I have my bag on my shoulder and he is putting his coat back on.

'I hate waste,' he says.

I watch in amazement while he carefully decants the remaining wine from our glasses back into the bottle. He rescues a third of a bottle and, as he screws the cap back on, looks up and sees the look on my face.

'What?'

I hesitate; I don't want to say what I'm thinking, but he keeps looking at me, challenging me to come out with it.

'I've been wondering why you wear a coat on a summer's day,' I say, to deflect the question.

He grins and plunges the bottle theatrically into one of his raincoat pockets.

I laugh. 'Ask a silly question…'

We establish that we're heading in different directions—he to the Cromwell Road exit and me to the one on Exhibition Road.

It is a quicker parting than either of us had reckoned and he rounds on me suddenly. 'Walk with me through the garden.' He nods to the door out onto the garden quadrangle that sits at the centre of the museum's north side, and which, I realise, would be en route for both of us.

Stepping into the sunshine I notice the age in Victor's face. Not old, but not the young version of his age that I had first credited him with. In fact he looks tired, there's a touch of grey in his otherwise tanned pallor, and the bags under his eyes, invisible indoors, stand out sharply.

'The answer isn't "no", is it?' There's a hint of panic in his voice, which makes me wonder if he might fear having failed in his mission and, if so, what does that say about the demands of this anonymous sponsor? Will there be consequences for poor Victor?

'We will be disappointed,' he says, as if he has read my thought, 'but our search will continue, and we will eventually succeed in what we have sworn to do.'

Having crossed the garden we re-enter the museum, and reach the crossroads where we must separate. I look at him and see him looking back at me. It's just an instinct, but it seems as though some light breaks between us, some radiance that puts us on the same side in whatever scheme is laying claim to us.

'It's not a "no",' I say, and from the happiness in the smile he gives back to me, I know it will soon be "yes".

Chapter Three

It begins on the bus ride home, the long debrief, where I launch a bout of self-recrimination for having found myself in this bizarre situation. What am I thinking? Am I really, seriously contemplating entering this deal? Am I crazy?

The bus stops and starts as often as I change my mind: either I'm an idiot whose vanity got in the way of common sense, or I would be an idiot if I didn't take advantage of this opportunity. It feels like a ping-pong match in my head. But somewhere along the way it slows and my head cools and I start fitting things together, making some kind of sense of it all and finding reasons to be kinder on myself.

By the time I'm back at the house, two lists are coming together in my mind: the things I know and the things I don't. Up in the studio I write them down. The second is a lot longer, which prompts a third: questions I should have asked.

But maybe I know as much as he was prepared to tell me? He wasn't going to reveal the name of the sponsor or the precise nature of the project. I know approximately how long it will last and how much I'll be paid: several times what I'm used to in an average year. I know I have to keep it a secret and that, in their view, it will take its toll on me in ways unspecified. But they've chosen me following exhaustive research and will pay me five thousand pounds just for saying yes even if I say no immediately afterwards. Under the terms stated, why wouldn't I say yes, at least for now?

I look to the river. In its sweep to the sea, its inert power and predictability, it measures out my life more exactly and sympathetically than the days and months of the year. It draws me to a meditation, detaches me from time, let's my mind wander beyond the river to an endless garden, along a path that turns and twists and reveals in sequence its infinite variant displays.

Somewhere in this radiant daydream is Victor. I think of him without his shoes or raincoat, as he might appear on a summer's day in a country garden. I picture him playing with two children and a dog, feigning to throw a ball but holding on to it. The dog runs a few yards, sees it's been conned and turns back to face him again. The children laugh, then Victor throws the ball and the children yell for the dog to fetch. Everyone's happy; Victor is the kindly uncle who plays tricks.

There's subterfuge and forcefulness, but also kindness and understanding. I won't accuse him of empathy, however. Was that quite necessary? But I am, apparently—trumpet blast—the chosen one! What a laugh, how can I refuse?

My afternoon whiles away in a soporific, post-alcohol fuzz of warm air and a quivering breeze. I sit on the balcony, beyond the insulating pane of glass, closer to the river, vaguely studying an exhibition catalogue, listening to the cries of adults in small motorboats, who zip about shouting instructions at school-age rowers.

When Alex arrives home I tell him I've reserved a table at our local Nepalese restaurant. It will put him in a good mood and the fact we're in public will force him to behave when I tell him about Victor.

We arrive early and find the place empty. I feel mildly ridiculous announcing my reservation to the waiter.

'I think it went well,' I say, with as much sincerity as I can muster. I'm sure I must be blushing.

He nods and tells me he's had a shock today. An old school friend has died. He looks sad, like he's working hard on looking sad. I tell him I'm sorry to hear it.

'It's a while since we were close,' he says, meaning at least a decade. He reaches for the wine menu, anticipating the waiter's approach.

I tell him the story of my meeting with Victor and he listens, warming slightly to the salient points. But he's preoccupied, and I don't believe it's because of the dead school chum. Normally he would be all over my conversation by now, his opinions slapped on every detail. He would have me repeating key phrases, as though testing my veracity, or answering a barrage of judgemental questions while I attempt to respond to his snap hypotheses, before summoning himself for the final pronouncement, the one that would become his fixed opinion, his last word.

When I tell him I'm thinking of accepting the commission, he nods. I tell him he would have to keep it secret and he nods again, but he's piloting on auto.

'What's wrong?'

'I told you,' he says.

'You told me a school friend had died, but that isn't it.'

He apologises for it being so transparent, and reassures me that a school friend has died, that he didn't make that up, although it wasn't someone he'd ever been that close to, but then goes on to tell me his firm is being merged with another.

'It'll be a bloodbath.' He likes dramatising things and I tell him so. 'I may be forced out.' He holds my gaze, maybe hoping to extract sympathy.

I ask him what he will do. He tells me he will have to fight his corner, marshal support, call in favours; the same language he used on a previous occasion when it was his firm doing the buying out. 'Sorry,' he says, and looks down.

'For what?'

'For not being much use to you over this commission.'

He reaches across the table and takes my hand. I feel him squeeze it gently and I squeeze back and smile. It seems to be a day for reaching out across tables.

'It's okay. I was worried you would get annoyed and become impossible, so this is preferable.' I laugh and squeeze his hand again. He tightens his grip in response, almost, but not quite, to a point that becomes uncomfortable.

'I think you'd better say yes,' he says, and puts on one of his rueful expressions. Mostly they're ironic, to emphasise the exposure of a weakness in one of my arguments, as if he regrets that I've got it wrong. But this one's for real.

When we get home I go up to the studio. It's a nightly ritual whereby I close down for the day in preparation for the next. It's a purely mental process, the physical closure having been completed when I call it a day, anytime from early afternoon to mid-evening, and consists of moving amongst the work, observing it, touching it, smelling it, absorbing it. I like to feel it, to draw it into me, to see if it blends with me.

I study the G7 leaders and wonder how long it'll take to finish. I'd like to throw them in the river, but as a matter of principle I always finish anything I start, however misguided it begins to feel. At some point in my career I got this mantra into my head that the more a project feels wrong at the start, the more it feels right by the end. It's part truth and part superstition, but it works: it keeps me going after I want to give up. I recite it to myself again now, knowing that to do so will help me sleep better.

Checking my emails one last time—an odd habit since few come in during the evening and I won't deal with any until the morning anyway—I notice one from v.kun, the name on the email that invited me to meet the 'representative' who turned out to be Victor.

Dear Ms West

I'm delighted to report that Victor greatly enjoyed meeting you today. I'm so glad the pair of you hit it off; I had a hunch you would.

Although your agreement was not explicitly voiced, I have made arrangements to transfer the £5,000 he mentioned, this being our gesture of good faith. It should be in your account by the time you read this. As Victor made clear, you are at liberty to walk away and keep the money if you wish.

I have confidence that you will not.

My pleasure at the progress we are making is unconfined and I look forward to our future dealings.

Once again, no name at the end. But is the V for Victor, and therefore less disguised than I had assumed? But why persist with referring to himself in the third person? And how the hell did they get my bank details?

Their presumption is in character, I am coming to realise. Maybe it's a house style. I should feel annoyed, scared even, but they've given me £5,000 for nothing and in truth I had already decided to say yes. So instead of getting angry, I put the computer to sleep, turn off the lights and make my way to the bedroom.

And catch myself smiling all the way.

Chapter Four

Can we meet?

It's all it says. No Ms West, no preliminaries.

Alex has gone. Somewhere amidst his preoccupation with corporate power politics, he let me know he supported my decision. It felt more like abandonment: a default statement issued in haste to free himself for bigger concerns. But I suppose I can't have it both ways; his indifference amounts to permission, his attention would have ended in a fight.

So, all the things he would have said, if he'd been bothered, I now find myself saying. Nobody hands out £5,000 for nothing. They know where I am, who I am and have my bank details for fuck's sake. Meanwhile, I don't know who they are, where they're from, whether it's really just Victor working on his own, or if he and this 'sponsor' are part of some secret, dubious organisation.

I'm in though; I know I am. I want to believe in them. Almost like religion: if I believe, it will be true. Except with religion you can never be disappointed; if it isn't true you will never know, whereas Victor is flesh and blood, maybe as false as any god but no doubt provable one way or the other.

So I send my reply. I tell him I want to meet, I want the commission and that I will do my best to justify their faith in me. I suggest the V&A again. Seconds later he replies. He wants to meet in my studio.

I get up from the computer and walk to the window. It's raining, and I watch the serried blobs of water running across the pane, chased by the frequent squalls, while out to the river, itself dull and full, and beyond to the bridge, indistinct and colourless, I see, on the opposite bank, a solitary dog walker, caught out by a downpour that wasn't forecast, bending into the gusts, holding onto a hood to prevent it blowing off.

It amuses me to think of Victor putting his raincoat to use for once. And if he comes here it will spare me the discomfort of a bus journey, hemmed amongst wet clothes, dripping umbrellas, and the faintly rank vapour of warm but damp people exchanging the air and misting the windows.

Turning from the outside view, I picture Victor in my studio, his presence in my home—the next stage of his invasion. I decide it's too soon to give this kind of access to someone so shadowy, whose motives are so unclear. It's one thing to want to believe, it's another to surrender entirely to the unknown.

I return to the computer and tap out a reply, saying that my studio is a mess and I would prefer not to meet here. I make it jokey and, ashamedly, a bit ditzy-girly.

Trust me.

It's all I get back. It cuts that he knows what I'm thinking. I don't want to give in, but how can I repel him? He's seen through my excuse, knows the truth and is asking me to trust him. Fucking well do something to earn it, I want to say.

So I go over it again, the reasons I said yes rather than no. It's not the rationale, it's not the money, in spite of Alexander's precarious position, it's not the need for adventure, it's not wanting to be wanted, and it's obviously not the project itself since I know nothing. Or maybe it's a bit of those, and they become relevant only because of one curious, unverifiable impulse: that, although I shouldn't possess this thought, a thought that my husband would rightly ridicule if he hadn't so conveniently tuned out, I do trust him.

I trust Victor. I say it out loud to see if it doesn't combust in the air the moment it's uttered. It survives; it's true. I shout it and it echoes around the high ceiling of the studio. I tap the keyboard and can hardly believe the two simple characters that appear on the screen: OK. I send. At once I feel defeated and liberated.

In less than two hours Victor occupies the space that is my sanctuary. I had been surprised at the warmth of our greeting and with the chatty, frothy way we compensated for any awkwardness. But now I see him poking around my space, making approving noises, I rebel.

'Victor,' I say, and wait for him to finish looking at a series of wood engravings I did a decade ago, 'I need to know what this is about.' I stop myself there, at a point where there is some severity in my voice, resisting the temptation to undo the effect with some tagged on apology.

He smiles and waves a hand as if to say, of course. I invite him to sit with me at the computer table, the only place in the studio that has more than one chair.

'This is what I expected,' he says. 'I like the space; I like your work. A lot,' he adds. 'And I am sure we have a great future.' His smile is warm and alluring, as though he knows that having won my confidence he can extend his repertoire of charm. I thank him, but keep my tone businesslike.

'You are right to be wary, and brave to accept.' He sounds sincere and complacent.

'I can still back out,' I say, and make myself unfold my arms.

He tells me I won't want to, that clearing the first hurdle was the real act of courage. Once people take such a leap of faith they rarely, if ever, go back. His mouth chewed the word 'real' like a dog with a steak.

'How do you know I'm not simply desperate?' I laugh, hoping to return to the lightness of our first minutes.

He barely flickers at the question, and instead looks at me like a father who knows his child is a genius. I bask in his pride, and it warms me. The easy praise he gave earlier was quietly absorbed, but this new look of his makes me blush.

'Let me start at the beginning,' he says, 'or at least, somewhere near. By the way, do you have anything to drink?' By which he doesn't mean the cup of tea, now half drunk, I gave him when he arrived.

'Do you mind if I smoke,' I say. He pulls a face but tells me it's my house. I tell him where he can find a bottle of wine and two glasses, while I stand on the balcony smoking, enjoying the rich humid air, the sun now bright in the open sky, vaporising the fresh rainwater. The wide blue atmosphere has changed the colour of the river: no longer a dull sludge, now a sparkling blue dragon's tail.

The early days of any project are always the most exhilarating. I'd read somewhere about stages in a project, one of those supposedly satirical corporate humour pieces that glorify an unhappy truth under the guise of subverting it. It starts with excitement, then disillusionment, a hunt for the blameworthy, and ends with scapegoats and all the wrong people reaping rewards. How I love not being part of that world, Alex's world. My world is of hard slog and dogged, isolated, self-doubting perseverance, for little more than the release and fulfilment that hopefully, and uncertainly, awaits a hard won completion. It is why I have no fear of the hardship Victor has promised; it is addictive, I enjoy it, it's why I do what I do.

He returns with the wine, sits and pours. He's serene, as though he's waited, pent up for this moment and now it's here he can relax. He smiles at me.

'My grandfather came to Britain in 1939,' he says. 'He claimed dual nationality: Hungarian by birth, brought up in Poland by his mother after his father died of tuberculosis. But he always kept his other nationality secret, depending on which country he was in. Aged only eighteen, at the end of World War One, he went to Germany and made a modest fortune selling rubber—quite an achievement in early 1920s Germany—until the Nazis took over and he returned to Hungary. For a few years he was a prominent political journalist on the leading Social Democratic newspaper in Budapest, but Hungary's lurch towards fascism in the late 1930s, made his life in Budapest increasingly untenable and he left.

'Initially he intended to go to America, but a mix up in Lisbon resulted in him being on a ship to Britain, and here he stayed, not least because he met my grandmother. Within months, Britain was at war with Germany and my grandfather joined the Royal Air Force, as a Polish citizen. Hungary was, by then, firmly pro-German, and Hungarians were viewed with suspicion, at risk of internment along with Germans and Italians.

'I never knew him, and nor did my father. He was with the ground personnel at Debden airfield when, in a raid in August 1940, he was killed. My father was born two weeks later.

'He, in turn, was raised by my grandmother, a woman with an extended and close family that included her own mother—herself an immigrant a generation previously—two sisters, a brother, several aunts, uncles and cousins, many of whom also arrived in Britain during the 1930s, and a growing number of nieces and nephews. It could never quite fill the hole left where a father should have been, but it was a huge compensation. He was a boy surrounded by love and never lonely.

'My father excelled at school and won a scholarship to St Catharine's, Cambridge where he studied law. He joined a law firm after university and built a successful career, becoming a partner in a leading firm before founding his own. When my grandmother died he became the de facto leader of the family in Britain.'

Victor stalls, as though his brain has raced ahead of his speech into an emotional impasse. He hasn't touched his wine but he takes a drink now. It creates a pause, and a moment for the mental ambush that had stopped him to clear.

'Excuse me,' he says and smiles broadly—too broadly— and in overdoing it increases the sense that the emotional crux of the matter, and presumably the purpose of this enterprise, is getting close. 'There's no need to say more about my father as such.' He shrugs, as if to suggest that what he says next is of little consequence. 'Suffice to say he married my mother, lived happily and continues to do so. I was born in 1964 and my sister in 1971.'

He has another drink and I join him. There's a hint of relief about him now, as though some barrier has been overcome, even though the big reveal, as I'm now calling it to myself, a mixture of bravado and nervousness, like a guilty schoolgirl giggling before the head teacher, is imminent.

'You will have guessed,' he says, becoming serious, almost melancholic, 'my grandfather was Jewish, as is my father and the whole family.'

There's a faint, involuntary twitch in his right cheek, as though he's fighting something.

'Yes,' I say, 'I'd guessed.' I smile, wanting the smile to say that it's okay.

'I tell people I'm Jewish all the time, I'm quite open about it,' he says, a little too loud, forcing himself through his bluster to regain control, 'but I'm not at their mercy in the way I am with you.'

I am stunned. He sees it and his face changes to self-reproach.

'No, that's too dramatic. I'm not religious. I am ethnically Jewish but I do not believe in God. My family is split: those who believe and those who don't, but there's little debate about it, people accept one another's positions. It's the family that binds us.'

I think he's reassuring me that I don't have to worry about not being Jewish. He doesn't want to put me off. Am I really that important?

He reaches for his bag, a business bag, one he hasn't had about him before, and pulls out a thick A4 envelope. He folds the flap back and peers inside, rustling through some paper, until he pulls out a sheet. He holds it against his chest so I can only see the blank side, but from the heavy shading visible through the thin paper I can see it's a photograph.

'I want to show you this,' he says, 'this is what it is all about.'

He places the paper face up on the table, turning it towards me. The approximate date of the picture is obvious, a time defined for all time by the simplest of symbols. The grain in the picture, the uniforms, the man hanging from a makeshift gallows. Standard atrocity, except that around the hanging man, the German soldiers are taking photographs, the souvenir shot of their latest kill. And yet they look so normal, so little animation, so matter of fact, as though the putting to death of a man has to be collected on film in case it is otherwise forgotten.

'What are you thinking?' Victor asks.

I'm stuck. It's gruesome, horrific. But the words aren't enough, they come to mind too easily, too predictably.

I wonder if he's testing me. I must surely be failing.

'It's the fact they're taking photographs that makes it particularly...' I trail, aware again that I can only think of obvious words that merely dull the emotion.

'Precisely,' he says.

We look at each other. Something's shared and I understand.

'It's why we need you.'

I want to ask the question again, 'why me?' Meaning, why a non-Jew? Meaning, there must be other artists, better equipped to do justice to this, than me.

Victor has me in his gaze, an interrogative squint, but just before he speaks it softens and his eyes widen.

'It will be big,' he says, 'that's why we need you for at least a year.'

'What exactly do you have in mind?'

He leans forward.

'We are fighting the Nazis,' he thumps a clenched fist onto the table. 'Not German Nazis, or Italians, or Hungarians, or the neo-Nazis of Britain or France or Russia or Japan or America or wherever you may care to look. But the Nazi that exists in all the small impulses that in isolation we would call prejudice or intolerance or even bigotry, but when collected in bulk and fuelled by self-interest or greed or fear or jealousy, become an ideology characterised by extreme nationalism, xenophobia, racism, anti-semitism, ethnic cleansing and genocide.'

He pauses, almost breathless, as though he's finished, but leans forward another few inches. 'The little impulses that lie within us all. How do we stop them bulking up? That's the question.'

I feel queasy. This is a job for politicians, not artists. I remember him saying they wanted someone political but not too political, and right now I don't feel political enough. I see him looking at me, worried.

'This is overwhelming,' I say, and shake my head, 'where would I start, and what can I achieve? You make it sound like we're out to change human nature.'

'We are most definitely not trying to change human nature,' he says, as though I've committed a faux pas. 'That would be futile. We work with human nature. Just as you can fight disease with disease, we use the good part of human nature to fight the bad.'

He glares at me, to reinforce his point rather than to continue the admonishment. But, perhaps realising the possibility of misinterpretation, he breaks into a grin. 'I'm sorry, I ran away with myself. I always feel as though time is running out.'

I think of the cosmos, the 4.5 billion years of the Earth, evolution, the fact that there's seven billion of us on this planet, soon to be ten billion, and his words reverberate: 'time is running out.'

But what can a work of art do? I want to say it but I only think it.

'People make choices,' he says, 'we want them to make good ones, by which I mean ones that grow love in the world, not hate. Human nature is static, it can love and it can hate; when it hates you get this.' He points at the picture.

Looking again, I notice, for the first time, a small boy in the corner of the frame, eyes staring at the camera, apparently more interested in the photographer than the carcass of a man hanging six feet in front of him.

'Or it can be indifferent,' I say and turn the picture to face Victor. His eyes follow mine and he smiles.

'I think we are in business,' he says.

Chapter Five

In the end he leaves. I'd started to think he never would. We've talked about the possibilities, and I've joked about it being 'mission impossible' and he's joked about butterfly wings flapping and how my art is somehow going to 'go seismic.' Exactly the sort of abstract euphoria, uncontaminated by anything as concrete as experience, that these things start with. Meanwhile, we've knocked back the wine, which has provided its momentum to a conversation at constant risk of jumping track into a dimension beyond any reality I know.

And now he's gone, reality breaks through. Alone in the studio with the G7 leaders for company, I am frail and vulnerable. Victor may joke, but his expectations are obvious and my imagination suddenly a river run dry. It's been done before; it's impossible to be original. Nazis are evil! We know that.

But it's not all about Nazis, I remind myself, it's about the little impulses that bulk up, that start in fear and insecurity and end in persecution. But how to isolate them? How to represent them?

Are they a gift from history, a warning of how it can end, which, if heeded, will save us? Or are they an eruption from a far-from-extinct volcano, unpredictable, unstoppable and inevitable?

Or maybe, terrifyingly, they were a mere splutter, a minor grind of the plates forewarning of the super-volcano to come, the one that devastates everything and delivers us to extinction?

It's a relief when Alexander arrives home, hours later, after the alcohol has seeped from the system, leaving in its wake a vague and uneasy need for sleep. If I were to succumb now, I'd wake in the early hours and be awake and restless until morning. Alexander's presence gives me a reason not to drift off.

'I'm fighting the Nazis,' I say, by way of opening the conversation.

He doesn't respond, just goes to the fridge for the wine: the bottle that Victor and I have drunk.

'And was the wine for dutch courage?' he says, with unexpected good humour, a smile that looks happy rather than sarcastic. There's a bottle of red on the shelf and he takes that instead.

'How was your fight?' Although it's mine I want to talk about.

'On hold for now,' he says, 'but only just. We have some breathing space, that's all.'

He delivers short answers when he's confident. This breathing space must have been a significant victory. I move beside him and lay my hand on his arm.

'Well done.' He smiles, takes my hand.

'We have gained a tempo, so hope is not entirely extinguished.'

Another thing: when he talks of 'we' like this, it means he's hopeful, 'I' would translate as 'poor me.'

He pours a glass of wine and, as an afterthought, asks if I want one. I say yes, thinking: what the hell, just one.

'So, tell me about these Nazis you're fighting,' he says, grinning, as though expecting an anecdote.

And I find that everything is contained in that one short statement. Here we are, playing out a domestic scene like millions of others, a husband and wife sharing their news of the day, helped along by a glass of something, and he invites me to talk. Except that in the way he does it, the whole of my day, everything I'm wrestling with, all the doubts and the hopelessness, is placed in perspective, because what he has said makes sense of it.

Not that he knows. How could he? Indifference is here, in front of me, amusement even. Is this the small boy grown up, removed from the atrocity, finding recreation in its aftermath?

I tell my husband about Victor, his grandfather and father, the photo, his desire for something big, his theory of small impulses bulking up, his spirit, his hope, and the seriousness of the venture. I am out of breath when I finish, when I add that it has to be a secret.

I'd mentioned it before when he wasn't listening. He is now.

'That's very convenient, from his point of view,' he says.

'Meaning what?'

'Meaning that he has you working away for a year on a project in total secrecy, and for what? No promises, no defined outcome. You're his indulgence.'

'They're paying me one hundred thousand pounds…'

'The speech a minute ago seemed to be about rescuing humanity. But if it's about the money, that's fine.'

I'm about to say it's not about the money. Angry, reactive, like a child. But I stop myself from falling into the trap, as though a solemn responsibility has been passed to me and it's my duty now to stay calm and win the argument.

'I mention the money because it shows how serious they are. No one would hand out that kind of money as an indulgence.'

'It depends how rich they are,' he says, but the look on his face says he is listening, just.

'I've spent the afternoon fearing what I've taken on, almost wishing I hadn't, but now I know I have to do this. It's important.'

'The duty of an artist, and so forth,' says Alex. There's an ironic edge, but not aggressively so, almost as though to say it without irony would expose him to ridicule: the price you pay for sincerity in a world where everyone wants a laugh.

I look at Chagall, still sitting amongst the cigarette paraphernalia. It was real enough for him, escaping occupied France in the nick of time and only because his daughter was alive to the dangers ahead. You lose a moment and you die, you gain a moment and you live. It's all about what happens in those moments. I'm an artist; I know this. I can do this.

I pick up the cigarettes and lighter, take one and light it, smiling at Alexander, as though to say I am happy to be doing my 'duty' for art. Thinking about it, maybe for the first time, it's true. Properly true, not art bollocks true. I won't be in pursuit of some elusive, esoteric meaning, I'll be dealing with the moments that matter, the ones that are everything, that determine if we live or die. It's an honour, a privilege to be doing this.

Victor has promised to leave me alone, but he does it in a way that leaves me with a constant sense of his presence. He says he'll 'pop in' occasionally to make sure I'm okay, an assurance that could be achieved through a phone call, text or email.

He tells me there will be monthly 'display' meetings: my opportunity to show the work in progress, which I assume means his opportunity to appraise and report back to the sponsor.

I have no complaint, this is a less restrictive commission than many I have worked to, but his proprietorial attitude hangs over me, making it impossible to discount him even when he isn't there. It engenders a curious impression of the work and Victor merging as one, as of a pervasion that guides, unseen, unfelt but as constant as a shadow.

Still, he tells me I have complete freedom. He doesn't want to interfere, and the sponsor will, in due course, have something to say. Meanwhile, he, Victor, exists as a supporter, a friend even, and as a kind of proxy guardian. It creates an odd feeling of being both scrutinised and cared for.

He does, however, prime me with some reading.

'Everyone knows about gas chambers and piles of suitcases,' he says.

I nod. If I'm expecting a pile of books, I'm disappointed. He gives me a list and leaves me to assume that their acquisition is down to me. Some old thrift impulse prompts me to think about claiming expenses, but I laugh inwardly and remind myself that I'm actually earning some decent money for once. I like buying books and owning them, and for them not to be part of an expense or tax return for that matter, will make them more precious.

So I buy the books and read. There's a welcome side effect: I can sit in my studio in the evenings 'researching' while Alex prowls downstairs, making intermittent phone calls and working himself up into an increasingly filthy temper. The stay of execution, or whatever it was that had given him hope, is ending. I could ask, but I don't want to. I have a client and a project, and both are more important than my husband's business affairs.

As I pore through the books, every new piece of knowledge about the Nazis and the Holocaust makes them more incomprehensible. Three days into the reading and I am sketching ideas about my starting point: it's not the morbid fascination with the horror that terrorises the mind; it's not only the fact of the men, women and children subjected to mass shootings, gassings, clubbings, burnings and lynchings that maximises the fear; it's that this maelstrom of violence, this complete breakdown of a humane or civilised code, could spread with such virulence throughout a continent, even though the numbers of people who really, truly and sincerely desired it and drove it were vanishingly few.

On day four Victor drops by.

'No Hitler, no Holocaust,' he says. I take him to mean he approves of where I'm heading. 'But Hitler didn't do it by himself,' he adds.

This for him is the crux. One man bent a whole continent to his will. One man warped a democratic process and turned it into a terrifying dictatorship. One man held power over millions and generated a cascading, exponential whirlwind of death and destruction. Most bizarre was that one man could victimise, persecute and put to death millions of human beings and at the same time enact the most humane animal rights policies the world had hitherto known.

Victor agrees that it seems incomprehensible.

'But we don't expect you to comprehend,' he says. Thanks, I think.

Conforming to a stereotype of the conceptual artist, I have run away with an idea while failing to ask the most obvious question: what happens once I have spent a year producing art about the Nazis? Is there an exhibition? Does the 'sponsor' stash the work privately? Or what? At last, I put the question.

Victor looks ambushed, but tells me he's surprised I didn't ask before.

'There is, however, no answer,' he says.

Perhaps I hadn't asked because I somehow knew that the answer wouldn't be straightforward.

'Is there a range of possibilities?' I utter the question in as clipped a manner as I can without being rude. I am determined to make him work for his obfuscation.

'Both the things you suggested—the exhibition, the private stash—are possible. So are many other possibilities.'

'Like what?'

'Anything you can imagine,' he says, 'is theoretically a possibility in a situation where nothing has been decided.'

I smile. Strangely, I want to show that I'm cool with the arrangement. I'm warming to the sense of mystery and enjoying the freedom to do so while Alex's cold water scepticism is diverted elsewhere.

Victor looks at me and smiles back. I feel like he's pleased that I'm happy to voyage into the unknown with him. A tiny puncturing of complacency follows as the 'voice of Alex' breaks through, but I shut it down. I say again to myself that I trust Victor. I don't know why, but I do. He's playing games with me, testing me perhaps, but he's protecting his project until he knows he can trust me.

'First we need the work,' he says, reminding me that the range of possibilities exist only as a hypothesis in the absence of art.

'I'm ready,' I say. And I feel it too. In spite of there being no further instruction, no greater clarity as to the brief, and no answer as to where it's leading, the meeting feels a success. The absence of any attempt to control what I do is permission to do as I please. Surprisingly and almost shockingly, I'm aware of a nascent, stabbing thrill at the prospect of starting work in earnest.

'I know you are,' he says, and gets up to leave. 'You've been ready a long time,' he adds, as we part at the door. I hear his shoes against the pavement, abruptly silenced as I close the door, and wonder about his meaning. Is he saying that my artistic life to this point has been in preparation for this moment, readying me for this challenge? Or is he suggesting there's something in me I've never understood before, a latent urge that now finds its moment?

I don't suppose it matters either way. I am strangely in his power, but I'm happy, and tomorrow I start for real on my secret project. Or what is now mine and Alex's secret. But he won't tell, he's honourable in that regard.

Chapter Six

I'm hoping for a few things today: no Victor, no emails from the sponsor, no Alex. I want to work unhindered and uninterrupted. In sport they talk about getting in the zone, which sounds a bit ballsy for arty me, but since Victor's gone big on the need to be strong, I may as well embrace it.

I've never really thought of myself as 'arty'. I'm a practitioner, a maker of things, a creator; I move around my space producing stuff labelled art by other people. Am I a non-arty artist? Or am I fooling myself? Does my immersion in this world blind me to the person I am? The fish notices everything but the water, right?

Maybe it's because I shy from labels, but something in me rebels against the word artist. It straddles too many possibilities. Musicians, writers, choreographers, actors, even people who get pissed, are artists. Add an extra vowel and you have artistes: the hairdressers, chefs, and circus performers. In fact anyone with the remotest claim to a creative spark can be an artist or an artiste, even the barista who signs off lattes with a milky heart.

'I'm an artist,' I say to people who ask. They're generally interested enough to ask questions, prior to telling me stuff I don't want to hear, such as how crap at art they were at school. They won't tell you they're illiterate or innumerate or a shit driver or an incompetent lover, but being crap at art is something they shout about. If I'm with Alex and he tells people he's an investment analyst they fade out fast, the focus switches to me, and I find myself having to 'explain' my 'work'. In fact, he does a lot more than analyse, but if he tells people the truth they fix polite smiles to disguise the thought that he would barely be more of a pariah if he were a sex offender.

And that's how it is: people love artists but invest nothing of themselves in art; they hate investment bankers but let them rule the world.

I drill myself to get Victor as far out of mind as I can—to blot the unseen hand. He trusts me, apparently, so take him at his word, follow your instincts. My instinct is to start with facts about the Nazis' march of death across the continent: the horror stories of fantastical inhumanity that stand as a permanent and putrid scar on the human race's claim to civilisation.

A job title that would be laughable if it weren't so hideous was the 'Reich Commissioner for the Strengthening of the German Race'. In October 1939 Hitler appointed Heinrich Himmler to the post. Once Germany had conquered Poland, Himmler's brief was to get rid of racial inferiors and bring in ethnic Germans. In other words, he was to enable the master race to strut about its new homeland free from the offence of encountering anyone impure.

The resettlement programme that followed was carried out with a brutal disregard for the welfare of those deported. People were turned out of their homes, or off their land, and herded onto trucks. Able bodied men might be taken to Germany as forced labourers, others sent to an area of Poland known as the General Government and dumped in camps, where they might conveniently die of disease or hunger.

There wasn't yet an official programme of extermination, and more ethnic Poles than Jews were rounded up, but the carelessness as to whether deportees lived or died was a clear sign that the Nazi mind was rapidly hard wiring to the dehumanisation of 'undesirables'.

As I work through the history books, through eye-witness accounts and testimonies, my attention is captured by a story of a trainload that arrived in Cracow in December 1939. It was bitterly cold and the cattle trucks were draughty and unheated. When the train reached its destination the officials opened the trucks and found the frozen corpses of forty children.

It is a good subject. As I say that to myself, I come up against a barrier: that this abomination is a 'good subject'. Am I dishonouring the victims by exploiting their memory? Shouldn't the history stand for itself, unmediated by my twenty-first century, oh-so postmodern perspective? Or do I toughen up, banish the squeamishness and do my duty for art, truth and humanity?

What are my motives? The six-figure sum? Wasn't that the clincher? Please, no. I think back to the discussions with Alex and the threat he's under, and feel queasy.

But that wasn't it; I know it wasn't. I remember saying 'I trust Victor' as though that in itself was the reason. But how? How can Victor be the reason I'm doing this? What is it about his trust in me, his faith that I am the right person that makes this so compelling?

He sure moves in mysterious ways, Victor. An unseen hand and an invisible force. He is moving me, through a power of no power, or the power of mystery, or the alignment of my mind with the faith of his. It's not the money, I tell myself, it's not the money. What I want is for every persecuted, murdered, bullied, exploited, tortured, abused or oppressed person who ever lived to come back, to retake their rightful place as a free member of humankind, to have restored a life that was stolen, extinguished by those who abused their own right to life. I want the impossible because I want to believe it isn't impossible. If I preserve the memory of a death I regain something of the life.

So, what's the story of the frozen children? The one I will choose to tell and remember them by. Does it start with the rattle of the trucks on the rail, the rhythmic clatter that strikes the beat for their demise? Does it continue with their growing awareness that they are freezing, with their huddling together, the chattering of their teeth slowing as the cold hits bone and prepares to reap its harvest? I see them terrified, extracted from their lives, separated from their parents, riding to a place and a future they can only fearfully imagine, yet hoping to find safety.

They call out. Cries that no one will hear but themselves. Or maybe some adults in a neighbouring truck, but what can they do other than hear the pain and wish it away? In the midst of the huddle there's the face of one particular child, her eyes open, eyelids frosted, shivering uncontrollably. She wets herself, at first warm, then cold, then ice. The other children are quiet now, but she knows they're not asleep. She knows they're beyond sleep and it will soon come to her. She can't move, her limbs won't respond. She's the last, she's sure. She tries to cry out but her voice has gone. She feels something ebb within and finally loses all sense, as though to sleep, but her eyes still stare, her lids rimmed with pearls of ice.

I make a series of sketches, each stage of the story. I go to the balcony and light a cigarette. I need time with the river—and the nicotine—to think how the story can be rendered as art. A series of etchings would be too obvious, too linear. A film would open up more possibilities, but require performers, and children only come with a lot of well meaning, but bureaucratic licensing stipulations. Well, there's an irony: the child safety laws thwarting a film about Nazis killing children.

But I only need a child's face for an hour or two, and I can construct the rest around a few central images, photographs perhaps, or video shorts.

A sense of where I'm going emerges, followed by a burst of energy that accompanies the feeling that it'll work —even though I don't know exactly how: a real child incorporated within an animation, with sound. There'll be technical challenges, since this is a medium I've only dabbled in before, but it'll give me a narrative that is part literal and part metaphor, part figurative, part abstract. I stub out the cigarette and plunge back into the studio.

I tell Alex the story of the frozen children in the cattle truck. He wants to talk about his work.

He tells me that the takeover battle, as it's now officially called, has heated up. He says this while pacing the kitchen with a bottle of wine in one hand, which he uses to refresh a glass in the other. He's urgent, he's 'up for it', and he's oblivious to anything I say. I want to tell him about the rhythm of the train being like the rhythm of a heartbeat, except the heartbeat slows and the train continues, unrelenting, until the heartbeat stops. But the train running now is the one he's on.

'Bastards,' he says. When he's in a good mood he says it sardonically, when he's in a bad mood, like now, hatefully. Allies are dumping him apparently. He doesn't use the word 'dumping' though; he uses 'chickening out' and 'welching'. As long as I know they're cowards, that's the point he's most insistent on.

'Who's left?' I ask, meaning who is still on Alex's side.

He pours another glass, slows the pace, and even stops to pour me one. The torrent has been stemmed, momentarily at least, and I see the almost imperceptible slump in his shoulders. No one else would notice it, only someone who has watched him at close quarters in a thousand different moods over however many years? Sixteen?

'They're all on my side,' he says, raising himself again, 'just too shit scared to say anything.'

'So there's no one, really,' I say and get ready for the blast.

But it doesn't come. He tells me, quietly, calmly even, that there's a legal angle he's raised that will have to be worked through and may have costly implications for 'them'. He's thinking about Jarndyce and Jarndyce in Bleak House, I can see it in his eyes. He loves that book, he loves the idea of legal processes taking forever until there's nothing left to fight for because the lawyers have taken the lot. It's hard to tell whether he's latching on in desperation or if it's a strategy he believes.

'By the time they've unscrambled that one the world will have moved on and the deal will no longer be hot.'

He lifts his glass and sips, and, for the first time since opening the bottle, he rolls it around his mouth to appreciate it.

'And, yes, it's a good place to start,' he says.

It takes a moment to realise that he's bounced back to my conversation. So non-sequential of him—he must be suffering. But he remembered, which is astonishing.

He asks about Victor and I realise this is the key thing for him. In future, start with Victor, that's how to secure his attention.

'I had no contact with him today,' I say, truthfully. 'I think he's leaving me to it, for now.'

Alex shakes his head but says nothing. I wonder if he's been thwarted in something.

'What?'

He almost smiles. He knows I know he has something to say about Victor.

'I was thinking about him,' he says. I grin and he cracks a real smile.

'What?' I say again.

'Do you think it's a hoax?'

I look at him, say nothing, and let my face fall into an open mouth 'eh'? shape.

'Seriously,' he says. And he is.

'They've put five grand in my account,' I say.

'Okay, so they're rich and can afford an expensive prank.'

I don't know where this has come from. Is it another note of desperation, like his legal ruse to avoid the takeover? Should I view this conversation as evidence that my husband is cracking up?

'What possible motive could they have?'

'Are you sure he hasn't been secretly filming you?'

I tell him he's mad. I don't actually mean mad as in mad. I mean that it's a crazy idea, as in ha ha. I tell him he's bringing his corporate paranoia home with him and he should do me the courtesy of leaving it on the doorstep when he steps inside the house.

'I'm just saying,' he says, 'that when someone gives you money and sets you off on some wild goose chase, it can't help but raise suspicion.'

'It raises questions,' I admit. 'But a "wild goose chase" would be rather wonderful if a goose were actually caught.'

I smile at him, pleased with myself, knowing I haven't addressed his real meaning.

'The danger may not be in clear sight,' he says, in a new conspiracy thriller voice, 'but it's a weird set up, that's for sure.'

'It's mysterious,' I concede, putting on a Cheshire cat grin. It will infuriate him knowing I find the intrigue exciting.

But he looks at me with concern. 'I'd just rather you were the fox than the goose,' he says.

True, I think, although I wonder if he's thinking of his own situation.

The next few days pass quickly. It's not straightforward procuring a child who would be plausible as an East European Jew, without offering an explanation as to what you want them for. There are question and answer traps that need to be avoided. I decide to explain it as close to the truth as possible: it's a short film about the victims of dictatorial regimes, and although a Holocaust connection could be gleaned from the fragmentary, almost subliminal use of sound and symbolism, it isn't explicit. Since the sound and symbolism I have in mind would inevitably suggest the Holocaust, this is technically a lie. However I convince myself I have a formula that tells as much of the truth as is necessary, balanced against my need to honour Victor's stipulation that no one should know.

I know I'm playing with words and meanings. In explanation to others, it's a film about persecution, not about the Holocaust—I say this to disguise the centrality of the Holocaust—but in my own mind it isn't only about the Holocaust, it is about the facility within us all to be both persecutor and persecuted. It's a lie that tells the truth.

Eat your heart out Dr Goebbels.

This will have to be a one-off session. I won't be able to engage children, actors or any third parties repeatedly. To do so once suggests an isolated piece of work, more than once and it's a project—at which point it becomes a secret I may struggle to protect.

I decide to find someone through personal contacts—a regular child, not a child actor—enabling me to sidestep registers and the local authority. Not that I'm trying to avoid paying anyone, but anyone connected to an agency will ask to put the work in their portfolio. If I agree, it will be hawked around to God knows who, and if I don't, they probably won't be interested in doing it.

Sitting in the living room one evening, winding down from a day reworking my sketches, I get a phone call from a woman called Natalie. Within moments, and with urgency, she is telling me about her daughter: Nina lacks confidence; she's becoming withdrawn; she has few friends; she's falling behind at school except in art where she excels. Natalie thinks Nina will benefit 'exponentially' from the opportunity to be part of a real artist's work.

I feel pain in Natalie's voice: the clipped, too-fast explanation; the way she talks through short sighs, and I find myself picturing Nina. From an impulse to feel sorry for her, emerges the realisation that she could be just right. I like the sound of a girl under-confident, vulnerable, haunted even. My imagination flies.

I recite to her my prepared, semi-truthful, script, with a growing sense of the hollowness in my words as they emerge from my mouth. But Natalie listens with interest.

'I'll probably only need her for an hour,' I say. There's a pause at the other end and, though silent, it sounds like disappointment. 'I can show Nina around the studio, let her see how things are done.' I add.

'That would be great,' says Natalie, 'really kind, thank you.'

There's another pause.

'Anything you want to ask me?' I say, quickly.

Natalie wants to know more of what the artwork is about. It's the question I didn't want and she may sense me hedging around, doing my best to provide a respectful answer without saying anything.

'It's just that,' she says, and hesitates, 'we are Jewish.'

'Oh,' is all I say. I want to say more but the words get stuck. I'm guarded: they will be more interested, more questioning; wonderful qualities in a normal relationship, but not if the only replies you can give are to make you more of a liar.

'So we won't just be pretending,' says Natalie, giving a lift to her voice, as though to make light of it, or to tell me she's only giving me this information to reassure me of her daughter's authenticity.

'That's good,' I say, and wonder how that would not be good. Has three days working with the Nazis made me so self-conscious?

'It is a sympathetic work, isn't it?' she says, 'sympathetic to Jews, I mean.'

'Yes,' I say and relax, relieved that she's voiced her fear, and for the opportunity to speak truthfully, 'I promise you it is.'

The tension evaporates. I must have said it well because I sense Natalie is reassured.

Natalie and Nina turn up on Saturday, as arranged. They've taken a two-bus journey from Belsize Park, an endless stop-start trip that would numb my excitement, but theirs seem undiminished. Natalie is tall and elegant, at odds with her darting eyes and chattering speech; a sparrow inhabiting the body of a swan.

We do the polite thing of thanking each other, as though already sure the venture will be a success. I guide them through the house, stopping at the kitchen where I introduce them to Alex. He's in a good mood, although he's about to set off for the office, officially to complete a report, but, since he could probably do that at home, I assume some takeover related skullduggery too complicated to explain.

'Hello Nina,' he says, making a fuss of her by giving her his big friendly smile, the one he saves for kids because he thinks that's how you communicate with them, even when they're teenagers. It's impressive, however, since it means he's remembered her name. It works, miraculously: Nina giggles back, although she may be humouring him—she does seem very polite. Alex even offers to make drinks and promises to bring them up to the studio.

Nina has already captured my interest beyond my expectation of her. She darts around like her mother, sharp and charming, not at all the ill-at-ease person I'd anticipated. Perhaps I'd read too much into the struggling-at-school description and made assumptions about her lack of confidence, but still, the contrast between Natalie's description and Nina's behaviour can't all be down to my imagination. I counsel myself to suspend judgement: Natalie is her mother and I've met her ten minutes ago, and maybe this is just the buzz of excitement that comes with a new adventure.

Leading them up to my studio, I can feel mother and daughter's growing eagerness. Whatever's going on, it's gratifying to know this is a thrill for them both. As we walk in, Nina's mouth opens and shapes a 'wow'. I know I'm lucky: to have a space like this in my home is unusual but, even so, I'm surprised it's making such a big impression.

'This is a great space,' says Natalie, her head swivelling to take everything in.

'Great view of the river,' says Nina, skipping to the window.

'Every artist should have a studio overlooking a river,' I say to her. She smiles and nods gently. She's just turned thirteen so should be old enough not to take me literally, but the knowingness in that nod and on her face and in her eyes, tells me she understands exactly what I mean.

'Something to look at during those creative blocks?' says Natalie and laughs.

I smile at her. 'It's a great comfort in all kinds of ways,' I say and leave unsaid what I'm thinking: that her daughter is way ahead of her.

I do the tour as promised. Natalie is exhaustingly interested, and Nina is captivated. I'm almost embarrassed at how admiring they are of everything I show them. But whereas Natalie swoons and exhorts, Nina looks deep and absorbs. Natalie's eyes are alive and searching, Nina's full of wonder.

Alex arrives with a tray. He has a domesticated look, and I catch an approving glance from Natalie. He's not normally like this, I want to say, but don't. I thank him, and for a moment, as he turns to go, his nice-guy cameo complete, I feel some part of me soften towards him.

'Let me show you my tool shed,' I say. I watch Natalie's features stall and Nina's turn to puzzlement. I'm playing for this moment, as I often do with visitors.

'No one expects an artist to have a tool shed,' I say, in the style of Monty Python's 'no one expects the Spanish Inquisition'. They relax, sensing the digression might be relevant after all. I'm not sure if Nina understood the reference but the voice made her laugh. I take it as a compliment: she must have warmed to me to laugh at that. I walk to the back of the studio and open a walk-in cupboard to reveal power drills, a workbench, a drill press, a band saw, a lump hammer, sheets of metal, wood, spray paint cans, a hand torch, various planes and cutters, a hand-tool box, a chain saw and a sewing machine.

I see Natalie forming a question.

'For installations, mainly, and the occasional sculpted figure for animations,' I say. She nods. 'I don't sculpt in the traditional sense, but I can knock up a mean looking metal-man from junkyard scrap.'

Nina laughs again. I am her new heroine and I smile at her.

I explain to Nina the story of the frozen children in the Cracow train, but without mentioning Cracow or that it is a factual as opposed to fictional story.

'It's the part I want you to play,' I tell her, 'the last child to die; the one who knows everyone around her is dead, and waits, terrified and helpless, for the same fate.'

I look at her, thirteen, and wonder if she can give me what I want. Her face has changed, the smile gone.

'Sorry, have I frightened you?' I say and half turn to Natalie, worried that she may be anxious on Nina's behalf.

'No,' says Nina, 'I'm fine.' She's beaming again and I know she's telling the truth. I realise she's given me a performance. She's going to be good, and I practically swoon.

I'd created the set before they arrived: lights, cameras, ladder, backdrop. It's simple stuff; the variables to play around with are light levels, angles and, of course, Nina. I tell her she will need patience: she's to be shot—still and movie—from a dozen angles, at every gradation of lighting between hard and diffuse, from front and side, and in every body position we can think of.

'I'm experimenting,' I say.

'I'm ready,' she says.

And she is. Every emotion I ask for she gives me. As I swoop on her with the camera she doesn't lose her assurance or recede. She becomes more vital, the emotion within her slender frame maps onto her face so vividly I wonder about the life force at her core, a trembling intensity available at will. So frail and so strong.

Natalie remains remarkably still. I've known her for a fraction of an afternoon, but already I feel I know enough to be sure this is uncharacteristic. Is it out of respect for my work, my need to concentrate, my need to create a rapport with Nina? Or, is she, as I am, transfixed by her daughter? Is this as much of a surprise to her as it is to me?

I put down the SLR and pick up the camcorder. I decide to ask Nina for something I hadn't planned, since I'd assumed it would be too ambitious a request for a random thirteen year old, before Nina turned out to be so adept. I want her to transform her emotional state during a shot, to move from sadness to fear, first suddenly and then gradually.

While I alter the lighting, I catch her in the corner of my eye practicing. I steal glances as I continue to fiddle, not wanting to look at her directly in case I distract her. She has it perfectly, first time—the exactitude, the confidence—a joy to watch. Don't peak too soon, I think, but the thought fades and I smile to myself, knowing she has it.

She is a dream, and Natalie too, whose quietness stills to silence while the camcorder rolls.

'That's it,' I say, eventually, 'all done.' It breaks the spell, like a clap of thunder on a warm summer evening.

I can see, feel even, the regret in both Natalie and Nina for the time having passed.

'You were fantastic,' I say to Nina, and I know from the way I'm bubbling over that she won't doubt me. She throws her arms around me and squeezes. It's another confident gesture that belies her mother's description.

Natalie thanks me and lingers. She wants to talk to me, but something stops her. I realise she'd like to talk about Nina, but when Nina isn't present.

'Give me a call in a day or two,' I say.

And they leave. There's still a buzz in the air as they disappear outside, but as I close the door their departure feels like a loss. I wonder if it's the same for them as they walk up the road to catch the return bus. Something happened this afternoon—it happened to me, and I want it to have happened to them too.

Victor sits, thinking, his face struck immobile, all animation confined to his right hand, which is tapping on my desk.

He's invited himself around to one of 'our'—I would say 'his'—'display meetings'. It's too soon for me, but I can't refuse and, after all, would I want him to be uninterested?

'Tell me more about this girl, Nina,' he says.

I pick my words carefully, not wanting to further inflame a sensitivity I'd hoped, optimistically, not to agitate—the one about confidentiality.

I start to explain that Nina and her mother would have no idea that the work with them was part of anything bigger, but Victor cuts me off.

'Just tell me about Nina,' he says.

I'm tempted to ask what exactly he wants to know, but his tetchiness cautions me against this. So I tell him about Natalie's initial phone call, what she told me about Nina, how that contrasted with my experience, and how remarkable she was as a model.

'She was magical,' I say.

'Natalie. What about her?'

'Well…' I'm thinking suddenly that it's not Nina he's worried about. Nina may tell other children, but the fact that she's sat for an artist would probably be more interesting than what she sat for. But a mother, a proud mother, one who wanted to glorify her daughter's role with as much, possibly embellished detail, as possible? She's more of a risk. I start to say again that Natalie and Nina know only that I am an artist working on one isolated piece.

'It doesn't matter.' He waves a carefree hand, his face relaxed once more.

'You don't sound like it doesn't matter.'

'I needed a moment, that's all,' he says. 'To think it through.'

'So it's okay, me involving Nina?'

He smiles and nods and tells me it's fine, that I surprised him by starting with a film. He hadn't expected that.

'If, as you say, they're ignorant of the bigger project,' he says, 'there's no conceivable threat.'

'So you trust my judgement after all?' I am pleasantly surprised, but still sceptical.

'Of course, but I don't know what you mean by "after all".'

It's my turn to smile, and he reciprocates. It's a warm, encompassing smile and it encourages me to ask a question that formed in my mind a few seconds ago.

'What exactly is this "conceivable threat?"'

His eyes retreat. He's closed down. Is it too hard a question? Is it something he's protecting me from? Is it a stipulation of our sponsor that everyone must obey without knowing why?

'The integrity of our mission must not be compromised,' he says.

'Meaning?'

'It has to be secret, that is its essence.'

To me it sounds like flannel followed by bullshit, and pompous with it. I weigh whether it is worth pursuing further. I don't know if he's on the verge of saying something meaningful, or I am on the verge of annoying him.

I'm aware of him studying my face, but I can't guess what he's looking for.

'I'm sorry,' he says, 'I know my answers are not satisfactory.'

But he offers no more and I'm caught in too many minds to frame another question. The conversation stumbles and falls and I decide the best thing is to move onto the 'display'.

I have sketches, which provoke a resurgence of interest. They're preliminary and it would be hard for anyone to visualise where they're going, but Victor gets it. I tell him about the animation and how I plan to 'sit' Nina within it. It's all very abstract but Victor is warming to it without me having to explain in tortuous detail what I hope to achieve.

Which is good, since, in my experience, once you have to explain what someone fails to grasp intuitively, the more doubt and confusion you create.

I show him the photos of Nina.

'The camera was a foot from her face,' I say, as we look into the pure swim of her eyes, 'and she hardly blinked. She let herself flow into the camera, as though its lens were a doorway to another world.'

I fluster, thinking that I may be saying too much, and worried I'm gushing, but Victor is studying the picture, apparently oblivious.

'You can tell,' he says, 'and in return, she's drawing me to her.' He turns to me, his face open in acclamation. 'Show me more.'

I move through the folder, pausing for several seconds over each picture. As the images pass by, there's a consistency to Victor's responses: a slow perusal, a slight nod and a murmur.

'Let me pick some out,' I say, moving from slideshow to file view.

'No, let me see them all.'

I tell him there are hundreds, but he insists.

'I have all day.' Unlike me, I think, but don't say it.

He sits and watches as two hundred and eighty-four images of Nina scroll past. He doesn't talk, or shift restlessly. Gradually I almost forget he's there and find myself calmed, engrossed in the photographs.

It becomes a meditation, the two of us side by side watching a young girl's face, witnesses to some gift of mind and body that can draw so precisely on such a range of human emotion. As I watch with Victor, the grip Nina already has on me tightens: she's so effortless, so natural, so innocent, but, from somewhere deep, so knowing too. How can she be so unworldly and yet able to summon expressions that betray our darkest fears?

The slideshow ends and Victor gives his deepest nod and longest murmur. His eyes remain on the screen, scanning the thumbnails as though to strengthen the memory of what he's seen.

'You haven't seen the movies yet,' I say.

'The movies?' He turns to me, his face woken from a trance, as though a grief that arrived with the end of the slideshow is reprieved.

The first film is of Nina lying on her side opening and closing her eyes. It's a minute long, as they all are; short films to be spliced into animations. I've envisaged a staccato effect: multiple screens showing different edits of the various films on loops, sequenced to ensure no two screens show the same footage simultaneously.

But Victor and I watch the raw film footage, in a sequence from first to last. They're all silent and, as I watch, I'm reminded of the moments at which I directed Nina: to not add a double blink as she opened her eyes, something she didn't know she did; the look on her face the exact moment I told her to believe she might live; and the moment when she knew she would die. We watch her face change from hopeful to desperate, from loved to forsaken, from impudent to broken. Everything I asked she gave, sometimes in an instant and sometimes slowly, her face altering in gradients as the camera closed in.

The final film, the one with the beads of ice around her eyelids, is the longest. In a single two minute shot she alters her expression from pain to fear—from anger to sadness—from resignation to numbness—from chilled to frozen—from life to death. As the end approaches, her face goes from slackened to solid and her eyes from mobile to inert. She holds that look for half a minute while the camera silently records her face—she is like someone long dead, freshly cracked out from permafrost.

'It's as though she's expired right before our eyes,' says Victor.

I get up and walk to the window, to look out over the river. Victor follows me. I assume he too feels the need for some release.

'I think of it as your river.'

'That's funny, so do I.' I find myself grinning at him, at the coincidence of thought, and at the ridiculousness of appropriating a river as one's own, never mind one as world famous as this.

He puts his hand on my shoulder. No more than a touch, although there's a soothing strength behind his gentleness.

'You made the right decision,' he says, 'Nina is perfect.'

I thank him. I have a suspicion that earlier, when he said he trusted my judgement, he was making a show of having faith in me, as if it was important to do so to build the relationship, but now, thanks to Nina, his sincerity is as true as the water that flows past us to the sea.

As we silently observe the river, I feel his hand move across to the nape of my neck, where he presses a little more firmly. It's the touch of a lover except, as I look up, there is nothing of the lover in his face, just warmth and— strange word, I catch myself thinking as I think it— comradeship.

Chapter Seven

With Victor gone I'm left in the studio to catch up on what I'd planned today, but it's a losing battle. With the concentration broken and that fragile thing—momentum—disrupted, whatever it was that propelled me earlier has gone. But this is familiar territory, and I know if I give myself a firm talking-to I can restore the will and salvage something of the day.

Alas, it is not to be. I hear Alex arrive home. It's not his usual time, but the concept of 'usual' has taken a battering of late so this seems less a surprise, more a confirmation of the volatile nature of his world at present. I'm glad he's missed Victor, but guiltily so: I want them to meet in theory, but I'm never quite ready for it. I'm afraid that each may judge me by my association with the other.

I tell myself it shouldn't matter—to me, that is. I am me and they are them and they can damn well take responsibility for themselves and leave me out of it.

Alex's moods can be interpreted from the pattern of noises he makes when he's elsewhere in the house—even, as now, when he's two floors away downstairs. It can take a while to percolate through to consciousness, but when it does, after the shutting of a door, for instance, signalling the selection of one room entered as opposed to another, or if music is heard rather than TV, or a briefcase dropped rather than parked, such as now, it serves as an alert to be mindful of.

Almost the last thing he would do on arriving home is to come up to my studio, since he knows I'll be busy and not want to break off. He'll climb the stairs to the first floor, where our bedroom and wardrobes are, and call up to tell me he's home. This is a surplus communication since I already know, but it's a companionable ritual I respond to willingly before carrying on.

Today I hear his footsteps on the first flight, then the relative quiet as he crosses the landing to the bedroom door. But the call doesn't come, and I realise he is, in fact, climbing the stairs to the studio.

I save the file I'm looking at, so there's no chance of it somehow modifying while my attention turns to him. It's a compulsion born of the occasions—possibly only one—I've lost something important for reasons I can't explain, but suspect were to do with poor digital housekeeping.

Something significant is afoot, and as Alex presents himself in the doorway, the confirmation is manifest. He looks shocking and, if I'm not mistaken, he's been drinking.

'It's over,' he says.

No prizes for guessing what, but I'd imagined the end was further away.

'Complete wipeout,' he says, and slumps into the other chair.

'Are you alright?' Obviously not, but I'm hoping he won't choose now to take me literally.

'I'll be fine,' he says, 'just need a few days to get used to it.' He smiles a non-smile, one of those that communicates bravery in the face of shit.

'So what actually happened?'

And the floodgates open. 'Spineless bastards' have surrendered. 'Foreign bastards' have taken over. It's been a 'bloodbath' and 'every poor bastard has been fucked over.' If they'd had the guts... if they'd listened... if... if... everything's an 'if', but like he said at the start, it's over.

'Nothing to do anymore but move on,' he says, turning up his palms.

I look at him and wonder about the implications. I'm thinking of the house, mainly. I hedge around, not wanting to sound too concerned about me before he's finished venting about him.

'Where does this leave us?' I say, finally.

He grins, an unexpectedly genuine look of pleasure.

'A couple of us pulled a neat trick with some share options,' he says. 'We're fine.'

'You mean you knew how it was going to play out?'

'I saw the possibility. You have to have a fall-back and this one worked out pretty smartly.' His eyes are almost twinkling.

I ask him how much and he skirts around, teasing, before telling me it's 'close to seven figures'—more than he got in bonus even during the fat years, and enough to pay off a mortgage which, although easily our biggest outgoing, has been whittled away over time, and now stands at a fraction of what it was.

So we sail on almost as though nothing has happened. His pride dented, our bank balance swollen, the house secure and a 'bloodbath' behind that looks entirely bloodless from my point of view. Someone must suffer, somewhere down the line, I assume, but I'll snuff out that thought; it's a guilt trip too far for now.

'Relieved?' I ask.

'Too early for that,' he says, but the dishevelled look he arrived with is lifting.

'Oh fuck,' he says, as some new displeasure takes hold. I don't know what, but it's nothing to do with me so I don't enquire—and he's off back downstairs.

I feel good somehow. Is it because a domestic disaster is averted? Or is it in celebration of the fact that my clever husband has turned a catastrophe into—let's not call it a triumph—a successful rearguard operation? These are good things, relatively speaking, but not the source of my unexpected buoyancy. As I light up a cigarette and take in the expanse of my studio, appreciating, as though for the first time, its light and space, I arrive at the real reason: in talking to me for a few short minutes his mood changed from forlorn to sanguine while he told me that the house, our life, is saved. 'We're fine.' And in those words and the manner he said them, I realise I matter to him, and this is a reminder that he matters to me.

I dream of Nina, and of Victor. I mix them in my mind; a mind that likes, in sleep, to sort things out and categorise. It's a variation of a recurring dream, one in which I'm a librarian or a zoologist or a social historian, constantly finding new examples to be put in order, always against a clock.

Tonight 'the system' demands I categorise Nina and Victor. They stand in front of me, their papers in their hands. A man behind me shouts 'Jew' and I shout 'there's no such category' and he shouts again, 'Jew.' I shout 'Man' and 'Girl' but he still shouts 'Jew'. He points at the clock. 'Man' and 'Girl' I repeat, 'Jew is not a category.' And then I am screaming: 'there's no such category.'

But he points at the clock and says, 'Make a new category.' He is insistent, unceasing, immovable and angry. I pull a lever and a new category appears: 'Jew'. Nina and Victor walk with their papers to the door marked 'Jew'. It opens and they're gone.

And I wake up.

My research continues, alongside the production of what I'm calling the 'Nina piece'—a working title. I have no ideas for a name beyond that, but tell myself to wait until all the pieces are finished and we have our exhibition—if that is where we end up—by which point some structural imperative will throw up a naming system.

There's something grimly, indecently compelling about Nazi atrocities. They say you can become inured to life's grimness—compassion fatigued social workers, battle-hardened soldiers, institutionalised care workers, or whatever—but the more I learn about the Nazis the greater the weight of horror. With each story the revulsion grows, the sense of terror multiplies and the incomprehensibility overwhelms. In the past, I've felt squeamish thinking about the guillotine or the torture instruments of the middle ages, the conditions in the trenches in the First World War, but nothing piles fear onto abomination onto dread onto repugnance onto savagery onto desperate, heart-rending sadness and desolation like the history of the Nazis.

Where to begin? I wonder about Robert Ley, a man who lends himself to an artwork if ever anyone did. Some people don't need to be satirised because their life is such a bizarre performance nothing further can be achieved. Robert Ley lived one of those lives: implausible, horrific and pathetic. If ever there's a poster boy for the despot psyche Robert Ley has to be it.

He was the leader of the German Labour Front, a body set up by Hitler to enforce state control of the trade union movement—in effect, to emasculate it. Enduringly loyal to Hitler, his only real achievement was to retain the Fuhrer's patronage, since in everything else he was incompetent—as well as a drunk and corrupt. Of the latter, he would use confiscated funds to buy paintings and houses, including the purchase of a landed estate near Cologne whose buildings he knocked down to make way for a new style Nazi utopia over which he presided in the manner of a feudal landlord.

But it was his outlandish personal behaviour that perhaps serves best as exemplar and microcosm to the crazed morality of the Nazi regime.

Drinking bouts with his cronies frequently ended in drunken brawls, often spilling over during official engagements resulting, on one occasion, in a visiting dignitary being beaten up. In 1937 the Duke and Duchess of Windsor, during their infamous, apparently regime endorsing visit, were hosted by Robert Ley who, predictably, got drunk. Grabbing the keys to his Mercedes he took them for a spin and drove them straight through a set of locked factory gates, smashing them off their hinges.

This proved too much for Hitler, who replaced him with Goring for the remainder of the Duke and Duchess's visit. Despite this, Ley retained Hitler's favour because of his faithfulness. A key characteristic of Hitler's leadership was that loyalty was rewarded almost regardless of anything else.

Possibly the most bizarre Robert Ley story, and the one that interests me for it's artistic possibilities, concerns his second wife. Ley was a notorious womaniser and had a string of affairs during his first marriage, one of which was with a singer, Inge Spilker, whose body became the source of total infatuation on his part. He divorced his first wife and married Inge, still in thrall to her physical attributes— her beauty as famous as Ley's ugliness. He commissioned a portrait of her, topless, which he would eagerly flaunt for the appreciation of visitors, official and social.

Life for Inge became intolerable. Ley's drunken licentiousness reached a peak one evening, when, in the presence of guests, he ordered her to strip naked so that he could show off the beautiful body of the woman he had married. Angered by her reluctance to obey, he ripped off her clothes and proudly exhibited her to the astonished gathering.

For Inge the humiliations led to her spiralling decline. She took to alcohol and drugs, and finally took her own life, shooting herself at the culmination of another drunkenly violent row with Ley. Robert Ley then fucked her dead body before handing her over to the undertakers.

I made up that last sentence, but somehow I just bet it's true. And even if it isn't, the fact that I should ascribe it to him is a truth of sorts.

Victor is fascinated by the Robert Ley story. It transpires he's big on signifiers and sees in Ley a representative of a side of human nature that is at the 'core,' he says, of 'our project.'

'An outstanding example of the status seeking toady: talentless and useless, devoid of humility, filled with grandiose ideas that he's incapable of realising on his own initiative; all while securing his niche by brown-nosing upwards and dumping on those below. An archetype for the Nazi follower par excellence.'

Victor's angry, but ardent. This isn't a mere spilling over of resentment, a venting recrimination, a howl into the wind; it's an observation on the way in which human frailty can turn itself inside out: from weakness, the facade of strength; from fear, the growth of malice.

'This is it,' he says, 'this is it.' His eyes burn and his hands cut the air. 'Our sponsor will approve.'

The introduction into the conversation of the sponsor reminds me of the surreal nature of this enterprise. I'd almost forgotten this mystery figure, someone I'd variously thought of as Victor himself or as the man behind the curtain in the Wizard of Oz, but about whom I'd stopped thinking since immersing myself in the work. I look down and see Victor's shoes, gleaming as usual, and wonder again what, or who exactly, I'm involved with.

'Will I ever meet this sponsor?'

Victor's excitement stalls. The vitality in his features turns contemplative, and he looks at me in a way I haven't seen since our first meetings. Victor extends the silence beyond what is necessary. I shift in my seat, aware of my discomfort, a sensation I thought we had got beyond.

'The way things are going, I expect so,' he says, and breaks into an affirmative nod, as though he's surprised himself by what he's said. He finishes with a new smile and the tension dissipates.

I take it as a compliment. I have his approval and the prospect of one day meeting this 'sponsor' seems to have advanced. I feel bolder.

'Why the mystery?'

'It's no mystery, our sponsor wants to stay out of sight, that's all.'

I don't know if it's my imagination but there may have been a touch of irritation in Victor's reply. Oddly, and unusually for me, it spurs me on.

'Why should the sponsor want to stay out of sight of me?'

'Out of sight of you,' he says, 'and of everyone.'

'Is this person always so secretive?'

I brace myself for the answer. I know I'm treading on sensitivities and I'm sure Victor's undercurrent of annoyance will surface soon. I'm not sure why I'm doing it; Victor isn't going to tell me. Maybe I want to stretch him a little, make him work.

'Yes,' he says, and smiles. He does another of those nods, as if to say I've sparked a more honest response than he wanted to give.

But I'm not getting anywhere, at least not anywhere nearer to meeting the sponsor. 'Doesn't he trust me?'

I've used the masculine pronoun; quit fencing around with this 'person'. Maybe he'll fall for it.

'Is there a reason for our sponsor not to trust you?'

He's grinning. He knows my game and he's playing it back. I sigh and put out a defeated 'I tried' kind of smile.

'Seriously,' I say, and I mean it to be completely, literally serious, the kind of serious Alex would be proud of, 'whoever this sponsor is, can you tell him, or her, that I would love to meet? Can you pass that on for me please, Victor?'

'Of course,' he says, 'but it won't make any difference.' He softens and adds, 'I am sure the day will come and you will be more than satisfied.'

I wonder exactly what he thinks will satisfy me, but the conversation isn't worth pursuing further, I know that. But an idea occurs, a crazy idea. Having invoked Alex only a moment ago, I now want to veer as far off track as I can from anything Alex would do at this juncture. When Victor leaves, I'm going to follow him.

My objective isn't clear but my motive is: I want to unravel at least something of the mystery of Victor and the sponsor. If I can follow him to his house or the sponsor's house, and even if I can do nothing but note the address, I will have some detail to base my imaginings on, some connector to link my existence with theirs, some material knowledge to help me feel at less of a disadvantage.

It hinges on my hope that Victor doesn't drive when he visits me. I've always imagined him not driving but now, faced with a practicality, such a hunch counts for nothing. How often do mental pictures about people or their houses or families, or any other imaginary construct, fail to turn out in reality?

I say goodbye to him in a manner I hope is normal, probably trying too hard not to betray nervousness. Once the door closes behind him, I lunge at the hall cupboard and grab an old coat and hat. I tie my hair back and put on sunglasses. It's a look even Alex would struggle at first to recognise. My calculation is that Victor won't be scanning for someone following him, and my cover should survive the casual widescreen glance of a man on the move for whom people on the street are no more than the backdrop to everyday life.

In a child-like, sugar-rush state I dub myself Super Agent Sylvia (SAS) and head out of the door. I'm sure Victor was about to turn right after leaving the house, which means that if he hasn't already jumped into a car, he will be about half way to the end of the street. The parking situation is competitive, so if he's come by car he could have a fair walk to retrieve it.

Victor, it turns out, is a fast walker and is already well past the halfway mark. This adventure is going to be energetic. The street runs parallel to the river before meeting a pedestrianised riverside garden. I expect him to turn left at the end onto another street and head away from the river towards the bus stops or the tube station and the likeliest parking places.

But he doesn't. He walks through the gate into the garden and picks up the riverside path. He doglegs to the right, briefly out of sight behind a wall, before appearing again, and during those seconds I break into a jog to prevent too big a gap opening.

In common, I imagine, with anyone who's ever followed someone, I'm banking on him not turning round while he's walking. No one ever does that, right? Maybe if they lose their way and have to backtrack, but even then their concentration will be on the matter at hand, not the nobodies, the invisible multitude who inhabit the periphery of our self-absorbed lives.

The people with cause to glance behind are those who expect to be followed: the guilty, paranoid, famous. I don't think Victor falls into those categories. The longer Victor walks, the better. It will be at the bus stops, the tube carriages, the stoplights at pedestrian intersections, where problems arise.

Walking across one of the few exposed places in this huge city, I catch a blast from a stiff breeze. It's a warm day but the sudden wind off the river, combined with my nervous excitement, makes me shiver. The hat I grabbed for a disguise now feels like part of my armour and I pull it closer around my head.

Victor continues to sprint away. There's no sign of undue effort; he seems to glide as much as walk. An elegant man, I tell myself, and feel a surge of fondness for someone who has come to represent in my mind some higher plane, some symbol of a rarefied existence. I smile at the irony of projecting this onto him in the absence of knowing him—and that this deficit is the reason I'm on his tail now. I realise I have unconsciously slowed to my normal pace. I administer the mental crack of a riding crop and skip forward.

We pass the rowing clubs and their slipways, and the pubs with their brightly flowering hanging baskets, and Victor has passed up all opportunities to turn away from the river. His first staging post appears to be the bridge, which presumably means he's planning to head south of the river: for buses and tube trains north of the river, turning off sooner would have been quicker.

I'm right: he turns to walk across the bridge. My guess is that he'll cross the road to pick up a southbound bus, something I need to prepare myself for: to mount the same bus will be my first real test. I mentally rehearse a 'fancy meeting you again, I'm just off to see blah…' response in case I'm busted.

But he doesn't cross the road, and when he reaches the other side of the bridge he takes the steps down to the riverside path. He walks back upriver, the direction he's come from, but on the opposite bank. This is crazy; there's no obvious purpose. This runs counter to all the assumptions I've made about where he might be going—an admittedly open list, but based on the idea that the likeliest destination is home.

His pace slows. This is the unpopulated, unpaved side of the river, the preserve of dog walkers and joggers, trees and bushes, puddles and mud. No place for shiny shoes, although it won't be the first time I've seen him on this stretch. But working on the supposition we've passed that phase of our relationship, this makes no sense whatsoever. Almost anywhere Victor might be headed to from here could have been reached more quickly and less muddily by another route.

I slow. For the next quarter mile or so he's hemmed in on a path between the river and the grounds of a school, so there's little danger of me losing him. But then I realise the trap I'm setting myself: what if he does still come here to spy on me? Just because I've stopped looking out for him doesn't mean he isn't there. The danger is that once he's finished his observation he'll return the way he came, and with the path so tight he won't fail to see me. Face to face, and feet apart, my disguise is bound to fail.

But it's too irresistible. I have to know if I'm right. He's surprised me this far and may do again. I continue on his trail, hesitantly, deliberately keeping him only just in sight as he rounds a long bend. At this range he becomes nothing more than a distant figure flickering through the cover of the trees, which is exactly how I want to appear in reverse, should he look round.

He stops. I stop. He's in the same place as before. He looks across the water towards our house. I retreat a little, to the point I'm confident I can turn and disappear without drawing attention, when, if, he makes his return journey.

From here, our house is a distant group of windows, set in a terrace. I remember picking him out with the binoculars, watching him avoid my gaze, or so I thought—a moment open to reinterpretation since I now wonder if this is a habit of his that has nothing to do with me.

But now he's looking, or half looking. It's not easy to see. I've made such an effort to hide in the cover of the trees, I've rendered him almost invisible. I take up a position where I too could be contemplating the river, meaning I have my back to the bank and my attention only half focused in Victor's direction. Part of me thinks I should walk up bold as brass and ask him what he's doing, but that could give the game away. I'm not through following him—if this escapade ends in frustration there could still be a next time.

I shift to my left for a clearer view through the leaves. Victor is standing statue-like staring across the water. He holds the pose for maybe fifteen seconds before looking towards the bridge, which will bring me into his field of view. I quickly look out over the water, before slowly angling my head back in his direction to watch him from the corner of my eye. But he's gone. By the time I've snaked my head around far enough to see where he was, he's vanished.

I turn round further and see, with horror, he's coming back along the path. If I rush off now and walk at the pace required to stay ahead, I'll look like a startled rabbit. But I can't let him see me. Instead, I step forward to the edge of the embankment, where it slopes down to the river. I do it casually, but purposefully, as though something in the water has caught my interest. I squat and bring my left hand up to my cheek, to create the impression I am propping my head as I peer into the water, though, in reality, it's to cover the side of my face exposed to Victor's advance.

I daren't look, and wonder how long I can hold the pose without it seeming false. I hear the footsteps, a crack of a twig. I sense he's moving at his walking warp speed, which has to be good, and then he seems to be just behind. My heart thumps as I wait to hear him either approach me or walk on down the path. Seconds elapse and there's no approach, another second and his footfall recedes. I wait a few more seconds before stealing a glance and note, with utter relief, that he is on his way around the river's bend.

Chapter Eight

If Victor is a mystery, Alex is becoming an enigma. Where once he was a mouthpiece for the virtues of the capitalist economy—broadly on board for the general self-enriching merry go round, although not one to strike postures of denial about its darker side—he's now turned vengeful and wants to destroy the system. I'm paraphrasing, but it's no exaggeration that he's angry and wants to get his own back.

He's pursuing some new legal angle and he's constantly on some communications blitz which, from a distance—and I try hard not to get too close—sounds like he's moved from the inside pissing out to the outside pissing in, with some alacrity.

Meanwhile, his language to me is all about the need to 'rescue rationality,' and 'save civilisation'. I did ask if revenge was the right motive for someone on a mission to restore enlightened values, but he either didn't understand the question—unlikely—or it was too inconvenient a truth. He smiled and walked off.

But in the two weeks since Alex got fired, and the four since I started this weird commission, an oddly uplifting new regularity has established itself between us. It's as if a sharp jolt has been administered to the unchanging slow fade of our lives—not that we're old, but it's always struck me that by the time people hit middle age nothing much changes until they reach the departure lounge, or, at least, retirement. Unless—just as an example—you count shopping online, as opposed to pushing a trolley round a supermarket, as marking a lifestyle change.

We're both on new paths, and, curiously, the sense of sharing something is tangible. I'm guessing Alex's mood will get worse before it gets better, but nowadays his temper is directed at the world, not me. It's a subtle change and one that refashions our marriage: whereas in the past he would come home and behave as if I was somehow responsible for any bad luck, ill will or setback in his professional sphere, he now behaves as if I am the one entity—persons, companies, institutions—wholly innocent. I've become the ally; the one true ally; the person with whom he enjoys a special relationship.

Victor's been back twice since I followed him, both nerve shredding encounters. The first, because I couldn't shake off the idea that he knew I'd followed. From the moment he arrived I found myself playing up the friendly chitchat to the extent that my attempt to portray normality had become self-consciously abnormal. He asked if I was okay and I told him about Alex losing his job. An unexpectedly welcome alibi and Victor bought it, as far as I could tell. The second, because he actually met Alex—a potential face-off I'd been fearing—and while Alex put in a performance of monosyllabic inscrutability I knew harboured a still hostile suspicion, he was superficially polite, and Victor, who must have felt uneasy, just took it as the what-do-you-expect behaviour of a recently sacked banker. Not sure how many more embarrassments this alibi will be good for, but at last the ice is broken between my paymaster and my husband.

On each occasion, Victor's departure gives me an opportunity to set my mind at rest. I need to know if the walk round to the other side of the river is something he does regularly. If so, it's safe to assume it was unconnected to me following him. But if not, if it was a one off, it's the horror scenario: he knew all along, and it was a decoy to stop me following him anywhere that mattered. What's more, he's now sitting on the knowledge, saying nothing.

The first time, bingo. I stake out the far bank with my binoculars and in twenty minutes, almost the exact amount of time I would have calculated given his walking pace, he's there. He doesn't do anything though. He stands, looks—

somewhat meditatively—but not obviously towards me, and pirouettes and leaves.

The second time, nothing. I give it an hour to allow for him getting distracted along the way, but he doesn't appear.

This strikes me as a good news, bad news situation. The good news is that he doesn't always go there, so if I follow him again I have a chance of catching him on a day when he really does go somewhere, somewhere that helps fill the void that sits behind my mental picture of him. The bad news, of course, is that walking over to the far bank at the end of our meetings is a weird thing to do. There appears to be no purpose to it—yet there has to be, and one that may or may not relate to me. How does that make me feel?

I go to the bathroom and examine myself in the mirror. I'm smiling. I feel okay. The more surreal things get, the more the adrenalin pumps. I should be fearful, but I'm not. If I told Alex he'd go back into his you-must-be-nuts routine. Perhaps I am.

Maybe I should mention it to Victor next time? Just say, matter of fact, oh, by the way, I happened to notice, smiley-smiley. Keep it unthreatening, as though a mere flicker of idle curiosity had crossed my mind, the passing whim of a distracted observation. It might flush him out—ha! you were following me—or it may even prompt the truth, a story I would love to hear.

Perhaps I'll save it. First, I'll follow him again and see where that takes us.

Meanwhile I've been studying some more. The Victor conundrum combined with stories of Nazi atrocity ought to be fertile ground artistically speaking. But Victor is becoming a fixation and the Nazis are so relentlessly and numbingly death metal that every attempt to work is undermined by a wavering concentration and mounting sense of inadequacy in the face of the scale of the task.

None of which was helped by Natalie turning up out of the blue. To be strictly accurate she phoned ten minutes before arriving to say she was 'in the area' and could she pop by, but this was to give a gloss of spontaneity to an obviously planned visit, thought about and worried over—the phone call presumably a last minute decision to avoid any awkwardness arising from her doorstepping me.

I'd sent her a couple of email updates about the work, including screenshots, and these had produced an appreciation that was oddly muted compared with the rapturous one on the day. On arrival, her appearance was as I remember—a curious mix of being the picture of elegance while moving in spasms—but in her voice there was a distinct change. It was slower, more deliberate, maybe more guarded.

I led her into the living room, not wanting to take her to the studio, which was littered with half drawn, half painted, half storyboarded versions of several potential pieces, the sum total of which stood as incontrovertible evidence of a Nazi undertaking. I felt a curious guilt about the need to keep it secret, not like an alcoholic hiding whisky bottles or a heretic guarding a place of worship, but closer to concealing a person—a Jew from the Nazis, perhaps—which was when it dawned that I was concealing the Nazis from a Jew.

She started telling me about her life with Nina. She'd parted with the husband and father when Nina was six, the result of Natalie delivering him an ultimatum. Natalie smiled as she told me this, as though proud, no shadow of discomfort passing her face as she talked about this man. I wondered at first about what she'd done. I wanted to judge her. In her description was a hard luck story at odds with a disclosure too neatly, painlessly delivered.

'His work was his life,' she said.

I found myself thinking how important someone's vocation was to them and how you would interfere with it at your peril.

'It was his whole life; it was all he did. Even when he wasn't "at work", he was parked by his phone and you could see him willing it to ring. A call or a message, it didn't matter, and when it happened it would energise him, as though the whole of the rest of his life,' she spat these last words, 'was a giant bore.' She forced a laugh. 'I am exaggerating; of course, there was nothing giant about it at all. "It"—that is, Nina and me—was nothing more than a supplementary to what he considered to be his "life's work".' Her face creased, her sarcasm still scalding all these years later.

'And what was this work?' she continued. 'I never knew. He wouldn't talk about it. He couldn't muster the enthusiasm to tell me, his wife, what he did for a living. I heard snatches of conversation, of course. I heard about property, pipelines, ships, cargoes, consignments, but always general, subtly veiled, never anything specific enough to give you that aha moment. For a while I thought he must be a crook—maybe I wanted to believe he was—but I never saw anything suspicious.'

I looked at her, my sympathy growing, reluctantly at first, then wholeheartedly. Why had I wanted to judge her? What had she triggered in me that had put me in competition with her? I could identify with being the addendum and felt thankful that for me it had existed only in moments and phases rather than the devouring entirety Natalie was describing.

'So he upped and left,' she said, 'and actually looked grateful I'd pushed him into it. It was as if he daren't end it. Ironically, in that gratitude, I caught a glimpse of conscience. There was little acrimony because we both knew it was not so much that it was over; we were simply ending something that had never begun. There were no lawyers: he paid up and still does, the money hitting my account on the first of every month, uprated annually in line with inflation. All he asks for is a copy of Nina's school

93

report cards, which she conscientiously sends him each term. He is as precise and predictable as an ex as he was as a husband. But almost no contact. He sends a card and a large cheque on her birthday and at Christmas, always on time.'

Natalie's fragile stoicism almost breaks; her eyes lower and her voice drops. 'She always cashes it and she always makes a point of buying something nice "from Daddy". It's where we differ: she sees it as evidence of her father being present in her life; I see it as confirmation of his absence. Where she sees his love, I see his heartlessness.'

She told me she and Nina were happy. No new stepdaddy, nor would there be. Any pretenders to the position were quickly disabused. She was emphatic on this point, almost grimly determined, and I suppressed an urge to ask.

She came eventually to Nina. She repeated the portrayal of her as a withdrawn and struggling pupil. I began to offer my perspective, but, as I tried to put my point of view, I was quickly talked over. Of course, she said, I would have seen a different side to her: art is what she excels at, it's where she derives the little confidence she has.

I still doubted her, but I let it drop. I didn't know what I needed to say, and I didn't want to get into an argument with Natalie by uttering an ill-advised contradiction to what she held as an article of faith.

Besides, it felt like the time had come for her to get to the point, the upshot of which, I was sure, would determine whether the matter was worth interrogation.

But it was an hour later, when I closed the door on Natalie, having agreed to her request—plea might be a better word—for Nina to be my pupil, that I stood in the hall and shook my head and wondered what the devil I'd let myself in for. At first Natalie had talked of Nina being my apprentice, to which I'd said I didn't need one and, in any case, Nina was too young. I was also labouring under an old fashioned misapprehension that apprentices had to be paid, which caused Natalie amusement.

'No one pays apprentices. They call them interns or probationers and get them to work for nothing. I will pay you.'

I told her I didn't want paying, which inadvertently led Natalie to assume I was on the verge of saying yes. I repeated that she was too young and Natalie asked me to forget she'd said apprentice, she really only meant for Nina to be my pupil.

'Apprentice sounds more formal, or structured,' she said, 'and I suppose that's what I was hoping for: that she might become involved in your work, like an assistant.'

If it sounds like I was worn down by a mother's determination to do the best for her daughter, that would be half right. The other half was all about Nina and me. I was protective, I was involved, my heart had been a tightening gyre during the near dispute with her mother and I couldn't say no.

I couldn't say yes either. So I told her maybe, that I'd think about it. But she knew I wanted it to be a yes. As she left, I could see in her stride she thought she'd won me, which she had. The trouble being, the part that was hidden from her, the part she wouldn't have been able to guess, was that it wasn't really my yes to grant.

I'd won Victor round before, or more accurately Nina had, but explicitly on the basis of it being a one off, and now I had to convince him that allowing her to share in the project as it evolved over months was a good idea. I'd sprung a trap for myself, arising from a characteristic of mine I am sometimes proud of, sometimes hampered by: in trying to be kind I have set up a potential cruelty; to disappoint them now would be to unravel my double-dealing, however well intentioned I think I am.

There was the option of taking literally the idea of Nina as a pupil, keeping her out of the studio and sitting her at the kitchen table where I could teach her. As soon as the thought was alive I knew it was unworkable: how would I explain to Nina that the studio was off limits, and how would I explain to Natalie the fudge to our agreement, tacit though it was but by no means intangible?

'It's fine,' he says, and dissolves my anxieties in one surprising instant.

I'd fumbled my explanation, the words coming out in the wrong order and with none of the confidence I felt rehearsing them. I told him that it would work because I would impress on Nina, and Natalie, that exhibitions are sensitive, that secrecy is a requirement, that surprise is vital and that it's important that no third party can compromise the project in any way, or even steal the idea. I told him that I believe Natalie and Nina can be trusted, that Natalie is investing her faith in me and wouldn't dare jeopardise the good she believes I can do for Nina. Finally, I said that I believe I can be good for Nina and want to help her.

'You will be good for her,' he says, 'and you have my blessing.'

'Are you sure?' I can see he is, but I can't quite believe I've managed to persuade him so easily. He smiles.

'Onto business,' he says, and the matter's closed.

I'm almost drunkenly euphoric at having extracted myself from the hole I'd dug. The pain I foresaw is replaced by a vision of pleasure: me letting Natalie know that I'm willing, no delighted, to be able to take Nina on.

There is an exquisite relief in finding oneself released from guilt, especially for a crime committed in error and out of weakness. That relief now transposes into boldness and I decide the time is right to follow Victor again.

It's the same routine as before: I close the door on him, smiling and chirpy, and grab the coat, hat and sunglasses. In seconds I'm on the street and, as before, he's striding away.

But this time he takes a left, away from the river path. He walks through the underpass below the Great West Road. He takes a left through a garden square and heads north. He crosses the main road and continues north. He must be heading for the Underground at Stamford Brook. This is it, I think, and the thrill carries me with such excitement I find myself closing the gap on him.

I slow down and play a guessing game: east or west? I fancy east. He goes through the barrier and heads for the eastbound platform. Suddenly, I'm playing this game of spies, this new, fun adventure, this real world tailing of a man of mystery, following him to his lair.

The out of body thrill is brought down a notch when we reach the platform. Three minutes to the next train, three minutes to plan how to remain close enough to Victor to not lose him but far enough away to not attract attention. I let him walk ahead up the platform.

With the train approaching, Victor remains motionless until the moment it slows and people anticipate which doors to aim for. My plan is to wait for Victor to choose his and then get in at the far end of whichever carriage he gets on.

It's a strange moment when a state of thrill-induced exhilaration gives way to fear—when your body runs from hot to cold in the flicker of a moment—but that's what I feel as the train door closes and I look down the carriage to see Victor looking straight at me. It would be so easy to give a fancy-seeing-you-again wave, it was what I'd planned, but I don't. I'm rooted, my right hand hanging from the rail, aware I must have turned either crimson or white with the shock, waiting for him to acknowledge me, waiting for the moment when I have to walk down the carriage and talk to him and pretend a nonchalance I'm sure I won't be capable of. But he turns away, his face unmoved, his eyes blank, and I breath out realising my disguise has done its job.

My guess is that he will change trains further down the line, and I'll have to repeat the process. He may not have recognised me, but I am now part of the scenery; I am in his consciousness, a random figure maybe, but to pop into his field of vision again on another train would run the risk of him taking a closer interest. But how can I avoid it?

The train is three quarters full, which means I can remain standing without looking out of place. Not everyone wants to sit and I'm not alone, there are two servant-class women—it's usually easy to spot them: foreign, but not alert like tourists, nicely, but cheaply dressed, hair tied functionally, complexions drained, eye sockets dark with fatigue—off to clean or au pair or wait or nanny or any of the multitude of low paid, under the radar occupations this city depends on to function. They're standing in the next doorway, between Victor and me, helpfully providing a screen between my part of the train and his.

I avoid looking at Victor. He can't get out of a moving train, so constant vigilance is unnecessary. He could surprise me and get out at a stop where there's no interchange, he could surprise me even further and go all the way across the city to Plaistow or Hornchurch, but these are surely long shots. The danger is that he's heading out of London via a main line station and he's off to Cambridge or Birmingham or somewhere. If so, I won't get there on my Oyster card. Working out which train to buy a ticket for before it's too late will be almost impossible.

I half expect him to make a move at Hammersmith, but he doesn't and I next fix an alert in my mind for Earl's Court. Here the two women get off, but Victor stays put. I feel exposed in their absence and Victor seems to glance my way. Two male tourists jump on and one asks if they're going the right way for Westminster. I nod and mouth 'yes,' not wanting to risk Victor hearing my voice. His friend asks me, with a big Disney cartoon smile, if I am a Londoner. I nod again, smile and look down, faking shyness. It feels rude. He's hoping to talk to an actual native, and I'm desperate to shut the conversation down. Soon enough he may learn that no one talks on the tube and the fact I even acknowledged him is a bonus.

As the train slows for South Kensington, Victor stands up. His exit from the train is unobstructed whereas mine is crowded with people impatient to get on. By the time I'm on the platform, Victor is yards ahead, sprinting away. I imagine him heading for the Piccadilly line and, while I decide to follow my hunch and go there if I lose him, another thought comes to mind, one that plays on my fear: that he knows, and he's leading me, deliberately. Wouldn't it be a perfect turn on his part, a masterclass in the art of reversal, a feat of cool to match his sense of style, to lead me to the Victoria and Albert and there to confront my little game? If I'm not mistaken, he's slowing down. He doesn't want to lose me. The predator predated. But I'm wrong, he's not going up to the street, he's going down, following the dark blue for Piccadilly, descending from the relatively airy atmosphere of the District Line's cut and cover into the tubular underworld.

Heading north on the Piccadilly line, and a new problem: overcrowding. Victor jams himself in through one door leaving me staring at the other two to the same carriage, both crushed. In normal circumstances, I would wait for the next train but instead I squeeze, or rather, force, my way into the block of bodies. No one says anything, but a glance up reveals the scowling face of a young man in business dress who, somewhat incongruously, is wearing a backpack that now presses into the face of a woman behind him. It's urgent, I want to say, to excuse pressing myself into his personal space. Cancel urgent, let's call it a mental necessity, the gratification of an overdriven curiosity.

At Green Park Victor gets off and it's soon clear he's heading for the Jubilee line. It's not difficult tracking him through the interconnecting tube tunnels, as it's the last place anyone would look over their shoulder to see what's coming behind. There's something very direct and confident about his stride that tells of a man who knows the route by heart. I'm the predator once more and it's starting to feel fun again. I tell myself not to get cocky.

He's going northbound and the train this time is half empty. I attempt to bury myself in a seat next to a woman who has three shopping bags on her lap. It feels like I'm at least half hidden, but when she gets off at St John's Wood I feel the full blast of exposure. I could shuffle up two seats and hide behind a man with a briefcase, but that might feel weird to him and the movement might catch Victor's eye. I remain where I am and pretend to be interested in my phone.

The train pulls in at Swiss Cottage and by now I'm alert to any station that might be a getting-off stop, a destination rather than an interchange. In the corner of my eye Victor is still. Not yet it seems. The doors open and he's out of his seat and off the train. There's still time, I tell myself, and I'm right: I step onto the platform just as the doors close behind me, neatly side-stepping two smartly uniformed schoolgirls as I go.

But the station is chillingly empty. Half a dozen people left the train here and they're now dispersed, leaving me to follow Victor like a solitary stalker, hearing the clacking of my shoes on the hard surface, a sound that gets louder and louder with each step. I try to walk quietly, but the brisk, clicking beat, now infernal, keeps rising, hammering at my conscience until I can hear nothing else.

Finally we're above ground and Victor is striding past the Hampstead Theatre. I'm relieved to be outside, where my footsteps meet the hum of the city and their sound recedes. At the same time I'm nervous, knowing, surely, that a destination is near, but also, unexpectedly, I find myself preparing for a disappointment: I follow him until he goes into a house and…so what? What will I have proved? I will have filled in something of the Victor enigma but to what end? A logic that was compelling in the abstract, now seems anti-climactic in its actuality.

I follow him along a street of tall, Victorian red-brick piles, most converted for apartments or non-residential use like a nursery or clinic. Victor marches on until he comes to a villa with a double pitch roof and a red tiled front, which is probably late Victorian or maybe Edwardian, certainly more recent than the monsters lining the early part of the street, but big nonetheless, and more homely.

He turns into the drive and disappears from view behind a dividing hedge. I cross the road, partly for a better viewpoint, but also to get what cover I can from a parked car and tree. I see Victor press what is presumably an entrance buzzer. In the wait for the door to be answered he turns his head and gazes idly around. I duck so that I'm watching him through the car's windows, but he doesn't look in my direction. The door to the house opens, a man who has the look of a doorman waves him inside, and he's gone.

I make a note of the address and I look to see if there's a plate or sign fixed to the property that reveals the name of an organisation or institution, but there is none. The door is in an alcove and I cross the road to see if there are multiple buzzers or letterboxes. I walk slowly to give myself time to study the house without stopping. It's one bell and one letterbox. The doorman confuses things. Most people don't press a bell to access their own home, but maybe, if you have a servant, that is exactly what you do. If it isn't Victor's house, I should wait and follow him again when he leaves. But if it is his house I risk waiting a very long time for nothing. Either way, all I can do for now is wait.

I pass the gate, past the house altogether and decide to give it half an hour. I stand by a tree and smile at the thought that our roles are exactly reversed from when I first saw Victor. But I realise it's not a good place to stop: just as Alex and I were able to observe Victor that night, so he will be able to observe me. Walking further up the street I find a place to watch the road but not the house—in other words, I can see Victor if he leaves, but not be seen by him for as long as he stays.

The first few minutes of a wait are the worst. Time moves slowly until, inured to that feeling, it begins to move at a pace beyond consciousness, like a half-dream before falling into a deep sleep, a transition when time is suspended. And so it is, however many minutes later, my mind elsewhere, that I'm jolted back to the present by the strange, chilling sight of the man who might be the doorman, out on the street. He looks at me and I freeze. He seems to wave to me, but it's hard to be sure he means me. I look round, but there's no one else and I look back at him and he's beckoning. I walk forward, still half expecting, hoping maybe, that I'm not the object of his attention. Drawing near I see him smile and there's no mistaking that it's for me.

'Victor asks if you would like to come inside.'

Did he know all along? Have I been so obvious? I feel like a little girl caught in a scheme that seemed so clever and secret, but was in reality blatant and stupid.

The man doesn't wait for an answer, instead he gestures with an arm towards the house and I succumb. I mumble a thank you and tell myself to hold my dignity. I straighten my posture and walk toward the front door.

'This way, please,' he says, once we're in the entrance hall, indicating a half open door.

The house is dark and warm. The entrance hall is panelled, the staircase solid and wide. As we walk through the doorway, the richly patterned mosaic tiled floor gives way to a carpet. The man leads me into the room and I feel the soft squeeze of my shoe on the carpet, silent and luxurious. And there is Victor, standing alone by a large, mahogany partners desk centre stage at the far end of a substantial library.

I hear the door close behind and turn involuntarily. The man is gone. I turn back to face Victor, my stomach churning.

'Welcome,' he says, 'it's a pleasure to see you again so soon.'

He is practically laughing and I break into a smile. What else can I do? I feel foolish, but relieved at the absence of any reprimand in his voice.

'I'm sorry,' I say, automatically, not thinking what I'm saying.

'Sorry for what?' His look darkens, as though choosing this moment to go in for a kill. Does he want me to spell it out so he can see me squirm? I'm squirming inside alright, but struggling to say anything.

'For...' I shrug and flap my hands and attempt an apologetic look.

'You've done nothing wrong,' he says, the warmth returning to his voice. Was he playing with me? I want to call him a name, but don't yet feel sufficiently reinstated to risk doing that.

'I wanted to know more about you,' I say.

'Of course,' he says, 'that is only natural. And what more about me do you now know?'

It's an uncomfortable question. Any literal answer will only add to the embarrassment.

'I know you walk very fast,' I say, and he laughs. It feels like the 'right' answer: I've amused him, some ice has thawed and things feel more equal again.

He asks me what I think of the house and I tell him I like it. I'm telling the truth. It looks like a house retaining the style of the period it was built, although I imagine somewhere will be the ubiquitous modern kitchen with polished granite surfaces, sleek steel hood, sunken eco lights and maybe a fish tank.

'It isn't mine,' he says. I expect him to tell me whose it is, but he doesn't, instead ushering me to a door at the rear of the room. 'Come and look at the museum.'

I'm not expecting an actual museum—maybe a room with artefacts, perhaps a display cabinet or two—but what confronts me is a surprise: it really is a museum. It's a huge room with a central aisle of double sided mahogany and glass display cases; and in a continuous line around the walls, save for gaps for doorways, are a series of upright, floor to ceiling cabinets, also in mahogany.

Victor doesn't say anything, just becomes more solemn. I look around and see the killing fields of Cambodia, then Rwanda, then Bosnia, Armenia, India, USSR, China. No wonder his mood is serious, reverential even. Finally, starting at the far end, but occupying the larger part of the exhibition, the Holocaust.

At Victor's invitation I look around the room and notice a yellow star badge, the type Jews were required to wear in Nazi occupied Europe; a lock from a gate at Dachau; a Zyklon B gas canister; passport photos of Jewish forced labourers; a first English edition of Anne Frank's *Diary of a Young Girl*; an Iron Cross awarded to a German Jewish soldier for bravery in the First World War; a section of a roasting grille that victims were forced to lie on to be shot before their bodies were burned; and countless photos of forced marches, hangings, gassings and mass graves.

There's so much detail: gloves, glasses, letters, family photos, photos of Jewish districts before Nazi occupation, ration books, black market price lists, a Hanukkah lamp, a transit visa for a family fleeing to Shanghai, and a blood-stained swastika armband with a bullet hole. And so it goes on. All neatly labelled, with a few lines of explanatory text where necessary. On the only wall without a display case is a panel. On it a list of genocides, each with the estimated number of people killed. There's even a breakdown: numbers murdered; numbers who died as a result of deliberate acts of policy leading to starvation or disease. It's a museum, a memorial and a shrine.

I break off and look at Victor. I was aware of him watching me and now I catch him studying me as though I'm part of an experiment. Was that the purpose, to bring me here and see how I would take it?

'Did you put this collection together?' I ask.

'I've helped,' he says, and nods.

He tells me the owner of the house bought an already substantial collection and has added to it considerably. It was originally just stuff in boxes until the owner had the idea of mounting it as an exhibition.

I ask him whom the exhibition is for, since this doesn't look like a public museum.

'It's a private collection, that is all.' he says, 'open to family, although they mostly avoid it, and friends. And occasionally the owner brings round someone of importance.'

'Like?'

'Someone of influence, someone in a position to— what's the best way to put this?—someone who can benefit from the experience, and help others to benefit.' He looks at me with a new, kinder air, as though a new bond has formed. 'Someone like you,' he says.

I'm surprised and, I think, flattered. I want to ask how and why, in order to force the specifics out of him—the specifics of what is expected of me—but I know the answer lies in the commission and that he will say it's up to me. At the same time a new, freakish thought occurs, one both implausible and strangely believable.

'Did you mean to lead me here today?'

'I knew you were there,' he says, and smiles, almost giggles. Smug bastard.

He tells me that if the roles had been reversed he would have done the same and to take this as a compliment. It makes me feel better, but I'm unsure how it's a compliment to either of us. Not that I wish to see his anger, but its absence, replaced by kindness even, leaves me struggling with shame.

'You and I have conscience,' he says, 'our instinct is to fight the oppressor in the name of justice. For some people the fight, any fight, is for self-interest. A narrow self-interest, one that sees only metres ahead, one guided by the dictates of immediate circumstance, that is stupid, self-defeating and may ultimately open the door to evil. You followed me for justice.'

Did I? I don't quite say it aloud, instead I stand blinking in front of him.

'You have courage,' he says, 'moral courage. If you didn't you would right now be attempting to justify your actions, listing your complaints, sounding more and more hollow as you move further and further from the simple truth: that what you feel is the result of who you are and what you did.'

'I don't know,' I say, 'I feel bad; isn't that a measure of having done bad?'

'You're seeking a truth,' he says. 'I have made it all very cat and mouse and you were naturally curious. I know you meant no harm and I mean no harm to you. Neither of us is using the other for the blinkered self-interest I refer to, we operate from conscience. You chose to trust me as I chose to trust you and we are both right; the difference between us is that you don't yet know for certain; that is why you followed me.'

'Are you getting round to saying that if everyone operated from conscience there would be none of this?'

I draw my arm around in an arc to indicate the exhibition. I know for sure Victor won't believe it's that simple.

'See that book,' he says and points at Anne Frank's diary, 'her and her family were betrayed—by who remains unknown, although there are suspects—most probably because the Nazis put a bounty on the heads of Jews in hiding. By 1944, when the Nazis arrested her family, the people of Amsterdam were starving. You see where I'm going with this?'

He leans towards me with a look of such voraciousness I fear the consequences of giving a 'wrong' answer. I pause, hoping the question is rhetorical, but he nods, the cue for me to reply.

'That people were so desperate they would sell others to their deaths?'

'Indeed,' he says, and takes a sharp breath to add emphasis to the point he now wants to make, 'but however desperate, what they did was inexcusable. You would struggle to find anyone who wouldn't condemn the betrayers as weak-willed accomplices to murder, whose own act of evil is a match for the Nazis and who deserve to rot with them in hell. Conscience should have triumphed no matter what.

'But the truth is we don't know if it was someone who was starving; it may have been a Nazi sympathiser, someone who saw the Jews through the dehumanising prism of fascism, who had no ill-conscience about assisting the extermination of a pestilence. Of course, we can judge that the person shouldn't have been so blind, so corrupt, so easily seduced by myth and misinformation, but they were. The Nazis set the conditions for human nature at its ugliest to find expression—and you can argue people shouldn't have followed, shouldn't have fallen for it, shouldn't have allowed themselves to be bribed by it, shouldn't have been in fear of it—you can argue all these truths until they reek of their own sanctimony, but you cannot change the fact that human nature will cut between good and bad whether we like it or not, and it will cut to the good when conscience and self-interest can walk hand in hand.

'You know that old test don't you?' I look blank, wrong-footed once more by his habit of slipping between the real question and the rhetorical, 'it's the one where you imagine you live in an occupied territory and there are three choices: join the resistance; lie low and hope for the best; collaborate with the enemy. Now think about the people you know, which category would you put them in? Most find it surprisingly easy, and entertaining, to assign categories to the people they know. Somehow we have an instinct for people with fairweather principles: those polite, nice people who will help you when it doesn't cost them, but melt away, or worse, when the storms gather.'

I start thinking about people I know, starting with Alex. A resistance fighter, I'm certain. For all his negligence and belligerence, he's a defender of liberty and the sovereign rights of the individual. But would anyone else place him in that category?

'People's instincts may be wrong,' I say, 'people may not be predictable; people who look courageous may turn out weak; people who are timid may have stronger, deeper principles than anyone would guess.'

He looks at me, his eyes seeming to draw circles around my face.

'Are you concerned which category you would fall into?'

It hadn't occurred to me until he said it. I wouldn't sell out anyone in any circumstances and certainly not if their lives were at stake, that much I know without having to think about it. His suggestion, if that was what it is, seems like an affront. But something about the way he looks at me, the lilt in his eyes, the relaxed slope of his mouth, stops me from a snap reaction. He's ahead of me, as always.

'Which category would you put me in?'

'You've ducked the question,' he says, 'it's not about which category I would put you in, it's how confident are you of landing in the one you want?'

It's true. I am a resistance fighter, safe in my world, removed from the danger and the fear. How would I know? Do I really want to know? Victor does no more than ask the question and my certainty becomes vulnerable.

My mind casts back to the feelings I had when reading up on Reinhard Heydrich, appointed by Hitler as Reich Protector in Bohemia and Moravia, and nicknamed the 'Butcher of Prague' for his suppression of the Czech resistance movement. He rounded up and executed several hundred of the primary suspects and shipped another thousand or so citizens to concentration camps regardless of whether they were guilty or not. That the innocent were parcelled up with the guilty was a convenient by-product of the crackdown; this wasn't about dispensing justice, but destroying an opposition and, in so doing, sending a double-headed message to the people of Prague: to those who may follow, these are the consequences; to the rest, the actions of your resistance 'heroes' may rebound onto you. The subtext: collaboration in weeding out these insurgents is for everyone's benefit.

But it's what happened later that truly tests my conviction. In May 1942 two Czech exiles were parachuted into a field near Prague by British Special Operations to assassinate Heydrich. The Czech government in exile, along with the British, calculated that, if successful, the Nazis would exact a retribution that would stoke a sense of injustice and revive the resistance movement.

Despite almost bungling it, the assassins did their job. Heydrich wasn't killed outright as planned, but sustained injuries that he died of just over a week later. The assassins fled to a church where a local agent of British Special Operations, in return for a large reward, betrayed them to the Gestapo. They shot themselves after a lengthy gun battle. To Victor's categories I could add a fourth: double crossing bastards—one I could never belong to.

Hitler threatened the Czech President Hacha with the deportation of the entire Czech population should a similar incident occur. He was persuaded out of this on the grounds that this would be bad news for Czech arms production, which the Nazis controlled. But revenge, when it came, was brutal. The entire population of the village of Lidice was charged with sheltering the assassins; the men were shot, the women sent to a concentration camp and the children assessed for racial purity—the eighty-one of them who 'failed' the test were murdered. Lidice itself was burned to the ground. In another village, Lezacky, twenty-four men and women were shot. The Nazis executed a further 1,357 people for alleged involvement in the resistance, as well as using the incident as a prompt to round up and kill a thousand of Prague's Jews.

And, as I look at Victor, I weigh my courage. I wouldn't betray anyone and I wouldn't collaborate. Every act of resistance weakens the oppressor, but opens the way for a slaughter of innocents. Would I resist, or sit it out?

Victor is looking back at me. He knows my dilemma. He probably already knows my answer.

'The only thing necessary for the triumph of evil is for good people to do nothing,' I say. I believe it and always have. 'I only hope that my courage wouldn't desert me if the time came.'

Victor nods and brushes something from his jacket sleeve, as if casting off an unpleasant thought.

'Your courage would hold,' he says, 'I know because you have the conviction, but also the doubt. The people I fear are the ones without doubt; they are always the weak link. You can conquer a fear if you are aware of it or immune to it, but not if you are blind to it. Human nature always cuts both ways and you have just proved it to yourself. You are strong and you will fight, others are weak and they will succumb. The Nazis' achievement was to exploit the weakness of millions: the cowed masses, most of whom despised them, and all of whom, through fear, did nothing.

'It's a myth that they were ever hugely popular in Germany. There were fanatics who jumped on the bandwagon, of course. There were people who wanted to believe in them, and did—for a while. There were millions who voted for them while elections were allowed—but who and what were they voting for? War? The death of millions? The persecution of an entire race along with all the other "undesirables"? The abandonment of democracy? Only the fanatics wanted these things, but after a certain point their grip was so strong nothing could stop them. People's responses varied: there were those who maintained a denial of what was happening, to excuse a guilt at their compliance, and those who recognised the horror for what it was but had no wish to become victims themselves.'

Victor stops, looks at me and seems to force himself to relax. Is he embarrassed? Is he worried he's coming over as unfashionably heavy? I tell him I'm interested, I tell him I want to hear more.

'There was a history of anti-semitism in Germany that long pre-dated Hitler's rise to power and that the Nazis were keen to exploit. It's true that in many parts of Europe there was a suspicion of Jews, but in Germany, following its unification and the explosion of Nationalist sentiment that accompanied it, which coincided with social and economic turmoil, that suspicion became endemic. Calls for legal limits to be imposed on Jewish rights were widespread even among supposedly respectable politicians, who discovered they could gain popularity by turning up the rhetoric on Jews. By the 1890s the German Reichstag was considering proposals to limit Jews rights to education and to enter certain professions. They weren't enacted at this time, but prejudice against Jews was growing and the idea of state discrimination against Jews was active in the popular consciousness.

'Jews—as well as communists—were blamed for Germany's defeat in the First World War and the tide of anti-semitism reached new heights. Against this background, it is easy to paint a picture of the German people's complicity in the Holocaust. But it's what happened at critical junctures in the history of German Nazism that interests me and is important to our project.

'Theories to do with racial purity had been gaining currency in Germany since the back end of the nineteenth century. Hitler first became influenced when reading pamphlets during his time as a struggling artist in Vienna—and much of what he absorbed would be recycled in *Mein Kampf*. According to Hitler, the Third Reich would create a society shorn of the weak and undesirable in pursuit of a stronger race. That the Jews, whose culture by and large put great emphasis on education and betterment, should be subordinated to the uneducated low life bullyboys who rose in rank under the Nazis, in the name of improving the race, is one of history's bitterest ironies. That aside, the elimination of Jews from society may have been popular as a rallying cry, but when it became a concrete reality, something unexpected happened.

'The Nazis never enjoyed unconditional popular support. After the Depression, the working class were more likely to vote for the communists. The middle classes, however, feared the communists more than anything, being acutely aware of what had happened to their equivalents in Russia after the revolution, and they more or less fled to the Nazis as a way to block communist influence. The battleground was over who could oust what had become, by the 1930s, the reviled Weimar regime, and people voted to preserve or promote their interests—ideological notions about Judaism being of marginal concern. In fact, once the Nazis appreciated that they were gaining support from the middle classes, they reined in their anti-semitism, knowing that it played badly with this group. And after 1929, in the aftermath and fall-out of the Wall Street Crash, it wasn't eliciting much response in any part of the electorate.

'The lukewarm enthusiasm for anti-semitism continued beyond the Nazis seizure of power in 1933. By 1935 the Gestapo was reporting widespread dissatisfaction amongst the populace with the regime in general. The miserable economic conditions still prevailed and people had grown weary of the Nazis craven need for displays of support or financial contributions, which were often gathered under duress. There is little evidence that the population was much bothered by Jewish matters, one way or the other. Rumours of corruption among senior Nazis were rife and for those not ground down by the misery the regime was now something of a joke. The Nazi response was to crank up the anti-semitism in an effort to deflect people's anger towards the Jews.

'But it was never very successful among ordinary Germans. It played well with the die-hards in the Nazi Party, but it never resonated with people in general who saw the tactic for what it was. The Nazis held a major set-piece rally in Hamburg in 1935, trailed by a massive advertising campaign. The main speaker, a virulent Nazi named Julius Streicher, turned his anti-Jewish rhetoric up to maximum and although enthusiastically applauded by the Nazi cheerleaders placed strategically around the audience, the reception amongst ordinary members of the audience was one of indifference or revulsion. When, at one point, Streicher derided the baby of a Jewish man and a non Jewish woman as an "ape" people walked out. Others had, quite literally, fallen asleep.

'The general effect of this wave of anti-semitic propaganda was not the intended one. The regime did not gain in popularity and many people, notably the Catholic Church, sympathised with the Jews and made clear their belief that the persecution had gone too far. People began pointedly shopping in Jewish stores in defiance of Nazi propaganda, and in Mannheim-Neckarau shoppers engaged in a pitch fight with stormtroopers who attempted to prevent them entering Jewish shops. The middle classes, in particular, were horrified at the association of the Nazis with violence and were concerned about Germany's reputation abroad. By September 1935 the Nazis scaled down their violence against Jews realising it was losing rather than gaining them support, and focused instead on institutionalising anti-semitism through new laws of citizenship—the "Nuremberg Laws"—which further legitimised discrimination against Jews and effectively made Nazi Germany an apartheid state.

'The violence didn't disappear, of course, since belief in the mission amongst the hard-core proponents of racial purity was hardening, albeit in inverse proportion to the general population's growing distaste for it. As the years progressed it could be said German opinion went through a number of stages in relation to the Jewish question: first; a generalised public mood of anti-semitism, which saw widespread support for the idea that something-should-be-done about the Jews; second, a feeling of queasiness as laws were passed restricting Jewish rights, accompanied by the creeping realisation that the Third Reich's grip on power might not end well; third, a sense of horror, with the violence against Jews serving to demonstrate that organised thuggery was state sanctioned, and that, in the face of this, ordinary Germans were, or felt themselves to be, helpless. All of this is not to deny that for a great many the Nazi Party held out the prospect of achieving a degree of importance they would have been denied in normal circumstances and, for them, the opportunity to gain preferment by proving themselves loyal foot soldiers to Nazi ideology was too good to resist.

'So you end up with a noisy and visible minority, a silent and morally compromised majority and a state characterised by the corrupt use of power and the escalation of fear.

'A measure of the bizarre and terrifyingly ridiculous nature of Nazism is illustrated by their debate over part Jewishness—central to the new concept of citizenship rights based on racial purity. How do you classify people who were half Jewish, quarter Jewish or whatever? On the one hand, was Jewish blood so toxic that small amounts would seriously contaminate German blood or, on the other, was German blood so strong it overwhelmed all but the strongest concentrations of Jewish blood? If Jewish blood was deemed strong then what did that say about the Aryan master race, but if master race blood was so powerful then why worry about part Jewishness at all? An absurd argument because every premise on which it is based is nonsense, but that, of course, was not their conclusion.

'By 1938 the atmosphere of discrimination and intimidation towards Jews resulted in many thousands of them leaving Germany—with hindsight a relatively moderate solution to the presence of Jews in German society—but they were still a long way short of having expelled them all. Violence was on the increase once more, with the aim of forcing the remaining Jews to emigrate and, against this background, "Kristallnacht" took place.

'It began on 7 November 1938 when a seventeen year old Pole, Herschel Grynszpan, whose parents lived in Germany but who was himself living in Paris, discovered his parents had been deported from Germany to Poland. Incensed, he picked up a revolver, walked into the German embassy in Paris and shot the first diplomat he set eyes on. Goebbels instructed the press to feature the story as an attack by "world Jewry" on the Third Reich and that there would be severe "consequences" for all Jews living in Germany. It was a clear call to arms for the Nazi faithful.

'Hitler waited for the severely wounded diplomat to die, then used the moment to issue orders for an unprecedented orgy of violence and destruction targeted at Jews—except it was dressed up as a spontaneous explosion of anger towards Jews by the population at large, and not planned, co-ordinated or led by the Nazi high command at all.

'Across the country, party members and stormtroopers were celebrating the anniversary of the Munich putsch of 1923 when the command arrived, and were already drunk and boisterous. Within hours nearly every synagogue or other Jewish house of worship in the country was in flames, while shops had their plate glass windows smashed, leaving piles of smashed glass on pavements—so earning the name Kristallnacht or the Night of Broken Glass. Jewish Premises were broken into and trashed, and homes raided and the windows and furniture smashed, their owners beaten, thrown aside and threatened with being burned alive.

'Jewish gravestones were dug up and smashed. A Jewish orphanage in Esslingen was broken into by brownshirts wielding axes and sledgehammers and smashed to pieces, the traumatised children threatened with being thrown on the funeral pyre the Nazis had made out of their belongings. All over, Jews were chased out of their homes, their towns and their villages by jeering, laughing mobs.

'Disturbingly, the Party faithful's explosion of hateful violence was joined by others, especially the young, who had been subjected to years of indoctrination, through school and the Hitler Youth, and taught to believe that Jews were a subhuman, criminal sect. But because those who were responsible for the violence were everywhere visible, whereas those who would have nothing to do with it were quietly absent, the impression that the German people rose up against the Jews that night—the version put out by

Goebbels—was a misleading one. Many parents despaired of their children's involvement; the extreme violence was confined to particular anti-semitic strongholds; ordinary Germans resented the notion that the "uprising" was carried out in the name of a "people" that they, and most of their friends and family, were not a part of. The popular mood was of shock and revulsion. And the thing that most shocked people was its suddenness: for a number of years violent incidents against Jews had become relatively isolated, and the civilised German majority had not expected such an appalling outbreak. To confront the dreadful truth that the Nazis were, indeed, an evil regime, drew a reaction of disgust and contempt from the greater part of the populace.

'But it was too late. The Night of Broken Glass may have revolted the majority of Germans, but a significant minority had participated in it. German society was divided and the Nazis held the whip hand. Whilst disapproval was widespread, outspoken condemnation was not. The rule of terror had begun, and the one thing every German internalised that night was the need to keep quiet, while the one thing every Nazi internalised in the days that followed was that they could do whatever they liked to the Jews and no one was going to stop them. For years Hitler had personally distanced himself from his regime's hostile anti-semitism knowing it was unpopular with a large majority of Germans, but following the events of November 1938 he was confident enough to declare in January 1939 that if the Jews succeeded in tipping the world into war then it would result in the "annihilation of the Jewish race in Europe."

'The idea that there was any kind of Jewish conspiracy to foment a world war was a paranoid fantasy or propagandising delusion, depending on your point of view, but facts were never a critical component in the formation of Nazi ideology.'

Victor shakes his head; he looks tired. There's a sense that he's waited a long time to tell me this and it's draining him.

'The terrible thing,' he says, 'is when compliance becomes complicity. Hitler could have been stopped, but at a critical turning point, probably 1933 when he was invited into power by an old guard who thought they could contain him, he gained a momentum that would prove unstoppable, right through until he killed himself in his bunker. The deaths of millions would for decades scrape at the consciences of those who survived. They may have been driven into passivity through fear, they may have paid only lip service to the regime in public while privately decrying it, they may have reacted the way anyone would faced with the same circumstances—waiting for the storm to pass hoping it would leave them unscathed. But fate appointed them to the task—they were the chosen ones, the ones who failed humanity at its darkest hour, the ones who so graphically revealed a weakness at the heart of humankind.'

He looks at me. It's hard to tell if he's searching for my reaction, for my agreement or for some absolution, although I can't imagine for what. In his eyes there is history, on his face are the unresolved questions of why and how? I don't know what to say. He's saying something fundamental about the purpose of our project and I'm worried in case I fail him.

'You see, Sylvia, the civilised world—I'm speaking relatively, of course—learned lessons from The Third Reich's rise and fall. But those lessons are fading into the past. People have become lazy about democracy, complacent about freedom, blind to suffering that is no business of their own. News is turning into propaganda; public institutions are being chipped away by people for whom they are an inconvenience; the earth is burning up, filling up, and people are hated for being poor, for being rich, for being foreign, for being different, for trying too hard, for not trying, for living, for dying, for sleeping, for knowing, for not knowing, for disagreeing, for agreeing; in fact, just for being. Whoever you are, you represent something someone else hates and that hate is being turned up, amplified, choreographed and staged. Hate is part of the human condition, it is a universal: you will find it in every culture, you cannot remove the capacity for hatred, but you can stand up against it, build the institutions that contain it, tame the vested interests that feed from it and educate people as to where it might end if they do nothing until it's too late.'

He spreads his arms to embrace the room. It glares back: the vainglorious swastikas, the squalid ghettoes, the yellow stars, the couples paraded for 'race defilement', the tents of the Hitler Youth camps that stretch as far as the eye can see, the deathly censure on the face of Goebbels on finding out his photographer is a Jew, the emptied cattle trucks, the 'death marches', the emaciated faces of the doomed, the burial pits, the piled up carcasses of boys and girls, the smoke from chimneys and the clean, sharp air above the Birkenau gate on a bright winter's day.

It seems that something has ended. Something between us that has hovered since we first met. If I see him now as a man with a past, present and future, it's because I saw him before as more of an entity—someone who had entered my life and taken it over without surrendering anything of himself in return. Now he's no longer a loose sketch. He has clear lines and colour, he has filled in and, I think, causing myself a brief, inappropriate smirk, fattened.

'Whose house is this?' I ask, straightening to seem direct and businesslike.

'Take a guess,' he says, an eyebrow raised telling me to look no further than the obvious.

'Are you going to introduce me?'

'He's not at home. It's too soon anyway.'

He? Is this a slip or a calibrated reveal, the idea being to unveil him in stages, to warm me up gently for the eventual meeting?

'And this exhibition,' I say, 'is my work to be shut away in private?'

As soon as I ask the question, I regret the pejorative tone. I wave a hand as though to take it back, or apologise.

'There's nothing "shut away" about this, even though it is for private view,' says Victor. He doesn't look insulted, and maybe he understands, or maybe he thinks that I misunderstood: a comment from she who does not know of what she speaks? 'But no,' he says, 'we are thinking of something else entirely for you.'

He doesn't elaborate, preferring to sit guardedly, I think, behind his initial statement. I try and tease it from him, playing up to a newly assumed familiarity, but he doesn't budge.

On the way home on the train the phrase 'something else entirely' plays happily in my mind; an earworm I rotate and revel in the sound of.

But I also start thinking about the appearance of my fellow passengers and what judgements I could make about them. Some people are obsessed with clothes as a statement, but this is not what I mean. I'm thinking about the clues to identity, background, wealth, education, marital status, religion. I'm putting them together with hair: long, short, straight, curly, dressed, unkempt; and faces: angular, square, alert, tired, bored, vacant, intelligent, inquisitive. And how should I judge according to what really matters: collaborator, resistance fighter, bystander? Compliant, complicit, weak, strong? Killer or victim, doomed or destined to survive?

No answers, of course. As soon as I start the game I know I'll not dare consign anyone, even though it's easy to look at people and have an instinct. It's like a game where you watch passers-by and invent their life stories, safe in the knowledge they'll never know you're playing and you'll never know the truth.

'We are thinking of something else entirely for you'. It chimes away and I can see Victor's smile as he says it. There was something reassuring in the smile, something that told of being part of his movement. I've seen HQ and it worked out well. I'm vindicated, my faith renewed.

Chapter Nine

I ring Natalie and Nina answers. She greets me with my name before I've spoken and it takes a moment to realise it isn't Natalie. I'm thrown, not sure how to proceed—to ask for her mum seems curt, but to extend a conversation with Nina when she is the subject of the call feels false. I ask her how she is and she gabbles a little, and I ask her how school is and she chirps away, though less enthusiastically, and eventually I ask to speak to her mum.

'She isn't here.'

'Oh,' I say, 'and she's left you with her phone?'

'Of course,' says Nina, 'shouldn't she?'

I'm stuck. Why 'of course'? And did I imply she shouldn't?

'Most people take their mobile phone with them when they go out. Clue in the name,' I say, in what I hope is a good-humoured tone.

'Mum leaves hers with me, in case she gets any calls while she's out.' The logic of this is escaping me, but Nina continues, 'she might not hear if it's noisy, with it stuck in the bottom of her bag, so she leaves it with me so she doesn't miss anyone.'

Too many questions jump to mind: one is about voicemail, which I allow to pass. The one I ask is, 'What if she needs to make a call while she's out?'

'She has another phone for that,' says Nina. She says it so matter of fact I realise I've stumbled on something so normal to her that she has no idea how strange it may seem to anyone else.

'Okay,' is all I say, brightly, playing along with the idea of it all being what one would expect. But Nina becomes serious.

'No one else knows about the other phone,' she says, 'only Dad and me and a couple of others, I think, and now you. So you mustn't say anything to anyone.'

Again I'm floundering: the special phone no one knows about; the fact that one of the few who does is the absent father; the implication of being invited into this exclusive group, and have I really been invited or am I implicated by accident? What will Natalie say when she finds out?

'Is it okay, you telling me about the other phone?'

'I think so,' she says. But in a tone that communicates, I know so.

'Okay.'

'Sylvia, is this about you being my tutor?'

'Yes.' There's a pause, one I half expect Nina to fill, until I realise she's waiting for me to tell her what I've decided. It feels like a nervous pause, which is probably good if it means she hasn't been taking my answer for granted. 'I'd be delighted to be your tutor.'

As I say it, I feel an unexpected thrill: a flow of pleasure as I take Nina into my life.

Nina's static-like nervousness has subsided to true silence. She seems to disappear, to the point where I think the line has gone dead.

'Thank you,' she says, at last.

'I'm looking forward to it,' I say, and immediately regret the blandness of my reply, and add, rather more breathlessly, 'it'll be great, I promise.'

She goes silent again, broken a second or two later by a watery voice. 'Mum will be so pleased.'

'And you?'

'Me what?'

'Are you pleased?'

'Oh yes,' she gushes, as though her life hinged on the moment, 'I'm so happy I could die.'

I tell her we wouldn't want that, and she giggles. She's so sweet, I say to myself, wondering how much of her mum being 'so pleased' is Natalie taking pleasure in her daughter's acceptance, and how much is Nina's relief that she has secured her mother's approval.

'When can we start?'

By the time I eventually speak to Natalie, late in the evening, it is old news but she still sounds delighted.

'I knew you would,' she says, as though congratulating herself for having faith—whether in me or Nina isn't clear.

'I'm sorry you couldn't speak to me earlier,' she says, 'Nina explained that I don't take my phone with me in the evenings?'

'Yes,' I say, unsure if the question requires an answer and wondering if Natalie is going to volunteer an explanation.

She starts a conversation about when Nina can next come round. Weekdays she's in school, although evenings are free, as are most weekends.

'It's a long way for an evening.'

She apologises and says she only wants to fit in with whatever suits me. I tell her I'm flexible and that an evening a week plus some time over the weekend would be fine.

'Besides,' she says, 'her school's near you. It would be easy for her to come over after.'

I wonder why Nina comes all the way over here to go to school each day, and does she take the bus home every night? But the thought subsides, overtaken by the sense that Natalie has everything worked out.

'There's one more thing I need to tell you,' I say, and I hear a muted exclamation stick in Natalie's throat as she picks up on the ominous overture. 'The work is horrific, the subject matter that is. It's brutal, depraved stuff, the vilest acts human beings have ever committed. I'm distressed by it, and Nina is bound to be. I can shelter her from it as far as possible, but I can't hide it from her altogether.'

'She knows all about the Holocaust,' says Natalie, 'so don't worry. I trust you.'

Somewhere along the line I'd created an impression of Natalie as the over-protective mother, so the sanguine response comes as a mild surprise. Added to that, a couple of hours previously I'd discovered that Natalie leaves Nina alone in the house some evenings. Whatever it is about them, I'm hooked. I want to know more. And I wonder what other assumptions I've got wrong.

Once Natalie is off the phone, I sit with a drink and enjoy the evening as it spreads into night—a favourite time. In the excitement I've barely thought about Alex and I wonder how much of the day I should share with him.

He's in one of those phases of life where time is condensed, foreshortened and the sense of drifting downriver, for so many years—how many years?— predictable and stable, is upended by the unexpected need to navigate rapids. Every day is a day of reinvention, like a child greeting each sunrise as a new experience. It means exchanging his predictably unpredictable nature for genuine unpredictability. I see no sequences, no logical steps, no pattern and yet something of the Alex I knew and had almost forgotten has returned. Telling him about today will be an interesting experiment, a measure of where he's at.

'I followed Victor to his lair today.'

He repeats the word 'lair' back to me, which is good—it means he's listened and understood. My flippancy is defensive and I hope it'll disarm him and allow me to tell the story without interruption.

I tell Alex how I went undercover with what I thought was my cunning disguise, only to discover Victor knew I was following him.

'He led you on, knowing you were there?'

'I guess so,' I say, taken aback at how quickly Alex has latched on to this interpretation, worried he'll now want to make something of it.

'If he wasn't leading you he would have challenged you, or given you the slip.'

'I know. I still feel a bit foolish for having followed him for so long thinking how clever I was, only to discover I wasn't at all.'

I grin and he laughs; a spontaneous laugh, which shares in the absurdity rather than pointing up the stupidity.

I recount the journey, the wait outside, being called in, the red-tiled house and Victor's chilled-out attitude towards the whole adventure. Alex is listening, concentrating and not itching to interject.

He continues listening as I describe the museum and Victor's talk about the Nazi grip on power: how they seized and held it in spite of, not because of, their violent persecution of the Jews and others; their systematic moulding of the youth; the propaganda of dehumanisation; the barbaric rampage of the Night of Broken Glass; the horror of waking up as a German to discover that there was no longer anything that could be done to stop it; the terror that was unleashed that would result in tens of millions of dead across the world, and all of it spilling out from a small coterie of fanatics hung up on a theory that had as much scientific validity as the one that propelled the flat earth society.

Alex tells me the earth was believed to be spherical from as early as the fourth century BC, although if you ask people today, a ridiculous number think it was Columbus failing to fall off the edge of it in the fifteenth century that first alerted people to the fact. I'm puzzled why this passing analogy, a mere aside, is the point he chooses to pass comment on.

'Ignorance,' he says, 'breeds stupidity breeds violence. Propaganda exploits ignorance and amplifies it. The Nazis were the masters, but open a newspaper or switch on the radio or watch a news programme and you'll find the same traits, the same DNA, the same search for the "story", for someone to "blame", for someone to funnel hate towards.'

This isn't like Alex. He is capable of such thoughts, but he doesn't normally dwell on them.

'I wasn't expecting you to be quite so…' I leave it in the air, not wanting to inadvertently insult him.

'Connected?' he says. Interesting word, but I nod. 'I was reading about our takeover battle in the papers, and noticed the things they got wrong. Not disagreements in opinion or variance in speculation, but actual hard facts in print that were simply inaccurate. Meanwhile, I listen to politicians recycling myths about their opponents—again, not opinion, but untruths you would assume could only be delivered with a straight face if they had fallen for the myth themselves.

'Which is more frightening: the myth that is spread with the knowledge that it is wrong, or the myth that is spread out of sheer ignorance? Would you, for example, prefer a government of liars, or a government of the ignorant?'

Suddenly, again, I feel the project weighing on me. It's too much. Knowing the Nazis were evil is one thing, but using that knowledge to create something that is relevant today feels like a task forged in the pits of the earth as a punishment. Alex talks of the press, but aren't the press— superficial, sanctimonious and given to distortion as they are—at least notionally free?

Or is the tide turning? I think that's what Alex is saying. Victor talks of human nature: the good, the bad and what turns people from one to the other. What forces are working to give us freedom and a civilised world? What forces are rising that might abolish it? Are the people who are switching on the lights working faster than those switching them off? Are we competitive or co-operative, or are we both, depending on circumstances, and are those circumstances moving us towards or away from an enlightened state?

Are we always hanging by the slenderest thread? Is our democracy, decency, rule of law and freedom, prey to an aggregation of malign powers that could crush liberty and end our 'golden' age—and all the time we don't know it, blindsided until it's too late?

Alex comes to me and places his hand in the small of my back. I'm gazing vacantly from the window into the part of the street where I first saw Victor.

'I'm beginning to find Victor interesting,' he says, and smoothes the palm of his hand up my spine and to my neck. It means he wants sex and, for a change, I find I do too.

Chapter Ten

Once Germany was at war, any sign of a lingering opposition at home being of the slightest relevance evaporated. The Nazis were set fair to binge on atrocity and wasted no time establishing a pattern of mass executions carried out at the slightest pretext. Poland was first in line; a backward, subhuman race according to Nazi ideology; a people who deserved no better than what they got.

The statistics come as a terrifying surprise. What I thought I knew about the war was that Britain had stood alone for a year, brave and resilient in the face of the blitz and the threat of invasion, waiting, hoping, for a reversal that finally came when the Soviet Union and the Americans entered the war as allies. I was brought up on pictures of bombed British cities, Royal visits to ruins, the faces of the plucky survivors and an understanding of the terrible losses we as a nation had suffered. This narrative is more or less irrefutable, but it is only one truth and, in the context of Total War, a relatively small one.

What I didn't know was that five and a half million Polish civilians lost their lives as a direct result of crimes against humanity, committed not only by the Germans but also the Soviets during their occupation. The Germans hated the Soviets; the Soviets hated the Germans; the Soviets and the Germans both hated the Poles. Nearly half the total deaths were Polish Jews who qualified in two hate categories.

I find a story about some schoolboys who break a window in the local police station in Obluze. Fifty Polish schoolboys were subsequently arrested, none of whom would or could name the culprit. The SS ordered their parents to beat the boys, and when they refused the SS men beat the boys with their rifle butts, signing off by shooting dead ten of them and leaving their bodies lying in the open for a day in front of a church.

The Nazis, having easily won the war in Poland, were terrified of a guerrilla war and enacted the severest retaliatory measures, often not in response not to an actual incident but on suspicion one might occur—what became a pathological variation on getting one's retaliation in first. Hundreds of villages were burned to the ground, thousands of citizens executed. Where distaste for violence had existed in German society prior to the war, an apparent relish developed within the German military once war was underway and the ties that would normally bind civilised behaviour were unleashed.

Hitler ordered the creation of an 'Ethnic German Self-Protection' militia, which, along with SS task forces, presided over the mass shootings of Polish civilians. On one occasion, militiamen rounded up ten thousand Poles and Jews and brought them to Mniszek where they were taken to a gravel pit, lined up in batches and shot. Another eight thousand were shot in a wood near Karlshof. Everywhere in Poland, the Nazi machine set about enacting its leader's command to 'send man, woman and child of Polish descent to their deaths, pitilessly and remorselessly.'

In retaliation for the wounding of a German soldier in Wawer, a train was stopped at random and people pulled off—all wholly ignorant of and unconnected with the incident in question—and executed on the spot. Their bodies were left hanging upside down for days afterwards.

Where a fighting force needs discipline to succeed, an occupying force can bring terror through a sanctioned indiscipline. Hitler wanted his lebensraum, and the Polish people were occupying the designate area. 'Poland will be depopulated and settled with Germans,' he said.

The intelligentsia were rounded up and executed, including almost all journalists. Polish art and culture was destroyed. Two million Polish men were forcibly conscripted into the German army or used as forced labour. Aryan looking Polish children were taken from their mothers and placed in German families and about 100,000 non Jewish Poles were gassed at Auschwitz.

Dr Zygmunt Klukowski, whose diary of the occupation wasn't published in English until 1993, noted the sadistic pleasure that was openly visible on the faces of the Gestapo as they bludgeoned and whipped Poles imprisoned in an internment camp. Klukowski, personally, was lucky: having been brought to the camp from his hospital, he was subsequently released after convincing the Germans that he had a typhus outbreak that needed to be contained: failure to do so would endanger Germans and Poles alike, he said.

The background to the German soldiers' actions was a deadly combination of propaganda and the arrogance that comes with conquest. Poles were 'mentally subnormal', they lived in 'stinking holes' and they were in cahoots with the Jews. As the Germans encountered the poverty and poor living conditions of the Poles, the view of them as a backward, subhuman race who deserved extermination was confirmed. The Poles were cast as an inferior species and the contempt they were held in increased as the power the Germans wielded became more absolute.

If the number of non Jewish Poles exterminated in the Polish Holocaust comes as a surprise—and I find it astonishing and feel a pulse of guilt that it should—the Jewish Holocaust is horribly familiar. At least that's what I think until I begin researching the stories. The devil is in the detail. As is, I imagine, the lifeblood of my exhibition.

Numbers are one thing I realise. The millions of dead are statistics to shock and numb the mind. But people die one by one, each death the shutting down of someone's central nervous system: the surrender of sense, the wiping of memory; the destruction of a living, breathing person; someone nurtured and loved and educated and who stood on the earth as surely as I do; who had as many thoughts and feelings and hopes and dreams as I ever had. A mortal and unique existence, the source of love and grief for others, is obliterated, snuffed out, as though the right to kill existed, as if they weren't human at all.

How does this become art? What is my role, my responsibility? I'm not thinking about Victor, the sponsor, and their expectations, loose though they are, I'm thinking about me. How does the horror of history connect with me, the dabbler in paint and mixed media, and become vital? As I watch the river, the tide low, the banks exposed and the sense of it draining, I fear disappointment.

It's all in the stories. Stories of fact, not fiction; stories worse than the worst nightmares; stories I read with anger, humility, thankfulness and dread. The stories are not my life, nor likely to be, but I'm still surrounded each day by humans and their nature and the fact that the evolutionary timespan that dates from the Third Reich until now won't have banished the possibility. What rough beast indeed, lies still within us?

Once the Polish occupation was fully in train, many German soldiers became infected with the bestial fanaticism of their SS task force and militia comrades-in-arms, and found daily entertainment in the gratuitous persecution of any Jews they came across. A favourite was firing shots into Jewish houses, not necessarily at a specific target but just so as to enjoy the possibility that someone may have been at the end of the bullet. For a laugh, Jews were made to eat pork. For more than a laugh, and presumably no less gratifying, was the corralling of Jewish men in the street and forcing them to smear excrement over one another. Setting fire to beards was another favourite, as was cutting the Jewish star into a forehead with a knife.

The Warsaw ghetto was created in 1940 to contain the city's Jews in one area. It was sealed off from the rest of the city, with walls erected where natural barriers didn't exist, and fifteen checkpoints set up in order to police traffic in and out. For Jews, the traffic was one way, inwards —that is, until people were shipped out as part of the final solution. Overcrowding was rife, as was the never ending bullying and humiliation of Jews. Outbreaks of disease, such as typhus, were common in the squalid conditions: in June 1941 a quarter of the children in the ghetto shelters died.

Of the children who survived many were orphaned and would roam the streets, weeping, hoping to find somewhere to sleep. Corpses were left in the open, a sight so common people stopped bothering to move them. Eyewitness accounts spoke of the corpses being 'mere skeletons' while the living were 'nightmare figures, the ghosts of former human beings'. Altogether 140,000 people died in the ghetto.

Meanwhile German filmmakers were shooting propaganda for the good Germans back home, showing kind-hearted German soldiers bravely intervening to protect the Jews from the brutalities of the Polish police.

In spite of this, about 11,000 Jews survived in Warsaw until the end of the war, many helped by sympathetic non Jewish Poles. But these people operated at their own peril, not just from the Nazis but from other Poles who shared much of the Germans' anti-semitism, in spite of the fact that their countrymen, by the million, were subjected to the same fate as the Jews. It was a dog-eat-dog survival war in which few emerged with any credit, and certainly not the Polish Catholic church who distanced themselves from the Jews by decrying them as Bolsheviks. As a succession of institutions failed in the face of the anarchic murderousness of the Nazi machine, the spirit of common humanity was blown to the wind.

Nazi control and influence spread to other territories. In Romania, the fascist Iron Guard uprising resulted in an anti-Jewish rampage, during which two hundred Jewish men were taken to a slaughterhouse and subjected to exactly the same procedure used for slaughtering animals. Their carcasses were hung by the throat from meat hooks and labelled 'unfit for human consumption'.

Croatia, a new Nazi puppet state, began a massive programme of ethnic cleansing designed to eliminate Gypsies, Jews and the country's two million Serbs. After shooting dead three hundred Serbs in the village of Glina in July 1941, the Ustashe, Croatia's former insurgents, now appointed by Hitler as the country's rulers, offered an amnesty to surrounding villagers if they converted to Catholicism. About two hundred and fifty people turned up to the church in Glina for the ceremony, at which point the Ustashe made them lie down before smashing their skulls in with spiked clubs.

There were many incidents of Serb villagers herded into churches where the windows were boarded over before the building was set on fire and the people burned alive. Ustashe militias would routinely round up Serb men and gouge out their eyes or cut off women's breasts with penknives. In Croatian concentration camps the Ustashe would indulge in nightlong orgies of mass murder, with the encouragement of Franciscan monks—regular cheerleaders for ethnic cleansing—during which inmates were beaten to death with hammers. At the Loborgrad camp, the commander and his staff repeatedly raped fifteen hundred Jewish women.

On 27 June 1941 a German Colonel, Lothar von Bischoffshausen, entered the town of Kovno in Lithuania and witnessed a sight he, an experienced career soldier, found shocking. A crowd of people gathered around the forecourt of a petrol station, in the middle of which was a blond haired young man resting on a heavy wooden club. Around him lay at least a dozen dead or dying people whose blood ran down a drainage gully, washed away by water from a hose. To the side of this man was a line of about twenty men, guarded by armed civilians, each waiting to be clubbed to death, forced to witness the brutal executions of those in front of them; each one a sickening preview of their own death to come.

An SS man told the Colonel that this was a spontaneous uprising by locals against Soviet collaborators. It was nothing of the sort. In spite of German attempts to encourage local insurrection against Communists, Jews and resisters, the Lithuanians had been generally unobliging, and the SS Task Forces had largely resorted to carrying out the killings themselves. The execution was a staged SS event, the victims all Jews.

The Nazi experiments in killing with gas started as early as 1939. Psychiatric patients from Treskau were selected and taken to a Gestapo facility in Posen where they were crammed into a sealed room and killed with carbon monoxide. It is the first recorded mass killing in a gas chamber. By 1940 patients were being gassed regularly—so regularly rumour of what was happening spread and the intended victims began to struggle when the buses came for them. Sedation was administered to those who fought. The end, when it came, was slow and painful. An observer of a gassing at Hadamar described the men crammed together, the suffering as they struggled for air and their moment of clarity as they understood what was happening.

I wonder about the last moments of a murdered persons life. What goes through your mind? The numbed realisation that this really is it? The desperation to get out, which you know to be impossible? Hot, raw anger? An utter, forlorn helplessness? The shock of disbelief married to a solid awareness of exactly what is occurring? You had five minutes until consciousness was lost. You could condense a lot into that time.

Before gas chambers became the industrial scale killing factories of the final solution, shooting was the main method of execution. In July 1941 Hitler issued new decrees for the elimination of 'Jewish-Bolshevik subversion' and placed Himmler in charge. The shooting of civilians, always a stock response to any insurrection, real or imagined, was now ratcheted up to unprecedented levels. Himmler's SS Task Force brigades began to systematically shoot their way through the entire Jewish population, including, quite explicitly, all women and children. The programmed extermination was underway.

In Kamenetsk-Podolsk the task Force killed 23,600 men, women and children in three days at the end of August 1941. On the ravine of Babi Yar, outside Kiev, the Task Force killed 33,771 men, women and children in two days —all of whom had been ordered to assemble for 'resettlement'. A member of the unit responsible, Kurt Werner, later testified that having made every man, woman and child undress:

'Groups of Jews were sent down to each of these execution squads simultaneously. Each successive group of Jews had to lie down on top of the bodies of those that had already been shot. The marksmen stood behind the Jews and killed them with a shot in the neck. I still recall today the complete terror of the Jews when they first caught sight of the bodies as they reached the top edge of the ravine.'

Werner went on to talk about the nerves of steel required to do such dirty work, having to shoot continuously until every Jew was dead. His testimony suggests abhorrence at the task and some remorse, although whether genuine or manufactured is hard to tell.

The Nazis were surprisingly sympathetic to men who wouldn't take part in the murders. Those who refused weren't subjected to disciplinary action or told to expect any disadvantage to their career, but in spite of this policy most charged with the task chose to carry it out. Possibly the desire not to appear weak was a motive, possibly an undercurrent of anti-semitism, but there was also greed:

victims' possessions were looted, houses ransacked and property confiscated. None of this bounty would accrue to soldiers who sat it out or were assigned elsewhere.

And, of course, there was the perennial favourite, the get out of jail for moral qualms down the ages: if I don't do it they'll get someone else who will.

There are examples of German army commanders who would protest and succeed in stopping the murders, at least temporarily. In the village of Byelaya Tserkow, near Kiev, the men, women and older children were taken away and shot, leaving ninety of the young children, from babies up to six years old, shut away in an old church without adult supervision. A German Lieutenant Colonel was alerted to the children's presence, their pathetic cries having been heard by his men, and on inspection he found the children starving, without water, covered in flies and lying in excrement. He posted soldiers on the building with orders not to let anyone remove them, his motive being to ensure their safety. But he had flouted the command of Colonel Riedl, a fanatic of the first order and his decision was overturned, the children's murder officially authorised at a higher level.

Even so, the SS officer given the task of taking the children out to a wood and shooting them, objected. He said his own men had children and could not be expected to carry out the task. He suggested Ukrainian militiamen be recruited for the job. Nevertheless, he was present at the massacre. The children's wailing was, he said, indescribable, the scene unbearable.

He told of one small, fair-haired girl who took his hand and who was later shot. Some needed several bullets before they died.

That they were operating beyond the outer reaches of the moral universe was inescapable to all but the most hardened fanatics. Task Force leaders had a common complaint by the end of 1941: that the continual shooting of defenceless women and children was placing an intolerable strain on their men. Many had committed suicide, some had gone mad and most had come to rely on alcohol when carrying out their work.

In October 1941 Hans Kruger, the head of the Security Police, found himself with a problem. Ordered to create a Jewish ghetto in Stanislawow in Galicia he was informed there was insufficient housing for the town's thirty thousand Jews. His solution was to arrange them in a long line that led to two vast open graves in the town's cemetery, where they were shot by a combination of German police, ethnic Germans and nationalist Ukrainians. To maintain spirits amongst this motley band of murdering foot soldiers, whose killing spree would extend from morning until dusk, he laid on a table of food and alcohol, to be indulged in during break times, while he supervised the massacre with a hot dog in one hand and a bottle of vodka in the other.

The slaughter was as chaotic as one might expect. The Jews panicked and were shot as they attempted to climb the cemetery walls. Others jumped into the open graves where they were either shot or buried alive by bodies falling on them.

By the end of the day Kruger's men had shot over ten thousand men, women and children—the number of Jews that remained, now a manageable number—at which point he announced that Hitler had postponed the execution. They were then herded back to the ghetto, although many more were trampled to death in a panicked rush to exit the cemetery.

Kruger seems like a gift to my work. Grotesquely parodic except for the sheer terrorising reality of it, the image of a demented fanatic strutting around with his vodka and hot dog, commanding a drunken death squad, is frighteningly, surreally perfect as the representative Nazi, the man who encapsulates the unhinged hate fuelled madness of the Third Reich.

By autumn 1941, experiments in gassing people to death had moved into the realm of utilising carbon monoxide gasses from car exhausts. After a number of mental patients had been killed by pumping the fumes into a sealed room, Arthur Nebe, the head of Task Force B, came up with the idea of putting people in airtight vans and piping in the exhaust fumes.

Himmler gave an order for a camp to be created to serve as a base for the gas vans—a camp built for the express purpose of killing people. Soon there were more camps.

The purpose-built vans could hold up to sixty people. They would be loaded with Jews or Gypsies at the camp and driven several kilometres to woods, the passengers asphyxiating en route. At the destination the bodies would be tipped from the vans into ditches prepared by other Jewish inmates of the camp.

The van operators later testified that they would hear the Jews banging and screaming to be let out. When they arrived and opened up the back of the van, a cloud of smoke would drift out, and after it had cleared, they pulled out the bodies. According to one witness: 'You could see that they had fought desperately for their lives. The dead had to be dragged apart.'

Sometimes a mother would manage to wrap her baby tightly enough to prevent it from breathing the fumes. The German guards would pick up any surviving babies and smash their heads against the trees.

Chapter Eleven

She stands at the door, blinking, her face bright as morning sun. It's after school and I notice: her uniform, strangely incongruous, as though someone has mistakenly fitted her for a fancy dress party. I'm not used to schoolchildren and hadn't really thought of Nina as such until now, but as I watch her walking through the hall to the stairs I wonder how my life would be different with children.

The first thought is having to give up smoking. Probably a good thing. A strong enough reason is what I need. But that isn't the real point.

The termination was the worst day of my life: the wait to be called, the fact that my boyfriend, if he could be called that—shiftless; drug obsessed; a man of big dreams and little ambition—couldn't be with me. He dropped me off and ran back to his wife. I went through the procedure alone, including, afterwards, making my way past a group of protesters outside. The clinic was, indeed, clinical.

The following days I did nothing but drift, mentally and physically: an empty shell, something hollowed out within and alone. I walked around malls, something I never do. I normally shop like a man: in, find, buy and out. But I wasn't buying, I was hanging out in the vicinity of other human beings, imagining a solidarity with people who were going about their lives, carrying with them their failures and disappointments, but getting on.

It was several days before I felt like doing anything, never mind work. Part of me was gone, as was the someone else I thought I loved and who, though feckless, was a man I wanted to give myself to entirely. He was gentle and funny and loving and not in the least egotistical or aggressive or controlling, but belonged elsewhere; probably inside his own head, where I can only hope he made some kind of sense.

He had no choice but to leave me and return to his wife, once he'd decided he couldn't leave her. The logic was impossible otherwise. It forced his hand and it cast me adrift. I hated him for choosing her, until I understood he'd been honest with me and then I loved him all over again. It's true, he was thoroughly honest, at least about the things he knew, although there was so much of himself he didn't. And in that time, during the minutes he stood in front of me crying, telling me he was sorry, telling me he couldn't do it, I learned the difference between honesty and the truth. Have you ever said 'I love you' and not meant it? It's in all those questionnaires. He meant it every time he said it, and it may even have been true, but it was never truth enough.

As I complete my Nazi research, or, more accurately, put it aside because I can't take anymore, the sense of drift resurrects itself. I walk the riverbank repeatedly, around the circuit that takes me up to and across Hammersmith Bridge, along the opposite bank, down to Barnes Bridge and back home. Or I do it in reverse. Mornings clockwise, afternoons anti-clockwise. In between I nibble away at the work, sketching mainly or writing notes. Part of the process, I tell myself; but I'm stuck and I have to work through it somehow, telling myself to keep thinking, keep doodling, keep concentrating and something will come.

And today it's Nina. Cheerful, delightful and excited. I ask her about her school day and she's non-committal, but not in a downcast way. I'm still alert to her mother's description of the withdrawn girl falling behind, but if true she hides it well. I ask her if she likes her school.

'I have to like it,' she says, 'it costs too much not to.'

Nothing breaks in her features, no hint that this is anything but a matter of fact statement. I wonder if it's her voice or a projection of Natalie's I'm hearing.

'So art's your favourite subject?'

At this her face does change. Something dims and she looks down. 'Yes.'

I half expect her to look up again and resume her big, open smile, but she doesn't, or rather, as her forehead rises, it hesitates, and when her eyes meet mine they flicker and drop once more.

'What's the matter?' I wonder if I'm too direct. We hardly know one another and she may not want to confide in me. 'You don't have to say,' I add, smiling.

She looks up again, a glint in her eye and a small, nervous laugh. 'It's just that you're a real artist,' she says, and shrugs to convey the meaning, the implication, of what she's saying.

I want to gather her up in my arms, but I restrict it to a hand around her shoulder. I pull her into me.

'Don't be embarrassed,' I say, 'I was hopeless when I was thirteen. I didn't even like art lessons at that age.'

It's a small white lie. At thirteen I knew I wanted to be an artist but I was frustrated by my inability to perfect anything. I wasn't hopeless—I can that see now, but I felt it then—and I didn't like art lessons because my teacher picked fault, gnawing away at my confidence, making me feel like the one thing I wanted to do, that I thought I could do, that was really me, was beyond me. I was lucky to have better teachers later, but meanwhile I spent hours at home, in my bedroom, drawing and painting, trying to make myself into the person I thought I was.

Nina embraces me in return, which produces an unusual feeling, as though a pleasure valve within has opened for the first time. I let myself swim in the moment, putting off when I have to introduce her to the Nazis.

I have little idea of what to expect of her. I can make her useful with bits and pieces, and I want to continue to use her as a model, but what else?

I set her up with a sketchpad and some pencils and ask her if she'd like to draw the river scene for me.

'Just to get your interpretation,' I say, feeling like a fraud since I want to know is how hard it will be to teach her.

I leave her to it, seating her on a chair overlooking the river. I go downstairs, make myself a coffee, light a cigarette and sit in the living room leafing through old exhibition catalogues. I've set her a target of twenty minutes and as soon as the time is up—I decide it's important to set an example and reappear on the second—I climb the stairs and rejoin her.

When I open the door she darts half a look at me, before hurriedly adding something to the sketch. A second later she sets the pad down.

'Finished,' she says, and jumps up from her seat, guilty at having stolen the few extra seconds.

'Let's have a look.'

I ask her to explain what she's done and why she's made the choices she has. I expect to have to tell her what I mean by this, but she gets it immediately. Listening to her talking me through becomes a calming experience: she knows what she's doing, she's well taught and well read, and she's spent time thinking about and practicing the finer details. It shows. It isn't perfect—a word I use too often—but it's technically proficient and imaginative in its use of deep shadows around the far bank, turning a potentially bland view into one of mystery. Strangely, I find myself meditating on the thought of Victor standing in those shadows, swallowed by darkness.

I tell her it works, that it's fired my imagination. I point out that her perspective on the bridge has gone a little awry on the far side. She tells me that she could extend the shading of the trees to rebalance it. It's a cheat, but she's right. More important, she says it for fun, not defensively. A wave of feeling for this special girl runs through me, as does a pulse of trepidation about my desire to live up to her expectations and become a special teacher.

'You know some of what I'm about to tell you,' I say, and I tell her about my research into the Nazis, proceeding slowly at first, looking for signs of unease. I'm half persuaded by Natalie that Nina knows 'all about the Holocaust' and is capable of taking what I tell her in her stride, but I want to see it for myself. When we work on it, burying ourselves in it, making it visual, it will take on a new resonance; I know, I see it already in dreams that are merging more and more into nightmares.

As we walk around the studio, me relating the history to the sketches as I show them to her, she stays close, not crowding in, but a few inches nearer than I would expect of someone walking with me on a studio tour. At first I wonder if it's for reassurance, the physical proximity a protection from any distress, but there's nothing else about her to signal this. I wonder about the obvious: that she's Jewish; she knows the history and is familiar with it, and the sense of threat from the Nazi era, transmitted through the generations, is buried within, not surfacing consciously.

'Are you okay with this?' I say, eventually.

'Oh yes.' She snaps it back, almost with a jump. It's as though, by asking the question, I have sprung her from a daydream.

It's then I understand that she stays close not because she identifies as Jewish, but because she identifies with me. It's my steps she's treading in, it's the art that transfixes her. The Holocaust is old news, making art is the new project.

As I wind down the tour and talk about where next, she tells me some of what she knows. She holds herself upright as she talks, as though delivering a talk to a group, and she throws in little dramatic flourishes; it's part conversation, part performance and has the quality of a rehearsal.

She tells me about Treblinka: how it became overloaded and the Germans, quite literally, couldn't kill people fast enough—trainloads arrived quicker than the people could be 'processed.' The gas chambers broke down leaving people trapped for hours, naked and waiting to die. Meanwhile, all pretence of it being a transit camp was abandoned and people were shot at the railway station, or left in cattle trucks for days with no food or water, many dying of thirst or asphyxiation. Nina tells me about the SS setting up a small orchestra to play popular songs to drown the screams as people were whipped towards the gas chambers.

She tells me that the SS named a narrow alleyway that led from the undressing room to the gas chamber the 'Road to Heaven'.

At this she drops out of performance mode—a move I'm sure is unconscious—and looks up at me, as though seeking approval. She's listened and she's astute: her story a close relation to the ones I'd been telling her.

'I'm interested in the "Road to Heaven",' I say.

'Literally or metaphorically?'

The question takes me by surprise, not only because it reveals I've underestimated her—and, in so doing, forced me consider whether my prejudice extends to all thirteen year olds—but also because it makes me think more deeply about the 'Road to Heaven' and what it is that has grabbed my attention.

I don't answer directly, but tell her the phrase intrigues me because it's double-edged, open to interpretation, revealing a range of possible psychologies. We know the SS Task Forces had difficulty carrying out the mass shootings because of the moral qualms of the men involved, so, what of the SS guards at the camp? Was the 'Road to Heaven' an invocation of a religious belief in order to ease the guilt—as though they needed to believe they were helping their victims passage to the afterlife—or was it a sneering put-down for people whose ethnicity is intertwined with religion, as though to validate the ideal of racial purity through the extermination of those whose inferior beliefs brought a deserved scorn as they were processed to their deaths?

And for the guards who herded Jews along the 'Road to Heaven', how many, with a religious belief that Nazism hadn't displaced, found themselves chilled at the thought of their own eternal destination?

Nina walks to the window and looks out across the river.

'A great uncle of mine was killed over there,' she says, pointing to the far bank. 'I never knew him. My mother told me. He was out for a walk when he was set on—they never found out who—and stabbed. The killer left a Star of David pinned to his chest. Mother says that today they would call it a hate crime but back then it was a Jew slaying. Today the story would be big news, she says, but back then it got a paragraph before being forgotten.'

'I suppose that's some sort of progress,' I say.

'It's still hate,' she says, 'that hasn't changed.' She turns her face to me and offers a rueful smile. I meet it with one of my own and hers dissolves to a new alertness, a sudden excitement. 'Your work: it's not only about Jews or Nazis, it's wider than that, isn't it?'

It's as if she's given the answer before the question has been asked. If I were superstitious I would pinch myself at my good fortune in finding Nina. I tell her she's exactly right. It's not about the politics of Judaism or Nazism; it's about why any person could do such unspeakable things to another. The Nazis were simply the most famous and not even the most recent. Cambodia; Rwanda; Indonesia. These are the genocides, the horror stories, which make us recoil because of their scale. But violence is part of the human condition—the capacity to hate and commit a violent act is in us all. What I'm interested in, I tell her, is why some people act on it and others don't.

The sun's low now. It catches the trees, but not the river, and so makes the water look black, like tar, sliding past to the estuary and beyond, into the vast circulating ocean of the earth, where waters combine and defy rights of nationhood or ownership.

Nina takes in the view with me. I can only guess what she's thinking, but her eyes have softened. She gazes to the far bank, maybe imagining her great uncle, wanting him to wave from the past, signalling a more benign future, one in which a young girl can watch a sunset or meditate on a passing river, where she can create a life for herself and be in love with it, living as free as the air or water.

I envy her: I never knew my father. My mother would never talk about him except to say he'd died. Before I was adult enough to challenge her and force out the facts, she too was gone. My parents disappeared, denying me a history. Nina's past is filled in, unsparingly so, and she has a father who, though missing, isn't gone and can still be hoped for.

She turns from the window and gives me a look that says she's grateful for me not having interrupted her.

'It's time to go,' I say.

Alex has taken it on himself to walk Nina to the Underground station after her visits. It has become a habit, starting with her staying later and later, and always after seeking permission from Natalie, which is usually after the pair of us lose track of time and the 'request' has become more of a fait accompli.

'You're over-compensating,' I say to him, one night after he returns, 'she makes her own way home from school, it's no different.'

He points out that the worst bit is the underpass, which she doesn't have to negotiate on the way home from school, a place I confess to finding creepy. This, inconveniently, is true.

'If it helps her feel safe it's worth it,' he says, 'even if actual danger is remote.'

'Why not walk her through the underpass and then turn back?'

We're in familiar territory: Alex wants to be chivalrous; I want Nina to grow into an independent woman, unshackled by irrational fears of the world or self-limiting beliefs. One thing that reading a lot about the Nazis does for you is provide perspective on how dangerous our super scary, villain-on-every-street-corner society actually is.

'Which doesn't mean there aren't any villains out there,' says Alex.

Nina has got to know Alex and likes him, and Natalie seems reassured by the arrangement, so I'm left as the interfering one if I push it.

I make it a subversive joke. I say to Nina, 'He won't feel masculine if he doesn't do his duty,' and send them on their way with my blessing.

Nina is useful: she listens, she learns fast, she never looks fed up and, most remarkable, I can bounce ideas off her. She always has an opinion, often a sophisticated one. I've been sending her off with books to read and she reads them. The average time between me sending her away with a book and her talking to me in its language is about a week.

I was working on sketches for a painting of the clubbing to death of Jews at the Lithuanian petrol station, unsure which angle to go in on. Nina suggested making it a series, painting it from various of points of view. Hogarth's *A Rake's Progress* was fresh in her mind from a book I'd lent her on English engravers. Her interest was further aroused when I told her Hogarth's tomb was a five-minute walk from our house, an excursion we made one Saturday afternoon. I wouldn't have predicted that Hogarth could inspire a thirteen year old girl, thinking the book on engravers was a makeweight amongst the Pre-Raphaelites, Post-Impressionists and American Modernists I'd packed her off with, but she embraced everyone and everything, her desire to learn voracious and, on this occasion, relevant.

'It's the story,' she said.

She was right. In principle at least, since Hogarth is too linear for our purposes. We want more of a theatre-in-the-round effect, but her idea is the catalyst and when I tell her so her face brightens like a sunlit flower.

Victor shows up from time to time. It's routine now: he reviews what I've done, approves, goes away. He's always relaxed and friendly, the ice has broken between him and Alex—mainly thanks to Alex unfreezing—and he has developed this habit of looking at me when he leaves with an inscrutable air while delivering a parting compliment. The effect is to exaggerate the compliment, as though it is worth more because of the very lack of effusiveness in its delivery.

I haven't asked him much of late, there seems to be no need, or point. When he wants to tell me where the whole thing is going he will, meantime he won't. So there, I think, not harshly or petulantly, but with mild resignation. It feels better this way, to not feel the urge to push for clarity, instead to work steadily, accumulating the pieces, concentrating on the art one by one, not driven by anything other than the desire to bury myself in the process.

Victor is yet to meet Nina, which is no surprise since his visits are occasional rather than daily. He asks after her, and on one occasion I told him I felt privileged to be her tutor.

'Why's that?' he said. It was an odd question because he knew how highly I thought of her. I fumbled an answer, trying to say that because she had so much potential it was my honour to be her teacher. It sounded pompous and maybe the bit about her potential got lost.

'Is it because she's a Jewish girl helping you with the Holocaust. A kind of a mascot?'

I was struck dumb, literally. My thinking splintered into fragments as I tried to work through the permutations of whatever it was he was getting at. He stood there, not helping, obviously aware that he'd created a conflict, letting me flounder, until some voice in my head broke through and I found myself asking him: 'Is it because I'm not Jewish?'

149

I saw his face flicker, as if a certainty had broken down. The enigmatic coating had taken a scratch.

'As far as you know,' he said. It was his final word on the subject. Seconds later he was out of the door and on his way, but not before making a point of issuing his usual praise for the work in progress.

Alex joins me in the studio. It's late in the evening and I'm not working in any focused way. I've just come back from smoking on the balcony—since Nina started visiting I have stopped smoking in the studio—and have been prowling around, inspecting the day's work, making mental notes about priorities for the next day, and ruminating on Victor's strange interjection.

Alex asks me if I've had a good day. He's cheerful. He looks at the work and nods approvingly.

'You're a changed man.'

'Not really,' he says, 'just treading water for now.' But he looks so happy he's almost smug.

I look at him quizzically and he looks back at me with a giant 'what?' across his face.

I shake my head as though shaking something out of it. Something falls into place and I tell him it's so obvious. I wonder why it hadn't clicked before. I torture him by dragging the moment out, refusing to let him in on the realisation I have just arrived at.

'The weird thing is,' I say, 'that at work you were competitive and driven; out of work you're relaxed. You appear to change, but you're the same person.'

'Okay,' he says, extending the second syllable to let me know he's trying to get it, 'I'm a changed person and the same person, all at once?' He looks at me with a strained expression.

'Exactly.'

We laugh. He's enjoying the game, which is a sign in itself, and he's waiting for me to tell him what it's about. It's probably best not to test his newly found patience further.

'The real you, your inner core, if you like, doesn't change,' I say, 'but in one situation you behave like this, and in another like that.' I grin.

'Is that it?' he says.

Maybe I've been numbed by all the self-help bullshit that says you can become anything you want, and that if you fail it is, by implication, your fault. It's the mantra of our age.

'If I shoot someone I'm responsible for the consequences, but if I'm borderline psychotic, or plain hotheaded, then who's responsible for me getting my hands on a gun?'

'Okay,' he says again, in the same where-is-this-going voice.

'It's a loop. Human nature rides a loop, from perception to choice and back again. It can be in a good loop or a bad loop. I'm a hothead and I'm bound to lose control one day, meanwhile things happen that aggravate me and in a state of fear or panic or distress I reach for the gun that has been conveniently made available, and do real harm. Cut the loop—make my life less of a psycho-nightmare, make a gun less easy to own—and I harm no one.

'The Nazis created the worst loop ever, the one that spiralled from fear to persecution to extermination and mass death, and ultimately to self-destruction. Since that time we've been in a good loop—prosperity, freedom, democracy, respect for the law and human rights—but what if bad things are now feeding the loop? What if the loop, slowly, incrementally, almost imperceptibly, is turning bad? And what if the rest of us don't notice, or are asleep, or have been bought, or made dumb, and are now unknowingly complicit in a decline, one that feeds the darker side of our nature?

'I see the world as good, and I choose love and tolerance, I see the world as bad and I choose hate and the gun.'

I've said what I wanted to say and it seems so straightforward I can't understand how anyone would deny it. I look at my husband to see if he will.

Alex walks towards the window. The reflection from the lights in the studio makes it difficult to see out into the night, but he stops and looks nevertheless. I switch the lights off, which startles him, but he turns and nods his appreciation and I sidle up beside him and tell him I love him.

He puts his arm around me and we watch the river: the slow current, the flecks of light that bounce off the surface from the multitude of light sources that never go out in this city. The trees spike the far bank, their leaves thinning as summer shades into autumn. It's a clear night, and above the darkened, but never dark, sky, where our atmosphere hits the radiating universe, there's a suffused glow like a cosmic cloud.

'Nina told me a story today,' I say, 'about her great uncle who was stabbed to death for being a Jew, over there, on the far side. Natalie told her about it.'

'Why did she tell her,' he says.

'Part of her family history, I suppose, is there a reason she wouldn't?'

He doesn't answer but looks across the water, apparently searching the scene. What he expects to see is a mystery, it's as though he's looking for evidence.

'I'll go with love and tolerance,' he says at last. He must have been on a train of thought, which he has now rejected in favour of going back a stage in our conversation. He keeps his arm around me and I wrap mine around his waist. Watching the river wind around to the bridge, I'm seized with the thought that the night is beautiful and I'm lucky to be alive.

Chapter Twelve

Alex is out of the house a lot talking to journalists and film makers. They talk to him because he has money to invest and he wants to 'say something' about City culture and practices. Nothing illegal, nothing sordid or sensationalist—he isn't interested in hookers partying with banking bosses on the top floor of the Shard, a story he regards as apocryphal—he's more concerned with corporate creep: the phrase he uses several times a day, most days.

'I don't have stories about prostitutes,' I hear him say over the phone, 'or cocaine or five figure sums being spent on a bottle of champagne.'

I try not to get involved, just quietly celebrate this change in him or, should I say, this different side to him that has appeared since he found himself outside the temple. In truth he has plenty of stories about prostitutes, champagne and cocaine but, in his view, these things are clichés that do more to glamourise reputations than tarnish them. Everyone expects a certain type of rich person to blow piles of cash on hedonistic ephemera, all the more exciting because of the illegal undertones, what most people are unaware of is what these people do while dressed and sober.

I suppress the thought of him as a hypocrite—he was happy enough with the spoils when they were his—since it is uncomfortably clear that part of my desire to batten the hatches on this one is that I am implicated: I too lived off those spoils. The more I read about the bloody Nazis the more I confront my choices. The comparison is ridiculous —I would never harm another human being—but a voice rises up and asks, which side of the loop have I been feeding?

He could jump back on the money-go-round as easily as taking a walk by the river, but he doesn't, and that convinces me the shift is genuine, if it is a shift, of course: I remind myself that he is the same person transposed, not the same person changed.

He visits me in my studio at least once a day, which is several times a week more than he used to. He's around the house more often now, which partly explains it, but also his approach has altered. In the past, if he wanted to say something to me, he would holler up the stairs and expect me to drop whatever I was doing and present myself in his line of sight for what would often turn out to be a one sided discussion in which I was expected to tune in to his needs while he tuned out of mine. Now, he not only takes the trouble to manoeuvre himself so we're face to face, he also takes the time to listen. And he's stopped his habit of jumping about, restlessly looking to exit the conversation at the earliest opportunity.

His creep and my loop have met. It was a discussion that started with me telling him about Franz Stangl, the commandant of Treblinka who was given the task of closing down the camp after a riot among Jewish labourers had burnt down almost the entire structure, with the exception of the brick built gas chambers. Having packed his bags, he called together all the remaining labourers— many had been shot during the uprising—and insisted on saying goodbye to them, shaking many by the hand. It was, according to his testimony, a spontaneous act of goodwill. As soon as he was gone they were all murdered.

We're standing in front of my oil painting depicting the moment Stangl shook hands with the Jews on his last day, his oversize bags loaded into a sagging car behind him. It's in the tradition of cartoon satire, except I've made the faces of the Jews and Stangl entirely realistic, his features exclaiming congratulation on a job well done, theirs a sceptical, acquiescent ingratiation mingled with a desire to believe he's sincere and that they may yet survive.

'You see it all the time,' says Alex, 'not so extreme, but true nevertheless, that oppressors crave approval from the oppressed. It's as if they need permission to exercise their power from the very people they wish to exercise power over. Is it guilt or sadism? Or some self-bestowed entitlement that grows with status and power and gifts them the right to feel good about being a bastard?'

I'd never heard Alex deliver a speech like this in the entirety of our time together. I ask myself again if this can be real? Or am I listening to the embittered rationalisation of a man who was ultimately defeated, even if he did engineer a lucrative withdrawal?

He is so solidly with me, but so alien. Victor seems so solidly with me but remains enigmatic. All this attention, all this support, and yet some deep pull of anxiety tugs from way down below. I am lauded and paid, my husband is saintly; I have a wonderful, responsive child to think of, and I wake up full of purpose. But I don't dare believe in it, even though the evidence of my eyes asks me to accept it at face value.

He's talking about corporates, I'm talking about Nazis; not the same thing, we agree, even if they share a disposition towards world domination. What's more, the Nazis were co-ordinated from a central command structure, driven by ideology and hatred; the corporate world has emerged through generations of capitalist evolution—an emergent structure driven by self-interest.

He nods, he agrees, but he's still telling me that his creep and my loop are bedfellows: neither worships at the altar of democracy.

'Capitalists aren't crazy about genocide,' he says, 'it tends to shrink the market.'

Again, it strikes me that this may be some sort of progress.

Tonight he is late back from walking Nina to the station. Normally I wouldn't think twice about it: he may decide to extend his walk or stop for a drink on the way back. But while he was standing at the door waiting for Nina to put her coat on, there was something in his manner suggesting an urge to come straight back. It's nothing I could put my finger on, just one of those feelings you get when you've known someone a long time.

I think of phoning him, but the thought alone makes me doubt myself. Did I read the signals correctly? Will I sound fussy? Will it reopen the discussion about whether Nina needs accompanying?—not that it was acrimonious, but I know I was the loser, so a reprise of that would be unwelcome—or am I allowing my imagination to run away with me, the result of a foreboding that has crept up on me these past few weeks?

An hour later and I text him. A half hour unexplained absence can be put down to any number of trivialities, but by now, anyone, even Alex—old Alex at that—would accept that an explanation is due.

A message comes back to say he's sorry and everything's fine. No other explanation. I'm not a suspicious person —'everything's fine' is good enough for me—but I am curious, as he knows. Either he's been inconvenienced by someone or something and is too rushed to provide detail or he's up to something that's too complicated for a simple message.

Whichever, he's not in the pub or taking a walk along the river.

Another half hour and he walks through the door. It's immediately plain he's in high spirits: his face carries the look of something waiting to detonate.

He insists on telling the story from the start, from leaving home with Nina.

As normal, he walked her through the underpass, across the main road and up to the station. She was talking happily about school and how she was going to take up rowing in the new term. He was telling her it would be freezing cold on the river in winter and she had laughed, saying the teachers made them warm up before going out and they would be exercising too hard to get cold.

'Have you ever rowed, Alex?' she said, as they reached the station.

'No I haven't, Nina,' he said, echoing her name playfully.

She laughed, and a group of youths gathered by the station entrance stopped talking and started nudging each other.

One of them called him a paedo. The others sniggered. Alex and Nina kept walking, pretending ignorance and hoping not to provoke them.

'Do you suck his cock?' said one.

'Want to suck mine?' said another; the others laughed.

Alex would usually leave her at the entrance, but he decided to walk with her to the platform. As he fished for his Oyster card, the youths moved towards the barriers. They were pushing each other and sharing some half audible joke. It could have been about anything, but it felt like it was at their expense. Alex turned to them.

'That's enough,' he said.

It was a sternly delivered command and it shut them up, but it was soon clear they were heading for the same platform. Alex and Nina endured a five-minute wait with the youths snickering and jostling just feet away. When the train came, they took the precaution of walking up the platform to avoid having to sit near them. They boarded the train, found a seat and, with relief, realised that the youths hadn't followed.

It crosses my mind that if Alex hadn't been there, Nina would have passed the boys unnoticed and the incident wouldn't have happened. But I choose to keep that one to myself. Besides, this isn't the purpose of him telling me the story, that much is clear from the lack of conclusion in his voice, or of a punchline, or sign of him leaning back waiting for my reaction, or, most telling of all, the lack of real shock or censure about the boys' behaviour, unpleasant and disturbing as it would have been. This is the preamble, the youths a sideshow, the explanation of why he got on the train.

He skates over her reaction, saying that she didn't want to talk about it in an open carriage. Apparently she didn't want to talk about anything else either, so they sat out the journey in silence. He couldn't tell if this was because she was upset or shy about conducting conversations in public. He decided he might as well take her the whole way home.

'I was curious, it gave me an excuse,' he says, and his eyes tell me he can't wait to tell me what comes next.

They changed at South Kensington for the Piccadilly line and at Leicester Square for the Northern Line and eventually reached Belsize Park station. Once they were on foot and out of earshot of anyone else, Alex took the opportunity to check how she was.

'Oh, that,' she said, curling her lips in what Alex feared was displeasure at being asked the question, 'boys come out with that stuff all the time. It's so juvenile.'

He looked at her. She looked strong, defiant even, but he'd felt her anxiety earlier and he couldn't tell if this was bravado or genuine resilience.

Alex sighs. Some sort of disclosure is coming.

'They'd made me feel anxious,' he says, and pauses, as though weighing up whether to say out loud what he's thinking, 'but then I don't get called a paedo "all the time". Maybe I need to toughen up.'

We smile at the thought of tough Nina and soft Alex. Eventually, I tell him he did the right thing, that he was right not to leave her.

'She was okay because you made it okay.'

He nods, but moves on, smiling slyly: we're still not at the point of the story.

They walked to her house, a three storey Edwardian family terrace with a particularly fine stained glass door, situated on a road to the west of Haverstock Hill; not one of the mansions of classical Belsize, but far bigger than a mother and daughter living together would need. Nina let herself in with her key and called out to her mother.

Alex was surprised to find Natalie dressed in a hat, coat and gloves.

'We arrived just in time, two minutes later and she would have been gone.'

Nina rushed through an explanation of why Alex was with her, hurrying the tale, it seemed, to finish the story before her mother vanished into the night. Natalie went through a limited repertoire of concerned parental noises without sounding at all alarmed, but she did make a special point of thanking Alex for his trouble.

'It seemed odd,' he says, 'that she should react more to my plight than to Nina's.'

'Maybe you're being harsh. She could see there was nothing wrong with Nina, so why panic? She was being polite to you and she may have talked about it to Nina later. If only to find out what she may or may not know about sucking cock.'

He doesn't catch the intended humour and I sense the disapproval. Maybe travelling across town with a thirteen year old girl and being called a paedo has made him a bit touchy.

'I don't think there's any mystery there,' says Alex, 'from what she told me about the boys at school there's not much left for her to wonder about.'

'So much for innocence,' I say, meaning hers and his.

'But,' he says, in a tone that changes the subject, 'and you may not approve of the next bit.'

It's his stand-by method when introducing a subject he feels guilty about. He does it to prepare me, to encourage me to think 'is that all?' when he's finished. It's called, 'managing my expectations' and will be accompanied with the haven't-I-been-a-bad-boy-but-I'm-a-loveable-rogue-really look—except this time it isn't. This time he has the look of someone letting me in on a mystery.

'Natalie and I left the house together. At the gate she turned right, and I turned left intending to retrace the route to the station. I walked uphill for a bit, and was suddenly seized by a possibility. I turned, and saw her reach the far end of the street. She was walking quickly, as though late for something.

'I asked myself what she could be doing at this time of night. She'd been ready to leave the house before her daughter had returned home and it was only by accident we arrived before she'd gone. I know there are easy explanations, but something about her manner didn't feel right. She was polite, certainly, but I got the feeling I was in the way. As she turned left and disappeared around the corner, I decided to follow. I felt slightly ridiculous and I told myself it would probably be a fruitless excursion, but the idea had lodged and, in the end, I just thought, why not?'

Although he's prepared me for my disapproval, he knows I would be a hypocrite to voice any moral indignation: in having followed Victor, it was surely me who planted the seed. But now I'm wondering if I told him about Natalie's evening disappearances, the ones she goes on without her phone: a curious story, which I may have accidentally mentioned in spite of being sworn to secrecy. It would explain where he got his suspicion. I ransack my memory but find nothing incriminating. In any case he would have mentioned it just now, wouldn't he? Having convinced myself I've let nothing slip, I'm left with the curious realisation Alex has quite independently developed his own hunch about Natalie's movements.

Alex is looking at me, eyes wide, almost ablaze. He knows I've been sucked into the story and it's encouraged him, even though he doesn't know that I hold a piece of his jigsaw.

I grin. 'I assume it wasn't fruitless,' I say, prompting him to continue. His face loses some tension, but becomes more serious.

'I walked back down the hill to the end of the street, as quickly as I could without drawing attention. When I got there she'd crossed the road and was disappearing round a bend to the right. There were trees and cars; it wasn't difficult to merge with the background and keep her within range. She walked for another ten minutes, perhaps a bit less, a few more turns, mainly rights, until she came to a large, twin gabled, red tiled property. She walked across the drive and up to the door, which opened instantly. Someone must have been waiting.'

'The doorman perhaps,' he says, and gives me a look that says, 'so there you have it.'

It takes a second for the realisation to crawl up my spine.

'I thought of you and Victor immediately,' he says, 'but I wasn't sure, partly because I wasn't entirely sure where I was any more. I staked out the place for a while. No one else arrived and I concluded that the only thing I was likely to witness was Natalie going back home, which wouldn't have told me anything new. Instead of going back to Belsize Park I followed my nose down the road and, within minutes, I passed the Hampstead theatre and came to Swiss Cottage station.'

I ask him if he's got the address. He has. It's the same.

It's one of those moments in life where your sense of reality warps as you try to distil events into some pre-existing notion of what you think you know. While I'm sifting through the conversations with Victor about Nina, and trying to remember exactly what chain of people had led me to Natalie and hence Nina, Alex starts up about how he 'always' suspected there was 'something going on with Victor'.

'Don't reopen that,' I say. I have energy for dealing with where we are now; raking over the past, will make me weary and want to hide. I say this to him.

'I get that,' he says, 'but where you are and where you were, are connected you know.'

'Fuck off with being logical,' I say. It's harsh, but I want to think without being pressured.

He holds his hands up, but then smiles and apologises. I apologise back and tell him I know he's right, I just need a bit of time.

'Of course,' he says, and waits for me to tell him how I got in touch with Nina.

'I sent an email to a dozen or so people: artists, schoolteachers—no one who teaches at Nina's school—a couple of actors, and a couple of people who just seem to know everyone. That was it, next thing Natalie phones.'

'Didn't you ask her?'

'I don't think we had the conversation. I have a dim recollection that when I asked she was on another train of thought, keen to tell me all about Nina I expect, and off she went. Probably didn't even hear my question. I can remember thinking I must come back to it, but I didn't. Once I'd met Nina, I was taken with her and never really thought about it again.'

'But, from their point of view, what's the secret?' says Alex. 'Why allow you to assume that Natalie and Nina have no connection to Victor. Why would it matter to them if you knew from the start?'

We ponder the question, but we're not going to find the answer. I tell him that it was my idea to use a child. There was no prompt, direct or otherwise, from Victor, so he, or they, had no control over that part of the process.

We discuss the possibility of it being a coincidence. We factor in that they're all Jewish and Natalie's visit to a house that contains a Holocaust exhibition, and which presumably hosts gatherings from time to time, might be nothing more than one of those random occurrences that, however startling, do happen.

'We'll never work it out,' I say to him, 'and I can't ask either of them.'

'Why not?'

'How do I ask without admitting that you followed Natalie?'

I know I'm struggling to quell a sense of betrayal. There has always been, as Alex says, 'something going on with Victor,' but he's always had my trust in spite of it. This is another weirdness in a succession of weirdnesses and my belief in his sincerity has remained steadfast, so why doubt now? I don't believe the coincidence theory and I do believe that there will be an explanation that makes sense. At least I tell myself there will be. But maybe I just want to, maybe I'm a pawn in a bigger game? As soon as I think this I want to retract it, even though only from myself. Victor has always made me feel important. He has his secrets and maybe he's entitled to them, and not because he's paying me.

'You should tell Victor what you know and how you know it,' says Alex. 'It's me who followed Natalie, not you. And you can tell him it was accidental: I changed my mind about which way to go home and happened to find myself walking behind her, not following her at all.'

He would describe it as a harmless white lie, but I would describe it as a material one—the test being how I would feel about telling it, and I couldn't without my conscience stabbing me.

But we don't argue about it, which consolidates the sense that things have changed between us. As I put the lamps out in readiness for bed, I notice how the glow from one reflects in the window and catches me in silhouette—a figure that becomes simultaneously me and not me: a shadow in a room, in a time and place that is mine in this moment. I click the switch and I am gone, dissolved into darkness.

Maybe it's cowardice, or awkwardness—or is there a difference?—but I don't talk to Victor about it. So, Natalie and Victor are connected, and I don't know how or why, but what difference does it make, practically?

That there are new layers to Victor's mysteriousness doesn't change one essential fact: he's always been a puzzle. It has been said that one of the surprising things about life is that people are surprised by surprises. I chose to be involved in Victor's strange project and by chance I've found out that a mystery also hangs around Natalie. Should it be so surprising that the two connect?

Am I being naïve? Alex would probably say so, though he still doesn't know the Natalie phone story—I'm keeping my word to Nina on that. Maybe it's all part of an elaborate test: what I say independently to Victor and Natalie has to add up when they talk to each other. My carefulness in guarding the secrecy of the project when first talking to Natalie was marked as a pass; my affection for Nina, related effusively and, I sometimes imagine, annoyingly to Victor, is received with more pleasure than he dares admit.

I'm heading to central London to take photographs, looking for present day images to juxtapose with Nazi iconography. I want to establish distance: as though the past is, indeed, a foreign country, where they do things differently. Not one we would want to travel back to, but one that can catch up with us again if we're not careful. I take the bus for the obvious reason that there's more overground than underground to take pictures of. Even better: there's a seat at the front of the top deck.

It's a slow journey—I'm impatient and prefer the tube when I need to get somewhere on time—but there's a paradox about the tube versus bus debate: on the tube, where people face one another, you feel their isolation; on the bus, where people sit with their backs to one another, there's an odd sense of community.

Today the bus provides a perch from which to observe metropolitan life in its variety and banal indifference. It's the latter that triumphs, I realise, since my attention fails and all I think about is Victor and Natalie. It will be odd, being with him in future. Will I be able to mention Natalie's or even Nina's name without feeling self-conscious? And what of Natalie? She presumably knows 'our sponsor', which adds a new conversational hazard to look forward to.

Maybe I can catch them out. Careful planted references to the other, or subtly phrased questions, to see if one of them slips up. This seems like fun, but do I trust myself not to overdo it? What if I ham it up terribly, pushing the point until even an idiot would guess what I'm up to?

Me: Victor, I wonder what Natalie will be doing tonight?

Victor: She's coming round actually.

Me: Ha! Gotcha!

Victor: Curses.

I settle back in my seat, pleased to have talked myself into a happier frame of mind. My knowledge is my power not my weakness, I tell myself. I'm the hunter again, not the hunted.

'It's crap,' says an elderly woman behind me. She's talking about a book someone she knows has written. I find my attention drawn because the phrase is at odds with her cut-glass voice.

'It's complete crap,' says her companion, another woman of the same age and, to coin a phrase, station in life.

Neither sounds contemptuous, the verdicts delivered without emotion; matter of fact declarations, tinged with, if anything, fondness for the hapless author. The exchange summons to mind a circle of people unaffected by life's scarcities. The accents clipped and confident, the words flow without qualification or reflection. Maybe they belong

165

to a generation born before the war and who grew up as part of a stoical upper-middle class for whom temporary privation was an adventure. I wonder when 'crap' entered their vocabulary. Do they think themselves modern when they use it, especially on the upper deck of a London bus?

I want to turn around and look, to see if they resemble my image of them. I think back to Alex's attempt at a discussion on the tube with Nina. A different circumstance, but her reluctance to talk is a world away from these two who have no such reticence. The conversation moves on, without any lowering of tone, to a goddaughter's relationship breakdown.

'She left him at midnight on Monday. No warning, nothing. Got up all of a sudden and went. Took the car, left the children. Hasn't been seen or heard from since.'

'Good for her.'

I want to know more, but they get off on Kensington High Street. I catch sight of them walking along the pavement before disappearing beneath a shop canopy. They're younger than I imagined, post-war not pre-war, but as well postured as I expected, carrying their class down the street in a manner I first think of as anachronistic. But I see people give way to them, politeness prompted by deference, and it seems the square-shouldered advance of Kensington ladies still counts for something.

A man replaces them behind me and starts talking to himself. I smell alcohol.

'Is civilisation dead?' he asks. I ignore him and suffer the ensuing silence, but after the short yet endless pause it turns out he's taking both parts of the conversation.

'It is indeed, yes siree.'

'When did it die?'

'It died with God, yes siree.'

'Is God dead?'

'Yes siree.'

'So he can't save us?'

'No siree.'

'We're fucked?'

'We fucking well are, yes siree.'

By the time the bus reaches Kensington Palace Gardens I've had enough and get off. Standing up I catch a glimpse of the man. He's smart looking, his outer layer an expensive trench coat, and well groomed. Someone's looking after him. He's young, mid-twenties at a guess, educated. He's rocking in his seat and as I pass he looks up, but there's no look of enquiry, no signal he could engage me if he wanted to.

I want to take his picture and stop in front of him, thinking how best to phrase a request. He doesn't react, just carries on rocking, staring at me silently. I change my mind, smile at him nervously and carry on past.

'It sucks that we're fucked,' he says.

I take the first step down the stairs.

'Yes siree.'

The intended walk through Kensington Gardens and Hyde Park starts with a stern brief to myself on the need to be more disciplined. The bus journey was a failure, photographically speaking, and with the crisp winter sunshine lighting a glorious tranche of London parkland it would be easy to wander into the scene and forget the work.

But immediately I am gifted a perfect opportunity: a group of about twenty small children wearing school uniforms, partially covered by high visibility bibs, being marched down Broad Walk. The children are holding hands and the colour and symmetry of the group is irresistible, but I'm shooting with a lens that telephotos from wide angle to not much better than normal vision, and after a couple of hastily composed shots I move closer.

'Excuse me,' someone calls out. Through the viewfinder I see a teacher waving at me. I lower the camera. 'Can I help you?' she says.

She doesn't mean she wants to help me, but I decide to take her at face value. 'If you would, that would be most kind,' I say, and smile sweetly.

If you ask any photographer, they will tell you that the ethical situation on photographing people in public places is as follows: there's no law against it, so tough. Against that you have to weigh up the objector and how likely they are to turn nasty if you deliver a 'get used to it' message without sugaring the pill with a few niceties, like telling them what you're doing and why and explaining how taking their picture helps your project. Most people become interested, even flattered, and will offer you their email address.

The teacher marching towards me has a look of someone keener to tell me what's on her mind than finding out what's on mine.

'What do you think you're doing?' she says, but it's plain that the question is semi-rhetorical, a stock teacher's phrase that invites a statement of the obvious: if I tell her I'm taking pictures I'll be facetious, if I say 'nothing' I'll be impudent. It's a neat trick; I learned it at school.

'Let me explain,' I say. She looks at me suspiciously. The other adults in the party, teachers or assistants, have stopped and are watching, as are the children. She ushers me a few yards further up the path.

She grips my arm as we come to a halt.

'You do not take pictures of children,' she says, 'under any circumstances. I want you to delete them. I want to see you do it.' She points at the camera, as though there may be some confusion as to which piece of equipment we might be talking about.

The unofficial ethical guide to photographing people in public places would say that if someone asks you not to take their photograph, you comply. If they ask you to delete any you have already taken you politely ask them why and depending on the answer and whether or not you think the pictures are worth the hassle, you may choose to concede. All the time you will know that the law is on your side and it is imperative that you inform them of this. 'It's a free country' you will say 'but I don't want to embarrass you by publishing a photograph of you kissing someone you shouldn't, so I will kindly accede to your request.' Or something of the sort.

The teacher has played the children card, which means she may escalate and name the issue: child protection. Wait until I tell Alex. I smile to myself, not quite ready to take her seriously.

I ask her again if she'd like me to explain what I'm doing.

'I want you to delete those photos,' she says. My faint amusement dries up and I feel a rush of annoyance.

'You asked me what I was doing,' I say, 'but you won't let me answer.'

I'm pleased to have turned that one around on her and watch as she struggles for a response.

'If you don't, I'll report you,' she says, desperately and over-assertively, as though she's reached for the last weapon left in a depleted armoury.

I feel my cheeks flush with anger. She is ridiculous and petulant and I want to shout names at her, but I don't want to make a scene in front of the children. I want to take a picture of her to wind her up further, but I mustn't be the one who inflames the situation. I'm damned if I'm deleting the pictures, shit though they probably are.

'I'm an artist,' I say. I want to tell her the pictures may, in fact, never be used, but if they are they will be used responsibly, that the school's co-operation can be credited, that I have a perfect legal right to keep them and so forth. In fact I do mouth all these words but she isn't listening. She stands in front of me repeating over and over, quietly but with alarming hostility: 'I want you to delete those pictures,' and, 'if you don't I'll report you.'

I reciprocate with a matching *sotto voce* hostility, the gist of which is that if she'd asked nicely I might have considered it, but since she didn't there was no chance.

She pulls a phone from her bag and starts tapping the screen. I step back and she grabs my arm again. I pull my arm to release it from her grip and her phone falls to the ground, landing at my feet. She looks at me uncertainly. She doesn't want to bend in front of me. It's as if she expects me to pick it up for her. I flick it with my toe towards the grass, turn around and start walking.

My plan is simply to walk away. If she's stupid enough to call the police, or whoever she has in mind, she will have to wait for them and then explain my 'crime' only to be told there's nothing they can do. Meanwhile a school trip will be ruined.

'Come back,' she shouts, retrieving her phone. She repeats it, but louder, and I quicken my step.

She comes after me and I hear one of the other teachers call something. She breaks into a run and catches up with me, grabbing my arm again. I carry on walking, hauling her with me, aware I am close to losing my temper and hoping that, far enough away from the children, I would be justified in doing so.

In attempting to restrain me, while making a call and keeping control of a swinging shoulder bag, she trips. The only thing stopping her fall is me and she lunges with her other arm to grab on two-handed. I make an instinctive effort to catch her and we somehow manage to lock on to one another, but the bag crashes from her shoulder and her phone once more hits the ground.

I let go of her. I'm not expecting to be thanked and I'm not disappointed. The contents of her bag are spread across the path. A gust of wind blows some papers and I walk away as another teacher runs over to help her pick things up.

I break into a semi-jog, opening up as much distance between us as I can, and hoping it's enough to make her think twice about resuming the chase. Glancing over my shoulder, it looks like a disagreement has broken out between her and the other teacher. Another gust of wind blows a paper out of her reach, just as she stoops to pick it up. It gives me another few seconds to get away and, with luck, another few seconds for the other teacher to talk sense into her. At least that's what I'd like to think. Meanwhile, in the distance, are twenty children lined up beautifully in their bright yellow bibs. Damn you, stupid woman.

I branch off to the right, among trees that in summer would blanket the view, but at this time of year provide only sporadic cover. I can still see her, intermittently, through the thicket of trunks, more concerned with her papers and the other teacher. I keep jogging, glancing back, getting further away with every second, and it looks like she's given up. I slow to a walk. Eventually, with some relief, I see her walk back to the children.

Although mercifully rare, my altercations with people, especially strangers, whether in the car, a shop, the phone, or, like now, out on the street, always result in a compulsive need to regurgitate the incident over and over in my mind. I try and remember it correctly, to understand what I said and did and why I said it and did it.

The reason I do this, when most advice, in the absence of any harm being done, would be to forget it, is simple: I have to feel good about my part. I hate having a bad conscience and I have to cycle the whole thing through repeatedly until I convince myself that I have nothing to feel guilty about.

After a slowly de-escalating flight, from jog to brisk walk to stroll, I find a bench to sit, somewhere in the shade, so I can review the pictures and decide if the trauma was worth it. There are only two and, looking at them backwards, rather than in the order they were taken, it's clear that the last I took is a failure: the symmetry, that I thought I saw with my eye, isn't there. The children's attention is quite random, thus defeating any sense of there being a story. One of the teachers is blocking the end of the column in a way that ruins the balance. Worst of all, even though I'm looking at the twenty-centimetre square camera playback screen, it looks out of focus. I zoom in on one of the children and my suspicion is confirmed. I move the zoom around the whole frame and it's the same: a uniform focus error, not an outcome of a suddenly moving subject— which can work accidentally in the image's favour, unlike an error by the photographer, which can't.

While pressing the selector to go back to the previous image, I'm thinking about how crazy it was to have found myself in the middle of a park, witnessed by dozens, almost—I may be kidding myself here, it may have been more than 'almost'—making a spectacle of myself for a completely unusable couple of pictures. I could run back, chase down the teacher and yell, mock triumphantly, at her —'see what you fought for, they're fucking useless'—and make great ceremony of deleting them in front of her. 'Are you satisfied, you philistine?'

I think about how she might react, but the words I just imagined—'what you fought for'—come back to me and stop the train of thought. 'What she fought for,' and again, 'what she fought for.' I'm stuck on the thought that she was fighting for something, more specifically that she was fighting for her children. What I interpreted as a cocktail of ignorance and paranoia infused with self-righteousness, was a woman doing battle for the innocents in her charge, however crassly. She wasn't afraid to expose herself, unlike me, nor was she going to back down, as I probably, eventually, would have. She was a warrior, the cause she fought for more important than her comfort or dignity.

Maybe she is, maybe she isn't, but something in me, suddenly and unexpectedly, wants to give her the benefit of the doubt.

Looking at the screen, at the first image I took, I hope to see it differently, and wish for something of the story I've mentally constructed to come alive. Shockingly, and with perverse inevitably, it does. Where the last picture had everything wrong with it, this has everything right: an immaculate image. In an instant I feel the glow of a rare emotion, the one you get when something perfect has happened, the one that occurs in the space in time between your instinct telling you and your reason confirming it, when you believe something is true but daren't say so, even to yourself, in case it isn't.

In the few short seconds while I took the pictures, hurriedly and without forethought, the perfect image had fragmented into disarray and now, as I reverse the sequence in which I view them, it reassembles, regains its lines, its form and its symmetry. It is whole again.

The children are in line, although two are shivering together, their faces turned against the cold blasts of air that sweep across the park. The teacher is looking at me, her focus pin-sharp, her eyes picked out by the light from the sky behind me: a sentry who has spotted an enemy. The other teacher is no longer blocking the view of the children. She must have stopped between shots.

The story comes alive. The teacher's reaction alerted the children, which would explain why so many shifted their attention between frame one and two. I wonder how they felt: that there was someone they could trust to defend them, or confused that something they didn't understand was near and closing? Then there's the two shivering, whose separateness creates a subplot that somehow completes rather than imbalances the whole.

That the elements of the picture have arranged themselves so beautifully is a gift of fortune. The sharp focus picks up the fringe of moisture in the grass. The clouds of breath that gather above the children, made ghostly by the light of the pale sun, create the contrast that, with the bright yellow bibs, give the image a depth of luminescence I wouldn't have achieved if I'd spent an hour setting it up. I have one pure image and it is all the more precious for being accidental.

It was tempting to race back to the studio, upload the photo and view it on the big screen in the studio, imagining the thrill to be had from its upscaled, full-blown glory. What part of the story may yet reveal itself, what waits to be discovered in the detail and the saturations of colour and shade? And, most important, what can I do with it? My instinct suggests a central role, maybe as an emblem of the past brought to the present. Like many abstractions, the conversion into something that makes concrete sense requires instinct and reason, but it will have to wait.

I still need to collect the pictures I came for: the tourist traps, the London landmarks known throughout the world, the places that, if you say their name, people across the globe will nod in recognition. These locations mean London and, because they exist in the minds of everyone, they are real London, as real as the London of Charles Dickens, Jack the Ripper and Sherlock Holmes.

The list is easy and obvious: Hyde Park; Trafalgar Square; The Houses of Parliament; The British Museum; Buckingham Place; Covent Garden; Harrods; The Tower of London; Tower Bridge; St Paul's Cathedral; Westminster Abbey. I get round them all in a couple of hours, a combination of walking and hopping on and off the tube. I snap a few red buses and London Underground signs and I pop into Sir John Soane's Museum by jumping off the train at Holborn, while on my way to St Paul's. It's an indulgence, one I include for me, to signal solidarity with those who know the place and because it contains the original paintings of *A Rake's Progress*.

Reviewing the photos, hunched over a coffee in a quiet cafe down a lane near the cathedral, the doubts that hovered in my mind as I wandered from location to location grow in size and certainty. The pictures are flat and empty. The light had dulled since I'd left the park and so had my imagination. They look like tourist snaps—well composed ones, I console myself, but devoid of life or character. My unusual angles fail to generate energy or freshness, my establishing shots lacklustre, my close ups lifeless. I feel like an amateur: not technically, but as an artist. There's no story, no theme, nothing captured, nothing happening. A tourist snap might at least have some people in the foreground, striking postures for the camera and providing a focal point. These have nothing and no potential to connect history, genocide, the Nazis, civilisation and humanity, or whatever else my fucking exhibition is meant to be about.

I sit back in my chair and blow through pouting lips, to extract as much self-pity as I can from the situation, before leaning forward and planting my forehead on an upturned palm.

I think of Nina. Quite why, I'm unsure. Until I realise I don't want to disappoint her. I want to be her artist heroine, not some phoney also-ran of the art world, a mediocre talent at best, not so much to look up to as to jog past on the way to one's own glittering prizes.

Then it occurs to me, practically drops into my brain, that the missing element, the unifying theme, the story and the point of interest, all rolled into one, is Nina. Nina is the answer. Put her in the frame, take her on a tour of London and picture her against the sights, and maybe also the mundane districts, the marginal zones, the backyards that don't belong to the whole globe, the places to which the phrase 'world city' don't apply. Nina is the story, not the city. Put Nina in the city, anywhere in and around the city, and I have a narrative.

The excitement of this epiphany is matched only by the shock of her turning up at the weekend with Victor.

'We travelled together,' says Victor. The look on his face tells me he wants to provide an explanation, but not in front of Nina.

Nina smiles as she steps through the doorway, showing not a hint that anything out of the ordinary has just happened.

'Where's your mother?' I say to her.

'She's out,' she says, 'out and about somewhere.'

She smiles again, sweetly, innocently—and I mean that without irony—as if the whole fun being-in-the-world thing had been invented just now, for her.

I gently place a hand on her, bridging her shoulder and neck. 'It's lovely to see you,' I say, catching her eye. 'It's going to be an exhausting day, so I hope you're ready.'

I send her up to the studio, ostensibly to let her look over paintings I've worked on since she was last here. I lead Victor through to the living room.

As I turn to confront him with my 'what-the-fuck' face, I hear him call my name with an urgency I've not heard from him before. He is starting a plea. Facing me square on, arms are outstretched.

'It's not what you think,' he says. But the arms cross in front of him, his manner relaxes, a smile teases from the corner of his mouth and radiates to his eyes.

The corny line of the exposed adulterer has disarmed me. I struggle to resist a smile. 'What is it you think I think?' I stand my ground, playing the wronged wife as deadpan as I can.

'You think I've cheated on you,' he says.

'Haven't you?'

'Sort of.'

We sit. He crosses his legs, the shine of his uppermost shoe just a foot from my knee. I settle straight-backed, waiting for whatever his 'sort of' confession will amount to.

'I know I owe you an explanation,' he says, a formulation of words that suggests I'm not going to not get one, 'and, in time, I promise you one in full.'

I tell him he owes me some explanation right now.

'Indeed,' he says, and shifts in his seat. I can see him weighing up what he can tell me to satisfy the 'some' part of the explanation without giving the whole. 'There is an organisation,' he says, 'that exists to work for humanity and civilisation...'

'There are quite a few of those,' I interrupt, and name some, culminating in the United Nations.

'Yes, but you've heard of them,' he says, 'this one has no public profile. It exists in the margins, operating outside politics or nationhood. It's not strictly a secret organisation, but it is invisible.'

'And you're about to tell me that you are a member of this organisation.'

'There's no membership as such,' he says, and hesitates, as if expecting me to react to his pedantry, 'but yes, in essence. And our sponsor.'

'There's a surprise,' I say, the sarcasm leavened by my smile, which, in turn, sneaks out from the part of me that trusts him, that has always, perhaps unwisely or irrationally, wanted to believe in him.

I should make him work harder, but don't. I start with Nina and how she came to me; he waffles about friends of friends. I ask about the non-secret secret organisation and he talks of 'doing their bit' to avoid the 'world falling into an abyss.'

Nothing specific. I point this out to him, but without anger or hurt. How can I manufacture something that isn't there? I remember the relief I felt when I asked him if Nina could become part of the project—how scared I was,

177

to betray him, to disappoint her—and now I know he must have engineered it. What else did I expect? He plays these games and I fall conveniently in line; that's how it works. The emotion I'm aware is of disappointment in myself for having become quite such a pushover. What will Alex have to say about this?

But his face changes from teasing pseudo-innocence to a serious we-must-talk-about-this. It's as though he really does want to deliver the speech of the guilty party in a marriage.

'Soon I will explain everything,' he says, and his eyes lock with mine, sincere and solemn, as though sanctifying a bond.

It's still all you, isn't it? I think. I am the malleable one, the experimented upon, the one in the dark.

He keeps looking at me, a puzzle on his face, as though whatever I am thinking intrigues him. Perhaps he sees what I feel, perhaps he feels bad about what he sees; perhaps he doesn't like playing with the dice always loaded in his favour.

'But be prepared,' he says, 'the explanation will be more than you're expecting.'

His face dissolves to kindness. He's back to avuncular, which, if I'm honest, is how I like him best. Maybe it's the child in me still. Maybe it's because it's a role that Alex cannot or will not play.

'On past performance, my expectations are low,' I say.

He laughs. 'It's only because the time has not been right,' he says and pats me on the arm. Something Alex knows not to do, but somehow Victor gets away with it.

Being out and about with Nina prompts distant recollections of days out in childhood, or dreams of how those trips would have been: mindful invocations of the happiness I felt in the presence of my mother. So little of what I remember is clear, except an abiding sense of having been loved and cherished to the point, I would later realise, of being the surrogate for all that was missing in my mother's life. Now, it's as if it can be rewritten with Nina. She may be borrowed, but there's a sweet, deep consolation in being in charge of a girl who is the image of a child I would love to have called my own.

In Kensington Gardens she plays the game of observing passers-by and inventing their stories. 'She lives alone and eats chicken liver every day...' A thin woman on stilettos. 'She has four lovers, each has his own day of the week and none are allowed to visit outside their allotted hours...' A middle-aged woman wearing a black fedora and leopardskin smock. 'He phones his mum every day to reassure her he hasn't committed suicide after he was abandoned six months ago by his abusive girlfriend...' A pale young man eating a burger, who smiles shyly as we pass.

I don't mention having discovered the connection between her mother and Victor. She seems oblivious of subterfuge and should probably remain so. Nothing has changed as a result, either in the relationships between the adults or in the sense of a knock-on to her. If I broach the subject I may prompt her to ask questions I can't answer, provoking anxieties I'm keen to see her spared.

The irony is that I think she could handle it. If the chicanery of dealings between Victor, Natalie and myself were in the open, she would, I'm sure, make sense of it all. I say that because I believe we're all acting in good faith and an honest explanation of how we got to where we are would serve as an object lesson in the conflicts, contradictions and compromises that make up life.

I must resist thinking like a mother. It's not my place to instigate that conversation. As she walks beside me, chattering about the filming and her role, she's growing up perfectly well without my interference.

The filming is a dream. It's a bit Actors Studio at times, waiting for her to work herself into the frame of mind required, but whatever I ask she delivers. I ask for sad, I get it; for wistful, I get it. I ask for sad and faraway, as though remembering a long lost friend, and I get it. She is quite brilliant. I take photographs and movies. Paradoxically the photographs provide the dynamism and the movies the stasis: a long take of Nina looking towards the camera with a changeless expression creates a sense of immobility. A photograph of her, in its frozen moment, carries with it a suggestion of the before and after.

I set up a long take, filmed from a distance, of Nina walking across Westminster Bridge with the Houses of Parliament in the background. I ask her to look self-absorbed, as if going over in her mind an awkward conversation with a close friend, and to avoid eye contact with passers by.

We do two takes: one where I zoom in as she walks towards the camera and another where she just walks towards the camera. I decide to go for one more, where she fixes her eyes on the camera the whole way as though willing a saviour to appear from darkness to rescue her from a long and treacherous journey.

I start her a hundred yards away, dropping my arm to signal go. I've told her to move slowly and deliberately, drawing out each step, but not falling into a funereal rhythm; keep it smooth and flowing, dreamlike and faraway, as if from the past.

The lens foreshortens the view, but not so tight as to make it appear in close up. There's enough of the street and the Palace of Westminster to make the context clear. People notice her and at first I worry they'll alter the mood, intrude on what is an intimate frame, but they look and pass by and the effect of them looking and not being looked back at, as Nina stares resolutely towards the camera, heightens her insularity.

I enjoy the effect of what's being created as I shoot and sense the thrill of something that works better for its unforeseen elements than if it had merely gone to plan. Nina is glorious: so young, yet grown up; so innocent, yet weighted with history; her face wise and yearning; the softness around her cheeks and lips fringed with sunlight. She's a representation of life, love and the unpredictability of being, like the clouds blown above the river, that gather and drift and squall before vanishing in the atmosphere.

Then a man leans towards her. He halts and appears to say something. Nina continues to fix her eyes on the camera, her features unchanged, her focus locked on. The man steps backwards and seems once more to say something. Again Nina looks towards me as if nothing is happening. The man persists and I catch what appears to be a flash of temper. Nina is utterly unmoved. She is extraordinary in her resolve, but I feel a surge of fear and find myself weighing the need to intervene against the desire to capture the moment.

The man is unaware of my presence, that much is clear, his face turned to Nina's, not the direction of her gaze. He places a palm on her shoulder, as though to stop her, but she pushes forward, her eyes unyielding still in their pursuit of the camera. He says something else, this time his voice raised, since she flinches. It's a tiny, almost imperceptible, reaction to his invasion of her space, against which she summons blankness in defence. But it seems this defiance, if that's what you call a stone-faced resistance to provocation, becomes its own provocation, and suddenly, and horribly, I see him shouting at her.

I snap, and run towards her screaming her name. Even now she holds herself in role. The man turns, at last, and sees me as I close the last few yards between us. I see a sneer form around his mouth and his eyes fill with resentment—whether affected or genuine, it's impossible to tell—the kind of look that rises in bullies when they are met with resistance, as if disbelieving that they should be upbraided, that their victim is the one who deserves the blame.

'Leave her alone!' I shout and I repeat it, louder as I get nearer.

He has a who-are-you look.

'She's with me,' I say.

'Fucking mental, the pair of you,' he says and turns to Nina. 'Snotty bitch.'

I tell him to 'get away from her' and 'leave us alone.' I say it through angry, gritted teeth, just about holding down the volume to avoid attracting further attention, but aware that I have, in every meaningful sense, lost it.

He stalls, as though thinking of something to say.

'You do not harass girls in public,' I say, 'you don't do it, not ever, do you understand?'

He tries to tell me 'for my information' that he was asking her if she was okay.

'And then you started shouting at her,' I shout. I feel some certainty drain away and I shake my head and point up the street, 'just go.'

He turns, mutters, and walks away.

I'm shaking and close to tears.

'I'm sorry,' I say to Nina, wanting to excuse my outburst, one in stark contrast to her imperturbability. I feel, I realise, rather foolish.

But she puts her arms around me and hugs me.

'He was scary,' she says.

It's what I need to hear and the sense of foolishness lifts.

'You were brave,' I say.

She tightens her hug and I respond in kind. A moment later we relax our hold and look at each other.

'He said to me, "I'm talking to you" and then "do you not understand the English language?" and then "fucking stuck up bitch", then he repeated "talk to me bitch", like he

182

was in a trance, until you arrived and snapped him out of it.'

'Well done for being so brave,' I say and stroke her head.

'I didn't want to ruin the film,' she says, and now the tears flow. I hold her tight and feel her shake as she cries.

I knew by instinct something was wrong, but was misled by Nina's bravery and determination. Am I too harsh on myself? I ran to her aid as soon as it became critical. But could I have pre-empted it? She is unharmed physically but what about mentally? Do I have the right to ask her to do this? What would Natalie say?

'Never mind "ruin" it,' I say, 'you may have made it.' I smile at her hoping my spin will produce a happy reaction.

'Do you think so?' she says, her eyes widening.

In my studio, after Nina has gone on her way with Natalie, having talked proudly of her heroism in the face of the hateful man—a story Natalie took well—I look back over the day's work. In spite of the shock, we completed what we set out to do. Nina was determined, the desire not to succumb driving her on. And her focus became sharper, her face more heavenly, her expressions deeper and stronger, as though some life force had been summoned for a fight. Her defiance became an incarnation, a daring beauty of the spirit, and a pure expression of vitality in the face of tyranny. She wasn't going to give up for anything.

Chapter Thirteen

When the Red Army entered Auschwitz on 27 January 1945, they found a camp that had been hastily and incompletely dismantled. Over fifty thousand inmates had been evacuated on foot, many to die in the enforced death marches that followed. The SS had destroyed records, blown up crematoria and converted gas chambers into air raid shelters. But there were still survivors, some children and some Special Detachment prisoners, who the SS planned to shoot, but who, in the panic and confusion of the camp's last days, managed to disappear into the surrounding countryside. The Nazis had filled in the mass burial sites and turfed them over, but the Red Army had no difficulty spotting the six hundred corpses that lay outside in plain view. Other evidence pointed inescapably to the camp's purpose: the seven tons of human hair; the forty-four thousand pairs of shoes; the eight hundred thousand women's coats and dresses.

They found what they should have expected to find. There's a modern preoccupation for reordering the past for dramatic effect, one I suspect I had fallen victim to. Many films and many fictions have presented the liberation of the extermination camps as the moment when the world found out, when the seismic shock of discovery produced waves of international revulsion as though waking up to the Nazi's true project for the first time.

In truth, everyone knew. Maybe not graphically, or from first hand witnesses they trusted, but, shocked though they may have been, they could not have been surprised. News of the mass murder of Jews was everywhere by 1942. Diarists in Germany were recording it, and Anne Frank, in Amsterdam, wrote on 9 October that English radio was reporting the gassing of Jews. It wasn't even a secret that anyone was trying hard to keep: soldiers returning to

Germany from Poland talked freely about it. The people who worked on the railways, the station guards, the engine drivers, the timetable clerks, all knew which of the trains carried the Jews and where they were going. Everyone knew.

The people who carried the reports beyond Germany, to the US or Britain, encountered disbelief, and maybe people in the West found it difficult to believe something so unbelievable. But the reports kept pouring in and in November 1942 the Polish government-in-exile officially recognised the fact that Poles and Jews were being systematically murdered. By December 1942 the British Foreign Secretary, Anthony Eden, tabled a report on the genocide to Cabinet. Days later Allied propaganda bombarded the German people with broadcasts and leaflets telling them what was happening in their name. Goebbels and the Nazi propaganda machine didn't even bother to deny it.

Everyone knew, but no one could do a damn thing about it.

During 1943 Nazi propaganda began to rebound. People knew the war was going badly and the more hyperbolic the propaganda machine's output became, the less credible it was deemed to be. German Christians began to believe that their losses were a retribution for not doing more to stand up for the Jews. When Cologne cathedral was bombed many saw it as divine justice for the burning of synagogues in 1938. When Goebbels tried to stir up nationalist sentiment by issuing propaganda, largely true, about the raping and killing of Germans by Soviet soldiers, much of the reaction was blunted by feelings of guilt for what had been allowed to happen to the Jews. The feelings of indignant nationalism that had helped propel Hitler into power were being superseded by a spreading national shame. Added to that was the growing fear of what the allies would do once they won the war and sought

185

recompense. Everyone remembered the reparations Germany was forced to endure after the First World War, a war in which the atrocities committed by Germans could be said to be unexceptional by the standards of warfare, but what would be the consequences of defeat for the citizens of a country that had unleashed such barbarism?

The Hitler greeting started to be used in an openly ironic manner and by the middle of 1944 it had practically died out altogether. It signalled a truth in German society: that disillusionment was rife but popular uprisings almost nonexistent. Once the Allied troops landed in Normandy and the end became inevitable, the German people prepared for life under occupation. But how to live with the guilt? And how to protect oneself from the interrogations about how and why and what part one played in letting it, helping it, happen? The answer for many was simple: deny all knowledge.

You can ruin a dinner party by postulating that Germans were no different in essence from the French, or the British, or the Americans, or anyone else you care to name, and that had circumstances been different, had the accumulated burdens and manifestations of the quirks and legacies of history produced a random, decisive shift in the political, social and economic axis of the day, it might have been us, that is you and me, not some abstract, beastly other, who was coopted into the machine, wittingly or not, of mass murder.

We would never, they say. We are a civilised people. We won't make excuses for them and nor must you.

You have no wish to excuse, you say, but that doesn't mean the inexcusable couldn't have happened here, or there, or anywhere. You look at the faces round the table, of people whose imaginations are unprepared for such a scale of suffering, who are gathered for pleasure in a spirit of conviviality, a contrivance of the abundant, where the wine is passed and the subject changed before anyone takes irreparable offence.

Your fellow diners aren't racist or xenophobic or homophobic or prone to nationalist extremism, nor are they cruel or insensitive or uncaring or liable to see the world as composed of the worthy and the unworthy. They are responsible and educated and well mannered and conscientious and they love nature and the environment and they respond to appeals for aid from those less fortunate.

But try telling them that they too might become consorts or lackeys or sidekicks or sneaks or cheerleaders or gimps or even murderers in the service of a monstrous regime, if circumstances were different.

Alex's documentary is taking shape.

'Henry Ford,' he says, 'was once asked why he paid his workers so well. His answer was that they could afford to buy a car and give the money back to him.'

Pre-production may have started, thanks to Alex's funding, but the production company still haven't found a TV company willing to commit. Broadcasting a film that tackles the system itself, rather than the bad behaviour of individuals within the system, seems to be a risk too far for TV commissioners. You can talk about blowing cocaine up hookers' anuses to your heart's content, and the more examples you have the better, but try suggesting that the rules of the game are at fault because they create conditions in which reckless greed is inevitable, with adverse consequences for billions of other people—unlike whatever anyone does in private with white powder—and you hit a wall of nervousness.

What Alex wants to say is that capitalism used to achieve some approximation of balance between exploitation on the one hand and distribution on the other. Nowadays capitalism extracts its wealth and keeps it. Where this is going is anyone's guess, he says. He's hardly a socialist, as he points out, but he can't be the only person who thinks that manufacturing wealth out of nothing and redistributing what there is upwards is a recipe for some serious shit.

'You would have thought 2008 should have convinced everyone,' he says, 'but it seems that the deeper the catastrophe, the worse the guilt, the greater the denial.'

He talks about the state. 'The rise of the state,' he says, 'is the great civilising influence of modern history. Wherever you have the rule of law you have the opportunity for peace and prosperity and the opportunity for people to live comfortable lives. And, as the state develops, you have democracy, checks and balances, freedom, rights. That is until the state loses its power and democracy mutates into a counterfeit version of itself.'

He looks at me for confirmation. I look back at him half interested, half confused. I tell him I wasn't aware of an absence of state power. If anything, I say, it seems to have grown more oppressive.

'It's more oppressive because it's not the state in control. It's Big Global.'

'The people you spent your career with.'

He shrugs, as if to say 'shucks, but that's in the past'.

'St. Paul on the road to Damascus.' I laugh.

'This is serious.' And he is, deadly.

He talks about the 'humanitarian revolutions': the abolition of slavery; the universal franchise; the Geneva Convention; the United Nations; civil rights; human rights; equal rights.

'From the Enlightenment onwards there was a steady, if punctuated, movement towards a better world in which ordinary people got a better deal. It reached its zenith in the latter half of the twentieth century. But then the state began to shrink from those virtues. Ideals replaced by a new ideology that measured the quality of life almost exclusively in terms of wealth creation.'

'Didn't you deny that you were a socialist?'

His eyes shine, he almost leaps with excitement. 'That's my point,' he says, 'fifty years ago, if I'd said that the value of day to day human existence was more important than the freedom of the market, I wouldn't have been branded a socialist. Politicians across the spectrum would have agreed. But now the democratic institutions of state are in retreat, leaving society to the market, creating markets where there were none, in places where markets had hitherto failed. Human rights are under attack; workers rights; consumer rights; legal rights, withering in the name of the market. And the state is at the whim of Big Global. Remember Tony Blair?' I nod, unnecessarily. 'And his third way? It never happened. Big Global was running a circus. Turn a blind eye or sink your economy. The state turned lackey, and democracy—if we take that to mean enacting the will of the people—a sideshow, a magician's trick to distract an audience so they don't see what's happening under their noses.'

Alex glowers, not at me, but in accord with the anger of his speech. I'm surprised at his vehemence. He looks at me, must see my look reflected back, and calms himself.

'It's not a message that makes securing a commission for an hour of prime time TV straightforward.' He's moved from anger to irony, which means he hasn't given up. He'd have moved to name calling if that were the case.

'Can you not sneak it in subliminally among the cocaine and the hookers?' I say, hoping to humour him. He nods and grins and may even be thinking about it.

So, Alex has a film in the making and nowhere to show it, and I have an exhibition in the making and no idea where or how it will be shown.

I think about what Alex has told me and how the Weimar Republic, a fledgling democracy, was ripped apart in the aftermath of the Wall Street crash. Would Hitler have risen to power in a country where democratic government was more deeply rooted? Or should I be looking at it the other way around: is our democratic government still as deeply rooted as I would like to think?

I wonder about Alex and his conversion. Is it convenient for him that it's all about the system? Has he found a formula for exonerating himself? He talks of the denial in others, implying he's beyond that, that he has faced up to the underlying causes and is prepared to speak out, but what of his own behaviour?

And what of mine, for that matter? I knew only a fraction of the story, but what I knew meant I should have been able to imagine the rest, or at least have been curious about it. But I didn't ask, I didn't probe or investigate, I let it happen and lived off the rewards.

Strangely, we find ourselves in parallel: his film and my exhibition, projects through which we can absolve ourselves. Maybe I'm ahead of him with that thought, and maybe I'm ahead of myself: I don't feel guilty even though I think I must be.

Victor turns up once again to appraise the work in progress. He's in high spirits. He has been true to his word about offering support and not interfering, and my attitude to his visits has moved incrementally from apprehension to acceptance to pleasure. Today he excels himself and we laugh like friends sharing a joke no one else would get; the kind of in-joke others would find annoying, but also the kind that becomes a code that fortifies a relationship.

Alex appears at the door and finds us giggling. I feel like we've been caught doing something naughty. He smiles awkwardly, the smile of someone on the outside looking in, and asks if we would like a drink.

'I was about to put the kettle on,' he says.

Victor looks at me with a plea, and I know what he wants.

'A glass of wine, perhaps,' I say, and add, feeling the need, 'why don't you join us?'

He declines, but two minutes later he appears with a bottle of wine and three glasses.

We stand in a line at the window contemplating the river.

'How many lives has it witnessed?' says Victor. 'It sweeps by, century after century, buildings and settlements come and go, inhabitants are born and live and die, but the river is always there.'

'It's never the same water,' says Alex, 'never the same molecules: they flow past and are gone, the river has no memory...' he pauses, a look of uncertainty for once, 'but for those of us in its reach it helps in both remembering and forgetting.'

He looks as though something he'd always failed to grasp has been understood. I smile at him and look at Victor.

Victor's face opens fully to Alex for the first time. He nods and smiles.

'The molecules will come around again one day,' he says, 'we are the only impermanence.'

'And what about our molecules? Do they come around again?' says Alex.

'Are you talking science or spirituality?' says Victor.

'Alex doesn't talk spirituality,' I say, pre-empting the response Alex is bound to deliver. Victor may not believe in God, but there's no need for Alex to spoil the moment by telling him why he shouldn't.

'Me neither,' says Victor, and raises his glass, 'to our molecules, however they may reconstitute themselves.'

For half an hour we move around the studio, our wine glasses in hand, like guests at an art preview, stopping to look casually at my work, but in reality making it a social occasion. Victor's approval flows over everything. I don't know if the mood he arrived in has softened his

191

judgement, or if the wine has hit a sweet spot, or if the sudden connection between him and Alex has created an atmosphere he wants to surf a while longer, but he is good-naturedly uncritical in his assessment. No interrogation of meaning, no inquiry about context, no extemporisation about how an idea might be developed, no 'ifs', no 'buts', just superlatives and a look of a man immersed in the pleasure of the moment.

As he drains his glass, the bottle now empty, and places it on the table, he looks at me with a seriousness that startles after the gentle amiability of the previous minutes.

'It's going to work,' he says, 'not that I doubted it would, but now we have come this far I feel the certainty of it.'

The words are celebratory but the sombreness of the delivery snaps me back to what we are dealing with. Our meeting has been too pleasant, too charmed. We have chatted and entertained ourselves while casting glances over art that tackles some of the worst depravity in history. The future is about what we do with it. Victor says it will 'work' and I still don't know what he means by that.

His eyes catch mine and I know he's read my mind.

'Soon,' he says, holding the look for a second before turning to go.

Alex volunteers to cook and I hang on in the studio shuffling a few things around. The light outside has turned to dusk. It's a bonus hour, when the work of the day is done, but I make myself do more so I can tell myself I've got ahead. I sketch a storyboard for an animated motif I've been thinking about, trying to sequence it with an overlay of film or photography either of Nina or, possibly, the school-children in Kensington Gardens.

I pause, afflicted by a twist of conscience. Should I contact the school, always assuming I can work out which one it is? I suppose I want their blessing, as a courtesy. But what if they refuse? What if they decide to refer the question to the parents of each child? What if they all agree except one? In that event, if I go ahead regardless, what would have been the point of asking?

I stand and walk to the window, dimming the light to reduce the reflection. I see a figure on the far side of the river and know it is Victor. I pick up the binoculars.

His shape is now familiar and unmistakeable, even at this distance, and his wanderings to the far bank after his visits are part of a routine I find comforting. I still don't know why he goes there and, strangely, no longer want to ask. Maybe I don't want to know, maybe the mystery provides the solace, like a distant father that a child can't hope to know, but whose presence in life is a predictable and binding reassurance.

I don't need the binoculars to confirm it's him and since there's enough light in the studio to silhouette me against the window, in a shape that, even from his distance, would be unmistakably voyeuristic, I should put them down and carry on working. But if he looks and sees me, I can wave and see if he waves back. It would be an odd communication, one that prolongs a contact, but might provoke him to volunteer what he does out there.

As I watch him, willing a look in my direction, I see that he isn't alone. There's a figure behind, no two, moving towards him. He's staring into the current, his concentration fixed to the water. Suddenly he turns, and I realise he's been startled.

I feel a thump in my chest, my instinct telling me these two men—I can see their faces now—are dangerous.

'Alex! Come here!' I scream the words over my shoulder and they have the desired effect: I hear his thumping footfall on the stairs, two at a time. He arrives in the doorframe, his face adjusting to the sight of me standing still at the window.

'I'm fine. It's Victor,' I say and point.

I lift the binoculars again as Alex rushes to my side. I see Victor take a step back. One of the men is advancing on him, the other staying a yard behind. He's talking, but there's no smile. Victor takes another half step back, but he's running out of bank: another two steps and he'll be in the river.

'They're attacking him, I'm sure of it,' I say.

Alex looks around the studio.

'It's beside the computer,' I say, meaning my phone. He runs over to get it.

'He's got a knife. The other one's got a fucking knife. He's got a fucking knife!' I scream, again. 'Fuck. Shit. I can't look.'

Alex hands me the phone and seizes the binoculars.

'Call the cops.'

I'm shaking as I tap the screen. I'm rushing it and yet it's happening in slow motion. I misdial. Only three fucking numbers and I get it wrong. I scream my frustration.

'There's nothing happening. I think they're threatening him, but no more,' says Alex. 'Some kind of negotiation I think.'

I connect to the emergency service. I ask for the police and I'm put through. The woman answering wants my name. I want to tell her what's happening. I garble my name, she asks for an exact location.

'Fuck's sake, a man's life is in danger.'

Alex puts down the binoculars.

'I'm going out there,' he says.

'No. Alex.' I say. 'It's my husband,' I say to the woman. She tells me he must leave it to officers who are trained to deal with it. I relay this back to him. But he's already through the door.

She asks me to calm down. I do, realising I have to. She asks for details, but they're complicated. I don't have a postcode. It's on the opposite bank, I say, behind the school. It's not a precise location. I tell her my postcode and that the location is on the other side of the river to it, but she's beaten me to it: she's traced my phone. She tells

194

me units have despatched and abruptly puts me through to someone else.

This new person asks me to be as precise as I can. I tell her the nearest access point for a vehicle. She tells me an ambulance is on its way too. I break down at this. An ambulance? It hasn't happened yet, thank God. She's right but, God only knows, I wish for her to be wrong. She tells me her name is Chloe and asks me what's happening now. I pick up the binoculars, sick with fear.

Nothing. It looks like a discussion but I can't get a sense of how threatening it is. It looks calm from here, but that's only because there's no obvious movement from either of the two men. They're among the trees and it's getting darker and their features aren't easy to read. But the knife is still out. I say all this to Chloe and she is listening. 'Be brave Sylvia,' says Chloe, and I'm struck by her use of my name, 'I need you to keep telling me what's happening.'

The men look upstream and I see Victor look too. Scanning further up the bank I see a couple walking their dogs towards them. The discussion between Victor and the men reanimates and the man with the knife puts it away. The three of them shuffle as the couple approach.

'Keep talking to me,' says Chloe, making me feel like I'm at the top of a building preparing to jump. I tell her everything as it happens, on the assumption, although Chloe doesn't say so, that this is being relayed to the 'units'—wherever the fuck they are.

And it's as if I've stepped out of myself. I'm a commentator at a public event, involved but dispassionate, relaying information, describing what I see. Some part of me has shut off. Did Chloe do this to me? I can hear my voice telling her that the couple break their stride when they see the men. They're nervous of them, that is obvious. They look fearful of having stumbled into something they shouldn't have. I see them call the dogs, one of whom runs to Victor. Victor bends and grabs the dog by the scruff of

195

the neck and rubs it with both hands. He looks up at the couple. They relax. Some sort of conversation has broken out. Victor has initiated some doggy chat. I think he's playing for time, or he's trying to make some coded reference to the fact he's in trouble.

The couple put the dogs on leads and walk on. The men and Victor stand around in a strained, at ease arrangement, for no purpose other than to wait for the couple to be gone. Thirty yards down the path I see the woman turn her head back in the direction of Victor and the men.

The men close in on Victor. They are hurrying now. The light is fading and I can't see detail. I see Victor drop to his knees, but I can't tell if they told him to or if he chose to. One of the men stands behind him. Is it the man who had the knife? The shock of the premonition I have makes my throat close. Chloe tells me, quietly, calmly, authoritatively, to be brave. I tell her I can't look and I put the binoculars down. I feel myself shaking—is this hysteria? I wail at Chloe and she tells me to hang in there, the officers are minutes away. I shriek that it might be too late. She tells me to pick up the binoculars and talk to her.

It's so dark now I have trouble picking out the spot where they are, and I'm shivering with the fear of what I might see. At last I see their shapes and adjust the focus wheel in a futile attempt to make the image clearer. Victor is still kneeling, I'm sure. I can't see a knife. Now I think I catch a glint near his throat. I throw open the door to the balcony and step out. I scream, but the noise seems to hit a wall in front of me. The men look round. They heard it, just, but they don't know where it's coming from, they don't know I'm screaming at them. I scream again, but this time they don't react.

Putting down the binoculars to help me take the breath that will let me scream my loudest, I catch sight of a flashlight on the far bank. It's moving fast, someone running. The police at last. Chloe's voice tightens as she asks me to use the binoculars and I realise it can't be the police.

It's Alex. He must have grabbed the flashlight on his way out. 'Oh fuck oh fuck oh fuck oh fuck.' I pour the fucks into the phone, my voice growing shriller with each one. I think I'm on the edge of unconsciousness.

'I can't do it,' I scream.

'You can,' says Chloe. There's a snap in her voice. It's a command.

I raise the binoculars again. Alex is a hundred yards from them and I think the men have seen the flashlight, because something in their manner changes. One of them seems to reach across Victor. It's hard to tell, but their shapes merge for a moment. Victor is on his feet. He must have been hauled up. Alex is twenty yards away. The men and Victor turn to face the water. They think it's a jogger and are waiting for him to pass.

I see the flashlight appear behind the men and can just about see Alex behind it. He turns it on them. They turn around to face him, as does Victor. Nothing moves. Something must be being said.

Chloe tells me the police are on the scene. I should see their flashlights come into view any time now. I watch Alex, Victor and the men, but nothing's happening. I stare desperately back along the bank hoping to see a group of flashlights. One of the men walks towards Alex, holding something in front of him and I pray it isn't the knife. Alex jumps to one side and strikes out with his flashlight. The man backs away and I wonder if Alex managed to hit him. The man retreats to Victor and holds him, and I see the blade, lit by Alex's torch, pressed against Victor's neck.

I have no breath save a strangulated exhale that squeaks out, a sound I've never emitted in my life. Chloe tells me they're probably bargaining. If they haven't stabbed him yet it's because they don't want to. The officers will be there any minute to take over. Every piece of information I am able to relay helps them to prepare. And I'm doing a great job, she adds.

She could be right; it looks like a stand off. If there's anything preferable to having a knife at your neck it's not having it plunge in. The police torches are visible along the bank now. There must be at least ten. I'm impressed at the level of response. This is a whole lot better than the time I reported a break in at my neighbours. A sense of reassurance gives way to a new fear: it's coming to a head now and anything might happen.

Alex, I think, is shouting at the men. His flashlight beam darts from one to the other. Is he trying to play them off against one another? Has he detected a divide? Further down the bank the flashlights close, they will be visible to the men any minute, except, suddenly, they go out.

'I may have to leave you in a minute,' says Chloe.

You can't! I want to say. But she can and will. She starts talking about victim support, oblivious to the fact that she is my support right now. How did that happen?

Don't you want to know how it ends? I think. But she doesn't, not now at least. She's doing a job. I tell her I can hear a megaphone, although I can't hear what it's saying. I tell her the men look startled. They've obviously heard it. She says she's going, she says I've been great, and she's gone.

I reach inside and put the phone down. The voice of someone who knows what they're doing, knows how to talk to me, is gone. The loss of her is an abandonment and I'm a spectator now in every sense. Again I lift the binoculars. Some sense that I mustn't abandon Alex and Victor makes me force myself, when what I want to do is shut my eyes and wait and hope.

There's a flurry of short sharp movements. It's hard to tell what's happening, but the megaphone has obviously changed things. The torches, except Alex's, are still dimmed, but I can see shadows moving along the shore.

The police are fifty yards away. I can hear the megaphone. Someone grabs Victor again. Alex shines the torch. The knife is at Victor's throat. The advancing shadows are moving slowly. I hear the megaphone again and this time I catch a phrase: 'don't want to hurt you', before it fades on the breeze. No one moves. The megaphone again, this time the tone is softer. This is killing me. I can see what they're doing and it all makes sense, but I just want them to shoot the bastards and be done with it.

Alex lunges at the man with the knife. Fuck, no, Alex! But the other man does too. There's a tangle of men and a splash. The flashlights go up like stage lights. I see Alex rush to the water's edge; it must be Victor in the river. Can he swim? Alex jumps in. Half a dozen police tackle the men, who surrender without a fight; the others run downstream to draw level with Victor. Alex reaches Victor and gets hold of him. He's a good swimmer and the current isn't strong, so I'm not worried about Alex. But what happened in that final scuffle? Why did Alex lunge so suddenly? Can I see blood?

Alex pulls Victor onto a boathouse slipway and two police officers bend to help. I tighten in anticipation of their reaction to whatever state Victor is in. This nervous terror is almost blacking me out, but I'm not turning away. I see one of the officers gesticulate frantically, triggering another explosion of fear in me. But Alex stands and rubs his head. I know that gesture; it's relief. I see Victor move, then I see him struggle to his feet, aided by one of the officers. I lean forward and hang my torso over the balcony rail, overcome by an uncontrolled spasm of joy, before bursting into tears. It's like the end of the world has come and gone and somehow we're still here.

For hours I'm alone, fretting, drinking, unable to settle, waiting for news. I go to the balcony to shiver, letting the chatter of my teeth clatter in my head until I force myself to stop. I'm not cold. I finish one bottle of wine and start another before realising I'm no longer walking straight. So I shiver again and wait and smoke.

An hour into the vigil I call Alex. I've postponed the moment, not daring to, giving myself the excuse that there would be police and hospital procedurals to be gone through before he would be able to talk. As soon as I dial I hear his phone ring downstairs. I think of trying Victor, but even assuming it isn't waterlogged or lying at the bottom of the river, it feels wrong to pursue him instead of waiting for Alex. When the opportunity presents itself, Alex will call, I'm sure.

So it's a big surprise when the phone rings and the screen shows 'Victor'. I pack a thousandfold of relief into saying 'hi' only to hear Alex, and my voice drops into a rather flat, but still relieved, sigh.

'I'm fine,' he says, the tinge of sarcasm constrained by the knowledge that the situation overall is anything but.

'I'm sorry,' I say, 'but I could see you were alright.'

'It's okay,' he says, and there's something measured and consoling about his voice, the tone of a survivor who has entered into a new reality. 'Victor's fine,' he says, and when I break out shivering again, and attempt to speak with a voice slewed by sobs and alcohol, he keeps repeating, 'it's okay, it's okay.'

I start asking questions, firing them at him faster than he can answer and not really listening to the replies, just sifting the words for the essentials: life; death; injury.

'I'll be back in an hour,' he says, 'but don't wait up. I can give you the whole story in the morning.'

Nice try, Alex, I think. So, I'm drunk and annoying and it would be better for him if I were asleep when he gets home, but he can forget that. I stopper the remaining wine, make myself a sandwich and coffee, and settle down to wait.

But I crash, suddenly and heavily. I feel it enveloping me and I fight it, but it won't let go, it devours me, and in the final seconds something in my head drains, or evaporates, and my last thought before waking the next morning in the bed Alex must have carried me to, is that this is what it feels like to die.

'Good morning,' he says and smiles, placing a cup of coffee at my bedside. I lift my head and feel relief not to have a headache, just a washed out, disengaged imprecision, as though the parts of my brain that control thought and movement have departed for the heavens.

He reassures me that Victor suffered no physical injuries.

'I'm okay too,' he says, and grins.

I start to explain that I knew he was okay, that it was obvious even from the other side of the river, but he stops me.

'No need to keep digging,' he says, and strokes my arm. His hand is slow and soothing, and I want to close my eyes and purr, letting him gently stroke my skin as though his touch will smooth out the tangled nerves. But there's too much to know and I reach for his hand, curl my fingers around his, and tell him it's time for 'the whole story.'

'The "whole story" is something I can't actually tell you,' he says. 'What I know is that it wasn't random, his attackers knew who he was. Victor wasn't forthcoming about anything else, at least not to me, so I don't know why they were there, or what they wanted. When they put the knife to his throat they were telling me to fuck off and mind my own business or they'd kill him.'

I tell Alex that Victor had been on his knees before he arrived and one of them had stood behind him brandishing the knife.

'I thought they were going to slit his throat. It was you with your flashlight that stopped them. It looked like you'd interrupted an execution.'

Alex looks at me, surprised.

'Shall I tell you something weird?' he says, 'Victor's attackers didn't call him Victor. They called him Wilhelm.'

'My god, you mean it was mistaken identity?'

'No, they knew him. They knew he was Jewish, they made that plain, and they had a grievance against him about something, but I don't know what.'

'Didn't you and Victor give statements to the police?'

'Yes,' he says, 'but separately. I don't know what Victor told them.'

I start turning over conceivable explanations as to why Victor might be Wilhelm to them, but I don't want to lose track of the story, so I drop the thought and listen to Alex.

'When I arrived the three of them were facing the river as though nothing was amiss, like they were friends enjoying the twilight while out on an evening stroll.

'I shone the torch, and when I called out "Victor" I was hesitant, fearing maybe we'd got the whole thing wrong. They turned round and one of them said "who's Victor?" But there was a real edge to his voice, a sly aggressive tone, and if that wasn't the confirmation I needed, the look on Victor's face was.'

Alex adjusts his position on the edge of the bed and drops his voice.

'He was terrified. You know how he's always so poised? He'd lost it. Not in his bearing, which was still of a man taught from childhood to stand straight, but on his face and in his eyes. It was that look that really frightened me.

'I asked them what was going on? I didn't expect a straight answer, but it was the best I could think of. They told me to mind my own business and I told them I wasn't going to do that. I told them I'd come to meet Victor and I was taking him home with me. One of them said to the other, "I think he means Wilhelm", but without irony, which made me think the other must be a bit dim. Then he looked at me and said, "Wilhelm's ours". He came towards

202

me telling me to fuck off. He was brandishing the knife and when he was close enough I lashed out with the flashlight, catching part of his arm and glancing off his chin.

'He squealed and backed off and I found myself thinking it had been surprisingly easy to fight off a madman with a knife. I realised he was a coward and that I could win this. But he grabbed Victor and put the knife to his throat. He yelled "we have business with this Jew, that doesn't involve you" and turned to his accomplice, apparently pleased with his rhyme, before turning back to me and yelling that either I left now or he'd kill "Wilhelm".

'The other guy said that if they had to kill "Wilhelm" they'd also have to kill me. To which I told them to just fucking try it. You let go of Victor, I said, or I'll kill both of you. Crazy talk, I know, but I was reeling in the shock of the moment and that's how it came out. I started shining the torch beam into their eyes, thinking it might give me some psychological advantage. I found myself telling them to let go of Victor or I would "seek my vengeance".'

Alex shakes his head, disbelieving his own words. I can't believe what I'm hearing. I ask him if it occurred to him that they might simply have killed Victor and gone after him.

'Only afterwards,' he says, 'when I had time to dwell on how else it could have ended. But in that moment I was sure of myself.'

He stares at me like he needs me to believe in him. He's fighting the thought he knows I must be thinking: that he was a reckless fool, albeit a brave one.

'I think you saved his life,' I say, 'by showing up when you did.'

It worked out, so why dull the triumph by continuing a postmortem about where it could have gone wrong. Let the survivor bias prevail. I wasn't there, he was, who am I to judge? He looks relieved to hear it and smiles.

'I might have saved it twice,' he says. 'Victor claimed to me afterwards that he could swim, but if that was swimming I wouldn't like to see him drowning. When I first heard the megaphone I didn't know what was happening. I couldn't hear what was being said, but Victor's attackers knew it was the police. They tightened their grip on him and pushed the knife further up against his throat. They told me I shouldn't have phoned the police, that by doing so I'd signed "Wilhelm's" death sentence. They told me to tell the police to back off. I said I didn't phone them and that the police wouldn't pay any attention to me anyway. They knew they were cornered, but desperate for any way out.

'The megaphone started up again and this time I could hear what they were saying: they wanted to sort things out; they didn't want to hurt anyone. The man without the knife told the one with to drop it. It made him pause and I knew he was thinking about it, but he still wasn't prepared to be beaten. I moved closer, hoping to grab his arm if I could get close enough. The voice in the megaphone was almost seductive: we're here to help, here to listen.

'The man with the knife wanted to use Victor to do a deal, the other said they should throw the knife in the river and run for it. They glared at each other, no longer looking at me, and I jumped at the arm holding the knife. My plan was to launch myself hard enough to knock him to the ground while grabbing the arm so tight he couldn't use the knife. The police were yards away and I'd only have to hang on for seconds before they would reach me.

'It didn't go quite to plan. I got the arm, but he stayed on his feet, his other arm still round Victor. I shouted to the police that I'd got him and all the lights went on, but the knife was still close to Victor's neck. Then the other man grabbed the arm, also trying to stop him from stabbing Victor, but sending the three of us stumbling off balance down the embankment. The lights were blinding and I was sure the police were almost on top of us. Suddenly something gave, I saw the knife fall to the ground and heard a splash. I knew straight away that Victor had fallen in.

'The police stormed in as the men started blaming each other, but my focus was on Victor. I heard someone shout "man in the river". It was obvious Victor was struggling and I was the nearest, so I jumped in. I figured I knew this stretch of the river and if anyone was going to fish Victor out it should be me. I guess the rest you know.'

He looks at me. I tell him he was brave. He looks sheepish.

'We were given a change of clothes,' he says, 'and then it was all just paperwork. They were taking it ultra seriously, no question of that, but giving nothing away. Not a hint of who Victor's attackers might have been, or what will happen next.'

He stops, but something plays on his face, like there's more but he doesn't know whether to say it.

'What?'

'You'll probably think I'm reading too much into this,' he says, 'but although Victor was really keen to thank me for pulling him out of the river—a point he kept repeating —he never once mentioned me turning up there in the first place.'

Work is hard. I'm too distracted, and when I take refuge in the river, I see only the scene of the crime. A familiar contemplation, one that has rescued so many situations, is now indicted. So I light another cigarette, because it seems the only thing to do, and hope for something to resolve itself.

There's no word from Victor. Natalie and Nina show up, and Natalie pretends to be normal and fails. After several minutes of excruciatingly banal chitchat I take a leap and bring Victor into the conversation. Judging by the revival in speed of Natalie's gestures, she is as relieved as I am to hold a conversation in which we acknowledge we both know him.

'I'm sorry,' she says, bringing things back down again, 'that we dragged you into this.' Her face stiffens, but her eyes soften and an impulse to ask what exactly they have dragged Alex and me into is appeased. I sit, indicating to Natalie and Nina to do the same.

'What can you tell me?'

She struggles with the question. She glances at Nina and I expect her to send her away while we talk privately, but she doesn't. Nina looks curious and excited, as though something's about to happen that she's been looking forward to.

Natalie looks at me and then at Nina and back to me again.

'Victor will tell you,' she says, at which point the glow on Nina's face vanishes as fast as if she'd blown out candles on a birthday cake.

She folds her arms. 'Mum!'

Natalie looks at her and smiles.

'We want to take you into our confidence, completely,' she says, at which Nina's strop unwinds a notch, 'but Victor should be here to tell you because he's the one who knows the full story, the one with all the answers.'

I look at her blankly. 'I'm lost,' I say, knowing it sounds lame, but it's the best I can do and it does sum things up.

'I'll tell you two things,' she says, arching her back to raise her posture. 'The first is to do with my phone.'

I blink, which she picks up on and asks me what I'm thinking.

'Sorry,' I say, 'I'd forgotten about the phone.'

I trail off, stopping myself from adding 'at last, the truth,' not least because the truth might still not be what I'm about to get.

'I leave the phone when I go some place I don't want to be followed,' she says, 'or tracked.' She waits for a reaction. I'm thinking back to Nina's explanation at the time—that Natalie might miss calls because of background noise—and realise, with Nina sitting here looking anything but surprised, that she would have known the truth and is therefore part of this intrigue. 'I trust Nina completely,' she says.

'Of course,' I say.

'What I mean is that Nina knows about my life, about our life. I trust her to know everything there is to know.'

I smile at Nina through narrowed eyes. The mystery may be un-peeling slowly, but Nina has just grown up ten years in my mind. She looks coy and in that look I understand she has been more knowing, less innocent than I've taken her for. I've treated her as a child, an intelligent, gifted child, one I've had a delightfully grown-up relationship with, but nonetheless a child in age and being, and one who has been an active player in a grown up plan.

'You're full of surprises,' I say to her.

'It wasn't my place to tell you anything.' She looks at Natalie, but I keep my gaze on Nina, reminded that she is a girl of thirteen—a clever, adaptable, inscrutable girl, but, at heart, an honest one.

'She's a fast learner,' says Natalie.

'You're good,' I say to her, and she blushes. She's taken it as a sign of forgiveness, which I think it is, although I don't know for sure. I turn back to Natalie. 'So who's tracking you?'

'People who don't like what we do, who we are, what we stand for, or anything about us. Victor hadn't turned his off. Normally he would leave the phone behind, or switch it off and remove the battery, or deliberately park it somewhere as a decoy…'

'Shit.' I say it to myself as much as to Natalie. But she nods as if to confirm I've understood something correctly.

'They wouldn't have attacked him here,' she says, quickly. She's ahead of me: I hadn't had that thought, though I probably should have.

'How do you know?' I say it pointedly, accusingly. In the short silence that follows, I remember Victor's categories: the resisters; the do-nothings; the collaborators. I chose to be part of this and I chose it knowing I was entering the unknown. It was a leap of faith, blind and maybe foolish, except for one thing I did know, the thing that generated the excitement, the lure I couldn't say no to: that I was joining some form of resistance. I lower my voice. 'Don't answer. I'm sorry.' I smile, imagining it as gesture of renewed faith.

'You're too good, Sylvia,' says Natalie. 'You would be right to be angry, and that's why we must take you into our confidence now. As soon as Victor regains his mettle, that is. I promise.'

She smiles. A wide embracing smile, one that welcomes me to her. She reaches for my hand and I take it. It's firm, almost hard, but warm.

'That was the first thing,' I say, 'what's the second?'

She tosses her head back and transforms herself from friend to something more businesslike.

'I am your sponsor.'

She could have parted the river like the Red Sea and I'd have been less surprised.

I'm sure Victor said the sponsor was a 'he'. It's one of those times when I know I'm right at the same time as I begin to doubt it, as though I'm looking for an explanation as to why the evidence of my eyes and ears is wrong. It's not a trait Alex suffers from and I suppose some people are more sensitive to being mistaken than others. But I know I heard it right. And aside from her not being a 'he', what does it mean that it's Natalie? How far do I allow my willingness to be kept in the dark excuse the fact that they've played me good and proper?

But Nina's eyes are like the imaginary child of mine: the one that looks at me—the good and gracious mother, the protector and nurturer—with love and belief. That child will never exist and the dream will never be tested against anything as fickle as reality, but in the meantime there she is, a surrogate for a dream that wants to be true.

In the days following, when I'm alone and waiting for Victor to arrive and tell me the 'full story', I find myself laughing at Natalie's explanation. I think it is suppressed hysteria, if it isn't it's hysteria pure and simple. I laugh a lot and sometimes cry. The whole project is at a watershed. I am promised their complete confidence, which I interpret as an end to the almost surreal game playing and an exploding of the mystery. Alex risked his life to save Victor's and amidst the sense of fracture that has opened since, that simple fact, impossible to conceive of only days ago when the world was a safe and ordered place, seems like the singular focal point in a field of blurred reality.

When he arrives he does so with Natalie, but without Nina. He looks immaculate as ever, and seems as convivial. From the moment I greet Natalie I know things have shifted. It's subtle but decisive: she isn't a mother, but a comrade in arms, and her smile no longer carries her hopes for her daughter but shines with hope for us all.

My polite enquiry as to Victor's health is met with an emphatic reassurance that lacks detail. My question about the attackers, wrapped together with whats, hows and whens regarding police, prosecutions and mine and Alex's future involvement, is sped through as though of peripheral consequence.

'Is this what you mean by taking me into your confidence?' The tartness in my voice is deliberate and I eyeball them both, determined not to flinch.

'Minor issues,' says Victor, and he looks as if he has no intention of saying anything more, until Natalie prompts him. So he tells me that the attackers were members of an extremist group known for its virulent anti-semitism and that the police may struggle to press charges.

'What?' I shout, part question, part exclamation.

'That's how I thought you would react.'

'How should I react?' I say.

'It's complicated,' he says. And so he tells me that he doesn't want to appear in court as a witness. 'It would serve no purpose except to divert attention from where I wish to focus it.'

I tell him he can't just let them get away with it, that justice has to be done and be seen to be done, that the rule of law is the one institutional advance that separates our civilised world from that of the barbarians. 'When the law is corrupted you get Nazism.'

'Or when you get Nazism, the law becomes corrupted,' says Natalie. Her words seem to reinforce mine, but I'm not surprised when it turns out that they don't.

'Have you ever been involved in a serious legal case?' says Victor. I shake my head. 'It takes over your life. Everything becomes subservient to it. Challenging something in law is for rich, foolish people or people who have no choice or are too naïve to know what they're committing to. It exists for lawyers.'

'And,' I interrupt, 'for bringing evil to justice. What the hell do you have in mind, Victor? What they did was criminal and violent, you're talking as though you're suing a neighbour who's breached a planning agreement.' I sense my incredulity dying somewhere in the gap that seems to have opened between us.

'Freedom of speech,' he says. 'In a civilised democracy, it's of equal importance to the rule of law.'

He's lost me and as he turns to smile at Natalie I see him fish something out of his pocket.

'Can we adjourn the conversation to your studio?' he says, holding up a memory stick. 'I have something to show you.'

As Victor plays the film I watch initially in disbelief and then awe. He clicks on a file with the name 'River' which rings a distant alarm in my head, but still doesn't prepare me for what's to come. I see a riverside, then I see it from another angle. It is my riverside: I can see my house in the background. Then I see Victor walk into the foreground.

'You have to be joking,' I say, and it's all I say until the film finishes. The whole incident: the approach by the men; Victor being forced to kneel; the arrival of Alex; the struggle; the splash; the police; Alex diving into the river. The strangest thing is that after Alex has dived in to rescue Victor and the police have led the attackers away, the film continues, recording the empty space—from two angles— where it all happened. Empty space and silence. It continues for over a minute until Victor reaches over and exits the file.

'What do you think now?' he says.

'Fucking insane,' I say.

'Entrapment,' he says. 'When I told the police that the incident was on film they were initially pleased to have the evidence, then they did a volte-face realising that my having set it up created all kinds of difficulties. They were annoyed with me. They threatened to charge me.

'But they're not going to. If I'd been either a vengeful victim, or a cynical entrapper, it would, with respect to each outcome—either prosecute the attackers, or prosecute me —be different, but I'm neither. Too implicated to be relied on in court, but nevertheless too much a victim to be prosecuted for my recklessness.'

'They threatened to kill you,' I say, 'doesn't that override everything?'

Victor breaths deeply. 'Did you notice how quickly the police arrived after you phoned 999?'

'I was impressed.'

'They were on their way by the time you phoned. Natalie had put the call through as soon as she saw them on the path. We had two other cameras, neither of which we've used in the edited version you've seen, but which Natalie was watching back home on a phone that has no location capability, so she could report it as if she were witnessing it live.'

It's one of those times when you are surprised and yet not, like the inevitable has happened even though you never foresaw it. The world becomes different, questions crowd your mind and your only response is to ask the mundane.

'So how did I end up giving a running commentary to the police if Natalie was already on the line.'

Natalie leans forward, she wants to take up the story. 'They lost interest in me,' says Natalie. 'At first I couldn't believe it since I was giving important information. I was told someone else had come on the line and was reporting the incident, but several seconds ahead of me. This "someone else" was you of course, although I didn't know it, and you were actually watching it live whereas my feed had a delay.'

As the revelations pile up and details are explained, I feel a small sense of satisfaction grow, but the big questions remain unanswered. An almost nauseous frustration takes hold. Victor staked his life on making a movie of the event. For what? And what if he'd died? I practically shout these questions at him, finishing by asking what the hell he thought he was doing. He holds up his hands and asks me to be patient.

'They wouldn't have killed me,' he says.

'They had you kneeling on the floor. One of them was behind you with a knife ready to cut your throat.'

'The sound is poor,' he says, 'so you don't hear me ask him to name his price. We know these people. We have their measure when it comes to what motivates them. They

212

would like to kill me but their weakness is they have no money. I wasn't going to pay them a cent and I knew the police were coming.' He looks at me, a finality in the seriousness of his expression, until his face lightens and he adds: 'Alex turning up was touching, but rather inconvenient. Fortunately it worked out.'

I tell him what Alex said, that when he'd arrived Victor had looked terrified, his elegant demeanour in shreds. I admit that it's less obvious on the film, but the distance of the camera and the graininess of the image would make the detail less perceptible.

'Why were you so frightened if it was all under control?'

'It wasn't a situation without risk,' he says, 'so there was fear. But from that fear I created terror, as my audience demanded. Let me show you.'

Victor falls to his knees and looks at me with hollowed eyes and an open mouth, his lips trembling, the skin tight around his cheeks, his breathing hoarse and then whistles like a wind on a desolate moor. It's ghastly.

'Stop it. I get it,' I shout.

He stops trembling, relaxes his face but stays on his knees, his eyes still demonic as he continues. 'They had to succeed. They needed to feel powerful, to satisfy their desire for control, to enjoy the thrill of holding a life in their hands. I gave them an option: choose your lust, blood or money. By threatening blood they were offered money. I doubled their satisfaction. I helped them feel like gods. And all the more thrilling for me knowing it was to be so cruelly snatched from them. I gave them the illusion of control, while holding it all the while in my hands.'

I'm confused, alarmed at his transformations, both physical and mental, though paradoxically impressed that he has such range. He rises to his feet and smiles. He looks smug and I want to punch him, but the smugness gives way to the resumption of his charming persona and I surrender, grinning back while shaking my head.

'So where does freedom of speech come into all this?'

'We have a film of anti-semites threatening a man's life which, I must admit, has been pepped up somewhat by Alex's presence. One thing you can hear, loud and clear, is them shouting "fucking Jew" for his benefit. As I say, it worked out well.'

So Victor has a film of his own near death experience and wants to share it with the world. At least that's what I think he's saying.

'Even if it goes viral, how will that help?'

'Viral?' he says.

He looks at me. Natalie looks at me. They're waiting. They've been waiting for this moment for a while.

I stretch in the chair, a long easeful extension of arms and legs, before getting to my feet, walking to the window and looking out across the darkening river to the trees beyond.

'It was about this time,' I say.

Natalie joins me, leaving Victor at the table.

She asks how I feel about it now. I tell her it's better. I mean the view, and although I imagine she means the situation as a whole, the answer is curiously the same. Whatever I think of Victor and Natalie and this bizarre enterprise, the scene of the crime, the sight from my window, is not the reviled place it was threatening to become.

'And what about Alex?'

I laugh. 'He's still wandering around feeling heroic.'

'We'll leave out the bit about it being slightly inconvenient, then,' she laughs.

The laugh subsides and in its wake is an air of indecision. I know the Really Big Conversation now has to happen and I sense neither Victor nor Natalie knows how to start it.

I hear the chair scrape as Victor gets to his feet.

'He was heroic,' he says. 'No question.'

Over the next hours, as the darkness inks-in the shadows outside, and after I turn down the studio lights from work-bright to a sociable amber, and once we've fallen headlong into the discussion that changes everything, helped along by the bottle of wine Alex thoughtfully provides, it all becomes settled and clear and I am admitted to their world.

Victor is anxious to point out a 'technicality' relating to the 'gender specifics of the sponsor'. He tells me there is a 'sleeping' sponsor and an 'active' one. Natalie is the active one.

He pauses, looks at Natalie, who nods for him to continue. We all know I'm waiting to hear who the sleeping sponsor is.

'Our father,' he says.

For an uncomprehending moment I expect him to continue with the Lord's prayer, but in the glance between him and Natalie the meaning breaks through. They're grinning at me: two children whose guilty-but-innocent little secret is now out. And in those grins is the first sign of a likeness between them. It's so strong I can't believe I hadn't seen it before.

'Father's the one with the money,' says Natalie, 'but this is my project, so I am, de facto, the sponsor.'

'And Nina?' I say, 'how much of the plan is she in on?'

She starts telling me that Nina's interest in art is genuine and I respond by saying it's not something I need to be convinced about. 'She's a good actor, but she isn't that good.'

Natalie goes on to tell me that her and Nina were part of my network before the project had even been thought about.

'It's how we came to choose you in the first place. We'd been following you on twitter for ages. When you put the call out for a child model I was surprised, and a little worried, but the fastest way to seal the situation, as well as test that you weren't going rogue, was to step in with Nina, who was thrilled.'

And so the conversation continues.

The house with the genocide museum belongs to Victor and Natalie's mother and father.

'They want to meet you,' says Natalie. 'They're looking forward to it, which is amazing since they don't normally meet anyone.'

I echo back the word 'anyone', wondering how literally to take this.

'Anyone outside their existing world,' says Victor, 'the world they created for themselves during the early years of their marriage. It's not a small world. It consists of a large family and a kind of extended family of trusted associates and business partners, all of whom have remained steadfastly loyal for decades. Outside of that there is almost no one. For all those years the same people have run their house, driven their cars, managed their affairs…'

'Done their shopping,' says Natalie, sounding anxious to suggest they're normal people, with everyday concerns.

Victor looks annoyed at the interruption, but nods anyway. 'Suffice to say their feet rarely touch the London pavement, by which I mean almost any public space. They enjoy an exclusive, utterly private existence in an enclave of devoted friends and overpaid servants. The outside world barely touches them. If they attend a public institution it will be for a private function.'

'Do they not want to experience real life? Are they not curious about all the stuff that goes on beyond their closeted existence?'

Victor looks at Natalie and I can see he's weighing something up, as if the full admission that his parents are hermits is something he'd like to avoid. He seems to get some sort of permission from her, although I saw nothing transmit between them. 'Their life is real, as far as they're concerned, they have all they want, although inevitably some things have to be bought in, as it were.' He lowers his eyes, suggesting that the buying in is done grudgingly.

'Oh,' I say. I want to interrogate what this means, the difference between the 'real life' and the elements that are 'bought in'—when it hits me that I am an outsider who's been 'bought in'.

'It's not the same,' says Natalie. She's as good at reading my mind as Victor, but it makes me feel doubly aware of my status as a consequence. 'You aren't bought,' she says, 'you are recompensed.'

'Is there a difference? I'm still someone hired on a whim by a rich person.' My words echo waspishly through my head.

The air seems to suck itself from the room, drawing in a chill, as if some vapour from the river had risen up the bank and crawled in to fill a vacuum.

Victor swivels in reaction, his face grave. He leans forward.

'Sylvia,' he says, 'let me tell you a story.'

'If it'll help,' I say. He collects himself slowly; preparing me for a story that will take some time. I feel myself shiver and I look at Natalie whose face betrays something I just don't recognise. Victor begins.

'In 1938, in Vienna, two young people, a Jewish woman, Erika, and a non-Jewish man, Johann, fell in love. They shouldn't have: Jews were banned from virtually every aspect of public life; marriage between Jews and non-Jews was forbidden and Jews who were already married to non-Jews were encouraged to divorce. Erika's father was a secular Jew and a doctor by qualification, although no longer practicing, at least officially, and Johann's was a mathematician. Both Erika and Johann had been brought up to value education—science and the arts—and to hold enlightened views about democracy and justice.

'Johann grew up knowing that his name was a Germanic version of the Hebrew Johanan. Witnessing the Nazi invasion of his country and the enactment of laws that oppressed and denigrated Jews, he felt, through this mundane, unscientific association, strangely connected. He knew Erika from when she used to sit near him in the library, each working on their studies, in his case distracted by her presence. One day, coming across her in the neighbourhood, he smiled at her. She hurried past, head down. He saw her again a few weeks later in a spot near the river—a quiet place and relatively safe from disapproving or malicious eyes—and tried to make conversation. She was suspicious at first having more to lose if they were seen together, but his interest in her, the kindness in his manner, and the unfamiliar but pleasant feelings aroused, led her to trust him.

'Soon they were meeting secretly, exchanging fears about the shameless world they were growing up in. They talked about freedom and happiness, unattainable ideals in the dark and suffocating Nazi landscape, and slowly, in the eyes of the other, saw a glimpse of the impossible. In a few short days, in the way that falling in love compresses events and expands time, the talk was of "we" and "us" and how they could liberate themselves by being together.

'Erika's parents, who had hung on in Vienna in the hope that the anti-semitic tide that swelled following Anschluss would ebb away as the situation stabilised and people rediscovered their humanity, were finally forced to accept the need to escape following Kristallnacht, during which nearly all the synagogues in Austria were destroyed by brownshirt mobs and members of the Hitler Youth. The events of that night were terrible enough, worse was the look on the faces of their decent, law abiding Austrian neighbours in the coming days: pity, born of a knowledge that the Jews were damned, mixed with evasiveness out of a fear of contamination. Among Jews there was a stampede for exit visas during the following weeks, Erika's parents' intention was to leave for Budapest and join another branch of their family.

'For Johann and Erika, despite the dangers of her staying put, exile would be the end. In desperation Erika told her parents of her secret love affair and pleaded with them either to let her stay or for them to take Johann. The same night Johann confessed to his parents his love for Erika and begged for them to take Erika in, and either hide her or pass her off as one of the family.

'Johann's parents would not permit his leaving for Budapest nor give credence to keeping Erika: the practicalities were impossible, however sympathetic they were to her plight. Erika's parents' first reaction was to refuse to take the relationship seriously. Her father had secured the visas, they were all leaving together and that was the end of the matter.

'The couple laid siege to their respective parents with a campaign of pleading and protestation, until the families held a joint meeting. What the participants hoped to gain can only be speculated on: for Johann and Erika it was maybe to buy time and hope that a change of heart would occur; for the parents, perhaps they wanted to make up for their initial indifference to the call of young love and show that they took it seriously after all. Whatever anyone privately hoped, they would not have foreseen the solution they came up with. Somewhere along the way, amidst the arguments about practicalities and impracticalities, set against the ticking of the clock before the borders might finally be sealed, a simple but bizarre plan emerged.

'It would be the last time Erika would see her parents and the last time Johann's parents would see their son alive. They would acquire some false identity papers for Erika, then the couple would marry and move to Innsbruck and live as a normal Austrian man and wife. Erika didn't conform to any standard Jewish stereotype; Johann could pass as a poster boy for Aryan manhood. As a couple they wouldn't inspire suspicion. They could set up comfortably with money from their parents and get on with the business of being good Austrians. The universities were closing their doors, a war seemed inevitable, there was nothing to lose. Johann's parents, desperate to find a way to keep him in the country and fearful of what he might do if they barred him altogether, acquiesced. Erika's parents, although secular, had always imagined a Jewish boy for their daughter, but recognising the powerful emotions that had seized her and fearing a catastrophic misjudgement on her part if they opposed, reluctantly, although hopefully, agreed.

'Erika's parents went to Budapest, staying initially with her father's elder sister. Hungary wasn't friendly to Jews—many prominent Jews had been forced out of their positions long before 1940, when the country joined Germany and Italy as one of the Axis powers—but it wasn't persecuting them with the violence that occurred in Germany and Austria. It was relatively safe and would remain so until 1944 when Germany occupied the country in retaliation for Hungary conducting secret peace treaty talks with the United Kingdom and United States. Half a million Holocaust victims were from Hungary, including Erika's parents.

'Johann was drafted into military service a few months after the war broke out, having done what he could to delay the inevitable. He became an officer of the Wehrmacht and served as part of the occupying force in Norway before being sent to fight in the Balkans, where he was killed during a Partisan offensive in 1945—on the same day his and Erika's daughter celebrated her first birthday.

'Erika and the little girl survived the war. No one knew her in Innsbruck. She had been careful not to keep anything that would link her to her past. She was married to an army officer, a man who was fighting for the Reich and received the Knight's Cross along the way. In Nazi controlled Europe, where small mercies could be earned by selling a Jew for "resettlement," you could never be certain of being safe, but Erika carried herself with confidence and politeness, never giving cause for anyone to want to think of her as a Jew.

'Johann's reports back from Norway contained nothing of what war was capable. The worst fears hadn't materialised. Instead an almost fondness emerged, as though in gratitude for the surprisingly benign nature of what had become a foreign adventure. Where he'd expected to find military life insufferable he instead found camaraderie amongst fellow officers, most of whom were civilised, educated men, whose approval of the war sprung from a desire to see the new unified Germany win respect in the world, and much less from an endorsement of the malign aspects of Nazi politics that most seemed not particularly invested in. And since the war was going so well and would soon be over, the debate about how to get rid of the jumped up corporal-come-failed-artist who had, after all, served a useful purpose, could happily be set aside.

'It wasn't to last. Johann's death would begin a life sentence for Erika, not so much for his dying but for what happened before his death. After Norway, he went to fight in Yugoslavia alongside units comprising hardened veterans of the Polish campaign and fully signed up members of the Nazi project. He found himself in contact with SS officers, Hitler fanatics and Aryan supremacists. These men hated Jews and they hated Poles. They didn't much like Russians, Ukrainians or Lithuanians either. They enthusiastically met one another with the Hitler greeting and loved the spoils of war: money that could be made from selling the furniture of displaced or murdered Jews; gold from teeth; jewellery; clothing; anything plundered from someone else's life.

'The stories he heard were foul. Mass shootings; people, including children, herded into buildings that were then set alight, to be burned alive. He noticed that the people who told these stories divided into two types: those who relished the telling, as though permitted at last to exercise their latent bestiality; and those who told it as a horror story, fearing the judgement of the listener, anxiously describing a "dirty business" as though their involvement was accidental, reluctant, or simply arose because someone had to do it. Either way, something was normalising in the minds of these men: the more you kill, the easier it is to kill the next time.

'The Balkans became a mess of conflicting ethnicities and interests. The Germans rounded up the Jews for extermination; the Croatian Ustashe committed genocide against Serbs and Roma; the Chetniks ethnically cleansed Muslims and Croats; the Germans committed mass executions of civilians in retaliation for acts of resistance; and Yugoslav and Partisan forces carried out mass executions of collaborators and civilian refugees.

'Johann came home one leave and broke down. To be implicated was inescapable, he said. Even without putting a pistol to someone's head, which he didn't, he would be conducting searches, pulling people from their homes, burning any property deemed worthless, banishing the innocent to a fate elsewhere. He was part of a machine of war and destruction. A mad, out of control beast that rapaciously devoured, and, as it devoured, became bigger, its appetite increased and its regard to the consequences of its blood lust diminished. He would look into the eyes of his wife, the woman he loved, knowing that only a trick of circumstance made him her protector rather than her murderer.

'After the war, when the world no longer doubted the scale of Nazi atrocities, when the Nuremberg trials placed on record the excuses made by the perpetrators of history's worst crimes against humanity, Erika became haunted by the thought of Johann's complicity. She knew him as a peaceful, compassionate person, one who had been caught up in a maelstrom in which no sane person could survive without having to make some bargain with their conscience. But it wasn't enough. The mere knowledge of his involvement, however reluctant, however far removed from the firing squad or the gas chamber, drove stakes of shame into her already grief stricken heart. As a Jew she could have been excused the need to share the nation's shame, but as the secret Jewish wife and lover of an officer of the Reich, a woman who knew of the evil being done but who went on with her daily life regardless, she felt like a traitor. In common with millions of Germans and Austrians she would not talk about it. As her daughter grew up, Erika would speak only of the girl's father having died in the war. The link to previous generations was severed. The girl was denied a father by the war and denied a memory of a father by a stain of guilt that even the innocent could not escape.'

Victor stops and stares at me with a look that makes me shudder. Am I touched by this guilt? Am I responsible because I have allowed myself to be bought? Is that where he's going?

I tell them I need a cigarette and go to the balcony. It's dark now, but some light still glints off the river. Natalie joins me and shares a weak smile. It seems an odd thing to do. It's like the smile you give to someone who's lost a loved one.

'History's a bitch,' she says, and turns the smile into the kind of laugh that's meant to break the tension. I'm tense because I still don't know how my art fits in. The history is interesting but peripheral. I know enough already without listening to Victor's favourite stories.

'I think I'm worn down with it,' I say.

'They're a bit relentless, the Nazis,' says Natalie, 'but there's more,' she adds, and this time fixes me with a look that tells me to stay the course, that my attention will be rewarded.

Cigarette finished we go back inside. Victor speaks again, this time adopting a lighter tone, as though mindful of my wearying mood.

'Erika moved to the UK after the war. Her aunt, Agnes, her father's eldest sister, survived and managed to find her. Agnes had a daughter, who, in turn, had a son, Béla. That side of the family was about half a generation older than Erika's.

'Agnes also had a son, who'd fled to England just before the start of the war, fell in love, almost on arrival, with a British Jewish woman. He joined the RAF but was killed in 1940 although not before he fathered a son.' Victor breaks off for a moment and looks at me. I furrow my brow and shrug. 'The son won a scholarship,' he continues, 'to St Catharine's, Cambridge, and did a law degree.'

It connects. Like a punch to the solar plexus. I breathlessly spoon out the next words: 'Your father. So Agnes's son was killed at Debden airfield; your grandfather.'

Victor claps his hands. 'You have paid attention.'

I relax, glad Victor's family saga has reached a conclusion, the intricacies of which I was beginning to struggle with.

'There's more,' he says. 'Béla is Nina's great uncle, the man who was killed on the far bank. He was the second cousin to Erika's daughter, but twelve years older and, although part of the same family, they weren't of much interest to one another growing up. Béla made a success of his career in advertising, and a failure of his first marriage. As part of the fallout from this, he withdrew from the family, and at some point fell out with Father, after which he seemed lost to us. Later he met up again with Erika's daughter, now grown up and also largely peripheral within the family, having gone to university and chosen to mostly detach herself from Jewish society. It was a union that would make sense to people who didn't know them: both outsiders; he, the paternal figure she'd craved; she, the young woman who would reignite his zest for life. Perhaps unsurprisingly they ended up together and had a daughter.

'My memories of Béla are sketchy, ending in the early 1970s when I was still only nine or ten, the time he more or less vanished from our lives. He was taller than Father and louder. He seemed to have an opinion on everything and he was always immaculately turned out. I missed him when he was gone and I think my fastidiousness is something I owe to him. When he was murdered in 1978 it hit me hard, indeed all of us, Father included. We expected him to return to the fold one day, we thought his absence was temporary and waited with open arms allowing the time to be of his choosing.

'His wife held a small, very private funeral. She told Father we weren't welcome, that our interest in him was too late. At the time I thought this was cruel and unfair, vengeful even, but as I grew up I realised it arose from grief and loyalty, as though to spurn the family he had retreated from was the final gesture of her love for him. As far as I know, Father never met her again. I know I never did, although I did receive a small gift he'd willed to me, a simple act that has held me in his bond ever since.

'There was correspondence, apparently, in which she would exchange matter-of-fact details to do with life's events such as forwarding a new address or some cursory report on her daughter's progress. But there was never any discernible warmth. One day she died. She was in her fifties and had a heart attack, an event reported to Father by her solicitor several weeks later. He established that the daughter was taken care of financially—she was an adult by then—and, satisfied that she was, he closed the book, as it were. Until now.'

Victor is looking at me with some sort of intent, while I ruminate in the wake of a story that contains the sadness and familiarity of many diaspora tales. Natalie moves closer, stretching her limbs.

'Erika's daughter was called Naomi,' he says. I smile. It's good to have a name for her at last—a detail I felt was missing from the story up until now—but I also feel a wince of pain at the coincidence of it being my mother's name. It heightens the sadness somehow. But the smile dies at the sight of Victor and Natalie looking at me, eyes sparkling, mouths open.

My spine freezes, my face locks and all I can do is say, feebly, 'That was my mother's name.'

How did I not see it coming? After the expletives are uttered and the disbelief fades, once the tears have rolled and a semblance of calm descends, I find myself warmed and slightly detached, like I've taken too much codeine. I am a part of this scene and separate; here and not here; this is my life and it isn't; everything has crashed, but it seems to have crashed beautifully.

But still there's more, Victor tells me. There has to be, of course. There has to be an endless amount more, an infinity of who I am, who I am now for heaven's sake. God, this is weird. No, weird doesn't begin to describe it.

I've started shaking. Natalie reaches for my hand and I yield, inviting her touch, welcoming the embrace that follows. It feels like I'm hugging someone different from who she was minutes ago. It's the same person transformed; the angle of approach changed from outside to inside. Everything has changed, though materially we're the same.

'Your father wasn't murdered just because he was Jewish, possibly not because he was Jewish at all,' says Victor. 'He was meeting someone. The river was his favourite rendezvous in those days. The Common was too common, he liked to say. Whoever killed him stuck a Star of David to his breast, but that may have been a secondary or compounding consideration, maybe even to throw the police in the wrong direction. The case wasn't solved and I have no idea what line the investigation took or whether the police were ever close to finding the killer.

'I am quite sure your mother knew he was gay. I think we all did, and it was certainly implied by the tone of her communication after his death. My belief is that she'd always known. She wasn't a conventional woman in any sense, as I'm sure you will remember, and marrying a gay man would have suited her. After the failure of his first marriage to a woman who most definitely did not know—with consequences that were, in the end, inevitable—to be loved by a woman who not only knew but embraced the idea, was almost too good to be true. Each of them found a security in the other. It was still a marriage of convenience from his viewpoint but he didn't have to hide within it. She gave him a love he would never have got from any other woman and, as far as we can tell, never received from any man.'

I feel lightheaded and reach for the tabletop to steady myself. Natalie reinvigorates her attentions, rubbing my hand as though I'm a hypothermia victim. It works, in the sense that it makes me laugh. I glance into her eyes, which are now soft and watery.

'It's a lot to take in,' she says.

'Oh, I don't know,' I say, feeling giddy but stubbornly forbearing, 'so you two are my cousins, my father was gay and murdered right over there, my Grandfather fought for the Third Reich, and I'm apparently of Austrian descent and Jewish and have been all my life without knowing. Is that all?'

'You missed out the ancestors killed in the Holocaust,' says Victor. He's serious, though uncritical, and he brings a blush to my face.

'Of course,' I say. We're back to the project. For a few moments it was all about me, but now it's all about them again: the gone, the vanquished, the murdered, the desecrated, the annihilated.

'Victor!' says Natalie. He feigns hurt at the admonishment and breaks into a smile.

'We'll talk about that tomorrow,' he says, and reaches to hug me. He's not much of a hugger, but although it feels awkward, I hold on after he starts to let go. So he hugs me again, this time deeper and warmer—the embrace of the lost and found.

Chapter Fourteen

I don't sleep well and give up trying at 4.00 a.m. Exhausted, I make coffee, light a cigarette and go up to my studio. The trees on the far bank are silhouetted against the light polluted haze of the sky, the bank itself a shadowed blackness. I gaze hard into its depths as though to conjure the moment my father was knifed to death. My father? It's hard to make the connection. Knowing it and feeling it are not the same. I knew nothing of him, and now, knowing something, he remains, still, more a concept than an entity. Maybe it will change. There's so much to get used to and I'm old enough to know this won't be straightforward. I sip the coffee, which is thick and comforting, and catch myself enjoying the irony of my life thrown into flux, just as I'd reached an age I'd begun to think nothing much would change.

I suck at the cigarette, draw the smoke down deep and exhale. The first of the day is always the best—but it's so early this feels like the last of the previous day. I look at the cigarette and the coffee, drugs to get me up and running. I jab the end of the cigarette into the ashtray in anger. I'm gassing myself. Why make it easy for them? I'll quit.

After Victor and Natalie left, I went in search of Alex and found him sitting among a mess of papers. Hearing me enter the room he told me they were ready to begin shooting, but then he looked up and saw me.

'My God, what happened up there?'

'You won't believe it.'

At first he didn't. Not literally, which is to say he didn't think Natalie and Victor were making it up, but it took a lot to convince him they'd got their facts right. Maybe it was his habitual rigour, or a protective instinct, but it seemed he maintained the inquisition long after he knew it was true.

'Fuck,' he said at last, raising his eyebrows with a theatricality that said exactly how much of a fuck it really was. Then he added, 'so this means you're Jewish?'

Neither of us, we're sure, has uttered an anti-semitic word in our lives, so that's one hurdle we don't have to face. In truth, I'm unsure Jews or Jewishness had featured much in our thoughts until I began working on Victor and Natalie's project. But Alex's question is one I'd been pushing to the back of my mind.

'According to Hitler I'm Jewish enough to be exterminated.'

'According to you?'

'You know what?' I said, 'we're talking about whether or not I'm Jewish, but not whether I'm Austrian or Hungarian, both of which now have claims on me. Why is that?'

'Because we make it so?' He shrugged. He knew it was one of his obvious and literal non-responses, but something about the phrase tugged at the back of my mind, dragging out the memory of when Victor first talked to me about human nature.

'Because we make it so.' I echoed back without the question mark. He probably assumed I was being sarcastic, but he reached out to me, inviting me to sit with him. I could see he was working on some flippant, deflective comment and I hoped he'd resist. I scowled and his mood changed.

'Is it because ethnicity is more important to who we think we are than nationality?'

I smiled and accepted his arm around my shoulder.

'It can be more visible I suppose,' I said, 'but that doesn't explain it. I've always ticked the white British box, and maybe that wouldn't change even if I decided to be Jewish. Jews can be invisible, as Erika proved: as a white person I am always visible, as a Jew I have been invisible even to myself.'

Alex called it a 'mind fuck' and talked about an 'identity crisis.' He's half right, it feels like both of those things. But he couldn't put into words what it really is, which is no surprise since neither can I. It's too soon. I want it all to make perfect sense, but fear there will never be any sense at all.

'My life has been recast,' I said, 'and it's the weirdest feeling. As if I'm in my own biopic and been told my motivation has to change because they've rewritten the backstory.'

Alex leaned back, pulling his arm away. I knew what he was thinking: will this change me? But I don't think he knew how to broach it, or even dared to. Perhaps he knows I can't begin to give him an answer.

We talked a while longer before going to bed. We made love, as though that would fortify our defences against whatever might come. He was especially tender, more than usually concerned for my part in the proceedings, which could mean he feels some threat, or that the trajectory he's been on since quitting the bank has taken another turn upwards. But he has nothing to fear, there's no threat to him, and I told him so.

I look at the extinguished cigarette butt. There's a change, I say to myself, wondering immediately if it really is. Can I give up? Do I want to or was it just a whim of the moment, a neat thought, an urge to exercise some new power, to test some part of my new persona?

I stare at the river, slow and low, its eddies picked out in the reflected light. The tide has only just turned, a time when the water is said to be slack, although close up it is anything but, its discreet turbulence anticipating the flood of the incoming tide.

If I watch the river through to dawn, then past sunrise and into the morning, will things resolve? Even a little? Will I decide if I'm happy or sad or will I just continue being tired? Do I want this new family? Do I want to be Jewish?

Do I have a choice? What about Palestine? I've always thought a separate Palestinian state is desirable and Israel should get out of the West Bank—as much as I've ever thought about it, I now realise—but will that change? Am I who I am simply as a result of where I am and how I came to be? Alex would ride reason over the top of it all, invoking objectivity and rationality as weapons against arbitrariness and accident, but who is he kidding, how far along the evolutionary scale does he really think we've come? He was a banker for twenty years for God's sake, feeding off the entirely non-rational tendencies of our species.

Relax. Things will fall into place. Why do I believe that? Is it the absence of an existential threat? Is it a first world privilege to feel secure in the world, or is it a misplaced entitlement based on a complacent illusion? Are we desensitised to danger after decades of prosperity, sure that our superior way of life is under control and unchallengeable? Are we blind to the signs of reversal that are visible if we only want to look?

What of Victor and Natalie? Are they to become a new permanence in my life? I like them well enough, but do I want the commitment? I shrug and turn away from the window and head to the kitchen to make another cup of coffee. If I'm to give up smoking I'll have to double the coffee intake. I can't live drug free, plus I need to reward myself and, on that score, more chocolate and a few bottles of fine wine wouldn't go amiss.

Nina. Now there's a thought and one I'm surprised not to have fretted over already. As I wait for the machine to deliver the next shot, I recollect when she was last here with Natalie and how she'd been disappointed when her mother chose to put off telling me. Nina must have known, but for how long? She wanted to be part of the conversation that told me we were related. Dear child, it was to be a big moment for her.

When Victor and Natalie turn up mid-morning they enter the house with the briefest of greetings. No small talk. Smiles are forced. There's a brittleness in the air. I excuse myself by offering to make drinks and send them up to the studio. I hear them pass Alex on the stairs; the contrast between his friendly hello and their courteous but clipped response makes me flush with embarrassment.

He finds me in the kitchen and asks if something's wrong. I say I don't know.

'Could it be something you said yesterday?'

'No.' I stare hard at him.

'Maybe something you didn't realise, something that took a while for them to process.'

I throw my arms up; my continuing stare tells him the answer is still no.

'Pass me the milk.'

He does, plus the tray, the unsolicited offer of which is his contrition. I smile sarcastically, assemble the drinks and head upstairs.

As I enter the studio, they swing round towards me with rather too eager smiles, the kind that appear on faces following the curtailment of a private exchange.

'What's up?' I say, as matter of fact as I can. They look at each other but neither speaks. 'I can leave you to it if you like.'

'I'm sorry,' says Natalie, 'for our rudeness.' She looks at Victor as if to check that he's a willing party to the apology.

'Perhaps you can help us,' he says.

Welcome to the family, I think.

It's about Nina. One of the reasons for her wanting to be my model was that she hoped it would attract her father's attention. This is news to me and, apparently, Victor also. Natalie doesn't believe it will work, but has never seen any harm in allowing Nina to believe in the possibility, especially because she has so much to gain from the project in other ways. Victor sees no benefit in raising

Nina's expectations, although, curiously, believes in the possibility of it working.

'I'm not raising her expectations,' says Natalie, 'I'm just not crushing her dream.'

'You don't believe in her dream, but you think it's okay to indulge it.'

'How many times? I'm not indulging it. But I'm not going to create a rift between my daughter and me by denigrating something important to her.'

'You don't have to "denigrate" it, just prepare her for the possibility of it not happening. And if it does happen, it's all the more wonderful.'

'It won't happen.'

'You can't be so certain.'

'I can.'

'You're prejudiced against him.'

'With good cause.'

Natalie turns to me. She tells me that what I've heard is the third repeat of a now futile discussion.

'He won't listen.'

'I'm fed up of listening,' says Victor.

They look at each other, then switch their attention to me. But the tension seems to be receding. Maybe three repeats is what it takes to burn itself out. Eventually Natalie asks me what I think.

A scintilla of the past splices the present and crystallises in my mind. Everything descends, converges and breaks apart. I burst into tears. Irresistible eruptions of something I had no idea of. Victor and Natalie start apologising although they surely can't know what for. I hear them scolding themselves, until the noise in my head overwhelms and I convulse, submerged beneath a deep wail.

I'm torn. I fight it but I submit to it. I want it out but I want it put back. Slowly some control returns. Victor and Natalie come back into focus. They look horrified; they don't know what to do or what they did. It's not what you said, I try to say. I form words but they don't all come out. I tell them that Nina will always want her father to come good, that she will never give up the hope unless there's no reason to hope.

'Like, if he's dead,' I say, and break down again.

What is it about the past? Why can't it stay the fuck where it is? Did I say that, or just think it? Natalie revolves around me like a nervous nanny, inspecting, touching, withdrawing. I don't know what she expects to find. Her concern is sincere but I wish she would sit down.

'Work,' says Victor.

Natalie looks at him reproachfully, but I feel uplifted at the thought. He's either read me perfectly or, quite by accident, his insensitivity has chimed with what I need.

He's anxious to find out if my feelings towards the project have changed. I don't know—there could be so many answers—but the one thing I do know, which I'm sure he's driving at, is that my desire to complete feels more urgent than ever.

'I want to weave a thread that starts with the Nazis and runs to human nature and the world we live in,' I announce, as if I'm reading out some promo blurb, the words in my head sounding tinny and inadequate. 'Although I'd already decided that,' I add, as though to compensate for stating the obvious. They look at me kindly. 'Before all this,' I say, finally, and wave my arm in the air as if the air is the thing in question.

Victor takes a breath, which means he's preparing to speak at length, presumably about human nature. Natalie sees it too and interjects to ask me what exactly I have in mind.

She's cleared the way for me and it pushes me on to make the most of it. So I test my working theory, one I'm hopeful will dovetail with Victor's beliefs, which, instinctively, I've always shared, but now more consciously: that human nature is fixed and universal; that is to say, across all cultures, nationalities and races, people exhibit the same distribution of innate characteristics. You can't say all people are the same because they aren't, but you can say, for example, that on average all people in the northern hemisphere are the same as people in the southern hemisphere. Or, to put it more pertinently, in relation to the subject at hand, Jews are, on average, the same as gentiles. Or Germans. Or Aryans. And so on. The implication being that different circumstances bring out different conglomerations of the facets of human nature. Stability and abundance give rise to peace and love; chaos and scarcity to insecurity and hatred. Insecurity leads to fight or flight, a division into persecutors and the persecuted, the evil and the damned. There are cultural practices that grow independently, but all are consistent with one underlying human nature.

I've hardly looked up, partly out of concentration, partly not daring, but I see Victor and Natalie are on board so far. I take a breath, the hint of panic fluttering in my chest, and steady myself. I don't know what I'm so nervous of. I'm sure they won't debate the fundamentals. Maybe a shift in emphasis, a question of degree or nuance, an addition or subtraction of detail, but not a clash of principles. Have the stakes got higher because they are now family? Am I sucked into some weird relationship where I need the approval of a mother and father? Which is absurd, since Natalie is close to my age.

I resume by saying that if you look at the Nazi era through the psychology of the separate actors whose lives coincided at that point in history, you can explain things in ways that can't be explained by focusing purely on events, or following straight lines of cause and effect. Practically every element necessary for genocide coalesced in a deadly mix that contained all the failings and weaknesses of the human species. Circumstance met human nature and found it wanting.

Almost nobody wanted a war, but they got one, and fifty million people died. Nobody other than a small group of ideologically driven fanatics wanted the mass extermination of civilians, but that's what happened. Nobody wanted the wholesale laying to waste of towns and cities, the wilful destruction of millions of buildings and items of infrastructure, but once it was underway they were helpless to stop it. No soldier wanted to be the one who pulled a trigger to fire a bullet into a young girl's brain, but few tasked with the job refused. By 1944 only a vanishingly few people still believed in Hitler, but millions carried out his orders until the bitter end.

Psychologists talk of an empathy bypass to describe the process by which a person who normally cares for other people, ceases to do so. Triggers include vengeance, fear and disgust. The conditioning necessary includes ignorance, demonisation and dehumanisation. Propaganda prepares the ground through myth-making and local leaders provide the trigger through rabble rousing. People's fears are played on and they start to believe things because they want or need to.

People need to believe any harm they do can be justified. They will also believe any harm done to them is a wrong to be avenged. Thus everyone carries around a predisposition to believe that if they do a bad thing it is an aberration committed by an essentially good person whereas the bad things done to them are motivated by evil.

Pure evil is something of a myth. Most genocidal ideologues are just that: ideologically driven. A morally deplorable act—one you or I would describe as evil—is, to them, committed in service to a moral purpose.

Empathy erodes even where it isn't bypassed. Desensitisation occurs with repeat exposure to extreme conditions and a corrupt moral purpose becomes a routine even to people who take no sadistic pleasure in administering pain. Those who are sadists find that their pleasure circuits become ever more aroused as their victim tally mounts.

We can all switch off empathy and do it more often that we care to think. At one level there is the widespread anger at a terrorist atrocity, which mushrooms into an infectious desire for a bloody vengeance against anyone associated with the perpetrators, often on the grounds they share a religion or nationality. But it also happens at a mundane, everyday level when people get angry towards the people they are close to, or even love the most: in families; between couples; among friends.

Once the empathy circuit has blown its fuse, the most hurtful things may be said and done, only to be unsaid or, with luck, undone, once empathy returns. There are only a tiny number of people who are truly psychopathic, but the capability for something akin to a temporary rush of psychopathology lies below the surface in all of us, and may not be so deeply buried as we would admit or recognise.

It's in our nature, and there is no one immune to fear, anger, jealousy, or envy and nor is there anyone who can't feel outrage at becoming a victim of injustice. We identify 'in' groups and 'out' groups, and since we are prone to bouts of insensitivity to the people we supposedly care most about—our favourite 'in' people—it can hardly be a surprise that we can become utterly desensitised to the welfare of anyone on the 'out' side.

And when we hurt other people, we find ways of excusing ourselves. We rewrite the history to retrofit the facts to accommodate our view of ourselves as moral agents. The other person becomes deserving of the treatment we meted out, as though they brought it on themselves.

We are weak; we lack self-control. You put a human being in a situation where he or she perceives danger, either real or imagined, and fear becomes the driver. People quickly make up their minds how to stay safe in the face of a threat and a nobility of spirit is not always what we offer up.

Safety in numbers is an age-old survival strategy. Conform to the prevailing pattern. It's a great recipe for not standing out and becoming a target, but also a sure way for people to become trapped in an ideology that few agree with individually—thus, perversely, adding to its momentum. We admire people who act bravely, who put their welfare or lives on the line, but are as likely to consider them fools if they fail and suffer the consequences.

The darkest spectrum of our psychologies will not evolve away in the timeframe necessary to save us from a catastrophe of our own making. They are the same psychologies that have been present uninterrupted for thousands of years, and if the world is generally, on a day by day basis, a less violent and more civilised place now than hundreds or thousands of years ago, it isn't because human nature has advanced.

Why are we so poor at seeing ahead? Why do we fall for the myth when the truth isn't difficult to find? Why couldn't those Nazi enthusiasts see where it might be going before they were conscripted into the actuality of blowing out the brains of fellow human beings?

We know they hated it. Soldiers would vomit at their actions. They would defecate involuntarily. They turned to drink. They committed suicide. SS Task Force leaders complained that it was all too much for their men to stomach, and yet it was the logical end to an ideology many of them bought into willingly.

For those who were inured, who had learned to deal with it as an everyday occurrence, there was compensation in that it kept them out of the front line. Given the choice over which end of the gun to stand, few would choose the pointy one. Better to march others to the death pits, there to hold the pistol, hear its crack, see the fractal bursts of blood tracing the air and the bubbling final pulse in the blasted head before the victim falls into the pile of grey, dead corpses—former beings who breathed and thought and had lives only moments before, now carnage. Evil and alive, or innocent and dead? It's a basic calculation.

So, it isn't you, or us, and for that we are grateful. But a realignment of the wheels of history and it could be.

Then there was the other sort, the believers, the nobodies who had been given power and had taken up barbarity with zeal, for whom mercilessness became a joy. Were they the ones who would joke about the road to heaven, while herding the doomed, still pathetically hopeful, women and children into the 'showers', and who then sealed the doors and waited to hear the useless screams as the gas dropped?

There was no secret about the Nazi agenda. They were the superior race and the list of undesirables was long: in addition to Jews, Poles, Roma Gypsies and any other non Aryan race, you can add welfare recipients, the disabled, homosexuals, communists, freemasons and any religious group who refused to place Nazi ideology on a higher pedestal than their own deities.

Once you define the superior race you create a cast of inferiors. For some comes a sense of being magically promoted to an elevated vantage point in society. An ideology that excludes everyone else becomes a warm embrace, a sacrament to the soul, something to fight and kill for. And for others, those not so needy or credulous, once you know you are a member of the approved classification, life is easier and safer if you succumb than if you resist.

The pattern repeats wherever you find genocide in history. The slaughtered are reduced to a category; the dominant group sees the weaker one as subhuman. The list of genocide and mass murder locations in modern history is long and wide: Cambodia, Rwanda, Burundi, Bosnia, Soviet Union, Croatia, Southern Africa, Haiti, Dominican Republic, Guatemala, Mexico, Peru, China, Tasmania, North America, Argentina, Ethiopia, Democratic Republic of Congo, South West Africa, Japan, Laos, Australia, New Zealand, North Korea, Armenia, Assyria, Kurdistan, Greece, Bangladesh, Equatorial Guinea, East Timor, West New Guinea, Iraq. Add in actions that are against international humanitarian law, or in breach of human rights, and you implicate nearly every place on the planet. Human inhumanity knows no boundaries because human nature is everywhere. It is an inescapable reality that we are a flawed, semi-evolved species, wired for violence.

Natalie's eyes have encouraged me all the way through: she has nodded and smiled and everything in her manner has suggested she is pleased. Victor has grown more still, more withdrawn, his features coalescing into a frown that but for Natalie's warmth and support would have undermined my confidence. I look at him. Natalie notices and turns to him.

'I know I used the E word: empathy.' I say, and laugh. I'm about to say that I tried to think of alternatives and they all gave rise to horrendous convolutions so I gave up, but he cuts in.

'It's okay,' he says, and waves a hand like he's batting away a fly. He breaths out, touches his cuffs in turn and looks up, as if from a daze. I don't fill the silence and neither does Natalie. We watch him gather his thoughts. My stomach tightens.

'The scale of it,' he says, 'it's impossible.' He stops and I want to ask him, 'What scale? Why impossible?' but I hold back. He's struggling with something. Let him breath, I say to myself.

'I had such high hopes,' he says, 'as if I could change the world, but it can't be done.'

And that's it. He relaxes back into his chair as if the last several months have been nothing more than a day trip, and having finished the picnic we load up the car and go back home.

I'm flabbergasted. My head is so full of questions and doubts and theories as to why he should shut down like this that I'm unable to put any words together. I sense Natalie flinch, as if jumping out of her own logjam.

'Where has this "I" come from?' Now she's out of her chair and pointing at him, her face twitching. 'Sylvia's doing all the work and bloody good work too.' She mimics him: '"If I could change the world"—who do you think you are? The world was never going to change for you, so snap out of it. We,' she puts a stress on the word, 'have plenty more work to do, so park the self pity and let's get on with it.'

Victor emits what appears to be a small chuckle. I glance at Natalie who rolls her eyes and sits with a thump. He looks up at me and across to her.

'I think we've illustrated Sylvia's point,' he says.

'Did she make a point about grown men acting like children? I think I missed it,' says Natalie. She looks severe. She folds her arms and looks at me as if to say, don't let him off this hook.

'I was naïve,' he says, 'it's my biggest failing.'

Natalie's jaw drops; she can obviously think of bigger ones. But the look on Victor's face reveals that he hung that one out for her. She sees it, grimaces and looks back at me.

I move to Victor and place a hand on his shoulder. He leans his head into it then takes my hand in his. We know it seems so vast, we know we won't change the world and we know that if someone picks on some detail and casts a malicious spin, it might become the story that vanquishes ours and turns our project to dust.

'It will look like a giant vanity project,' he says. 'What was I thinking, filming a set up in which I could have been killed? The narcissism.' He drops his shoulders.

'Is it a vanity project?' says Natalie. She looks at him steadily, without a trace of accusation or comfort, and leaves the question suspended as if above him, as though our future might turn on his verdict.

It's a question that's never occurred to me. In all my dealings with Victor, from the mysterious beginnings when I found myself pledging a faith in spite of the warnings from Alex, through to his stunt on the riverbank when Alex ran to his rescue at risk to himself, I have always believed Victor is altruistic, that every sacrifice is to a valiant cause.

'No.' I hear the word, so simple and stark against the silence of the room. It is the answer, the one I was hoping for, the one I hope will bring him back from the brink of whatever doubting place he's gone to. I see him looking at me, moisture collecting in the well of his soft, kind eyes and I break from my daydream to realise that I said it, I uttered the word, the response on behalf of us all to Natalie's question.

'Thank you,' he says.

Before he can say anything else I find myself speaking again. It's one of those moments the words erupt from within, when they carry you without the need for you to think. It's when months of thinking and researching and working meet the moment when everything falls into place and you know at last that you have it.

I find myself telling them I want an exhibition. That I want my artworks alongside their museum pieces, but on a large scale, preferably in a disused Victorian warehouse or factory, the more forgotten the better. I want the claustrophobic airiness, the clank and echo of long gone history. I want brickwork and cast iron and dark, shadowy atmospherics, suggestive of the clatter of trains, ghettoes, buildings used for murder.

I want a budget, a big one. Sound, lighting, video booths, light boxes, panels, plinths, cases. And I need a team to mount the exhibition: professionals, experts, people who can make the whole thing work.

We need a strategy for getting people to come. We don't want a big preview launch and have nobody turn up, or a press call with no press. We have to put the word out that we have something that matters. False modesty aside, my name isn't a big enough draw, the promotion has to be about what we are trying to say, what Natalie and Victor, as sponsors, hope to achieve. People have to know it's a unique event, and important. And that there's a free bar.

I look at them. Victor has perked up; Natalie looks thoughtful. Have I stretched the line too far? How far am I straying from whatever they had in mind? Is it different now I'm family? Would I have dared say it if I still wasn't?

I was out, now I'm in, and everything has changed.

'That's more or less how we were seeing it,' says Victor, a grin radiating towards me like sun rising on the horizon.

'We knew you'd get there,' says Natalie.

Fucking hell, these people are annoying.

It turns out they weren't entirely 'seeing it' like that, but what they had been waiting for was the day I would turn from employee into partner. Unfortunately, the way they described it—as if it was some inevitability they'd predicted based on my psychological profile—is to make me feel just that again: an employee.

But the feeling passes. I tell them I need to concentrate on the work. I feel like I've worked blind until now, sensing my way but seeing nothing, hoping things will connect or can be made to connect, fearing being left with a mess of images and abstractions that crave attention but mean nothing. I need Victor and Natalie to handle the organisational side and I find myself telling them to get on with it.

'It's understood,' says Natalie, 'don't worry about a thing.' She smiles like it's a relief I've taken charge. I almost hear a 'yes, ma'am' in the brisk manner of her delivery. She wheels around sharply, crisp and controlled, ready for action, and, for a joyous few hours after her and Victor have left, I do stop worrying.

I spend an hour reorganising the studio, preparing the space for the next phase of work, assembling materials, drafting a plan with target dates for the completion of each piece. I start drafting a preliminary floor plan for the exhibition, when Alex pops his head round the door.

'Come in,' I say, 'I think I'm ahead now.'

I fold the paper, my surge of optimism still intact, and look back at Alex. His face tells a different story. He settles in a chair, lips pursed.

'There won't be a documentary,' he says. 'No one wants it.'

'Legal issues?'

'Not entirely,' he shrugs and heaves out the next words. 'Political issues.'

He tells me people are scared. They fear the disappearance of revenue, the change in the regulatory framework, the disapproval of vested interests.

'The powerful are free to express their opinions and have them transmitted the length and breadth of the land,' he says, 'the weak are obliged to exercise their freedom of expression in places where no one will hear them.'

'You think of yourself as weak?'

A look of sufferance flashes across his face and he nods. 'I guess so,' he says, his voice falling off at the end, the last syllable stretched and fading. One of the kings of the market, a man on the inside and invulnerable, now outside and impotent. Having enough money isn't even enough.

'What if…' I say, and the moment I do he looks at me like he's read my thought. By the look on his face it's what he wants to hear, so I tell him.

After we've thrashed the idea around for a while we agree on two things: that I will bring Alex's documentary into my exhibition; and alongside it will be a film about its failure, a representation of the voicelessness and invisibility of ordinary people. He winces at being described as ordinary, but the chastening experience of the last few months leaves him with little choice than to face the fact.

'The film is more important because you can't sell it; the fact you can't sell it becomes its point,' I say.

Alex is impressed with my logic. I'm getting the hang of this. I could have been awesome in another life.

The tendency to worry returns the following day as I contemplate the arrival of Nina. I'm weirdly nervous about meeting her. I keep examining myself in the mirror, rehearsing how it might go. I think of myself as a soloist at the Royal Albert Hall waiting for a performance, repeating rituals that only ratchet up the tension. But what am I really worried about? It can't be that the relationship will suddenly sour or that she will want to put distance between us. Something has changed, even though nothing has, so what is it? I crave some kind of instant self-therapy to untangle the knot of emotions that hold me now, immobilised and ready to retch, but I've no idea how to find it.

If ever I needed a cigarette or a drink or to go for a brisk walk it is now, but I'm going to resist the first two and the third isn't possible since she's due any minute.

I hear the doorbell.

As soon as I see her I realise she's different. She's quieter, more shy, more like the girl I was led to expect in the first place. We speak our hellos over each other. I take her to the living room and then change my mind and take her to the kitchen where I make a drink. She starts to sit then doesn't and I tell her she can sit if she wants so she does. I pour her an orange juice and ask if she wants ice, even though I'd long since given up asking because she always says no.

There are half smiles that hang uncertainly until our eyes meet, when they flicker briefly before tightening again. Items of small talk get repeated and then apologised for. It's not just me I realise, although I can't think why she would be so nervous. Eventually, having made myself a coffee, I sit down.

'Aunt. Sylvia.' She breaks into a giggle.

'Weird, isn't it?' I say.

We look at one another, measuring something of ourselves as we do so. There's a glorious charm about the following silence, broken only by the rustle of our clothes as we shift waiting for the conversation to begin.

Somewhere in the art, in our story, in the relationship we already have, is now the possibility of something greater and permanent. I've grown to cherish her as a child and friend and have been gifted her as a blood relative. I was mentor and nurturer before I was family member. I saw her talent and beauty before it became an obligation. Now that the quirks of history have brought us to this point, I realise I am wishing for her to love me as I do her.

'Let's do some work,' I say. I blurt it out and get to my feet. I have surprised myself and, by the look on her face, Nina too, but she jumps up ready to follow. 'You know something?' I say, and she looks at me eager and smiling, almost laughing, 'I couldn't be happier.'

'Me neither,' she says, and we walk up to the studio arm in arm.

The subsequent days become weeks, become months, become one day after another and all so similar—except for the weather and the river—that I find myself forever unable to name the day of the week. Holidays are junked and social engagements refused. I hardly watch the TV or read a newspaper. My daily walk is always the exact same circular route—up river, across Barnes Bridge, down river, across Hammersmith Bridge, up river and home—so I don't have to think where I'm going, I just go and think about what I'm doing, have done, will do. The schedule of works.

I notice one thing about myself. When I began my research into the Nazis the facts were utterly horrific, so visceral, and so vile, I would shake with anger and cry with pity, shocked at the pictures—some from contemporary photographs, some burning in my imagination—and uncomprehending that human beings, so many of them, could be harnessed in service to such barbarity. Now, as I work with those images, turning them into what I hesitate to call art, all the time trying to capture on the face of the murderer and the murdered the thought that hangs within, I am slipping past outrage and into numbness.

I fear doing a disservice: that as my temper cools the work will lose force. Victor disagrees, seeing an essential objectivity. He points to the picture of Nazi soldiers smashing babies against the trees.

'If all you felt was rage, you wouldn't have caught the guilt and terror on the faces of the soldiers. They are damned and they know it. They've crossed over and if they survive the war they'll never be able to come back. Their evil is their defeat, and you've found that. It's where your picture captures truth and gains its power.'

Calming, supportive words and I'm grateful, but maybe it's depression driving me. Driving me insane? Am I emotionally stunted, at least to anything external? Is everything out there now a blur, the only focus the hurt I feel inside? Have I taken in the sorrow and the pity of it all, and begun some bizarre collaboration in which my mind merges with the whole murderous hell until it becomes normal? Have I withdrawn my feelings, retracted them to some deep, inner point within, the depression a blanket drawn over me to dull the sharpness of pain, rendering it a non-locatable ache?

Is this how it works, is this internalisation? Am I expressing myself in ways that reflect a cold eye and a subliminal heart?

Slowly, as I work on, I find I'm bringing a new control to what I do, a sense that my work is more precise and the chaos of human contradiction and suffering is landing on the canvas in ways that seem naturally right. Is a numbed soul the pre-requisite for a perfect execution?

I'm growing more confident that what is in my head is coming out in the work, and to realise that the momentum, which has stopped and started in fits, is now rolling steadily and gathering speed. It's what I have wished for my whole career: to feel the work pouring out as though it is producing itself; through me instead of by me. Days pass, the depression that had threatened to sink me, turns to euphoria. I work on quickly, obsessively, desperate to capitalise, fearing that this swim of intoxication will shut down and leave me alone again, dependent on the prosaic and mortal skill of poor little me.

Do I now experience the past not as a neutral, but as someone nearer the front line? Am I constructing this edifice of art as a protection against a fear that has hitherto been general and now feels located, specific, targeted? I'm the same me, the same human being, the same human being as all the other human beings on this planet; my identity, as an artist, defined by choices and accidents, not by evolution or biology. But I've been changed, the identity switch has been thrown for me and I'm cast into a different category.

I'm working on the moments when Germans switched from one category to another, like the realisation that the Nazi party they'd once waved flags for had turned their lives to hell; that Hitler's promises had turned to shit; that the maelstrom of fear they'd helped create, now held them in its grip as surely as their enemies; and, though they could barely utter it to themselves, and though the blame would slither like an eel through decades, it was all their fault.

Was the pre-War rhetoric about Jewish annihilation fervently remembered by the soldier firing a bullet into a child's head?

Not all Germans, of course, but the ones who were sucked in, who bought the lies, who cheered the land grabs, the war, the persecutions even; the ones who had no idea where it would end because they were sold the idea of a master race that couldn't lose. They had it thrust on them —the dream of a fantasist, a failure in a previous life, a fanatical distorter of truth and narcissistic bully. A man who would be considered inadequate in most walks of life. But, as historians point out: no Hitler, no Holocaust. So how stupid does that make humanity? And how do we get smarter the next time and all the next times to come?

Stalin is reported to have said that one life lost is a tragedy, but a million lives lost is a statistic. In my manic state I decide I want to make tragic a million deaths, as though that is remotely possible, and I realise I need to be rescued from my own strain of grandiosity. What I want to find within each death, each execution, is the lifetime that's to end, to document the dispossessing of a human being in its wholeness, its entirety, the sense of a once-only life expiring: my life, your life, anybody's life. Every thought and feeling you or I ever had or will have, or are capable of having is ended in that moment, in that person. It is you and me and everyone we love and are loved by. We are not a statistic.

I focus on the Jew whose job it was to transport the bodies of his fellow Jews to the roasting grilles. After the last one was laid out he was instructed to strip and lie on the dead bodies, where he would be shot and then incinerated. He knew what was coming. I try to catch it in his face in the act of laying out the last body, then in the act of removing his clothes, then as he lay down and felt the cold contact of a dead, naked body while he waited for the click of a pistol. He would sense the barrel at the back of his head and wait those last few seconds before the end, maybe hoping for a miracle, maybe saying a prayer, maybe playing through some final memories of loved ones and better times, maybe screaming for mercy, maybe paralysed by terror and wishing for a quick end.

And what of his executioner? His eyes are dead; dead to death. Any humanity he may ever have had has retreated to a hard point inside. He's lost his fanaticism, he's stopped rationalising what he does, he just does it over and over, an auto killing machine, pulling the trigger, watching them fall, but not to gain any satisfaction, either from sadism or zealotry, but to make sure they're dead. Somewhere located in that hard point within is a tiny kernel of the boy who grew up with his mother's love all around him.

Everyone is dehumanised: the process of dehumanising an other, in turn dehumanises oneself; a hollowing out of human dignity and spirit that makes beasts of us all, although beasts would never behave like Nazis. But something has to end, or be cut off, or be deadened for genocide to begin.

During natural disasters people risk their lives to save people they don't know. It is a nobility of spirit that arises spontaneously and fights for life, for people to survive not die. It starts from a love of humankind and turns to heroism and self-sacrifice, a collective will to live. But start from somewhere else and it aggregates as a death wish. It is Victor's bulking up of the demons in our nature.

If the Nazis teach us anything, isn't it to see the signs before it's too late? To notice the imperceptible changes in mood sentiment, or attitude? These are the signifiers that previous generations, in their ignorance, were blind to.

Forewarned by their history, our failure to apprehend the gathering storm would be a reckless negligence.

Meanwhile I work on the faces of people who realised too late what they had become. Allied soldiers forced civilians living near the liberated camps, as some sort of penance, to visit the horror that had occurred under their noses. They would barely look as they shuffled past. Was it repugnance or were they constructing their wall of silence and denial? And were they so different from the civilians who dug up the mass graves at Treblinka because they'd heard that the Nazis, in their haste to close down the camp, had failed to remove the gold teeth from the rotting carcasses? They were still at it months after the end of the war, raking over the land, pulling up dismembered limbs, looking for treasure, rifling the murdered and maybe thinking to themselves that the poor wretches whose bodies they plundered had no use for their teeth now. Ghouls or desperados? Either way, how low can our species sink?

Every idea I have seems to work out. A hot streak indeed. But then guilt strikes. Am I the ghoul a few steps removed, not cutting the teeth from dead mouths, but exploiting the event nonetheless? Artists have always done so, and why should I feel bad about it? But, really, am I implicated, a profiteer?

I talk to Alex and he says what I expect him to say: he goes a bit blah-blah about it all being a lesson from history and every generation must be taught not to forget. He's right. How can he not be, but why do I feel distanced by his words? I want to scream, 'it's not enough, it's never enough, it will never be enough,' but he's calm and he's listening and he almost understands, so I don't.

Is it the Gentile part of me talking to the Jewish part? Are they different? It's a ridiculous thought: I inherit this new label, one I would never have had if Victor hadn't walked into my life, and it becomes me, and the history of a whole race is dumped in my lap, like it's a training manual for the persecuted.

I've been untouched up until now. My life a breeze, relatively speaking. I don't mean there's been no pain or hardship, but there hasn't been any primal fear or dread in the face of a hostile regime. Having been spared for so long but to learn now that I am a part rather than apart from it all, to have been so unaware for all this time, I feel a peculiar shamefulness, as though my standing aside has caused others to take the hit.

The work goes well, too well I fear. The days pass, the anxiousness subsides, the exhibition comes together almost too perfectly, and I start to think, in the chinks of time when I allow myself such an outrageous thought, that I just might have a success on my hands.

Chapter Fifteen

Victor arrives early, catching me off guard. He apologises and tells me that Natalie is following and may or may not be bringing Nina.

'They were having an argument; a mother daughter thing so I got out of the way.' I want to know what they were arguing about, but Victor isn't volunteering the information. 'It gives me an opportunity to say a few things,' he says, but with the look of a man standing on the edge of a lengthy drop.

He tells me he's never doubted me, that he was confident even before our first meeting, and everything since has confirmed his earliest judgement. I'm not sure whether it is my accomplishments or his power of assessment he is most pleased with, but there is a sincere compliment in there, so I smile and let him carry on. I could remind him that he has yet to see the largest single display so far, that being the purpose of this visit, and he might yet change his mind.

'I had to fight for this project,' he says. 'Father wasn't keen, Mother was lukewarm, and Natalie drove me crazy with an avalanche of questions that convinced me she was against the idea. Then, by chance, I discovered you, by which I mean the family connection, the artist bit came later, and it all changed. Natalie dropped her guard and began the research on you, and soon she was talking with me about the possibilities. I saw your work, I followed you, I decided you were the one and persuaded Natalie—though she'd already started to come round—and together we got Mother and Father on board.'

It's an interesting potted history, but I don't know where he's going, or why he's so keen to cram the conversation into the gap between him arriving and Natalie appearing later. I'm curious to know a few things, like how the psychological profile came about, and how he got my bank details and exactly how much following he did do, literally and metaphorically, and I'm wondering if some sort of a full explanation—or should that be confession—is in the offing. Otherwise, isn't he just trying to persuade me that I owe him a debt of gratitude?

He gets down on one knee and reaches out for my hand. I let him take it, not sure whether to be worried or amused. He fumbles in his pocket and pulls out a small, pocket-sized wooden box. It is hand painted, oval in shape with rounded edges at the top and bottom, rather like an elongated egg, its finely detailed floral pattern dark with age and lacquer.

'It has been an honour,' he says. I want to burst out laughing at the absurd theatrics, but manage to stifle it to a nervous giggle. He cracks a smile but as he composes himself to say whatever it is he really wants to say, it evaporates. 'I want you to have this,' he says, although continuing to hold it close. 'It's the only thing we have in the world that was once in your father's possession. He made a will, leaving everything to your mother except this, which, for some reason, he chose to give to me.'

I take the box from Victor. It's heavier than I expected. There's no hinge. The upper part is a lid that fits tightly over the lower part. I hold the two parts in each hand and pull gently, not wanting to jerk it open and spill whatever's inside. By shuffling my fingers I ease off the lid and look inside. It's a jewellery box and seated on a cushioned insert is an emerald and gold tiepin.

'He once showed it to me at his house. He bought it from a jeweller who told him the emerald would bring him love. Béla dismissed this as nonsense aimed at the gullible and superstitious.' Victor looks at me as I run the pad of my forefinger along the gold bar and across the emerald, which is seated in the midst of a cluster of small diamonds. 'It's beautiful, isn't it?'

255

'Yes,' I say, breathing the word. I rotate the box in my palm, its smooth contours almost spiritually soothing.

'Béla fell in love—with this at least. The tiepin and its unconventional box were irresistible. It was a perfect acquisition.'

I'm aware of Victor shifting his eyes from the box to me, even though I'm still concentrating on the jewel. I try the lid back on, and it pushes back into position with such exactitude, such a perfect fit, that I can almost hear the air pushed out as it closes tight.

'I think you should keep it,' I say, holding the box out to him.

'He was your father, it's yours.'

It doesn't feel like mine. I was never aware of my father and was told nothing of his character by my mother. But I know Béla gave the box to Victor knowing it would be treasured.

'He made out a will giving it to you. That's good enough for me,' I say.

Victor looks at me closely. His eyes tell me he's on the verge of saying something, but what comes out next isn't it.

'He made out his will before you were born. It's nothing more than an administrative oversight on his part that I ended up with it.'

I look at him. I'm thinking, nice try, and I can see that he reads my mind. He almost smiles.

'What would a girl do with a tiepin?'

'Okay,' he says, his face resigned, as though I've forced something out of him. 'I want you to have it because it is my most precious possession. And that is how much I have come to treasure our relationship.'

The words are said with severity and I realise he couldn't have said them otherwise. He turns away from me and I hear him steady his breathing. I am bewildered, caught between a love of the words and the shock of their delivery. I move behind him and place a hand gently on his back.

'That's a beautiful sentiment, Victor, but it's not enough.' I'm nervous, my voice trembles.

He turns to face me. He looks alarmed. 'Enough for what?' he says.

'You know,' I say, recovering. I let my eye twinkle, and he relaxes.

'We're talking about the box aren't we?'

'Yes,' I say, 'what else?'

'Because you know I'm a confirmed bachelor?'

'Of course I do,' I say, 'which is another good reason why you're keeping the box.'

He thinks about it for a moment. There's resistance still, but all of a sudden it breaks. 'I'll do you a deal,' he says, 'the box belongs to you, but I'll be its keeper.'

'Deal,' I say, and laugh.

'What?' he says.

'"Confirmed bachelor"?' I haven't heard that in years.'

Natalie arrives with Nina and wants a 'quick word' with Victor. She ushers Nina from the room and I take her up to the studio. There's no obvious sign of whatever their argument was about, but Nina looks more buoyant than her mother, and the chat with Victor is presumably connected.

I don't have to fish around. She's bursting with the news.

'My father's coming to the preview,' she says, 'I wrote and told him everything about you and me and how I was going to be in the exhibition. I didn't hear back for days, but then I got this really long reply, an amazing reply.' Her voice falters; she sits to compose herself. 'He apologised for everything, can you believe it? For him and mother splitting up, for not being a real father, for being selfish. He promised a new start, that he was going to make it up to me, and practically begged me to let him wipe the slate clean.'

She looks up, and suddenly she's a baby bird in a nest with its mouth open, eager and trusting and innocent of the dangers ahead. I know what the argument with her mother will have been about and I can guess how the conversation between Natalie and Victor will be going. I'm in the middle. She should be allowed to hope, but does a leopard really change its spots? Did he become overwhelmed with a rush of guilt after all these years, perhaps after a drink or two and in a moment when he happened to have a bit of time available? Will he think the preview is an opportunity to discharge that guilt, that to be with her when she has her big moment will make up for every missed birthday party, family holiday, school play, sports day, not to mention the thousands of mundane quiet evenings and weekends when a father is just there and the world is a more secure place? Does he think it can all be wiped clean in one big self-redemptive gesture?

I jam on the brakes, aware my mind has run away from me, from reason, and into a zone that is about me, not Nina. My father had an excuse; he was dead. I'm blaming Nina's father for being alive, being human, for wanting a redemption that I think he should work harder for. I sit next to her.

'Be gentle on him,' I say, 'this may be as big a moment for him as it is for you, but he won't go from the absent father to the perfect father overnight.'

I feel like I'm beseeching her and I look for a sign that I've pitched it right.

'Be gentle on him?' she laughs, 'I'm going to make him suffer like hell.'

I want to tell her he left her mother, not her, but I know that's not entirely true: he was never really with either of them in the first place. Perhaps his priorities have shifted, maybe after a couple of decades craving wealth and status, some vision of alternative happiness has broken through?

Or a sense of loss even, made more acute once that great leveller, plain old mortality, begins to kick in?

'What do you think is better?' I say, 'If you've never had a father, for him to be dead so you can lay him to rest, or for him to be alive so you can live in hope knowing you may forever be disappointed?'

She looks at me, a piercingly contemplative look. 'You mean who's luckier, you or me?'

'I suppose so,' I say and smile, 'but it's you today against me a generation ago.'

'I can't imagine you at my age,' she says. 'I can imagine mother because of photos and stories, but I don't really know anything about you, do I?'

She wriggles in her seat, her question part serious, part playful. As with her bravura promise to make her father suffer, she's testing herself but leaving an escape route, her confidence riding the surface of a vulnerable interior. I wonder how she would have coped if pushed back a generation or two, beyond mine, back to the war, in the face of the Nazis. How would she have fared? How would that contest between spirit and susceptibility have resolved?

The memoir of Rudolf Hoss, commandant at Auschwitz, comes to mind. He described a mother of four who, while being herded towards the 'delousing' shed, went up to him, pointed to her children and whispered 'how can you bring yourself to kill such beautiful, darling children? Have you no heart at all?' It stayed with him. Of all the hundreds of thousands of Jews he was proud to have killed so efficiently, this was a death he remembered. One death is a tragedy; a million deaths, a statistic. Did the mother jolt his heart into life, for a moment at least, before he shut it back down again? Did her curious acceptance of the inevitable, her desire to protect her children from the knowledge of it, and the nerve she showed in quietly permitting him to know she was his moral superior, leave its trace? When he finally recanted, days before his execution, and expressed remorse for having 'sinned gravely against humanity', maybe it was her face he saw, and perhaps his confession at that final point was heartfelt?

'Nina,' I say, 'up until a short while ago you knew things about me that I didn't.'

She laughs, but stops abruptly. 'I want to get to know you, properly that is.'

'Have I become more interesting since becoming a member of the family?'

Will she take the question at face value or will she understand the meaning behind it? I wonder if I'm expecting too much. Maybe she'll be working out how to answer without offending me?

'You mean,' she says, 'since you became one of us rather than one of them?' She grins.

I nod and smile. I'm impressed.

'But wasn't I one of "us" before?'

'I guess. But I didn't know.' I gaze at her and raise my eyebrows. She nearly said more, but now she looks blank.

'You're drawing the us round the family,' I say. 'What about the us as a community of artists, or as English, or British, or European, or inhabitants of this not terribly significant orbiting sphere, whose lives coincide in this sliver of time and space. You can draw us however you want. It's the whole of humanity, or it's just us two, depending on how you see it.'

She's silent, seeming to recede into herself, as though in search of something.

'I think about us and them a lot,' she says, at last. 'Why does anyone who isn't us have to become them?'

I take her hand. I want to answer the question even though I know I don't have the answer. In any case, she may be ahead of me. 'It's the way it is.'

I want to take it back. When the words formed in my head they seemed to have some philosophical weight, but out loud they sound pessimistic and despairing, and as they fade into the air, they become almost nihilistic. Nina is nodding, as though she's latched on to some unintended wisdom, and I want to tell her I didn't mean it that way, that there is hope, that human nature isn't something to be given up on, but she looks at me, her eyes searching, like a veil has lifted.

'That's it,' she says, 'that's what Victor says.'

She's looking at me as though expecting me to have got it. I shrug and smile.

'What?'

'You can't just want people to change. They are how they are and there's nothing you can do about that. But if you're waiting for people to do good rather than bad, you're doing nothing, you're allowing it to happen. You have to change things around them, change their perspective, change their motivation, give them more of a reason to do good than bad. Evil triumphs when good people do nothing—or when all they do is indulge in wishful thinking.'

When Victor and Natalie enter the room they're smiling. Nina and I are smiling. Natalie and Victor genuflect hammily to one another as they approach us, to let us know all's well. Victor laughs, Natalie presses a hand to Nina's shoulder and gently squeezes.

'We all seem happy,' I say as if to check I can believe what I'm seeing.

'We are happy,' says Natalie.

'And we want to see some art,' says Victor.

We sometimes talk of things 'going viral,' but maybe not to describe the way killing spread from the Nazis like a virus. They may have started it, but soon everyone was at it: Ukrainians, Hungarians, Russians, Romanians, Greeks, British, Americans, French, Japanese, Italians, Croatians, Serbians. The list goes on. Who wasn't? Kill and counter-kill was the order, culminating finally—or temporarily, God forbid?—in Nagasaki.

I take them around my death-craze collection, as I'm squeamishly calling it—pictures of killing and being killed:

A Jewish girl, forced to dance naked for Sobibor commandant Irmfried Eberl, who, in the minutes between the order to undress and the end of the dance, may have had a hope that her degradation could become her salvation, but who was shot anyway, her indignity a worthless cast off.

The Franciscan friars, whose long standing hatreds, repressed in honour of their Lord, and unshackled by war's grotesque liberations, cheer-led the Ustashe during night-long rampages at Jasenovac concentration camp in Croatia, where inmates were pursued and cornered in groups and made to wait their turn while forced to witness the fate of those before them, bludgeoned to death by the hammer wielding militiamen.

A bullet frozen in the air during the fraction of a second between the trigger pulled and the target's death, when a repetitive task for one becomes the defining state for the other—the killer doing what is unconscionable except in the chaos of war when it becomes mundane.

The faces of sadists setting light to the beards of Jews, for whom the totalitarian regime that besmirches the honour of their country becomes their badge of perverted courage.

The dead souls of soldiers, trapped by circumstance in the Nazi killing machine, knowing they are damned but who carry on regardless loading people onto cattle trucks.

So it goes on. The gravel pits, the gas, the vans, the trains, the showers. The churches—boarded up, people herded inside and set alight. And finally Kruger, strutting around the killing zone, issuing orders, with the bottle of vodka in one hand and the hot dog in the other.

'If he was squirting mustard instead of bullets it could be a Saturday night at the funfair,' says Victor.

He breaks the mood, which has been grim and quiet since the display began. They've commented on the pictures' dimensions and how they see them fitting with other parts of the exhibition, which pictures they see hanging together and whether stuff should be integrated or themed, grouped in sections or dispersed semi-randomly, but about the pictures themselves, the subject matter and their response, nothing is said. Is this a compliment?

I ask what they think. At first they look at each other silently. I turn to Nina.

'It's great,' she says.

Natalie strokes her head and turns to me. She says she's speechless, and she's smiling.

Victor nods. 'It's going to be everything we hoped.'

'Better than that,' says Natalie.

'We need a drink,' I say, and send Nina to the kitchen to fetch glasses and a bottle of wine, 'and if you see Alex, ask him to join us.'

I head for the balcony, inviting Victor and Natalie. The river is full and slowed almost to a stop, or so it seems. Victor inhales deeply and blows out long and with an emptying sigh. Natalie leans on the rail and lets the strands of her hair blow in the wind and wrap across her face. I wonder whether to ask about Nina and her father, but with the river glistening and the silence between us almost reverential, I subside into the peace of the moment.

Chapter Sixteen

I've rarely felt as liberated as I did during those final weeks. With most of the artwork complete I could concentrate on the exhibition's logistics and put death camps, death marches, death militias, death machines and every other instrument, artefact, architecture and system involved in the orchestration and industrialisation of death, to one side. It was a relief to become the director of operations, overseeing the activities of building contractors (plumbers, sanitary engineers, electricians, plasterers, carpenters, heating engineers), technicians (light and sound engineers, picture framers, display case manufacturers, film editors, projection system experts), lawyers, publicists, handlers, landlords, planners, health and safety officers, surveyors, caterers—not to mention dealing with Alex's new found strand of perfectionism and Victor's new found inertia.

My principal ally was Natalie, without whom it would never have happened. Whether that turned out to be a good or bad thing in the context of what did happen is a wretched, impossible question, one I can only push aside in the hope that the answer will come good in time and rescue us. Victor said he had a feeling, like a premonition, which we ignored but became all the more irritating when he wanted to 'rethink' the 'whole thing'. It was a feeling he would eventually set aside when he understood that his equivocation was a sign of failing courage. But Natalie was the one who made the phone calls, sent the emails, did the meetings and chased, cajoled and threatened people until they did what we wanted. She executed every move on my say so, and that—giving my say so—was most of what I had to do. In another life I'm coming back as a boss. Is it power or ease that makes it so seductive?

Victor gave notice that I was to meet the parents. He repeated what he'd said earlier, that they were looking forward to it.

'There's nothing to fear,' he said, and up to that point I hadn't thought there was.

A car arrived at 7.00 on a Thursday evening. The driver wore a lounge suit without a tie, which, to my unaccustomed mind, made him seem less of a chauffeur, which was tempered when he opened a rear car passenger door for me.

'Don't dress for the occasion,' said Victor, and I hadn't, so this sudden injection of formality had the effect of making me nervous. Should I have taken him at his word?

The journey was slow, or so it seemed. Stuck behind darkened glass in the back of a limousine, I saw bystanders and pedestrians in a new, defamiliarised way. They couldn't see me, not that they would know who I was if they could, but the sight of the car and the driver was enough. It was a subtle thing, but the sense of anonymity that I would feel in a normal car or taxi had gone. People would hold their glance or, having glanced once, return for a second look. But their faces stayed blank and by not allowing an expression to form they could hope to disguise that they were looking. At one point, halted at a traffic light, a man stared at the window, seemingly right at me, his eyes dark and cold, his face like marble. I could see him and although he might know someone was in there, he would see nothing. The voyeur was blind, the spied on the one who could see. I shivered. Exposed and hidden at once. Was the dark glass worth it?

You would get used to it though, wouldn't you? If you were transported into this life, wouldn't you soon give up looking out to see who was looking in at you?

And you could be anyone, famous or rich, or both. You could invent who you were and the peepers could decide who they wanted you to be. Just so long as distance was maintained, we could project whatever we wanted onto one another. But either way, I'm rich and you're on the pavement.

As we made our way through Kensington and Notting Hill it occurred that there weren't any other limousines around. Wasn't the tranche of London from Chelsea in the south to Hampstead in the north, with the exception of the odd district along the way, a hive for the world's wealthy? Where were they all? Why weren't the roads crammed with these symbols of exclusivity? There were plenty of vans and no shortage of seven-year-old Toyotas, five-year-old Fords and three-year-old Volkswagens; there were people on buses, bikes, in taxis; everywhere there were people on the move, but where was the money, the display of wealth? An occasional Land Cruiser and a smattering of nondescript Mercedes' and BMWs drove by, standard middle class choices, as likely to be financed as owned. Where were the Rolls Royces, the Lamborghinis and Ferraris? I see them all the time when I'm on the pavement.

Victor greeted me at the door. He fussed around and started talking me through what was about to happen, as though some kind of ceremonial was to take place. Natalie, he said, was on her way.

The plan was for Victor, Natalie and me to eat, then 'go in' to meet the parents.

'Don't you eat together?'

'Not with you here.'

I looked at him, stuck for a response, or, more accurately, torn between so many possible replies that the moment passed and I gave up. Victor either realised how bizarre his response was or read it in my face.

'It has to be one step at a time,' he said, 'Mother and Father have their routines and you being here at all is enough of a break for them.'

Dinner was slow and methodical. Someone, somewhere prepared the food, and a young, friendly, intelligent-seeming woman called Annette brought it to the table. She joined in the conversation and there seemed to be no divide, the discussion flowed without deference until we started to eat and Annette disappeared.

The discussions involving Annette were the liveliest of the evening, Victor and Natalie being oddly subdued. They made no comment on the food other than to ask if I was enjoying it, and my answer—a resounding yes—prompted no more than a thin-lipped smile of acknowledgement from Victor.

I asked if everything was okay and they said yes. I said they seemed quiet, and Natalie said she was always quiet when she ate. During the last phase of the meal the chink of cutlery on bone china rose to a crescendo, like an avant-garde rhythm section.

Victor announced that we would 'remove ourselves.' He led us to a red drawing room at the back of the house, a sumptuous, deeply carpeted, richly draped room from an era when soft furnishings really were soft. It overlooked an immaculate lawn, visible through French windows in the fading mid-evening light.

At Victor's prompt, I fell into a sofa, its cushions moulding themselves to my body as I landed, the feeling of relaxation gloriously welcome after the mild but sustained strain of dinner. I let it envelop me, determined to enjoy the moment, leaving Victor or Natalie to make the running with any conversation.

'It won't be long,' said Natalie, uncrossing the legs she'd crossed moments earlier. There was a hint of a smile and her attention darted to Victor who was idly staring at a decanter. If he'd wanted a drink he'd have said, but he didn't. He was killing time.

I cracked, and made some idle chat about the comfort of the sofa. Natalie told me it was an Italian design and was about to say more when the door opened and the man who had driven me appeared. He didn't say anything. Perhaps some signal was given, some communication I wasn't able to decode, but Natalie got to her feet and Victor headed towards the door, gesturing for me to accompany him.

'It's all a bit old school, I know,' said Natalie as we walked along a mosaic tiled corridor that traversed the rear of the house. More like being at school, was my thought. But it was, at last, an acknowledgement that I wasn't being perverse in finding the whole thing peculiar.

We reached a heavy oak door with the word library inscribed in gold lettering. Victor nodded to Natalie, she nodded back, and he turned the handle.

Looking back afterwards, what followed next had a perfect logic. I'm not sure what I'd expected, but not this. The meeting that had been trailed for so long, the culmination of a year's turmoil, a symbolic as well as an actual climax, a coming together of the active agents, the coterie of a secret movement, an event that had put Victor and Natalie on edge the whole evening, and that deserved a fanfare, a celebration, or at least a glass of champagne, was over and done with in a couple of minutes.

The door opened, the parents were arranged in chairs facing. On entering they rose, hands clasped in front. They were smiling—at me I realised. Victor and Natalie flanked me as we walked towards them. The parents didn't take their eyes off me—glisteningly bright beams of pleasure— and I felt something ignite inside, as if in the embrace of a loved one. The mother was six inches taller than the father and palely elegant. He was rounded and tanned. As I reached him he extended a hand. It was soft and warm; no vigorous shake, a connecting of limbs as though we had joined.

'It's a pleasure to meet you,' he said, and bowed slightly, before releasing his grip.

'An absolute honour,' said the mother, her hand offered and taken. Her long fingers, their porcelain refinement, could never be so warm as her husbands, but there was strength in her seeming fragility. She held on to me, leaned in fractionally as though to appraise, but not critically, just to be sure, then let go.

'Thank you for taking the trouble to meet us,' said the father.

'I can't tell you how much I'm looking forward to the exhibition,' said the mother.

They sat and Victor edged back towards the door.

'Catch up later,' said Natalie to her mother and turned. She turned to me, gestured towards the door and I understood that we were done.

If it is possible to punch the air metaphorically, it is what Victor and Natalie did as the library door closed behind us. Their relief was visceral, so far removed from the stiff courtesies of the early evening, and so unlike any behaviour I had witnessed in them previously. Victor hummed a tune and I thought Natalie might burst into song, but instead she laughed. They were children on the edge of hysteria and I looked on in astonishment. That the meeting with their parents might have seemed to me to be utterly extraordinary was obviously not uppermost in their minds.

'You don't understand,' said Natalie when I asked her what had happened to suddenly alter them—and never had she said a truer word—'they accepted you; it was in the balance until that moment.'

I looked at her, expecting the explanation to continue, but she was still surfing a wave that was all hers.

'What?' I said, 'what was in the balance?'

Victor caught my tone and took my arm. He guided me back to the drawing room where a bottle of champagne was sitting in a bucket of ice.

'You were always going to get paid,' he said, 'rest assured, that wasn't in doubt.' I looked at him, startled. The fact of him mentioning it was alarming enough. 'But the exhibition…' he released the cork and shook his head as he poured, 'was never a certainty until five minutes ago.'

He handed me a glass and one to Natalie.

'Cheers,' she said, and we chinked glasses.

Victor told me, solemnly and apologetically, gauging accurately my mood, that part of the reason why, for so long, they couldn't tell me where the project was going was that they didn't know.

'We had to lead them step by step, but without them thinking they were being led. Once we'd come up with the plan for the exhibition we could tell them it was your idea.'

'Which it was,' I reminded him.

'Of course. What I mean is, we were able to get their go ahead because the idea was yours not ours. Do you see?'

I took a sip, and found myself, unaccountably, giggling.

'It's a fucking good job you two are family,' I said.

'And talking of which,' he said, 'that was what happened in there. If they hadn't recognised you the whole thing would have been off.'

'Recognised me?'

'They knew you as a baby, up to when you were a toddler,' said Natalie.

'And you're saying they recognised me, all these years later?'

'Oh yes,' said Victor, nodding furiously, as if there could have been any doubt.

'You mean they didn't really believe you until they saw me for themselves?' I stifled the urge to laugh out loud. 'Do they think you two are imbeciles?'

'They believed us at the start,' said Natalie, 'otherwise we couldn't have commissioned you. But as the reality of doing it loomed, and the stakes got bigger, doubts grew, their confidence slipped, and paranoia set in.'

'Paranoia?'

'It's easily provoked. They're afraid. They don't go into the world even though there's a city of millions on their doorstep. They're in hiding, waiting to be discovered, although they couldn't tell you by who. It's a state of mind: someone, somewhere out there is after them, because someone, somewhere out there is after someone, so it might as well be them.'

I mention that they seemed so relaxed, so friendly, so genuine. Where was the paranoia?

Natalie smiled. 'They recognised you the moment you entered the room. Everything was going to be okay after that. You wouldn't have known it but part of their pleasure was the sheer relief.'

I started to wonder what they'd suspected, the absurdities of which grew in my mind with each second. 'Did they think I was an imposter?'

Victor looked at Natalie, who exchanged a glance. The way something ricocheted between them was enough. I started forming words, but there were too many ways of addressing the craziness of that scenario, the ridiculousness of me being some kind of suspect. Me, the innocent, the ingenue, the trusting one, the one who took the leap of faith, the person to whom all this had happened, not the person plotting.

'How could they possibly?' I said. It was weak reply that vocalised almost nothing of what I felt.

'I know it's unjust,' said Natalie, leaning in gently, perhaps understanding the offence better than I'd thought, 'and absurd. We'd told them we were certain we knew who you were, even when you didn't yourself.' She put down her glass, and stood straight, and I saw her mother in her, although a sterner version than the one I'd just met. 'I know this sounds terrible, but you weren't a person at all until you walked into that room, you were an entity, known as an artist, that we talked about, that we could have invented. They live in fear, their imaginations take flight, but they can recognise reality when they see it, and they did.'

Victor travelled back in the car with me. I think he'd envisaged us playing out a big scene where he would apologise again for the chicanery, building up to a climax where we high-five in celebration of it having been worth it —not that Victor, in his Jermyn Street shirts, Savile Row suits and handcrafted shoes, is a high-fiving guy—after which, I would step happily into the night, his crimes exonerated, his guilt leached.

'I don't know,' was all I said, after his initial, undoubtedly sincere, apology. I was holding back, reluctant to play my part.

He went quiet for a while and I watched the road go by, waiting for him to start again, half hoping he would say something new, or at least something I wasn't half expecting. I allowed a wry smile, thinking that this is how it is in families: you get into these annoying, predictable routines, until eventually, after you've played them over scores of times, they become something you rely on to keep you sane.

The silence continued and I made myself relax, unclenching my abdomen, making a point of watching the city spin past beyond the car window, appreciating what I could see, telling myself to enjoy the ride and to notice the details, the colours, faces, traffic lights turning from red to green—just one of the billions of small moments that happen every second on earth, but that mean something in the instant of their happening.

Something made me turn from the street, to switch my attention to the car's interior, to Victor. It might have been the unexpected length of his silence, or that he made a sound that was barely audible and I picked up without knowing. Whatever it was, I found him with a hand over his eyes and a tear on his cheek.

'Victor?'

He didn't reply. I placed a hand on his shoulder and waited. He shook, then he leant forward cupping his head in his hands, muttering something I couldn't hear, and sprang back upright, as if trying to snap out of whatever it was.

'What is it, Victor?' I looked at his watery, reddened eyes and he tried to look back, but his face looked lost, almost desperate. He pulled out a crisply folded handkerchief, flicked it open and held it against his forehead, his thumb and middle finger pressing the pure white fabric into the sockets of his eyes. He remained like that, bent and head-covered, as though insulating himself, then relaxed his grip and let the handkerchief fall into his lap. As he struggled to straighten I could see the muscles in his face trembling reflexively beneath the skin.

His mouth moved, but he wasn't finding the words. He glanced at me and I could see what was stopping him. He was embarrassed. Whatever it was he wanted to say would humiliate him.

'Just say it,' I said, 'trust me.' I gripped his arm.

'The centre cannot hold,' he said, at last, slowly, fixedly.

I stared at him.

'Yeats.'

'I know,' I said.

'Well, why are you looking at me like I'm an idiot?'

There was no aggression, the accusation was aimed at himself, not me.

'You're not an idiot,' I said, and moved my hand to lay it on the back of his. He turned it over to gently squeeze mine back. Half a smile appeared on his lips.

'I'm out of my depth,' he said, 'I've always prized order: a defined place to live and work; some organising principles; the ability to retrieve whatever I want, whenever I want; knowing I'm in charge of my day, every day; knowing things will work and get better, just because I want them to. But I'm losing control, everything is disordered, everything is spinning away from me and I can't keep it together.'

'Everything?'

He looked at me and seemed about to repeat himself, but hesitated and said, softly, 'you know what I mean.'

I didn't, entirely, but I took him to mean that with our project about to go out into the world, we would be at the mercy of whatever judgement came our way. It would be formed out of the accumulation of understandings, misunderstandings, personal quirks, political prejudices, half truths, snap assessments, spun myths, doting responses, complete accidents and the random timings of one thing leading to another, that add up to the sum total of consciousness that attaches to any cultural event. The one thing certain was that once we opened the door we would surrender control.

'We should be so lucky,' I said, and grinned at him knowingly. I could see he didn't get it, he really was stuck and I wasn't going to pull him out easily. 'We don't want people to not notice it, do we?'

His face was pale, drained of any sign of an inner life. For a moment I feared he was having a nervous breakdown. It did look like 'everything' was too much for him. A strange sense of pity rose in me. Strange because Victor had always been the one poised and in command, it was always me chasing his shadow, wondering if I was getting it right, fearing my inadequacy.

When he began this scheme, he must have lacked any sense of how he might react when the crunch came. What little of life had he previously known if he'd been so incapable of foreseeing the pain he now felt? Wouldn't most people reach his age and know the circumstances in which they would thrive, as opposed to those in which they'd struggle? I take his hand again. It's warm and gentle, and I wonder what it has cost him to live such an insular life.

'No,' he said, at last. It took a moment to realise it was an answer to my question. Something shifted behind his

274

eyes. The panic that had burned out and left him in a torpor was giving way, and like the first perennial to nose up from the ground at the end of winter, it was a telling detail, a sign of a turn.

His falling apart had started to feel like my failure, and his recovery, fragile and incomplete though it was, felt like a small triumph. I let my limbs soften and the blood rush back to my brain, telling myself that we were going to be okay. Victor was brave, he had fought and won, and, if the enemy was himself, that enemy was quiet now.

It was one year, three months, and twenty-two days since I'd first spied Victor's shoes glinting in the street outside our home. It had been a pleasant and clear June night, the darkness seeping into the late evening like dissolved black velvet. By late September, on the day we opened our exhibition, the chills of autumn were riding in the air, and it felt like the darkness, when it came, would be jagged and cold.

Alex was saintly—in his mood in general, and in his helpfulness. He'd put his documentary 'to bed' a week before, the final edit keeping him up until four in the morning every night for weeks, but once it was done he was satisfied. It's a measure of our different temperaments: my work keeps me awake at night only after it's finished, when I start turning over all the things I could have done differently; for Alex, completion had freed him and he was happy, which meant he was a pleasure.

Victor kept apologising for his 'vacillating' courage, not that I thought of it that way. A lesser man would have gone under, we all said, or words to that effect. Maybe he didn't quite believe us, maybe that's why he brought it up so often, but if reassurance was what he craved, he got it and it worked.

But along the way his fears transferred to me, and I lay awake at night with hordes of imaginary critics, marching to a single damning beat, thumping through my head.

Natalie said that I was the one with a reputation to burn. 'Go easy on yourself; the stakes are highest for you. Once it's over the rest of us will be forgotten.'

'Thanks,' I said, 'but excuse me while I work out if that makes it better or worse.'

She laughed, and added, 'if it's any consolation, I can't sleep either.'

We all suffered with the responsibility we felt for our subject. We didn't want to let it down. 'It' being, on the one hand, the discarded byproduct of human enterprise: the people who don't live freely, the dispossessed whose lives are blighted and brutally shortened. And on the other, 'it' is the downside of our instinct for survival, for competitive advantage that makes human nature a dangerous multi-sided weapon; one that, over thousands of millennia, out of the coalescence of the gas and dust of the universe into liquid and solid, has seeded the possibility for good and evil within all of us.

Knowing Natalie wasn't sleeping helped me get a sense of the burden being shared, but part of her reason was Nina. It was convenient for me to reach this point knowing that the girl I'd sought as a model, who I was about to expose to the world—the real implications of which I hadn't, at the time, remotely thought through—turned out to be the daughter of the sponsor. That should get me off the hook. But Nina had become my girl, and I don't mean as a daughter or niece, but as a product of me, my vision, tutelage, investment in time and, as the weeks turned to months, my love.

I guess it helped that she responded so adroitly to my teachings and assignments. But that wasn't the half of it. That could describe any professional relationship where someone's skill becomes of value and your appreciation flows to them without the personal ever much coming into it.

She gave me back parts of myself, things lost from long ago: a childhood, a motherhood, a daughterhood were all there, all along, without me knowing it. And that was it: the longer I struggled with human nature, its bulkings, its loops, its mad barbarisms and primal fears, the more urgent was the need to find something fragile to protect, like an endangered species—or the endangered species we will one day make of ourselves, if we haven't already.

Nina's fragility is deceptive. I see why her mother feared for her as a schoolchild, but also why I found a child whose behaviour was at odds with the hand-me-down description I'd been given. Like anyone, but maybe more than most, she needs to be nurtured and loved. Having to compete with angrier, wilder, pushier children is a vexation to her, one she overcomes by mentally removing herself. She succeeds, not by hiding or running, but by somehow overriding it. It's a mental trick I wish I'd learned growing up. But maybe you don't learn it, maybe you can or can't do it. It's a way of finding a place where you can't be hurt while still being in the midst of the things that seek to hurt you. Nina practices the art of rising above her tormentors and in that she is tougher than all of us.

I told Alex my theory about Nina and he listened, which at first seemed good. I'm sure he's come to care for her almost as much as I do, but he also gets annoyed at the 'pen mightier than the sword brigade' as he puts it, and went out of his way to tell me, at greater length than was necessary, that her approach wouldn't help much in the face of bullets and gas chambers.

'She doesn't have to deal with bullets and gas chambers, thank God,' I said.

'Not yet,' he said, and after seeing me react, added that he hoped she never would.

He's concerned we're spiralling towards a day when there will be 'heads on spikes' and he's on a mission to 'save democracy from itself.' According to him, while the rest of us, meaning Victor, Natalie and myself, are trying to 'fend off the next genocide' he's trying to head off the next 'toppling of the upper class.'

'Not that I'd miss them,' he said, 'but I don't want them murdered by a baying mob.'

The 'upper class' has, of course, been redefined to fit the modern trend towards city real estate rather than country seats. Ironically, in Alex's scenario, the Royal Family may escape the bloodbath. 'But possibly not us,' he said.

I'd wondered how seriously to take him, but his face had a pinched, rigid expression and he was completely invested in what he was saying.

'Democracy's failing, detached from the will of the people,' he said, and he did what he rarely does, what I would do, and he turned away towards the river. 'The people are losing.' He stood, silent and remote, as if in memoriam, until eventually he said, 'Let me show you my film.'

I'd thought I had a good idea about what his documentary contained: the withering state; the all-consuming rush of the market; the taken for granted freedoms of our civilised world shaking as their foundations are undermined. I expected all this to be cogently argued, the evidence presented with clarity and conviction and witnesses brought forward to testify that we were, indeed, on the road to hell. The overview, the big picture, the widescreen panorama. I was wrong. It was all about the details. The group of carers gathered to be told by a grim looking manager that their pay will be cut; the woman dismissed for being two minutes late to one of her three illegal, below minimum wage, jobs; the man with a nasty cough told he'll have to wait weeks for a hospital appointment; the single mother regularly beaten by her ex who is taken to court for not controlling her truanting son; the father whose benefits are suspended because he turns up late to a job centre interview; his family who eat from shoplifted tins for a week; the three families sharing a house in East London so they can afford the rent; the four young graduates sharing a house in East London so they can afford the rent; the three young professionals buying a flat in South London so they can afford the mortgage; the domestic servant enslaved by her abusive employer whose passport has been retained for 'safekeeping'; the young people working for nothing at a city firm; the older people working for millions at a city firm; the young people working for nothing at a media firm; the older people dismissed by the media firm for being too expensive; the newspaper headline that says the government planned to make sex with ten year olds legal; the betting firm offering money back if the murderer gets off; the poorly educated children of Anytown whose tales of abuse aren't believed; the men and women of Anytown who compete for insecure, zero hours jobs because all the decent ones have gone; the nurse who committed suicide after she was scapegoated by managers following her complaint about bad practice; the journalists sidelined and eventually fired after they broke the news of a serial abuser who happened to work for their organisation; the financial analyst replaced by an algorithm; the bright young law graduates replaced by algorithms; the middle aged middle manager whose job vanishes because of an algorithm; the bright young graduates who never get a job in their chosen field because it's full of people on forty hour contracts working sixty hours a week; the warehouse supervisors made redundant by machines; the factory operatives made redundant by machines. And so it went on.

The film ended and Alex jabbed the remote to switch off the screen. I waited for him to say something, aware of him twitching nervously, wondering why I was also tongue-tied. There was nothing prohibiting a conversation, but a barrier hung there nevertheless. It took a moment to work out what it was: role reversal. In the normal scheme, Alex has to pass judgement on what I do. We're familiar with that, we know how the ritual goes and the lines to recite, both when he likes something and when he doesn't.

Eventually the absurdity of this breakdown overcame me and I snorted in a failed attempt to suppress a nervous giggle. He looked offended at first, then smiled. He'd got there too.

'You can get your own back for all those years,' he said.

'It wasn't what I was expecting,' I said. This was a deliberate tease, because this is one of his standard openings, a well used warning shot, one that presages a response that lies somewhere along the spectrum between sceptical and hostile.

I told him exactly why it wasn't what I was expecting. He listened closely, more so than he would normally. This matters to him, I thought. I could see him weighing whether to be pleased that he hadn't been predictable, or displeased I'd typecast him in the first place. In the end I told him I liked it, that it was powerful.

'It's about people's future being stolen from them,' I said.

He stood sharply and sliced the air with his hand. 'That's it, that's the whole point.' Our first try at me passing judgement on his creative output had worked out.

'I wanted to show these people in their situations, but not show them blaming anyone. If I asked them what was to blame they came up with the usual suspects: governments, rich bastards, immigrants, big business. But I don't want to recycle all that because I don't believe in easy answers or the blame game. No one seems able to stitch it all together; no one can say what is behind it all. Everyone knows it's happening all round to almost everyone. They know it and yet they're clueless as to what to do. They feel hopeless at worst or resigned at best. My film is an attempt to show it. I don't mean to be political in the old fashioned right versus left sense. That's too simplistic. We're beyond that. We're trapped in a system where almost nobody gets what they want and nobody knows the way out.'

'Is there a way out?'

'There has to be, otherwise…' He waved in the direction of my studio.

When we assembled amidst the brick and cast iron expanses of the disused dockland warehouse that was ours for four months, prior to its redevelopment into apartments, the end of civilisation still seemed some way off. The building, a dark and shadowy remnant of empire, may have looked like a gothic Victorian nightmare made real, but the event was a twenty-first century gathering of cultural arbiters, art cognoscenti and on-trend fashionistas, all prompted in their judgements by champagne, fine wine and food, provided at ridiculous expense by a flamboyant and punctilious high end event caterer.

I pointed out to Victor, not entirely in jest, that the spread was costing more than my commission.

'They won't turn up otherwise,' he said, offhand, like it was a statement of such obviousness it needn't be said at all. Then he turned to me and smiled, looked me in the eyes, and said, 'you'll be getting a bonus, so not quite true anyway.'

'That's not what I meant,' I said. I nearly went on to say the money wasn't important, but realised, seeing him standing in front of me, his smile broadening to a grin, that he'd been looking forward to telling me and I had given him the opening.

'I know the money isn't important,' he said, 'but it's all we've got.' He shrugged, I laughed.

'Better be a big one then,' I said.

The warehouse was one of the earliest in London to be made without using wood and therefore constructed entirely of non-combustible materials. With the amount of temporary electrics and lighting we were suspending from roof spaces and attaching to girders, this felt like one less fear to contend with. In the final days I suffered terrible bouts of anxiety. Small worries would go viral in my head and become colossal forebodings. Insurance was expensive and if we ever had to claim we would find ourselves trapped in a bureaucracy that, pictorially represented, would resemble an Escher lithograph. For days I was convinced I couldn't do it, that something was certain to go catastrophically wrong: no one would turn up and if anyone did they'd hate it, but since they weren't going to anyway it didn't matter—in which case I could relax— except for the panic attack I was having. I vaguely hoped the whole thing could be called off, that some buried snag would arise rendering impossible the entire venture. Perhaps the council would step in, or the Mayor's office, and quote some obscure by-law that meant we had to be closed down.

But there we were, with a show and, astonishingly, an audience. It was called, 'One still does everything to avoid attracting attention.' I'd decided there was a place at the heart of the exhibition for my recently discovered family history, going back to the story of Erika hiding her Jewishness in Nazi Austria, as the wife of a soldier of the Reich, making every effort to remain beyond suspicion, beyond the point at which the Gestapo would think it worth their while to probe.

The quote was taken from the journal of a Hamburg woman Erika S. (the name a fortunate coincidence) who wrote despairingly of the torment experienced in waiting the war out, knowing unspeakable things were happening. She knew the regime represented everything that was anathema to her sense of humanity, that people were being sacrificed to 'Hitler's devilish cause' and that there had been a descent into 'one huge campaign of murder'. But like countless others she was trapped by a need to 'avoid attracting attention' in order to survive.

Erika S's story seemed to sum up not only my Erika but the hope and the hopelessness of the ordinary German people who flew Swastikas and joined the Nazi party, not for belief but protection: people who deserve to be condemned for their cowardice by every person alive today who can be certain they would have acted differently in the same circumstances.

The press call went well. It was in the afternoon before the evening preview and we had three nationals, four art magazines, a London paper, half a dozen freelancers and the BBC—TV and radio. They took their time, asked questions, listened, laughed at the right places and took seriously, very seriously, what we were doing. As far as it was possible to tell, they got it. Some promised to stay for the evening, those that didn't sounded genuinely apologetic. We were going to wait until dark and project the film of Victor's attack onto the side of the building. We'd shown them a trailer on a small screen inside and they'd stared at it in silence, the temptation to disbelieve confounded by the knowledge that it was true. At the end no one moved, although you could see eyes flickering towards Victor as though not quite believing he was for real. Join the club, I thought.

The previous night, in the empty building, after we'd made the final adjustments and rehearsed the sequence of events, I wandered through the exhibition in walking order, as though seeing it the way a visitor would, and I felt something settle. For the first time I was able to experience the whole shameful, pitiable, bloody and brutal collection of art and artefact as though I was disconnected from it. Who are you Sylvia West? Are you the artist? Why haven't I heard of you before? But, of course, I have. I just would never have connected you to this.

One of Sylvia's most absorbing pieces was a photograph of a group of schoolchildren in Kensington Gardens. It had a mist-like radiance, the air made into a white light, as though burned around the children, their figures etched into the print like x-rays. They were formed into a perfect line, their yellow bibs the only points of real colour, two shivering children the only movement. At the head was their teacher, staring at the camera, her eyes fixed in determination, as though to say they're safe, they're going to a place where you can't get them, into an eternity that shields them from you all.

Sylvia should be proud, I said to myself. She should be congratulated on the video of the man approaching Nina on the bridge, the Houses of Parliament static and huge in the background, the courage on the girl's face, the hatred in the gestures of the man, the way the camera slowly zooms in on her unyielding vulnerability, drawing the viewer to the story, invisible at a distance but visceral in close up. There are no words, just the expression of a girl steadfast against her tormentor.

I walked, as my visitor, to the darkest area of the exhibition, where the ambient light is low, dimmed spotlights trained on the pictures. The raw horror: the men waiting their turn to be clubbed to death; the babies heads smashed against the trees; the men forced to smear each other with excrement and their beards set alight; the orphan children taken to the woods and shot; the men put through the slaughterhouse procedure; the girl forced to dance naked before being shot; and Kruger, with a hot dog in one hand and a bottle of vodka in the other, conducting a mass shooting and piss-up, his men piling up the shot bodies behind him, the alcohol greasing and anaesthetising the insanity.

Could Sylvia have done any more justice to the subject? Surely any more would have been at a cost to herself and public decency? She wanted to shock but not offend, show the truth without being gratuitous, be explicit but not pornographically. She seems to have struck the balance.

My visitor entered the largest of the black boxes, and discovered the film of the frozen children. Sylvia's animation of the train and the other dying children, revolved around the face of her model, Nina, whose flickering, ebbing expression faded to complete stillness, as the last filament of human warmth in a death-cold carriage expired. My visitor cried, so I expelled her. I sat and stared at the final images of Nina, a long take accompanied by the sound of the train clattering as the ice crystals formed around her eyelids. The tears became mine. It felt like the end for me. I wondered if I would be the only person who would weep. Was it just me, the creator, the person close to it all, who carried the emotion, or would some of it cross over into the world? And, if so, would it make any difference anyway?

The press call led into the evening preview, allowing little time to adjust or, thankfully, get nervous. In less than an hour nearly everyone had turned up. The evening hit its stride. We made our speeches and received warm, extended rounds of applause. The champagne flowed, the canapés circulated and people mingled and talked and were happy. Alex told me it was going fantastically well. I wasn't sure; maybe they were being polite. And maybe they would put down their glasses of champagne, take a look, and think what I was thinking. Instead of sweetly floating in an atmosphere of gentle inebriation and convivial assembly, they might think about another intoxication: of exclusionary ideology, fanaticism and hatred.

I found Nina, in thrall to a stream of attentive admirers, not that it was a submission she seemed inclined to resist. But the admirer that mattered hadn't arrived.

'He'll be here,' I said.

'Everyone tells me that,' she said.

Natalie turned round from an adjacent group. She must have heard.

'If he said he was coming, he will. He doesn't make promises he won't keep,' she said, but added, 'he just doesn't make many in the first place.' She raised her eyebrows, emphasising this last point, more to me than Nina, but Nina managed a half-laugh anyway.

The evening swelled and contracted with bright introductions and small conversations. Some of these could have grown into bigger discussions except we were circulating and no one wanted to be sidelined for long. Where did you get your ideas? How much time did you spend on research? Is it really true that the Nazis did all those things? I made up the last one, but you never know, there may have been someone who wanted to ask it. Victor and Natalie had pulled out all the stops to gather these people and I wanted to play my part. I even wondered if I was getting good at it; soaking up attention didn't seem so hard. I had a little fantasy about being a 'kingpin' and wondered how I would change in a world where all eyes were looking out for me. I would be benevolent, bestow kindness; I would retain my humility. I would be a good supreme being.

Looking back, I realised the man in the oversized quilted jacket had bugged me all evening. Not directly, he never said a word to me. But he didn't appear to say anything to anyone else. He hung around on the edge of things. He smiled occasionally. He ate a lot, seeming to connect better with the waiters than anyone else. I wasn't watching him and wasn't aware until later that I'd noticed any of this, yet somehow I had taken it all in and somewhere below my threshold of consciousness he'd annoyed me.

Afterwards, everyone seemed to have an observation to report. How fidgety he was; how out of place; how he looked like a stray, as though he'd been passing and was drawn in by the food; how he was sweating, his socks didn't match and he walked with a lollop; how his proximity, as he hung around the edges of conversations, spread a sense of being eavesdropped. For someone you would pass in the street and not notice, he became an unmissable curiosity, widely assumed harmless, until he produced a gun in his left hand and a machete in the right.

I heard a voice raised, but thought nothing until I realised the conversation was dying in waves, like a singing round coming to its end. I turned and saw him. Everyone was facing him. Someone said something to him, it sounded like 'take it easy'. He said to shut up, pointed the gun. There were gasps, screams, and in front of me, a rivulet of piss ran down a bare brown leg, over the heel of a stiletto, before oozing into a puddle on the floor.

'I will kill you if I need to,' he said. 'Don't make it easy for me. No phones. Anyone using their phone will be shot.' The word 'terrorist' leapt to mind at the same moment I was seized by my own terror.

Suddenly it was a real word, not an overfamiliar staple of news broadcasts. It wasn't happening on a screen, it was happening to me, to all of us in this room, in this space we were collected in. As I looked at him I felt the horror. It was a feeling as solid and extreme as any in my life, yet, at the same time, I felt as though I wasn't part of it at all, as if it was some bizarre Sensorama experiment.

The terrorist told the men to move to his right and the women to the left. At first people hesitated, not quite understanding that a separation of the sexes was what he required, but he repeated the command and everyone began to move. Once separated, we were told to sit.

He gestured with his machete to a middle aged man in a tailored suit. 'Are you with your wife?'

'My partner,' the man said.

'Where is she?'

The man's eyes searched the female half of the floor. At first I thought he couldn't see her, but then I realised he was trying to avoid giving an answer. The terrorist walked to the women's side and picked someone out. He pointed his blade up towards her throat and his gun towards the man.

'Is this her?'

'No', said the man.

'Then tell me.' He jabbed the blade closer to the woman's throat.

'It's me,' said a woman, further away, 'I'm his partner.' She was trying to speak clearly, strongly, defiantly, but her voice quavered.

'I didn't ask you, I asked him,' he shouted, shaking the still pointing gun in his hand for effect. Then he turned back to the man. 'Take your clothes off.'

I heard a low groan and saw people look down. The man in the suit looked around him, as though hoping something, someone, would rescue him.

'Now,' he yelled. He brandished his machete and stepped towards the man, who peeled off his jacket.

'And the rest of you,' he waved his machete across the room. 'All of you, all of your clothes off.' Someone stood to do it. 'Sit down.'

'What do you want?' shouted one of the men. 'Name your price. I will pay it.'

'Come here,' said the terrorist. The man walked over to him. I felt nauseous. I could see the man was expecting to negotiate, but that wasn't what was about to happen. He hasn't killed anyone yet, I said to myself.

The man came to within a few feet of the terrorist.

'Take your clothes off.'

The man began removing his clothes, until he stood naked. He seemed brave. He'd done it without hesitation, without bluster, without embarrassment.

'Pick up your jacket and take out your wallet.'

The man did as he was told.

'Empty it.'

Again, he did as he was told. Cash, bank cards, membership cards, travel cards, store cards, scraps of paper, a photo of a child, landed on the floor.

'Not enough,' said the terrorist, and kicked the pile.

'I can get more. Whatever you want.'

The terrorist laughed. 'You.' He pointed at the first man, who still had his unbuttoned shirt and trousers on. 'Why aren't you undressed?' He fired a shot into the roof. It was a violent, sickeningly loud crack, an explosive shock. I jumped. Everyone did. The man pulled off his shirt and trousers. 'Come here.'

He lined the two men up next to one another, standing, facing the rest of us.

'These two men are good. Obedient.' he said. 'They are undressed, the rest of you still have your clothes on. Do I punish you or do I reward them? Is it carrot or is it stick? Hands up for carrot.'

There were a couple of half raised hands.

He glared. 'You put your hands up for carrot, or you put your hands up for stick.' He cut the air with the machete. 'One or the other. Anyone who doesn't put their hand up will be shot. Hands up for carrot.'

A few hands went up, and then, as far as I could see, every hand went up, including mine.

'Who's for stick?' No one raised a hand. 'Looks like you get your reward boys.' He walked to the space between where the two men were standing and the women were sitting. 'Let's make this a bit more multi-cultural.' He pointed his machete towards us, the hostages. I guessed that was what we'd become. 'You. And you.' He indicated two women, one black, one middle-eastern. 'Come here.'

He stood them next to the two men, touched their throats in turn with the point of his machete, and instructed them to remove the rest of their clothes, before turning to us, pointing his gun, and telling us to do the same. There was an abrupt flurry of movement as we all did as we were told.

'On your knees,' he said to the women, guiding them to a space in front of the men. 'Fellate,' he said.

There was a widespread, half-suppressed gasp. People looked around, as though appealing for some solidarity. No one moved. I caught sight of Alex murmuring under his breath to a man next to him. It looked conspiratorial. I feared the terrorist would see him, but at the same time, I hoped Alex had a plan, some way of relieving us of this terror. Then I worried he might be the one about to make the sacrifice. Couldn't someone else be the brave fool this time?

If we all charged him he would be overwhelmed. But how would it be coordinated? Who would lead that charge? If I led, would anyone follow? We would all want to be part of the heroic wave, the one that brought him to the ground, that wrestled the machete off him and took his gun. That's the heroic wave that survives the charge, rather than the earlier one that dies in the attempt.

'Fellate!' He pushed the head of the black woman towards one of the flaccid penises. 'And you.' He pushed the blade up to the back of the other woman's neck, forcing her onwards. 'Suck cock.'

The women looked at each other and up at the men, their expressions of revulsion mingled with sorrow at the knowledge of what had to happen.

One of the men turned to the terrorist.

'This makes no sense. What is it you want?' His tone was pleading, but also incredulous. What is it you want? What the fuck can you possibly be gaining from this?

The terrorist gave an exaggerated nod as if to say that he was taking the question seriously. He paced along the line between the men and the women, looking closely at people as he passed, as though examining them, but giving nothing away as to what he might be looking for. There was silence except for the rustle of his clothes as he walked. It was as if people were afraid even to breathe.

'I want this moment,' he said, and nodded again, as though satisfied with an answer that had, that second, crystallised in his mind. Then he ran back to the head of the line, and pressed the blade of his machete against the back of the middle-eastern woman and shouted, 'Suck some fucking cock!'

So it began. I looked away, as, it seemed, did most. An incongruous act of politeness by surrendered spectators; a bizarre outbreak of manners in the face of tyranny. Wouldn't this indignity force someone to risk breaking cover? Something had to give. Where was this going? Were we all fearing the worst while hoping someone else would help us escape it?

I heard a siren in the distance. Had somebody managed to send out a message? It receded. But surely a surreptitious text was possible. He couldn't see the spaces between us where a phone could be placed and a message tapped out. Making us sit had made it easier for us. Was this his mistake? With his sex show distracting him, the time was ideal. I looked around: nothing, not a sign, although, by my logic, I shouldn't be able to see it anyway. There was something inert in every posture; nobody moving, or shuffling, or shifting concentration. Just a blank where human ingenuity had been numbed. Maybe it had to be me? My bag was a foot away. I looked up to see where he was. His attention was flitting between the fellating couples and us, the putative audience.

The penises were still flaccid, I noticed. The men's faces oddly relaxed. A failed erection was a desirable state rather than an embarrassment for once. But the women were exchanging glances: they were sharing a worry, and it hit me, in a grinding twist of foreboding, that they were right.

The terrorist was disappointed. His reward had been spurned. He was insulted. He walked behind the men, yelling about ingratitude. I saw him raise an arm, but that was all I saw since the men were now between him and me. But I heard the gun, and saw the top of the man's head spurt red and a trace of blood arc through the air before a red splurge, like a volcanic mud pool, throbbed from his head, the last beat of his heart, before he collapsed forward onto the middle-eastern woman beneath him.

The flaccid penis next to him flowed with urine, the woman in front buried her head in her arms and screamed. Screams were everywhere, but they died almost instantly— in case they weren't allowed. A stench filled the air: bowels had opened. People were shaking, crying. The terrorist pushed the end of his blade against the other man's throat.

'Beg,' he said.

'Please…' said the man, but that was as far as he got. The blade was stabbed in, the man span and fell, the blood spluttered and spurted. A splat of it fell across my face.

The next silence came in so fast and hard I imagined it as the one we may all hear in that tiny interval between facing our death and the execution of the moment. A heavy dread held me, incapacitated me. I couldn't reach for any phone; I was rigid.

The terrorist pointed to Victor.

'Wilhelm,' he said. 'Come here.'

Fucking Wilhelm. Another few minutes and the image would be projected onto the side of the building, just as programmed. Did he know? How could he know? Had he timed it deliberately?

Surely it had to be coincidence? Then I looked hard at Victor who was looking at me. An insane thought ran through my head: that he'd set this up. Had it all gone grotesquely, grievously wrong? I searched his face, trying to read the truth in his eyes, hoping to find some glimmer that this could yet be controlled. But as he looked at me again, his head bowed, resigned, a look beyond terror, it was clear this had nothing to do with him and he was looking at me to tell me so.

The terrorist brought Victor forward and stood him between the corpses on the floor. I saw Alex and the man next to him exchange a glance. Something had to happen. I got a weird almost divine feeling of nerves reassembling within me, as though the paralysis had been a preparation in readiness for a fight.

Then he pointed his blade at me.

'Let's diversify some more, change it up a little,' he said. 'The girl, come here.'

He wasn't pointing at me, but Nina, who was behind me and to my side.

'I'll do it,' said Natalie. She stumbled to her feet.

'Do what?' he said, his face screwed up: malicious, sneering, contemptuous.

'Whatever,' she said, and started moving forward. I could see her thighs trembling, she could hardly walk.

The terrorist stepped towards her and flashed his machete, warning her to stop.

'I want the girl,' he said, 'Wilhelm wants the girl.' He grinned and glanced at Victor.

Nina had the look she had on Westminster Bridge that day. I could see she had an idea, or an aim, or some semblance of intent that enabled her to hope that what she was doing could work out. I almost burst into tears at the thought and at the brave, pathetic futility of it. She got to her feet and walked. The fear was in her eyes, but her movement was pure and graceful.

It was then that I felt the faintest of draughts. If I hadn't have been naked I probably wouldn't have noticed. I looked towards the door, but couldn't see anything. The terrorist was positioning Nina in front of Victor. I thought I saw a shadow outside the door and looked to Alex to see if he'd seen it too. The terrorist was making Victor kneel in front of Nina as the shadow emerged into the gallery space. It was a man in a suit. The terrorist told Nina to dance. The man in the suit walked slowly forward. I daren't look at Alex. I hoped no one would move or give the man away. We must all have been watching him and maybe we were all sharing the same thought, that we could protect him by not noticing. The terrorist told Victor to masturbate. The man kept walking. Nina kept dancing, her attention fixed forward even though she would have been able to see the man's approach with a small tilt of her head. Suddenly I knew who it must be. I prayed for Nina not to see him. The terrorist told her to touch herself. The man kept walking. Victor had managed to get himself half hard. The terrorist was grinning. Nina danced.

The terrorist turned, he must have heard something. The man was almost on top of him. He surged forward for the last two metres and wrapped himself around the terrorist, the momentum crashing them both to the floor. The gun fired. Alex and the man next to him leapt up. The terrorist was trying to get himself out from under the man. Nina screamed and jumped back as Alex and the other man reached the terrorist and stamped on his arm, forcing him to release the gun. Alex picked up the gun as the other man wrestled the terrorist. He squirmed free and charged Alex with the machete and Alex shot him point blank. He landed next to Nina who jumped aside to avoid the last defiant motion of his machete, a final muscular spasm, a last ditch gesture of hate.

Nina's father was gasping for breath. A pool of blood had spread from his abdomen. Natalie ran towards Nina, whose eyes were locked on her father, her naked body trembling, so fragile, so breakable, but willing herself towards her father, to touch him, to fall onto his body, to immerse herself completely in the battle for his life, to cling to him after the blood stopped pooling, after he stopped breathing, after Natalie bent to console her, after the wails of grief split the air, after she'd told him she loved him, again and again, and that he wasn't dead because he couldn't be, and that she had never doubted he loved her, and that he would get better and they would all live together again, and that she would die without him.

Chapter Seventeen

I was in my studio, gazing blankly across the river, thinking the same thoughts I'd thought every day for weeks, when a rowing eight came into view from upstream. It's a habit I have of lifting the binoculars during idle moments to examine the faces of the boys and girls—children from one of the clutch of schools situated close enough to the river —who daily row to and fro across my field of view.

Sometimes they're straining every muscle and tendon to pull the boat through the water at racing speed, sometimes they're pulling at half speed, counting the strokes, concentrating on timing and technique, and sometimes they're just drifting, waiting for the next phase, the next command from a megaphoned coach patrolling the river in one of a flotilla of motorised dinghies that buzz from boat to boat issuing instruction, encouragement and admonishment by turn.

The eight girls eased, their exhaustion visible. Their instinct was to slump over their oars, but a sharp command forced them to paddle on for half a minute, before being told to stop. I picked up the binoculars and scanned the boat, starting at the stern.

Some of the girls had tied their hair back in a pony tail and threaded it through the back of their caps, two wore headbands, two had tied their hair up on top, the cox wore a bobble hat. Aside from the cox, who would freeze to death without the extra layers, I wondered about the thinking behind this: the blondes and the red head had the ponytails; the black girls wore their hair up and the dark haired white girls wore the headbands. Did they make their choices conscious of identity? Looking at them as they relaxed, at last able to look around and speak to one another, it seemed from the smiles, the awkward backward facing embraces, the gestures and touches of camaraderie, all of which seemed to cross the hairstyle lines, that the answer was probably not.

It was one special girl I'd been looking out for; in the bow, a dark haired girl with a headband, Nina. A blonde sat in front of her, stretched back so she was looking up at the sky. Nina had clasped her hands in hers and was bent over her. They burst out laughing and several of the other girls turned in response. Some retort must have been made and a wave of laughter and broad smiles spread along the boat. I felt a twinge of nostalgia, or maybe envy, for long gone schooldays, that were not, as I recall, packed with such moments.

I wondered what they would be learning. Was it togetherness, teamwork, the whole-being-greater-than-the-sum? Was it to compete, to be the best, to garner plaudits from peers and opponents? Was it to win graciously instead of arrogantly? Or to lose with dignity rather than petulantly? Or how to wear one's advantages without becoming superior? Or to be good in the world rather than bad? Or to love what you can do rather than hate what you can't?

Nina was due round in the late afternoon along with Natalie and Victor. She had come a long way in the weeks since her father had died. Natalie held a suicide watch for several days and although Victor and I tried hard to convince her that the words Nina had uttered as she clung to her dead father's body were not to be taken literally, we knew it was hopeless; for Natalie the microscopic risk presented itself as a mountainside of premonition.

And what about the psychological damage? How would she react to the trauma? Better than the rest of us, seemed to be the answer. As the grief slowly eased and the tears became less frequent, and as she began sleeping through the night most nights, the nightmares becoming spasmodic rather than regular, we noticed a change in her.

It was as if she'd thought her way through an obstacle and emerged somewhere new—while the rest of us were continually treading the same defunct path. For her, sadness didn't dissolve into torpor as it had for me. I wanted to close the exhibition, close my studio, close myself off to anything that looked like the art world. I was tired of police, press, politicians and what felt like a million intrusions, but most of all I was fed up of feeling responsible. Not that a single person ever said or insinuated as much, but I couldn't shake it. It was my exhibition, my name on the banners, ninety percent of it was my work and people had been killed because of it.

I was stuck, but Nina wasn't. I think the death of her father opened a sluice out of which flowed the still water of a divided upbringing. It's impossible to be sure about something so deeply personal, something that would reverberate within her indefinitely, settling and unsettling the composition of her young mind, until maybe finding a meaning she could fix on, but it appeared that with her relationship with him now over, and nothing left to hope for, he had become the hero who could no longer disappoint her.

She was rowing, and appeared good at it. Had I always thought of her as a sensitive creature, too delicate for something so demanding of brute force and a high pain threshold? Where was the evidence? She was slimly athletic and strong in mind, perhaps lacking the weight to join the list of Olympians her school was proud of having produced, but she could hold her own in the bow seat, that was clear.

As I looked on, the recent past was invisible in her features. The distant past of her race, my race, was a vanished entity, and any sense of race as a distinction, with the pain of the past, or the fear of the future, absent on every face in the boat, however they tied their hair. The future looked fine. For a flickering moment, it looked beautiful.

Victor and Natalie's parents would never again be tempted from their gilded cage, the consequence of their attempted foray into the world of people simply catapulting them back into hiding, their every fear confirmed: barbarity was everywhere, society a mixing ground where beasts and butchers become one.

'We tried,' said Victor, the sadness swimming in his eyes, 'and we can never be accused of doing nothing.'

He'd arrived with news of some decent press and we crowded around my computer as he navigated to the relevant sites. In the days following the preview the news was dominated by the atrocity, with the art a backdrop, treated as though it were no more than an irony that such a show should attract the murderous attentions of an ideological fanatic. There were too many complications— too many foreigners present; too many rich people; too many arty types; too many of the 'metropolitan elite'; too many Jews; too many of what seemed like an endless list; and not nearly enough victims—for them to feel truly inclined to sanctify the attack as a national tragedy warranting an unrestrained outpouring of public grief.

The newspapers moved quickly from shock and outrage that this should be happening on 'our' streets, to a who's-to-blame hunt that held that politicians, the police and the security services were responsible—the precise order of culpability depending on which paper—and that 'heads must roll.' Miraculously, I escaped this register of the 'criminally negligent,' although one commentator accused me of incitement on the grounds that the exhibition had 'an insidious pro-Jewish sub-text'.

Alex brought up the wine and we settled to read, like a family gathering round the TV for a favourite programme. Victor was right, the stories were an improvement, and there were several of them. It was as if they'd respectfully conspired to allow a specified time to elapse before passing judgement. These were arts stories, not news stories, and it was gratifying to see that the news hadn't obliterated the art. Without a mob in the background, reason and understanding emerged. The attack had heightened the poignancy people felt towards the work, which created a double-edged response in me: how could I decline the compliment paid to me as an artist, but how could I enjoy praise more freely offered because people had died?

I looked at Nina who was looking away from the screen. She was holding something back, fighting it, I placed an arm around her and she leant into me.

'He never got to see it,' she said, and the tears burst through. She cried for a minute before wiping her eyes with her hands. She looked up, drew breath and said, 'I'm proud of him,' before crying again, but this time through a broad, determined smile, one that sought to draw on her father's spirit as if it could have passed on from him to her.

There was huge interest in Nina and her relationship with me, artist to model. The story snared everyone who wrote about it, not that they knew the precise and unorthodox circumstances by which Victor and Natalie gave birth to the arrangement. In every photograph and video she is someone different, a new persona, the wearer of a new expression, like watching a chrysalis unfold a hundred times over, and each time, when the butterfly emerges, it has a new shape, a new colour scheme and pattern of flight. It was always her, but as if she were every girl, as though she could live a hundred lives and still not exhaust the possibilities: a stand-in for all the girls who were denied the chance to live just the one life. I had come to imagine her as a light swirling in the sky, an aurora made of the ghosts of them all.

I was proud of her and proud to have been her artist. I stepped back from the desk and looked at Natalie, Victor, Alex and Nina, crowding round the computer screen, taking in the news that we had created an exhibition that had at last earned the notices we had hoped for. I was proud of all of us.

'Let's take a walk,' said Victor.

I looked at him, wondering why.

'I think you know where,' he said.

The weather was pleasant for late autumn. We wore coats, but without the need to huddle into them we strode along the path towards the bridge, caressed by the gentle air of an evening warm enough to carry a scent of the passing season.

We walked to the end of our street, through to the riverside path, past the sailing club, the sculling club, the rowing clubs, past the school boathouse, the pubs, past Eric Ravilious's house, William Morris's house, past the slipways, the jetties, the houseboats, through the park, over the bridge, along the path behind the school playing fields, past the slipway Alex had dragged Victor ashore from, until we stood on the spot my father had been murdered, the spot where Victor, through his subterfuge, had become Wilhelm.

The walk was without conversation, except for exclamations of surprise or apology as we stepped into or around the hazards: the people coming out of the pubs, the tourists posing for photographs, the cyclists for whom the no cycling signs didn't exist, the joggers, the dogs and the man whose name none of us could recall but who we were sure had been in several films. I felt the freedom of someone lucky to have survived a disaster, experiencing a period of remission, the guilt turned down low, hope up high. Something had settled and I sensed it had for us all.

Crossing the bridge, I looked up at the clouds scudding across a darkening sky that dissolved above, hollow and infinite. I followed the curve of the river to the next bend and thought of it winding its way through the city, past rich people and poor people, past rule makers and rule breakers, and past the half dilapidated warehouse that contained our exhibition. It's all air and water and land, and out of it we exist—and maybe, somewhere down the line, we'll save ourselves.

Had we reached an ending? Is there solace in knowing an end creates a space for something else? We end something, we start something; we lose something, we find something. Just so long as we can breathe the air we mostly never notice, the air that circulates the globe, heats and cools us and carries moisture and fragrance. The air our lungs exchange every second, every minute, an exchange every human being shares, as one of us.

'You left your lights on,' said Nina looking across the water to my studio. The strengthening gloom of the evening rendered it ablaze, the brightest by far among the rows of windows that pack the opposite bank. She pointed to its reflection shimmering towards us across the water. 'It'll reach us when it's completely dark,' she said and crouched to view it from a lower angle.

Silence was all that was required. I could see Victor rehearsing something in his head, but he knew it wasn't necessary. Natalie crouched with Nina and put her arm around her. I walked to the edge of the embankment, where Victor and Alex came and stood beside me. I sat, as did Alex. Victor, after a moment's hesitation that suggested he had no intention of muddying his coat, relented and joined us. We watched the reflection from my studio light spread towards us just as Nina said it would.